Rowe is a paranormal star!" ~J.R. Ward

D1520680

Praise for Not Quite Dead

"[Rowe] has penned a winner with *Not Quite Dead*, the first novel in her new NightHunter vampire series...an action-packed, sensual, paranormal romance that will captivate readers from the outset... Brimming with vampires, danger, resurrection, Louisiana bayou, humor, surprising plot twists, fantasy, romance and love, this story is a must-read!" ~ *Romance Junkies:*

Praise for Darkness Possessed

"A story that will keep you on the edge of your seat, and characters you won't soon forget!" - Paige Tyler, *USA Today* Bestselling Author of the X-OPS Series

"*Darkness Possessed*...is an action-packed, adrenaline pumping paranormal romance that will keep you on the edge of your seat... Suspense, danger, evil, life threatening situations, magic, hunky Calydons, humor, fantasy, mystery, scorching sensuality, romance, and love – what more could you ask for in a story? Readers – take my advice – do not miss this dark, sexy tale!" ~*Romance Junkie*s

Praise for Darkness Unleashed

"Once more, award winning author Stephanie Rowe pens a winner with *Darkness Unleashed*, the seventh book in her amazing Order of the Blade series...[an] action-packed, sensual story that will keep you perched on the edge of your seat, eagerly turning pages to discover the outcome...one of the best paranormal books I have read this year." ~*Dottie, Romancejunkies.com*

Praise for Forever in Darkness

"Stephanie Rowe has done it again. The Order Of The Blade series is one of the best urban fantasy/paranormal series I have read. Ian's story held me riveted from page one. It is sure to delight all her fans. Keep them coming!" ~ *Alexx Mom Cat's Gateway Book Blog*

Praise for Darkness Awakened

"A fast-paced plot with strong characters, blazing sexual tension and sprinkled with witty banter, Darkness Awakened sucked me in and kept me hooked until the very last page." ~ *Literary Escapism*

"Rarely do I find a book that so captivates my attention, that makes me laugh out loud, and cry when things look bad. And the sex, wow! It took my breath away... The pace kept me on the edge of my seat, and turning the pages. I did not want to put this book down... [Darkness Awakened] is a must read." ~ D. Alexx Miller, Alexx Mom Cat's Gateway Book Blog

Praise for Darkness Seduced

"[D]ark, edgy, sexy … sizzles on the page…sex with soul shattering connections that leave the reader a little breathless!...Darkness Seduced delivers tight plot lines, well written, witty and lyrical - Rowe lays down some seriously dark and sexy tracks. There is no doubt that this series will have a cult following. " ~ *Guilty Indulgence Book Club*

"I was absolutely enthralled by this book…heart stopping action fueled by dangerous passions and hunky, primal men…If you're looking for a book that will grab hold of you and not let go until it has been totally devoured, look no further than Darkness Seduced."~*When Pen Met Paper Reviews*

† II †

PRAISE FOR DARKNESS SURRENDERED

"Book three of the Order of the Blades series is…superbly original and excellent, yet the passion, struggle and the depth of emotion that Ana and Elijah face is so brutal, yet is also pretty awe inspiring. I was swept away by Stephanie's depth of character detail and emotion. I absolutely loved the roller-coaster that Stephanie, Ana and Elijah took me on." ~ *Becky Johnson, Bex 'n' Books!*

"Darkness Surrendered drew me so deeply into the story that I felt Ana and Elijah's emotions as if they were my own…they completely engulfed me in their story…Ingenious plot turns and edge of your seat suspense…make Darkness Surrendered one of the best novels I have read in years." ~*Tamara Hoffa, Sizzling Hot Book Reviews*

PRAISE FOR ICE

"Ice, by Stephanie Rowe, is a thrill ride!" ~ Lisa Jackson, #1 *New York Times* bestselling author

"Passion explodes even in the face of spiraling danger as Rowe offers a chilling thrill-ride through a vivid--and unforgiving--Alaskan wilderness." ~ Cheyenne McCray, *New York Times* bestselling author

"Ice delivers pulse-pounding chills and hot romance as it races toward its exciting climax!" ~ JoAnn Ross, *New York Times* bestselling author

"Stephanie Rowe explodes onto the romantic suspense scene with this edgy, sexy and gripping thriller. From the very first page, the suspense is chilling, and there's enough sizzling passion between the two main characters to melt the thickest arctic ice. Get ready for a tense and dangerous adventure." ~ *Fresh Fiction*

"Stephanie Rowe makes her entry into Romantic Suspense, and what an awesome entry! From the very first pages to the end, heart-stopping danger and passion grab the heart. ... sends shivers down the spine... magnificent... mind-chilling suspense... riveting... A wonderful romance through and through!" ~ *Merrimon Book Reviews*

"[a] thrilling entry into romantic suspense... Rowe comes through with crackling tension as the killer closes in." ~ *Publisher's Weekly*

PRAISE FOR CHILL

"*Chill* is a riveting story of danger, betrayal, intrigue and the healing powers of love… *Chill* has everything a reader needs – death, threats, thefts, attraction and hot, sweet romance." ~ Jeanne Stone Hunter, *My Book Addiction Reviews*

"Once again Rowe has delivered a story with adrenalin-inducing action, suspense and a dark edged hero that will melt your heart and send a chill down your spine." ~ Sharon Stogner, *Love Romance Passion*

"*Chill* packs page turning suspense with tremendous emotional impact. Buy a box of Kleenex before you read *Chill*, because you will definitely need it! …*Chill* had a wonderfully complicated plot, full of twist and turns. " ~ Tamara Hoffa, *Sizzling Hot Book Reviews*

PRAISE FOR NO KNIGHT NEEDED

"*No Knight Needed* is m-a-g-i-c-a-l! Hands down, it is one of the best romances I have read. I can't wait till it comes out and I can tell the world about it." ~*Sharon Stogner, Love Romance Passion*

"*No Knight Needed* is contemporary romance at its best….There was not a moment that I wasn't completely engrossed in the novel, the story, the characters. I very audibly cheered for them and did not shed just one tear, nope, rather bucket fulls. My heart at times broke for them. The narrative and dialogue surrounding these 'tender' moments in particular were so beautifully crafted, poetic even; it was this that had me blubbering. And of course on the flip side of the heart-wrenching events, was the amazing, witty humour….If it's not obvious by now, then just to be clear, I love this book! I would most definitely and happily reread, which is an absolute first for me in this genre." ~*Becky Johnson, Bex 'N' Books*

"*No Knight Needed* is an amazing story of love and life…I literally laughed out loud, cried and cheered.… *No Knight Needed* is a must read and must re-read." *~Jeanne Stone-Hunter, My Book Addiction Reviews*

Darkness Awakened

ISBN 10: 0-9886566-5-5

ISBN 13: 978-0-9886566-5-9

Acknowledgements

Special thanks to my core team of amazing people, without whom I would never have been able to create this book. Each of you is so important, and your contribution was exactly what I needed. I'm so grateful to all of you! Your emails of support, or yelling at me because I hadn't sent you more of the book yet, or just your advice on covers, back cover copy and all things needed to whip this book into shape—every last one of them made a difference to me. I appreciate each one of you so much! Special thanks to Sharon Stogner, Jeanne Hunter, Tamara Hoffa, Rachel Unterman and Jan Leyh, not only for their help, but for their friendship and behind-the-scenes support. Huge thanks also to Anita Nallathamby, Loretta Gilbert, Summer Steelman, D. Alexx Miller, Janet Juengling-Snell, Jenn Shanks Pray and Jodi Moore. There are so many people I want to thank, but the people who simply must be called out are Denise Fluhr, Noelle Norris, Alencia Bates, Krizia Columna, Shell Bryce, and Ashley Cuesta. Thank you also to the following for all their help: Judi Pflughoeft, Sarah Whitten, Julie Simpson, Mary Lynn Ostrum, Maureen Downey and Mariann Medina. Thank you also to Jean Bowden, Dottie Jones, Phyllis Marshall, Nicole Telhiard, Holly Collins, and Rebecca Johnson. And so much thanks to my newest team members: Heidi Hoffman, Sandi Foss, Dana Simmons, Kasey Richardson, Valerie Glass, Caryn Santee, Leslie Barnes, Bridget Koan, and Evelyn Newman. You guys are the best! Thanks so much to Pete Davis at Los Zombios for such an amazing cover, and for all his hard work on the technical side to make this book come to life. Mom, you're the best. It means so much that you believe in me. I love you. Special thanks also to my amazing daughter, who I love more than words could ever express. You are my world, sweet girl, in all ways

Dedication

For Bill Berman, an amazing man with a great heart, beautiful soul and a love for books that help make the world a brighter place.

DARKNESS AWAKENED

THE ORDER OF THE BLADE

STEPHANIE

ROWE

CHAPTER 1

Death was stalking them.

Quinn Masters sprinted through the thick mountain woods of southern Oregon, trailed by the six young Calydon warriors he was training. Dodging overhanging branches coated with moss, Quinn scanned the night with his senses. He searched for the scent that shouldn't be there, for the noise that was out of place, as he hunted ruthlessly for the threat that had triggered his internal warnings.

He could find nothing amiss, but his gut knew that was a lie. His legendary instincts were often all that had kept him and his team alive, and they were all over this situation. Something was seriously wrong, but what the hell was it?

Quinn mentally scanned the team behind him to see if any of them had gone rogue, but he sensed only gritty determination as they followed him through the woods. Their minds were focused solely on their goal of being selected to join the Order of the Blade, the elite group of Calydons tasked with the mission of saving innocents from rogue Calydons, no matter the cost. Each trainee was intent on passing the tests, to be heralded as worthy of risking his life for humanity, morally strong enough to kill friends that had gone rogue, and deadly enough to defeat the opponents that no other creature could stop.

Someday, some of these trainees might be immortal warriors feared by all, loved by none, and haunted by what they had to do in the line of duty. Tonight, they were young, unskilled, and in grave danger, because whatever was after them was deadly as hell.

Quinn's mind was in overdrive, his adrenaline jacked, as he methodically and swiftly assessed every detail of his surroundings. He sorted through the rich scents of dampness and pine, of dirt and sweat, but came up with nothing. What was the threat that was making his skin crawl? He knew it was out there, and he would find it.

"What is it?" one of the trainees asked.

Silence. Quinn sent the order with such force that he heard the young warrior grunt with pain.

He halted at the bottom of the rocky ridge that was the highest point in his three hundred acres of untamed land. Silently ordering his charges to be still, he studied the overhang of rocks and roots that loomed a hundred yards above them. These were Quinn's woods, his territory, a sanctum he opened once every twenty years for a month of intensive training and testing with the young Calydons whom the Order had selected as potential candidates to join the team.

His land was a well-protected hideaway that no enemy dared enter. It was a safe zone where the rookies could make mistakes and not die for them.

Until tonight. Until now. Something that stank of evil and rot was in his woods, and it was fixated on the youth under his protection. *Just try it.* He sent the message out into the night. The air thickened, and he knew he'd been heard.

He grinned. *Bring it on, asshole.*

The ridge was the natural place to make a stand, an easy site for even these young warriors to defend successfully. But as Quinn eyed the ledge, the swords branded on his forearms burned in anticipation of battle. The air felt heavy and ponderous, like it was coated with sludge. The ridge was darker than it should have been, as if a thick cloud of malevolence had cloaked it in death. The wind was too calm. The animals eerily silent. The trees dangerously still.

Whatever had encroached upon his property was waiting for them on the top of the cliff. It knew his land, and it knew the ridge was where he'd take the trainees to fight.

Quinn narrowed his eyes, tempted to call out his swords and take out the bastard arrogant enough to trespass on his land and threaten his charges. He'd need only a split second to call his weapons to life, transforming the brands into deadly steel blades designed for only his hands. Each Calydon was chosen by his weapon, and Quinn wielded his swords with lethal precision.

He took one step toward the cliff, and then stopped instantly as a deadly certainty reverberated through him. His trainees would die on that ridge tonight if he took them up there.

Anger rippled through him. *Screw that.* They were his to keep alive, and they weren't going down. He'd get them out, and then come back for the battle.

Quinn quickly assessed his options and decided the river was the nearest exit. He could get them there fast, before the intruder realized what he was doing.

Quinn sent a silent order to his trainees as he spun around and sprinted toward the raging waters that were running violently from the winter rains. Tense and agitated, the rookies were loud behind him, their feet snapping branches and splashing through mud. Adrenaline was interfering with their ability to maintain silence. Quinn sent out a wave of calming energy to them, but there was so much electricity in the air that his attempt was useless.

Swearing, he pushed them harder, knowing that whatever was stalking them would be fast on their tail. He had to get the rookies clear before their enemy caught up.

The roar of rushing water filled the night as they approached the river. The sound was drowning out the other noises in the woods, including the sounds that would tell Quinn if their enemy was near. Swearing, he concentrated on scent, but he could smell only the dampness from the river, the fertility of the moisture-laden earth, and the salty sweat of his trainees. He could see nothing amiss in his woods, and his instincts were telling him they were safe for right now, but he knew it had to be a lie. There was no way that the threat from the ridge wasn't tracking them, despite the fact that his gut was broadcasting the all-clear signal. The only explanation could be that the bastard was trying to screw with Quinn's instincts.

He almost laughed at the realization that the intruder was trying to mess with his gut. *Nice try, scumbag.* There was a reason he was never wrong, and it was because he had talents that went far deeper than any stalker would be able to access.

As Quinn barreled toward the river, he shut down his external senses and reached deeper inside for the guidance that made him one of the most formidable warriors in the Order. No rhyme, no reason, no external facts guided those instincts, and yet they were infallible.

He opened his soul to his surroundings, allowing that deeper part of himself to access messages he couldn't otherwise identify. The night became still and silent as he allowed the fullness of his intuition to guide him. The moment he tapped into his deeper senses, he was able to detect the threat behind him. It was powerful and deadly, and his brush with it cast a tinge of evil into his mind, like poisoned tentacles. Renewed urgency filled him with the need to get his charges into the river. "Go!" he yelled as he half-slid down the embankment toward the muddy water. "Now!"

Quinn skidded to a stop at the edge of the water

and whirled around as his trainees came sprinting down the hill, moving with impressive speed for a team so young. He grinned with satisfaction as they neared, knowing they were almost safe—

His gut suddenly roared a warning, and Quinn heard the soft intake of air behind them. So faint, barely a whisper in the night, but he caught it. Someone had been waiting for them to pass by. *Son of a bitch.*

"It's a trap!" Quinn sprinted back up the slippery mud bank toward the rookies. He called forth one of his swords. The blade sprang out of his skin with a flash of black light and a loud crack. The jeweled handle slammed into the palm of his hand with satisfying force. He raised his blade as his trainees scrambled for position, shouting in confusion when a small metal disc burst out of the woods in a spinning blur and cracked into the head of the nearest kid.

The neophyte dropped instantly.

Another Calydon trainee swung at it with a battle axe, and the whirring metal disc skillfully dodged it before slicing through the kid's neck.

"Back to back!" Quinn shouted at his team, ordering them into a defensive formation. "Track it!" Quinn bolted into the fray as the best trainee charged the flying disc, hurling his dagger with brilliant speed and accuracy.

But the spinning disc was viciously fast, ducking and weaving, and the youth was dead before he even hit the earth. Sparkling with the moonlight, the disc spun around and clipped another trainee, and another, moving so quickly Quinn had to tap into his heightened senses to be able to track it.

"Try me, you bastard!" Quinn roared as the shadowed disc whirled around and spun right for the last trainee with dizzying speed.

Quinn leapt in front of the weapon and struck with unerring precision, smashing his blade into the metal object. The disc crashed into his sword so hard that the impact drove him to his knees. The disc ricocheted into the forest floor with a thump that cleaved a gash in the earth. Quinn immediately leapt to his feet and jammed his sword into the spinning metal, neutralizing it before it could take flight again.

His blade buried deep within, the disc finally stopped spinning. As it stilled, Quinn got his first look at the weapon that had just decimated an entire team of Calydon trainees in milliseconds.

He went ice cold at what he saw.

It was the six-pointed throwing star belonging to Elijah Ross, one of Quinn's Order of the Blade blood brothers, an immortal warrior who'd been by his side for centuries. A man he considered one of his best friends.

No, it was impossible. Elijah would never go rogue. *Ever.*

"What is it?" The sole trainee still standing moved swiftly into place behind Quinn to protect his back, his grip solid on his spear despite the carnage he'd just witnessed.

"Stay alert. I'm checking." Quinn pulled his sword free of the throwing star and squatted so he could study it more carefully. As he did, a feeling of stunned disbelief settled over him. There was no mistaking the intricate designs etched on the points of the star. It was Elijah's weapon.

Every Calydon weapon was unique, and Quinn had been through so many battles with Elijah that he could draw the damn thing in his sleep. "Son of a bitch," he said softly, running his finger over the cold steel.

Elijah had stood beside Quinn facing death thousands of times over the last five hundred years. He'd entrust his life to Elijah without question, under any circumstance. Elijah was an Order brother responsible for protecting the world, at all costs…and now he'd murdered five Calydons?

No. *Impossible.* Quinn gripped his sword as dark denial roared through him. There was no possibility Elijah had gone rogue. *No chance.* He knew his blood brother too well to be fooled into thinking that was what had just happened. He'd made the mistake once of believing someone he cared about had gone rogue, and he would never do it again.

Now was his chance to do it right. Finally. The chance he'd been seeking for five hundred years.

But he also knew that a Calydon weapon could be wielded only by the warrior it had chosen. No one else could have thrown it—

A faint hum filled the air, and Quinn jerked his gaze up at the sound of Elijah's second throwing star taking flight. He leapt to his feet as the final remaining trainee raised his own weapon, clearly sensing the same threat.

Quinn moved in tight beside the kid, searching the darkened woods for his best friend as he reached out with his mind to connect to him. *Elijah. Where are you?*

He felt the faint flicker of response from Elijah's mind, but it was distorted. Tainted. Wrong. Quinn's adrenaline spiked and he turned sharply, trying to pinpoint where Elijah was. *Stand down, Elijah. Now.*

Another surge of energy from Elijah touched Quinn's mind, and this time it was violent and dark, filled with loathing. Quinn shoved the rookie behind him, snapping into assault mode as he pinpointed his teammate's location.

Instinctively responding to the threat emanating so violently from Elijah, Quinn whipped back his arm to hurl his sword into the dark woods to take him out…but centuries-old truths made him pause. Elijah would never murder the trainees, and he was too controlled to go rogue. Something was off.

Quinn would not make the same mistake again of judging too soon.

He didn't throw his sword. Instead, he waited. He gave his blood brother the chance he hadn't given his uncle so long ago. *Elijah. Talk to me—*

The second throwing star slammed into the back of Quinn's neck and he crumpled to the earth, his sword still clutched in his hand.

☒☒☒☒

"What the hell happened here?" The familiar voice Gideon Roarke, a fellow Order member, jerked Quinn back to consciousness.

Fighting through the fog still enveloping his brain, Quinn wrenched his eyes open, slitting his lids against the setting sun peeking through the dense foliage. Pain throbbed at his neck, and the furious roar of the nearby river jolted his memory of what had just happened. *Elijah.*

He lunged to his feet, his sword exploding into his hand in a flash of black light. He spun around, blade ready—

On the ground was the body of the lone trainee who had survived the initial assault. The youth was on his back, eyes closed, as if he were taking an afternoon nap, but the stillness of his features left no doubt. *Dead.* Elijah had killed every single one of them.

Quinn whirled around, reaching out with his mind, searching for Elijah, for an indicator that would give away his location so Quinn would know where he was.

But there was no response. No flicker of life. Elijah was gone. The threat was over.

Quinn closed his eyes as sudden dizziness assaulted him and he stumbled, fighting for balance.

"What happened?" Gideon asked again, and this time, Quinn heard the muted fury in his voice.

Quinn jerked his gaze toward his Order blood brother who, along with Elijah, had been his closest friend for the last five hundred years. Gideon was wearing his customary jeans, black T-shirt and heavy boots, splashed with mud and smelling of sweat and anger. At the time the three of them had performed the blood ritual, they'd been rookies with the Order, and they'd needed each other to survive. In the five hundred years since, the bond of friendship had never weakened. Quinn had trusted them both with his life so many times, and they'd always had his back.

Until now.

Until Elijah had tried to murder him.

Was Gideon next? His arms were flexed, his feet spread in a battle stance. The aggression pouring off him triggered a defensive response in Quinn.

He spun toward Gideon, moving so swiftly that he had the tip of his blade pressed against Gideon's throat before the other Calydon could move. "Back off," he growled.

Shit. Quinn's head was spinning. The back of his neck hurt like he'd been upended by an axe. Darkness flickered at the edge of his vision, and he fought for balance. It was only by sheer force of will that he kept his blade steady, his adrenaline racing at the sight of the next man who might betray him.

Gideon stilled. "Who killed the trainees?" His gaze flicked past Quinn to the ground behind him, and anger curled his lips.

"You tell me," Quinn said softly, his grip tightening on the jeweled handle. He pressed his hand to the back of his neck where Elijah's weapon had hit, and he winced in pain. He had a deep skull fracture and a severed spinal cord that were just barely healed. Well, that'd explain the weakness. It was time to heal that shit and fast. He kept his sword up, maintaining the façade that he didn't feel like hell and that a stiff breeze wouldn't knock him on his ass.

Gideon's blue gaze jerked back to Quinn, and understanding flashed across his face. "Quinn," he said quietly. "I'm not responsible for this."

"Then why are you here?" Quinn's head was throbbing so intensely, he could barely focus on Gideon, but he fought to concentrate, to read the expression on Gideon's face, to assess his feelings. He tried to touch his mind, but Gideon's shields were up.

As blood brothers, it took a supreme and intentional effort to cut each other off from their thoughts, and Gideon was doing it right now. As was Elijah. Warning flooded Quinn and he readied himself for another attack, this time from Gideon.

Gideon met Quinn's gaze with unflinching force. "I'm here because it's my turn to take over the training," he said. "I had nothing to do with this," he repeated, his voice even and balanced, although the muscles in his neck were rigid.

"Your turn?" Quinn blinked at the explanation. Gideon had been scheduled to arrive three days after the attack. He'd been unconscious for *three days?* Shit. Elijah had nearly killed him.

Betrayal churned like bile, and Quinn was hit with such a wave of weakness that he almost went down to his knees. He ground his jaw, fighting for composure, for the appearance of strength. *Do not show weakness.* Not now. Not until he figured out who he could trust. "Neutralize yourself."

Gideon's blue eyes widened beneath his black skullcap. "You're kidding."

"Now, or you die." The forest was spinning now, and Quinn flexed his quads, bracing himself against the dizziness. He had to make sure it was safe before he collapsed. He had to disarm Gideon. The thought that Gideon might be rogue reviled him, matched only by his revulsion that Elijah might have killed everyone he was supposed to protect.

"You're a real ass before you've had your coffee,"

Gideon muttered as he flexed his left arm, showing a black brand in the shape of a double-bladed throwing axe. "You really want me to disarm myself—"

"Now." The forest was starting to spin more fiercely, and Quinn had to concentrate to keep from tilting over. Damn. He had new respect for the weapons of his kind. He'd never been hit like this. Kinda sucked, actually.

Gideon held out his arms and a metal throwing axe covered in intricate carvings exploded out of each forearm in a flash of black light, and then slammed into each palm.

For a moment, the two warriors stood immobile, eyes locked, weapons out. Quinn felt Gideon reach out to touch his mind, and Quinn immediately wove a barrier of protection, a shield strong enough to keep out even a warrior he was blood-bonded with.

"You don't trust me." Gideon observed.

"No. But don't take it personally."

Gideon's eyes narrowed, and Quinn pressed the tip of the sword harder into his skin, until a trickle of blood slid down his teammate's neck. He was ready for Gideon to attack. No Calydon could stand down from the open threat Quinn was offering, and Gideon was as cold and heartless as any Order member in existence.

But to his surprise, Gideon raised one axe to eye level, then opened his palm and let the weapon drop to the forest floor. He repeated the process with his other axe, which landed with a soft thud on the muddy ground beside the first one.

Neither man moved, waiting as both axes shimmered brightly. Gideon made no effort to pick them up, and after a moment, each blade disintegrated into the forest floor. By losing his weapons that way, it would be several minutes before Gideon could call forth another axe. He was defenseless, with the tip of Quinn's sword embedded in his neck.

The statement of an innocent man.

"Now do you want to tell me what the hell's going on?" Gideon's voice was calm. His blue gaze was penetrating and unwavering as he softened the shields around his mind, allowing Quinn to feel his innocence, and his outrage over the deaths. "I don't know what happened here, but I know I still trust you with my life. And you can still trust me with yours. Talk to me, Quinn."

Quinn felt his friend's innocence in the very core of his being. *Jesus. Gideon was innocent.* With a sigh of exhaustion, Quinn lowered his sword, keeping a tight grip on it so it didn't fall to the earth like Gideon's had. Except under a few specific circumstances, a Calydon weapon not physically connected to its owner would disintegrate within moments, a safeguard that kept the weapons from being taken and used against them.

Gideon nodded his acceptance of the truce, not bothering to wipe the blood off his neck. "There are six dead trainees out here, with their heads nearly sliced off. What went down?"

The trainees. Quinn braced himself on his sword, and then turned to see how bad it was, now that he wasn't worried about Gideon sinking an axe into his head. The bodies of his charges were strewn about, marked by Elijah's weapon. The arm of one of the trainees was flayed open, but the others were intact.

He whistled softly. Quinn had seen carnage like this before, a trail of death left by a rogue Calydon. He'd even seen it done by warriors he'd considered friends before they'd gone rogue. It was nothing new, not by a long shot.

But never in his life would he have expected to witness this kind of destruction by the hand of Elijah. There had to be a reason. Scanning the area for clues, for excuses, for explanations, he slowly walked over and squatted next to the trainee with the damaged arm, lifting his flayed arm. "His weapon's been stolen."

"Look at your arm," Gideon said.

At Gideon's words, Quinn's left forearm vibrated with sudden burning, as the fading adrenaline allowed the first sensations of pain to register. Quinn glanced down and saw his sleeve was sliced open, revealing a gaping wound in his forearm.

His left sword had been stolen as well.

That's what this had been about? Harvesting weapons? But that made no sense. Even if the weapons were taken, they couldn't be used in battle because they would work only for their chosen owner. What in the hell was going on? *Elijah.* He opened his mind, thrusting his mental energy ruthlessly out into the world. *Talk to me!*

There was no response. Not even a flicker from a blood brother that he should be able to sense from a thousand miles away.

"You died." Gideon sounded shocked. "I felt it for a minute three days ago, but it was gone so fast I thought I'd misread it." He rubbed the back of his hand over his brow. "Damn. I'm glad you're immortal."

"Immortality is never absolute. You know that." Gideon was right, though. Apparently, Quinn *had* died from Elijah's blow, however momentarily, because Calydon weapons could be taken only at the moment of death. Hell. He'd really died? That was enough to make a guy sit up and take notice. "First time I've ever died, I gotta admit." If a Calydon weapon was stolen at the exact moment of death, they could be salvaged, because there was no owner for them to revert to after disintegration.

"I never thought anything could take you down." Gideon ran his hand over his skullcap, and shook his head to clear it. "Hell, man. What was able to get a jump on you? Demon?"

Quinn ground his teeth as he tugged the skin on his arm back together and wound his belt around it to hold it together long enough to heal. "It was Elijah."

Gideon made a sharp grunt of disbelief. "Impossible.

He'd never go rogue. We'd know it by now."

Quinn tested his arm. It was weak and hurt like hell, but it was functional. "I saw his throwing star."

Gideon stared at him, frowning as he realized Quinn was serious. "You're sure?"

"I saw it kill the trainees. It was his weapon." They both knew that Calydon weapons would perform only for their owner, and their mate, of course, but none of them had mates. They wouldn't be that stupid.

Quinn opened his mind to Gideon and replayed the scene from that night in his head, so Gideon could see what had happened.

Gideon was silent as he watched the scene unfold, but emotions were raging in his blue eyes. When it was over, Gideon braced his hands against a nearby tree and dropped his head between his arms, closing his eyes, fighting to exert the control that the Order members were so legendary for. No words needed to be said. They both understood the magnitude of what had happened.

Their trio was supposed to be eternal. None of them were supposed to go rogue, and they tracked each other carefully to make sure no one was close to crossing the line. Elijah had been nowhere near rogue, and they both knew it. If he had gone rogue, and it looked like he had, it would be their fault for not seeing it coming, and it would be their failure when Elijah had to be assassinated to protect the world from him.

"You think he met his *sheva?* Bonding with his soul mate would turn him rogue." Gideon spoke the words as if it poisoned him to even think it.

"No chance. He's too careful. And if he did meet his mate, he'd have let us know before he bonded with her." Quinn met his teammate's gaze. "Like we all would do."

"There's no other explanation for how he could go rogue so quickly," Gideon said. "If he's met and bonded with his *sheva*, he could be rogue already."

Quinn's adrenaline surged at the thought of Elijah meeting his *sheva*, the woman destined to be his soul mate. God help them all if that was what had happened… No. That wasn't it. Elijah would never bond. He would have told them before he got sucked in. It had to be something else. "I have no idea what's going on," Quinn said as he crouched beside the trainee with the missing weapon and studied the damage, "but I'm going to ask Elijah when I find him." He gave Gideon a bitter smile. "Then I'm going to strangle the asshole for killing me."

Gideon jerked his head up to stare at Quinn. "You're going after him yourself? You're not going to report this to Dante?"

Dante Sinclair was their leader. He was a tough son of a bitch, a warrior strong enough to control a race of immortal beings destined to live and die by violence. Dante had been Quinn's mentor for five hundred years. Yeah, Quinn respected Dante and the mission he'd set forth for the Order, but he didn't always agree with the big boss's theories.

Especially when it came to rogues, and the unilateral edict to take them all out, instantly, no matter what the cost. Quinn had followed that edict one time too many, and his regret still haunted him. He would never give Dante the right to apply his arbitrary rule to Elijah's fate, no matter how many centuries of evidence supported that decision.

He stood up. "If we report to Dante, he'll pull you and me off the run and have someone else do it. Someone who won't give Elijah a chance."

"Hell." Gideon let out his breath. "*We* can't give him a chance. He slaughtered six people, seven if we count you. He's rogue. You know Calydons don't come back once we cross over into insanity."

"So, he killed me." Quinn shrugged. "That doesn't mean he's rogue, and if he is, that doesn't mean he can't come back."

Gideon swore. "Quinn, let it go. It's been five hundred years and no rogue has ever come back. Whatever you think you saw back then was a kid's imagination. Elijah is done. Look at what he did. See for yourself." He gestured to the carnage, but Quinn didn't bother to look.

He knew the evidence was there. He'd seen it. But he would not believe Elijah deserved to die, not until he'd exhausted all other possibilities. "He wouldn't go rogue."

Gideon raised his brows. "If he wasn't rogue, that means he did this in his sane mind."

"Then he had a reason." He would not condemn his teammate, not the man who'd been through hell and back with him. "Something else is going on, and I'm going to find out what it is." Quinn reached inside the de-weaponed trainee's jacket to find his ID tag. He made a point of not learning their names in case he had to kill them someday.

It was hard enough to do his job when a Calydon or a kid he didn't know went rogue. It was a hell of a lot tougher when they were friends, so he tried not to get personal if he could help it. It was the only way to survive his mission.

Gideon ground his teeth and didn't move to help him. Quinn could feel the turmoil inside Gideon as he struggled to understand what had happened. It was the same way he was feeling.

"I'm not due to report to Dante on the trainees' progress for two more days," Quinn said evenly. "That gives me forty-eight hours to find Elijah." Quinn located the ID tag. "Ajax Drachman." Drachman. The name sounded familiar. He knew he'd heard it before tonight, before the kid had shown up at his door. What was the kid's deal? Quinn checked another trainee. Roger Filcox. The name meant nothing to him. Not like Drachman. "Why did my weapon and Drachman's get stolen, but not the others?"

"Six dead innocents." Gideon ignored Quinn's

question as he strode over to a trainee and yanked the kid's shirt open so he could record the tag. "I'm reporting Elijah to Dante. We need to send out everyone to find him. He has to die." His voice became hard as he said the words. "We have no choice. It's our duty."

"Screw that." Quinn gave Gideon a cold stare across the bodies. "If Elijah can be brought back from the edge, we're going to do it. We owe him, like we all owe each other."

A shadow passed over Gideon's face. "You two aren't the only ones I owe. I have a duty to the innocents he might kill next. Innocents like these kids."

"For hell's sake, Gideon, this is *Elijah*. You can't condemn him outright. You know you can't." Quinn walked among the bodies, studying them, trying to think, trying to figure out Elijah's motivation, but he came up with no answers. There were no excuses for what his blood brother had done. The only explanation was that he had gone rogue, and, for him to murder his best friend, he had to be so far over the line that there was nothing left of the man who had been his friend. Quinn swore and slammed his sword into the earth in frustration. "I don't get it."

"Me neither." Gideon walked up and slammed his hand onto Quinn's shoulder. They stood side by side at the edge of the clearing, guarding the bodies they'd sworn to protect when the trainees had been given over to them. The kids they'd failed. The youths that Quinn had led to their deaths.

Why had he led them the wrong way? He was always right, but he'd made the wrong choice. Why? What had screwed with his instincts? Quinn listened to the wind whirling through the trees, and he opened his senses to the woods, trying to uncover the mask that had rendered his instincts inoperable. The forest smelled of death and treachery, and Quinn stood straighter. "Can you smell that? There's a shift of equilibrium. An imbalance. Something's not right."

Gideon's eyes narrowed, but he turned his head to the woods, closed his eyes and raised his face to the breeze. Quinn picked up the slight vibration as Gideon opened all his senses, reaching out on a metaphysical level to test the world.

After a moment, Gideon opened his eyes, staring into the forest. "You're right. I feel something dark lurking beneath the surface of the earth."

Hot damn. Quinn slammed his fist into his palm, psyched by the discovery. There really was something else going on. "We need to find Elijah and get answers," he said. "Killing him straight up isn't the solution. He's involved. He'll know."

The muscles in Gideon's jaw were working, the tendons in his neck rigid. "What if he kills other innocents while we search for him?" His eyes were dark with the agony of what he knew he had to do. "I can't let you go after him."

Quinn knew it was tearing Gideon up to make the decision that would result in the death of either his friend or maybe more innocents. Screw that. Quinn didn't have the same morals or ethics as Gideon, and he sure as hell had never claimed to be the most devoted follower of the Order's rigid code of conduct.

He was here for one reason, and that was to make sure the past didn't happen again. Now was his chance. He was certain Elijah was innocent. How and why he was so sure, he couldn't articulate. But his gut told him that Elijah needed a chance, and there was no way Quinn was walking away from his friend. He hadn't listened to his gut five hundred years ago, and that decision had led to the death of the man he considered his father.

Not again. Not this time. Today, there was only one choice Quinn could live with.

"It shouldn't be like this," Gideon said. "Elijah

shouldn't die without a trial. He shouldn't die at anyone's hands but ours."

"He isn't going to."

Gideon shot him a sharp look, and knowledge flared in his eyes as he realized what Quinn was about to do. He started to call out his axe to stop Quinn, but then his loyalty to Elijah made him hesitate, the barest pause. That split second of doubt gave Quinn the chance he needed.

Quinn belted Gideon in the back of his head with the butt of his sword before Gideon could react, knocking out his blood brother. He caught his friend as he slumped, and then eased the Calydon to the muddy ground. "Sorry, mate, but I couldn't let you make a choice we'd both regret."

He'd held back on the blow, so Gideon would be out for only about half a day, giving Quinn time to get a good lead on tracking Elijah. Once Gideon awoke, he'd do as he should and go straight to Dante, but they both would rest better with the knowledge that Quinn had a head start on finding Elijah first. The team would be dispatched after Elijah within minutes of Gideon's report, and the race would be on.

Quinn checked to make sure Gideon was still breathing, and then started sprinting toward his cabin to gather what he needed to go after Elijah. He had to slow after only a few steps, still reeling from the deathblow that Elijah had delivered him.

Nice. The life of his best friend was at stake, and he was going into battle with only one sword and a hangover from hell. He was at a fraction of his regular strength, and a posse of the most deadly warriors alive would be on his tail in less than a day.

Time to man up.

His weapon shimmered brightly in his grip, and then dissolved into the air. His brand burned like fire as the sword returned to his body, resting until the next time he needed it.

His blade sheathed, Quinn broke into an easy lope, forcing blood to surge to his muscles. If he did find Elijah, could he even bring him back from the edge? Or would he have to do what he did to his uncle so long ago?

Quinn swore.

There was no room for mistakes, not this time.

Dear God, let me be right.

Grace Matthews clenched the nylon strap of her backpack more tightly, her hand trembling with exhaustion. Or cold. Or fear. She didn't even know anymore. It didn't even matter.

All that mattered was that she'd made it to the place that rumors said didn't even exist. It was here. This address. This house.

But was *he* here? And if he was, could he help her? *Would* he help her? If he wouldn't, if he couldn't, her sister would die. Oh, God. *Ana.* Grace's throat tightened and tears welled up in her eyes.

She immediately lifted her chin and blinked away the tears. She wouldn't give up now. She'd found his home. She would make him help. There was no other option.

Grace took a shuddering breath and squared her shoulders, staring at the long, dirt driveway that disappeared into the shadowy woods. Trepidation rippled through her, and she wished for a moment that she'd arrived before night had fallen, before darkness shifted the playing field even further out of her favor.

As if a few bright rays of sunlight would help her if he decided she wasn't welcome.

She was only a human. Mostly.

Quinn Masters was one of the most deadly members of the Order of the Blade.

The odds were not in favor of the girl if the big, bad warrior got cranky about her invading his inner sanctum…

which was so not a constructive thought. She had to focus on positive thoughts, not envision her miserable demise at the hands of Quinn Masters.

For all she knew, this wasn't even his house. Rumors of where the Order members lived abounded on the Web. Most were false leads, and Grace could usually see through those fakes because she was an Illusionist, a magical being whose very essence was grounded in the disparity between reality and illusion.

Grace knew truth, and she knew lies, because she was one of those dreaded, hunted, shunned creatures who could cast false pictures into the world around her. She could create dark, twisted images that brought terrible things onto those who were exposed to them. They were horrible scenes that were so hard to suppress and so terrifyingly difficult to hide from the world...and from herself.

The moment she'd read that well-hidden nugget on that archaic website that Quinn Masters' home was located in this remote area of southeastern Oregon, she'd felt it was true. She'd been certain he was her answer. His name had practically pulsed on her computer screen, calling to her. She fought daily to pretend she wasn't a monster who deserved all the assassinations her kind had experienced over the centuries, but when her talents had shown her the truth about where she could find Quinn, she'd been thankful for who she was.

For that one minute, for one brief moment in her whole life, she'd been happy to be what she was. Deliriously happy. Insanely grateful.

Then grim reality had intruded, and the weight of all she carried had descended upon her once again.

After reading that tidbit about Quinn's home, Grace had embraced that last chance she'd been given, no matter how risky, far-fetched or unlikely it was. She'd paused long enough to throw critical necessities into a backpack, and then she'd taken off that very minute to search for the elusive warrior no one in mainstream society had talked to in years. One who was only rumored to exist. One who was said to be deadly and brutal, like all the other Order members. A warrior no sane person would try to track down.

If she was wrong that Quinn lived here and that he was sane, and if the nearby townspeople were right that the half-man who lived here really did hunt people at night... *God, please don't let me be wrong.*

The human world buzzed with rumors of the metaphysical. Humans knew about beings like the Calydons and Illusionists, but they didn't truly understand what they were, or what their powers were. Calydons were fierce immortal warriors created by violence thousands of years ago and destined to die by violence as well. They lived on the fringes of society, too dangerous to mingle with most other beings. They cared little about mixing it up with the human world, taking care of their own agendas within the dangerous subculture of the Otherworld.

Illusionists were different. They fit nowhere. Everyone feared them, everyone hated them. All they could do was try to hide and assimilate, hoping that no one figured out what they really were. It was easier to blend in as a human than to fight off vigilantes who wanted these threats to humanity wiped out.

Because that's exactly what Grace could be if she lost control: a threat to humanity.

The night settled darkly around Grace as she began to walk down the long driveway. Her boots scuffed on the pebbles, and her feet sank into the muddy earth. A cool mist drifted against her cheeks, and she shivered, pulling her jacket more tightly around her as the woods thickened. She wished she'd brought a heavier coat and warmer clothes.

God, she wanted to be home right now, not heading down some god-forsaken path into who knew what hell.

But what did she have to go home to?

She'd already been fired from her job at the yoga studio, because having one of their instructors related to an Otherworld murderer had seriously cut down on class attendance. Not that she'd minded. She couldn't afford to be noticed, and the news was too high profile. She'd taken her yoga mat and quietly slid off into the shadows, praying that somehow, someway, she could fix this without being noticed by the wrong people, the people who had been hunting her since she was fourteen.

As tempting as it was to run back to her home, crawl under her light blue comforter and hide, what was the point? What was there to return to?

To more news reports on the murders her missing sister was being held accountable for?

To another death threat for being related to a rumored killer with metaphysical powers?

To more nights in the empty house she shared with Ana, dreading the phone call that her sister had been apprehended and killed?

No.

Sitting around waiting for news of Ana's death wasn't an option. Grace was going to find her, prove her innocence, and bring her back safely. The house would remain empty until both sisters were back in it.

Grace wiped her palms on her jeans, hunched her shoulders against the damp wind, and crunched over the broken sticks that littered the driveway. She winced with each loud crack of another stick, knowing Quinn would be aware of her presence long before she reached his house.

He probably already knew she was there.

She glanced into the dark pine trees lining the road, wondering if he was in one of them.

Stalking her.

A trickle of fear crept down her spine and sudden pressure began to dig at her temples, signaling the ominous building of another illusion.

Oh, crap. *Not now.* Grace dropped to her knees and pressed her palms against her head, fighting against the swell of fear that was so dangerous to her. She tried to call upon years of practice to quell the emotions that would trigger the side of her that was so destructive, so deadly, the stuff of nightmares.

Normally, easy enough.

Now? The pain in her head intensified, like needles hammering relentlessly at her. Too many weeks of fear and stress were wearing down her defenses, and the threat of Quinn stalking her was too much. Her protective instincts were being triggered. Too strong. Too fast. The illusion was her body's natural defense to threats: throw up a mirage and run away while her attackers were caught in its thrall.

Grace's illusions wouldn't simply distract her adversaries. They would *kill*. The enemy, sure. But also friends, loved ones, and possibly even herself. Illusions were impotent unless you believed they were real, but Grace's were so vivid and powerful that even she couldn't convince her subconscious that they weren't real. The result: torture, agony and death to anyone unlucky enough to witness them. A great way to start any day.

She absolutely did not have time to kill herself right now. Who would save her sister if she were dead? Seriously! "Come *on*, Grace!"

She had to calm down. Had to slow her heart rate. Had to chill. She pressed her palms to her eyes. "My life is fine," she said. "Quinn's not going to kill me. Ana's going to be fine—" Raw fear for her sister's safety churned in her belly, and the pressure in her head became stronger. Faint blue light began to pulse in the air around her, a light that was the final precursor to one of her deadly illusions. "Dammit!"

She breathed deeply, inhaling the fresh, earthy scent of damp ground that reminded her of where she grew up, and she forced her mind back to the past, to the happy memories that always soothed her. She envisioned playing with her sister in the Vermont woods when they were little, watching Ana create fun illusions in the meadows. She saw Ana's butterfly illusions, the bunny rabbit ones, all those happy images her sister had made for Grace when she'd been struggling. Her dear, sweet little sister, gifted by some miracle with uplifting illusions instead of dark ones.

Grace breathed deeply, using the scent of pine and fresh dirt to anchor her in the memories of her past, of a time when nature brought her peace and love. She kept her mind relentlessly focused on the happy memories, listening to the sound of her sister's laughter mingled with her own. Finally, she felt her body begin to believe that everything was okay, that there was no imminent threat to her safety. Her muscles relaxed, her heart rate slowed, and the pressure in her head began to ease.

Her shoulders shook with relief, and she slumped to the dirt, exhausted by the battle. How many more times could she beat back her illusions? It was becoming increasingly difficult to control them since Ana had disappeared. Without being able to rely on Ana's calming images to ease her stress, the increasing worry about her sister was putting her dangerously close to the edge. Grace knew she was fighting a losing battle with the monster she'd kept at bay for almost a decade and a half.

"Just a little longer," she told herself. "You can do it." But even as she said it, doubt niggled at her and fear rippled through her. How bad would it be when she finally lost it? How many people would she kill? Would she be her own next victim?

The wind whispered through the pine trees, drawing Grace's attention back to her surroundings, reminding her she was invading the land of a warrior who had hidden himself away so effectively because he didn't want to deal with people like her. People with emotional baggage, people with needs, people who wanted something from him. People who would slow him down and distract him from his brutal mission.

She looked down the darkened road, and her hands slowly closed into determined fists. "I'm sorry to bother you," she told the night, in case he was listening, "but my sister needs help. I won't let you turn me down."

The wind rippled through the branches, like the forest was laughing softly at her, trying to chase her back down the driveway.

Grace tugged her lightweight running jacket tighter around her body, shivering under the cold mist. She resisted the temptation to look toward the street where the farmer had dropped her off, a nice old man who'd given her a ride after her too-old car had broken down and she hadn't wanted to wait to have it fixed. Her escort had refused to drive any closer to the lair of the man-beast, leaving it up to her to hike the rest of the way to his home.

There is no retreat. Instead, she faced the rutted, shadowed driveway and resumed her trek towards the one man who could save her sister.

She had one thing to offer Quinn to get him to help her. If it didn't work, her sister was dead. And most likely, so was she.

Quinn raced soundlessly through the thick woods, his injuries long forgotten, urgency coursing through him as he neared his house. He covered the last thirty yards, leapt over a fallen tree, and then reached the edge of the clearing by his cabin.

There she was.

He stopped dead, fading back into the trees as he stared at the woman he'd scented when he was still two hours away, a lure that had eviscerated all weakness from his body and fueled him into a dead sprint back to his house.

His lungs heaving with the effort of pushing his severely damaged body so hard, Quinn stood rigidly as he studied the woman whose scent had called to him through the dark night. She'd yanked him out of his thoughts about Elijah and galvanized him with energy he hadn't been able to summon on his own.

And now he'd found her.

She'd wedged herself up against the back corner of his porch, barely protected from the cold rain and wet wind. Her knees were pulled up against her chest, her delicate arms wrapped tightly around them as if she could hold onto her body heat by sheer force of will. Her shoulders were hunched, her forehead pressed against her knees while damp tangles of dark brown hair tumbled over her arms.

Her chest moved once. Twice. A trembling, aching breath into lungs that were too cold and too exhausted to work as well as they should.

He took a step toward her, and another, then three more before he realized what he was doing. He froze, suddenly aware of his urgent need to get to her. To help her. To fill her with heat and breathe safety into her trembling body. To whisk her off his porch and into his cabin.

Into his bed.

Quinn stiffened at the thought. Into his bed? Since when? He didn't engage when it came to women. Not anymore. The risk was too high for him, and for all Calydons. Any woman he met could be his mate, his fate, his doom. His *sheva.*

He was never tempted.

Until now.

Until this cold, vulnerable stranger had appeared inexplicably on his doorstep. He should be pulling out his sword, not thinking that the fastest way to get her warm would be to run his hands over her bare skin and infuse her whole body with the heat from his.

But his sword remained quiet. His instincts warned

him of nothing.

What the hell was going on? She had to be a threat. Nothing else made sense. Women didn't stumble onto his home, and he didn't get a hard-on from simply catching a whiff of one from miles away.

His aching quads braced against the cold air, he inhaled her scent again, searching for answers to a thousand questions. She smelled delicate, with a hint of something sweet, and a flavoring of the bitterness of true desperation. He could practically taste her anguish, a cold, acrid weight in the air, and he knew she was in trouble.

His hands flexed with the need to close the distance between them, to crouch by her side, to give her his protection. But he didn't move. He didn't dare. He had to figure out why he was so compelled by her, why he was responding like this, especially at a time when he couldn't afford any distraction.

She moaned softly and curled into an even tighter ball. His muscles tightened, his entire soul burning with the need to help her. Quinn narrowed his eyes and pried his gaze off her to search the woods.

With the life of his blood brother in his hands, an Order posse soon to be after him, and his own body still half in the grave, he should be so focused on business that a woman could dance naked on his chest and he still wouldn't notice. It shouldn't be possible for a woman he didn't even know, hadn't met, and barely even seen to rock him on his ass like this simply because he'd caught a whiff of her scent.

He was disciplined, dammit, and disciplined warriors didn't fall for that shit. It made no sense.

His intense need for her felt too similar to the compulsion that had sent him to the river three nights ago. Another trap? He'd suspected it from the moment he'd first reacted to her scent, but he'd been unable to resist the temptation, and he'd hauled ass to get back to his house.

Yeah, true, he'd also needed to get back to his cabin to retrieve his supplies to go after Elijah. The fact that she'd imbued him with new strength had been a bonus he wasn't going to deny.

But now he had to be sure. A trap or not? Quinn laughed softly. Shit. He hoped it was. If it wasn't, there was only one other reason he could think of that could explain his reaction to her, and that would be if she was his mate. His *sheva*. His ticket to certain destruction.

No chance.

He wouldn't allow it.

He had no time for dealing with that destiny right now. It was time to get in, get out, and go after Elijah. His amusement faded as he took a final survey of the woods. There was no lurking threat he could detect. Maybe he'd made it back before he'd been expected, or maybe an ambush had been aborted.

Either way, he had to get into his house, get his stuff, and move on. His gaze returned to the woman, and he noticed a drop of water sliding down the side of her neck, trickling over her skin like the most seductive of caresses. He swore, realizing she wasn't going to leave. She'd freeze to death before she'd abandon her perch.

He knew he had to go to her. He couldn't let her die on his front step. Not this woman. Not her.

He would make it fast, he would make it efficient, he would stay on target for his mission, but he would get her safe.

Keeping alert for any indication that this was a setup, Quinn stepped out of the woods and into the clearing. He'd made no sound, not even a whisper of his clothing, and yet she sensed him.

She sat up, her gaze finding him instantly in the dim light, despite his stealthy approach. They made eye contact, and the world seemed to stop for a split second. The moment he saw those silvery eyes, something thumped in his chest. Something visceral and male howled inside him, raging to be set free.

As he strode up, she unfolded herself from her cramped position and pulled herself to her feet, her gaze never leaving his. Her face was wary, her body tense, but she lifted her chin ever so slightly and set her hands on her hips, telling him that she wasn't leaving.

Her courage and determination, held together by that tiny, shivering frame, made satisfaction thud through him. There was a warrior in that slim, exhausted body.

She said nothing as he approached, and neither of them spoke as he came to a stop in front of her.

Up close, he was riveted. Her dark eyelashes were clumped from the rain. Her skin was pale, too pale. Her face was carrying the weight of a thousand burdens. But beneath that pain, those nightmares, that hell, lay a delicate femininity that called to him. The luminescent glow of her skin, the sensual curve of her mouth, the sheen of rain on her cheekbones, the simple silver hoops in her ears... It awoke in him something so male, so carnal, so primal, he wanted to throw her up against the wall and consume her until their bodies melted together in a single, scorching fire.

She searched his face with the same intensity that was raging through him. He felt like she was tearing through his shields, cataloguing everything about him, all the way down to his soul.

He studied her carefully, and she let him, not flinching when his gaze traveled down her body. His blood pulsed as he noted the curve of her breasts under her rain-slicked jacket, the sensuous curve of her hips, and even the mud on her jeans and boots. He almost groaned at his need to palm her hips, drag her over to him, and mark her with his kiss. Loose strands of thick dark hair curled around her neck and shoulders, like it was clinging to her for safety.

Protectiveness surged from deep inside him and he clenched his fists against the urge to sweep her into his arms and carry her inside, away from whatever hardships had brought her to his doorstep.

Double hell. He'd hoped his reaction would lessen when he got close to her, but it had intensified. He'd never felt like this before. He'd never had this response to a woman.

What the hell was going on? *Sheva*. The word was like a demon, whispering through his mind. He shut it out. He would never allow himself to bond with his mate. If that was what was going on, she was out of there immediately, before they were both destroyed forever.

Intent on sending her away, he looked again at her face, and then realized he was irrevocably ensnared. Her beautiful silver eyes were aching with a soul-deep pain that shattered what little defenses he had against her. He simply couldn't abandon her.

It didn't matter what she wanted. It didn't matter why she was there. She was coming inside. He would make sure it didn't interfere with his mission. He would make dead sure it turned out right. No matter what.

Without a word, he grabbed her backpack off the floor, surprised at how heavy it was. Either she had tossed her free weights in it, or she had packed her life into it.

He had a bad feeling it wasn't a set of dumbbells.

Quinn walked past her and unlocked his front door. He shoved it open, then stood back. Letting her decide. Hoping she would walk away and spare them both.

She took a deep breath, glanced at his face one more time, then walked past him and into his cabin.

Hell.

He paused to take one more survey of his woods, found nothing amiss, and then he followed her into his home and shut the door behind them.

Chapter 2

Quinn Masters was far more than Grace had been prepared for.

She could feel the heat from his stare as he followed her into the cabin, and her skin felt like it was on fire. From the moment she'd lifted her head and seen him striding toward her, she'd known she was in trouble. The lithe glide of his muscular body across the bare ground, the riveting intensity of his dark eyes, his hard jaw, his dauntingly broad shoulders…she was way out of her league.

His presence radiated strength and power, his eyes burned with sharp intelligence, and his body pulsed with raw maleness that took root deep in her soul. One sight of him, and she'd been consumed with such intense desire she'd been unable to do anything but stare, her pulse jumping with each step that had brought him closer to her.

She was viscerally aware of him as he followed her inside, his heavy boots silent on the wood floor. The door closed with the softest click, and Grace jumped, awareness and anticipation flooding her senses. She was locked in. With him. On his turf.

For a moment, there was no movement behind her, and she knew he was standing by the door, not moving, not talking. Waiting? Watching?

Her heart started to hammer with fear and a sensual

heat that had no business existing in a moment like this. Sweat broke out on her palms, despite the intense cold still racking her body. *Come on, Grace, pull it together.*

She made herself look around the cabin, forcing herself to see him as a man, not an immortal warrior who could rattle her with one, scorching look.

It was a one-room cabin, a small space that didn't seem large enough for the enormity of his presence. She saw a utility kitchen in one corner. *Okay, Grace, see? He makes food. That's pretty ordinary, right?* A king-size bed took up most of the remaining space, and a closed door led to what must have been the bathroom. Her gaze went back to the bed, and she felt her cheeks burning as she forced herself to turn away.

Taking up one entire wall was a huge stone fireplace. The thick, braided rug in front of the hearth looked soft and inviting. She had a sudden vision of flames reaching up high in that fireplace, of golden light flickering over Quinn's skin, of her stretching out beside him on that rug—*Oh, God, Grace! What is wrong with you?*

She jerked around, hoping desperately he couldn't read her mind and hear her embarrassing and completely out of character "Calydon Fan Girl" thoughts.

Quinn was standing in front of the closed door, water dripping from his leather jacket and dark jeans. He flicked the water out of his hair with a quick jerk of his head. Outside, he had seemed large, a man who could control the very forest surrounding them. Inside the small space, he was indomitable. His gray T-shirt was drenched, plastered to his muscular chest. Whiskers shadowed his jaw. But it was his eyes that once again compelled her.

They were dark, almost black, and he was watching her with such intense focus she felt like she would never be able to shake him.

She lifted her chin. "I'm Grace Matthews."

He raised one dark eyebrow and a muscle ticked

in his cheek. "Grace Matthews," he repeated softly, almost as if he were rolling her name around in his mouth and sampling it, like the most delectable offering.

His voice was deep and rough, and goose bumps popped up on her arms. He was so male, so tough, and yet his voice seemed to thrum through her, easing the fear licking at her composure and her focus. She managed her first deep breath in hours, and he nodded with satisfaction. "You're cold," he observed.

She became aware of how violently she was shaking and how tightly she was hugging herself. A man like Quinn Masters would have no time for someone who was weak. She quickly pried her arms away from her body and shoved her hands in her pockets. "I'm fine," she said firmly. "Just a little chilly."

He smiled then, a brief flash that made his whole face soften and relax. "Are you now?" He walked past her, grabbed the comforter off the bed and held it out to her.

She blinked in surprise, and her throat tightened at the kindness that reminded her of a life long forgotten, a time when she wasn't on her own, fighting to survive. His small gesture made something inside her crumble, and suddenly she had the most ridiculous urge to cry.

She hadn't succumbed to tears even once since Ana had disappeared. She'd worked hard to stay strong and to maintain her focus. Then some stranger handed her a blanket and it made her want to start sobbing? She had no time for tears. She really didn't. She cleared her throat and managed a small smile. "Thanks." She shrugged off her drenched coat, and he took it from her hand as he gave her the blanket.

"No problem." Watching her as if he were taking note of every detail about her, he tossed her jacket over a hook by the fireplace, then made quick work of starting a fire while she wrapped herself in the thick blanket that smelled of wood smoke, man and warmth.

Within moments, the small cabin was filled with flickering orange light, the roar of flames, and the crackle of dried logs burning. The reflection from the fire danced over Quinn's skin just as she'd envisioned it, and his gaze locked on hers, as if he were thinking the same thing.

Heat rose inside the comforter wrapped so tightly around her, and suddenly she wanted to peel it off her body and—

His eyes narrowed and his expression changed from smoldering heat to utter and intense coldness. Gone was the humanity of that quick smile he'd given her, replaced by the calculating warrior who saw her only as a threat, or an impediment. She knew then why he hadn't said much so far. He wasn't ready. He was still assessing her and figuring her out before deciding his avenue of attack.

Suddenly cold again, she hugged her arms tighter, trying to stop herself from trembling. But even her belly was aching from shivering. She'd been too cold for too long. This part of Oregon wasn't supposed to be this cold in the winter. Warm and rainy, not below freezing with the forecast of an ice storm.

Quinn walked to the kitchen, where he grabbed three bagels and a couple bottles of water. She sighed and eased over to the fire, trying to get warm and collect herself. She'd have one chance to ask for his help, one opportunity to play her hand. She had to get the timing right, the delivery perfect, all of it carefully executed. What kind of request would he respond to? She needed to analyze him exactly as he'd been evaluating her.

Quinn headed back in her direction, and her belly fluttered as he neared. But all he did was shove a bagel and a bottle of water at her before easing himself onto his bed, the only place to sit in the room. The faded blue blankets were askew from when he'd ripped off the comforter, and one of the pillows was on the floor.

He opened his water, took a big bite of the bagel

and leaned back, grimacing slightly when his back hit the headboard. His body was solid and well-muscled as he hooked his arm over the pine bed frame. There was a scar above his right eye and his nose looked like it had been shattered more than once, giving him the air of a soldier who had endured the worst and had come out the victor.

His brown eyes regarded her coldly. Waiting. "So, Grace Matthews," he said finally, "what do you want?"

It was time.

She willed herself courage, then dragged herself and the comforter across the room and perched on the edge of the bed, decadently close to his legs. He was sprawled carelessly over the mattress, as if he hadn't had the energy to hold himself up a moment longer. He hadn't bothered to take off his muddy boots and didn't even seem to notice that oversight.

Or maybe that's how he always slept: owning his space, fully dressed, and ready to go to battle in a split second.

She faced him, tucking her feet up under her to keep her boots from brushing against his heavily muscled thigh. She met his gaze, trying to keep the desperation out of her voice. "I need your help."

His face grew hard and unreadable, and she flinched at the sudden thread of warning in the air. *Get the hell away from me.* The message was clear and it was pushing at her like a hot poker, driving her to jump to her feet and run to the door.

But she had no choice. He was her last option. There was nowhere else to go. She braced her feet on the floor and ordered her body to stay where it was. "No."

His brow wrinkled in a brief show of confusion. "No, what?"

"I'm not *getting the hell away from you,* as you so eloquently put it."

Tension snapped through his body and he jerked

upright. *"You heard that?"*

"Of course. How could I not? I'd have to be dead not to."

He cursed and shoved to his feet with a groan of pain that made her frown. "Are you all right?" she asked.

He ignored her question, running his hand through his hair in agitation. "How the hell did you hear my thoughts?"

She blinked. "Your thoughts? You didn't say that out loud?"

"No. I didn't." He leaned over her suddenly, his hands on the blankets on either side of her hips, invading her space. "Tell me—" He stopped suddenly and he bent closer and inhaled. "You smell unbelievable."

"I can't read thoughts," she whispered, her heart racing at the intimacy of his position. His face was inches from hers, his lips barely a breath away. She could feel the heat from his body radiating through the air like a hot wind on her face. Her spine curled at the deep rumble of his voice, at the intensity of his emotions, stripping right through her and burning her skin.

She edged backwards, even as she wanted to lean into him, to press her nose against his neck, to inhale the scent that was him. Her response to his nearness was terrifying. What was wrong with her? Was her reaction simply because he was a Calydon? She'd heard they were intensely sensual, but he made her feel like she was spinning out of control, catapulting down a crevasse to fall under his dangerous spell.

He cursed and stood up, jerking his hands back to his sides. His jaw was clenched, shadowed with coarse whiskers. The fire gave enough light that she could see now that his jeans were black, and his hip-length leather jacket was creased, battered and ripped to shreds over his left forearm. It looked like it had been worn so much that it had become part of his body. Like it belonged on him.

He shifted and a flash of pain crossed his features before he could school them into a neutral expression.

"You're hurt?" Concern flared inside her and she grabbed his hand instinctively before she could think about it, her fingers closing over the roughness of his palm. Shock rattled her as soon as their skin touched, and she was falling—

His hand tightened around hers, and his eyes darkened. For a moment, the world fell away and it was just him, just the heat of his hand and—

He growled and yanked his hand out of hers. "You need to leave. Now. I have...things I need to do. Someone to find and kill." He added the last as if trying to scare her, then he turned away, grabbed a heavy parka from a corner armoire she hadn't noticed, and held it out. "This will keep you dry and warm. Now, get out."

She stood up and faced him, making no move to take the coat, realizing she probably had about two seconds before he picked her up and tossed her out the door. Here was her moment. Succeed or fail. It was now. "I'm here because I need your help finding my sister." She couldn't keep the fear, the anguish, and the worry out of her voice. "She's missing."

Softness flickered through those dark eyes, and his hand went to her face. His fingers drifted over her cheek with the lightest touch, making her throat tighten at the tender intimacy. She froze, afraid any movement from her would destroy the moment, drive him away.

Then he cursed, dropped his hand and strode past her. He swept her backpack off the floor and yanked open the front door. "Out."

She didn't move, digging her fingernails into the palms of her hands at the hostile expression on Quinn's face. His eyes were cold and harsh, a reflection of the Calydon warrior he was. A man who had killed many, and never flinched.

She lifted her chin and let him see the truth in her face as to why she was here, why she'd picked *him*. "In case you haven't heard the news out here in the woods, your teammate Elijah Ross was found murdered last night. I think my sister did it."

Quinn felt like she'd sucker-punched him in the gut. "Elijah's dead?"

She nodded. "Yes, I'm so sorry."

"No." Impossible. He would have known that, wouldn't he? Yeah, he'd blocked his connection with Elijah because he didn't want his blood brother to know he'd survived the attack until he was ready to use their connection to hunt him down, but he was damn sure he would have sensed Elijah's death. He folded his arms over his chest, suspicions glaring in his mind as he quickly recovered from the shock of her words. What was Grace trying to pull? "He's not dead."

"I wasn't sure you'd believe me, so I brought the paper." Keeping a wary eye on him, she held out her hand for her backpack, which he still gripped in his fist.

"I'll check." He unzipped the bag, leaping at the chance to see if he could learn anything about this woman who'd read his damn mind and nearly gotten herself seduced when she'd curled up on his bed in that comforter, looking so damn vulnerable and sexy he'd nearly forgotten everything that mattered. Like, you know, saving his blood brother, redeeming his uncle's death, fulfilling his life's mission, and, of course, staying the hell away from any woman who could be his *sheva*.

Inside the black nylon bag, a folded newspaper was wedged down beside a pair of jeans and a pair of thick socks. He caught a whiff of her scent from the clothes, and his groin hardened instantly. Hell. He'd been in a constant state of arousal since he'd first scented her, and it was making him jumpy as hell.

He needed to chill. It was most likely a simple explanation. It'd been too damn long since he'd been with a woman, and she was the one who was here. That was it. Nothing else.

The need for women pulsed hot in the veins of all Calydons, but any female they took up with could be their *sheva*. Many tried to stay away from women completely, despite the burning passion that drove them. It was a constant battle that few Calydons could win over the long term. Like Quinn's fellow Order member Ian, who'd wound up meeting his *sheva* despite all the safeguards he'd taken, and he'd died for his mistake. Quinn swore, still pissed at how Ian's situation had unraveled. It was another strike against his theory, against the odds of succeeding on the mission that had galvanized him for five hundred years.

Quinn had held off women for a long time, and the urge to grab Grace and sink himself into her was pulsing so hard and so deep that he could barely restrain himself.

Lust. Simple damn lust.

That was all he could afford for it to be, because he had much more important shit to deal with right now.

He let her bag drop to his feet and opened the newspaper. Dated today, Elijah's mug shot was on the front page, and Quinn stared into the eyes of the man he knew so well. The teammate who'd pulled him from death countless times, who knew secrets about him no one else did.

Quinn traced his thumb over the black and white image as he carefully unwound the mental shields he'd erected and opened his mind to his blood brother. *Elijah, you with me?*

There was no response. Not even a pulse of energy. Simply emptiness. Like Elijah had never existed. Quinn had connected with Elijah during the attack, but he hadn't been able to pull anything on him since he'd woken up. Not a damn thing, for the first time since they'd blood bonded five hundred years ago. *Elijah.* He sent the call with renewed force. *Where the hell are you?* He swore in frustration when there was nothing and looked back down at the photo, a dark dread settling over him. Was it really possible that he was dead? "Son of a bitch."

Sympathy softened Grace's face as she touched his arm. He froze at the unexpected intimacy.

"I'm sorry he's dead," she said, empathy so full in her voice that he was actually confused. No one spoke to him like that, like they thought he was some emotion-laden beast. "I know what it feels like to lose someone you love. It sucks beyond belief."

The deep pain in her voice tugged at him. Instead of brushing her hand away, he turned his head enough to look at her, surprised to see the sadness in her eyes. She smiled at him, and he wanted to open his arms to her and offer her comfort from her suffering. "Who died in your life?" he asked quietly.

"My parents."

"Sucks." He set his hand over hers and squeezed lightly. He knew that kind of pain. It did suck, no matter how many times you had to face it.

She nodded. "Yes." Her grip tightened on his arm, her fingers so delicate, yet surprisingly powerful. "That's why I can't lose Ana. I can't let her die. She's all I have left."

He felt the truth in her words, and they felt far too similar to the plea that had been issued to him five hundred years ago by his uncle, the one Quinn had ignored just before he'd ruined the lives of everyone he cared about. Was Grace his chance for redemption?

No. She couldn't be. It was Elijah. That was his mission. He had to stay focused. He forced himself to peel her hand off his arm and set it back gently by her side. "I'm sorry about your sister."

"I'm not. It's not over yet." She tucked her hands into the front pockets of her jeans, as if she couldn't quite resist touching him without locking her hands down. "I need your help."

"You want me to save your sister? The woman who supposedly killed Elijah?" He raised his brows. "How's that going to work, then?"

"She's being forced," Grace said hurriedly. "She would never hurt anyone on her own. She's not capable of it."

"Yeah, well, neither is Elijah. How sure are you that you're right?" Quinn's neck was still throbbing, his body starting to shut down after being pushed so hard when it hadn't yet recovered. He needed to rebuild his stores of energy and soon.

Grace's eyes glowed with passion and commitment. "I don't have a single shred of doubt about Ana," she said firmly. "There's no chance she has hurt anyone, at least not willingly."

"If she's so incapable of doing it, then why is she a suspect?" He eased down on the bed, saw Grace's furrowed brow, and realized he was grimacing in pain. He shut that down fast and opened the paper to read it more carefully.

Grace cleared her throat. "People have seen her at the murders. She has the same eyes I do. They stand out."

Oh, yeah, he'd noticed her eyes. Damn near drowned in them more than once already.

"Have they seen her kill anyone?" Below the picture of Elijah were several photos of the crime scene. Police tape, trees, the back of a ramshackle building. There was a blurred outline of a man's body, as if the newspaper reporter hadn't been permitted to get close enough for a quality photo.

"No," Grace said. "That's not how it would work with her."

"Then what's her deal?" He scanned the story quickly. Elijah had been killed less than three hours away from Quinn's cabin at a bar called The Gun Rack, and he was thought to have been dead for less than an hour before he'd been found.

He'd been murdered two days after he'd harvested the weapons and left Quinn for dead. Elijah, murdered? Who the hell could take him down? He glanced at Grace, who still hadn't answered his question. "What's your sister? Demon?"

Her cheeks flushed. "No, she has a gentle spirit. She doesn't have any offensive powers."

"Then she couldn't have killed him." Quinn frowned as he read a quote from the local sheriff, that all evidence pointed to it being another murder by a local woman, Ana Matthews, who had supposedly been roaming around the Pacific Northwest killing other men. He recognized two of the names as other Calydons.

His instincts began to burn as he read the rest of the story. Dead Calydons turning up around the city? He hadn't heard anything about it, and the newspaper claimed the honor of being the one to break the story. "Son of a bitch," he muttered. How had the Order not known what had been going on? And what about the ones the press didn't know about? Like the trainees?

Hell.

He read quickly. Ten minutes after the first police officers had arrived, while they were standing around assessing the crime scene, the body had vanished. They'd turned around and it was simply gone. Everyone had assumed it had disappeared as Calydon bodies did after death.

Grim reality began to set in. If Elijah had been killed, that was exactly what would have happened with his body. He was so old that two hours was about as long as he would have lasted before disintegrating into the earth.

"Damn." He threw the newspaper aside. "He's not dead. I would know it." If Elijah was dead, then Quinn had failed him. *Failed.* It couldn't be over. He couldn't have screwed up like that.

"Ana is my sister's name. Anastasia Matthews." Grace hadn't moved from her spot in the middle of the room. Her hands were still in her pockets and she was watching him, her brows furrowed in concentration, but that soft look of empathy was still on her face.

He was relieved she hadn't moved closer, but frustrated at the same time. He wanted to grab her, haul her over him, and release his frustrations about Elijah into her, to own her, body, soul, mind and—

Shit. He couldn't even concentrate with her around. "Grace. Your sister couldn't have killed Elijah. No one could kill him except for an Order member. He's too good. Elijah is my problem, not yours, and I need to—"

"Ana disappeared six weeks ago," she interrupted, "and this is the fifth death the police are blaming on her. There's a bounty out on her, double if she's brought in dead." Grace moved over to the bed and wrapped her hand tightly around the post on the footboard, as if it were the only thing holding her up. "On the news report of Elijah's death, I saw things she'd left behind, things that are only hers, so I know she was there when he died." Her voice cracked slightly and she looked up at the ceiling, trying to keep her composure.

But it was a lie. She was terrified, vulnerable and alone, and she had to be desperate, since she'd dared come to him for help. Quinn gritted his teeth against the need to comfort her. He didn't have time for this. He *couldn't* have time for this.

Grace looked at him again, her silver eyes aching with pain. "I *know* she wouldn't kill anyone. Someone is forcing her to do this, or using her powers to aid a murderer. If you find my sister, you'll find the person responsible for your friend's death. It wasn't her. Someone else is involved."

He narrowed his eyes at her certainty about her sister. "What exactly is your sister's power?"

Grace's cheeks turned red. "Um—"

What did she not want him to know? "Grace?"

She finally met his gaze. "She brings peace and harmony to everyone around her."

"Peace and harmony?" he echoed. How in the hell would that be useful in taking down immortal warriors? "What is she? A freaking angel who happens to carry around a machete?"

Grace shook her head. "She's very powerful," she said evasively.

"Very powerful," he repeated. "That's all you're going to tell me?" The woman was holding out on him. He knew it without a doubt. The question was: what was she trying to hide and why? "What exactly is she?"

Grace shrugged. "Does it matter? Doesn't it make sense to just find her?"

"I haven't decided what makes sense." Quinn reread the article while he thought, but the more he considered Grace's story, the more it seemed to fit. Just as Grace believed her sister wouldn't kill anyone on her own, he was damned sure Elijah would never go rogue, and he'd never turn traitor. But the disturbance he'd felt in his woods hadn't been happy angel dust, so it hadn't been Ana's sister he'd been sensing. Having a third party involved made sense. Big sense. It was exactly what he'd wanted—an indication that he was right to give Elijah a chance.

He tapped his finger on the paper. "So, we've got a missing angel—" He didn't miss Grace's telling flinch at his word choice, telling him that her sister was no damn angel. "And we've got a bunch of dead Calydons who couldn't have been killed by her." And he had Elijah going on a murderous rampage *after* all the other deaths had already occurred. The first death had occurred several months ago, and Elijah had been fine then.

He smacked the paper with his palm. "Hot damn, sweetheart. We've got another player, one we don't know.

I can feel it—" He grinned and looked up at Grace, then tensed when he realized she'd worked her way closer to him.

She was, in fact, standing directly in front of him, leaning into his space. Her hands were still in her pockets, but her gaze was fastened on his face, and he caught a whiff of her scent, calling for him, and damned if every part of his body didn't respond faster than a dog after a bone.

Sheva. The thought whispered through his mind again, and he shot to his feet. He set his hands on her shoulders and made her step back, but damn, she felt so good under his palms. She stared at him, desire flaring in those silver eyes of hers, and he couldn't stop from letting his thumbs drift over her shoulders.

"Stop," she whispered.

"Shit, yeah." He forced himself to release her and walked across the room, needing space from her, from her temptation. "I don't believe Elijah is dead. I would know."

"Quinn—"

"No." He glared at her. "I would know," he repeated. "I'm going to find him, and if your sister is with him, I'll get her, too. And I'll get answers from them both." As an Order member with obligations to his team, and as a blood brother on a mission to save Elijah, agreeing to get her sister was more than Quinn should offer, but he could do no less. Not for this woman who had descended into his life and rattled him so inexplicably.

Or not so inexplicably, if she was the woman he'd been avoiding his whole life.

Gratitude flashed on her face and her eyes lit up with such appreciation he knew she was going to hug him. Having her arms wrapped around him and her body pressed up against his…hell. They'd both be damned if that got started.

He spun away from her and stalked across the room.

"Thank you," she said quietly.

"You're welcome." *Thank you?* No one had thanked him for a damn thing in five hundred years. Who the hell thanked an Order of the Blade member? Crumbled in fear, yeah. Despised, certainly. Lusted after, yeah, that too. But *thanked?*

He didn't know what to make of her. He really didn't. A part of him, a dangerous, foolhardy part of him, wanted to slide that deadbolt on his door and spend the next forty-eight hours locked down with her, finding out every damn secret she had in her mind, her soul and her body.

Yeah, because that wouldn't be a risky thing to do, given the level of sensuality and desire between them, and that little incident of the mind reading. She was setting off every one of his alarms, and he had a bad, bad feeling about exactly what she might be. His mate. His destiny. His doom.

Screw that shit. He was cutting her loose, before the risk became a grim reality that would destroy them both forever. But the mere thought of ditching her made him want to toss her over his shoulder like some caveman and keep her by his side.

Again, not a good sign for a warrior who'd had no trouble doing the "love 'em and leave 'em" thing for the last few centuries. Self-preservation always trumped lust... until he'd met her.

"I'm heading out." He opened a hidden wall cabinet and pulled out a large pack, already stashed full of everything he would need. As he slung it over his shoulder, he caught a glimpse of her with her tousled brown hair and delicate frame. Something softened in his chest, something that hadn't been soft since he'd murdered his own uncle. "You can stay here tonight and leave in the morning," he offered in a move completely uncharacteristic of an anti-social bastard who never shared his space. "If I find your sister, she'll tell you what happened. If she doesn't contact you, then..." He forced himself to shrug. "It means I'm still looking." Or it could mean he'd had to kill her sister, but shit, he didn't want to go down that road.

He was tired of crap like that. He really was.

"What?" Her eyes flashed with awareness, and then disbelief. "You're going without me?"

"Hell, yes."

She set her hands on her hips and glared at him. "You expect me to sit here and do nothing while my sister's life is in danger? The person manipulating her could make you their next target! I'm coming."

He headed toward the door. "There's no chance you're coming with me, or even coming near me again. Trust me, it has to be this way." He grabbed the doorknob and started to turn it—

"Stop!"

The urgency in her voice made his instincts ignite instantly, and he had his sword out and in his hand before he was even aware he'd done it. "What's wrong?"

Grace was staring at the front door, her hand over her heart. "Something's out there."

✖✖✖

Quinn didn't question Grace for an instant. Her conviction was too certain.

There was a threat in his woods.

He immediately tuned his senses to the outdoors. He heard the rain drumming on his roof, so loud he couldn't hear anything else. The scent of damp earth and moss was so strong it blocked all other odors. He frowned, realizing that the scents and sounds of nature were being magnified to mask others and provide cover. Shit! Was the Order already there for him? Or had Elijah come to finish the job? Or was it someone else? Something else?

His spine tingling with anticipation, he reached for the lock to head out to investigate, driven by the need to find out what was going on—

"No! Don't go!" Grace grabbed his arm, jerking his focus off the woods and onto her.

He swore under his breath when he looked into her worried face, realizing that if he went outside, he'd be leaving Grace alone. Unprotected.

Unacceptable.

He didn't bother to question his need to make sure she was safe. It was too strong to ignore. He simply couldn't leave her behind. He would have to manage the situation to both address the threat outside and keep Grace safe. "Stay here."

Quinn slammed the deadbolt shut, strode across the room, then threw his shoulder against the bed and shoved it to the side. He passed his hands over the knotted pine floor until he found the right location and pressed a trigger spot until one of the knots popped up. Using the knot as a handle, he straddled several boards, braced himself, then wrenched up six boards and the half-ton steel door they hid, revealing a dark tunnel below.

He grabbed her backpack and tossed it down the hole along with his. "This way out."

But Grace didn't move, and she wasn't even looking at him. She was staring at the front wall. "An illusion is building outside," she said. "In your woods."

He paused with his hand extended toward her. "What did you say?"

"An illusion." Her gaze was riveted at the wall, as if she could see something visible only to her. "Something powerful. It's building. I can feel it." She frowned. "It's not Ana. It's too dark. It's a bad one. I—" She closed her eyes and suddenly went down to her knees, fingers digging into her temples as she hunched over. "Oh, God. Not again."

He sprinted over to Grace and crouched beside her, gripping her shoulders. "What's wrong with you?"

She shook her head. "It's the illusion. I can't stop—

" Her voice broke off as she groaned with pain.

The illusion? What the hell was going on here? Quinn tightened his grip on her and pulled her against him, keeping his sword ready and angled at the door. He ratcheted up his senses, searching even the most minute rhythms in the night for a clue on what was stalking them. He still felt compelled to go outside and search his woods, but that urge couldn't compete with his need to keep his ass right where he could make sure Grace was safe—

Flames exploded around them, his furniture igniting from the intense heat. He yanked Grace into the curve of his body, trying to shield her. They were surrounded by flames in every direction. Jesus. They were going to die right there—

What the hell kind of thought was that? Giving up? Panic? Shit. Quinn realized then that the fire must be the illusion Grace had sensed building in his woods. It was working him, trying to mess with his emotions, to make him believe that this unbeatable fire was going to kill him.

Screw that. Nothing was unbeatable, and any contradictory thought was not his own. "It's an illusion," he told himself as he tucked Grace's head under his chin, pressing her face against him to block the smoke. Illusion or not, he could feel it burning his chest. Crap. It was a strong one if it could actually cause physical harm. He'd never run into that before. "We'll walk right out past it," he said. "Come on."

Grace grabbed his arm. "No, we can't. This illusion is too powerful. Your body will burn just as if it's a real fire, because your mind believes it's real."

"No illusion is strong enough to cause actual physical harm." But he couldn't deny the fact his eyes were stinging from the smoke and his skin was searing hot. His body was reacting as if the fire were real. His mind was too, because all he could think about was that it looked like there was no way out.

Again, those weren't his thoughts, thanks so much. He wasn't going along with that crap. He was getting them out.

He'd just decided to take them out the front door straight through the flames, when he realized that it could be a trap, sending them straight into danger, just like when he took the trainees to the river. He paused, suddenly not sure whether he could trust his instincts, or whether they'd lead him astray like they'd done by the river. "They're trying to flush us out."

"No—" Grace's protest descended into a wracking cough, and his own lungs began to strain from the smoke. His eyes stung, and he realized she was right about the illusion: it was physically manifesting its energy to harm him.

And it was taking down Grace as well.

Not allowed. That illusion was going down *now.*

Keeping Grace tucked against the shield of his body, he drew his concentration deep within and began to focus. He applied the centuries of training he'd had learning how to control his body and his senses in an effort to access his instincts more purely. He slowed his breathing and narrowed his mind until he was focused only on his physical senses. Then he turned them off one by one, like flicking off a light switch, until he was in a world of gray silence, the place he sometimes retreated to so he could get a clear read from his instincts without the clutter of the outside world.

Now he was blind and deaf. Moving on memory alone. The illusion could not touch him, because it was powerless if it couldn't prey upon his mind to delude him. He sheathed his sword, and then swept Grace into his arms. "Come on." He strode toward the trap door hidden beneath his bed. "Shut down your senses." He couldn't hear his own voice, other than inside his head. He didn't know if she was responding. Was she even okay?

His concentration shattered as he thought about Grace being hurt, and all his senses roared back to life. He felt a flash of heat and opened his eyes to see roaring flames reaching up to the ceiling. He smelled the acrid odor of burning rubber, his nostrils stung from the fiery smoke, and his skin bubbled from the heat. Grace twisted in his grip, battling to get free, her panic wrenching at his concentration.

"Stay with me," he ordered, then forced his mind to slow again so he could focus on his senses, shutting them down so he was once again cut off from the illusion. Then he tightened his grip on Grace, shouldered the bed aside, and jammed his sword between two boards. He twisted the sword, felt the faint click, and then the floorboards popped up, revealing a steel trap door. Bracing himself, he wretched it open revealing what he knew would look like a bottomless chasm. Without hesitation, he instantly threw them both into the pit. They dead-dropped sixty feet as he fought to control their position in the air so he would take the impact when they hit.

Unable to judge the landing with his senses shut off, he hit so hard on his back that the force of the impact snapped his head into the ground, his neck still weak from Elijah's deathblow. His concentration shattered at the impact, but he kept his grip tight on Grace, absorbing the shock so she wouldn't get hurt.

She gasped, and then scrambled to get off him, groaning with pain. His shields compromised, the smoke burned his eyes, and he saw flames licking down the sides of the pit toward them. "Damn shit looks real." He pointed to a tunnel on the right. "Head that way."

He didn't wait to see if she obeyed as he gathered himself, then leapt back up to the door. He caught the edge, grimacing as his fingers fried on the hot steel, then grabbed the heavy steel door and yanked it shut so it looked like ordinary floorboard from the top. Then he dropped, landing easily in a crouch now that he could use his sight to judge the distance.

Grace was huddled against the wall, crushing her head between her hands, flaming rocks crashing down around her. Fear for her safety galvanized him, and he picked her up and locked her down against him. "Hang on."

She wrapped her legs around his hips and looped her arms around his neck, burying her face in his chest. He wrapped one arm around her waist to make sure she was secure, threw both their packs over his shoulder, then shut down his senses against the flames roaring all around them.

"Hang tight," he ordered, and then he sank deep into his memories, calling up the exact layout of his tunnels, not daring to use his eyesight to find their path until he knew they were clear of the illusion.

He broke into a sprint, hurling them both down the only tunnel that led to safety, ignoring the six that led nowhere, that existed for the sole purpose of distracting pursuers.

Ten steps forward. Turn right.

He counted the rhythm in his head, moving on recall alone, not even able to feel his feet strike the floor. He tripped once on a rock he hadn't remembered, and then they were off again. He'd practiced this tunnel in the dark, but he'd never tried to do it blind, deaf and without a sense of smell.

He'd sure as hell never done it carrying a woman who scared the crap out of him, and never when he was three days out from an injury that had sent him briefly into the afterlife.

But he kept up a steady pace, his breathing even, his legs moving in a natural rhythm he'd perfected to be most efficient for running long distances. To his surprise, Grace's grip never weakened, leaving his arms free to block the walls that occasionally had the audacity to jump in his damn way after a missed navigation.

It wasn't until they'd covered almost thirty miles that he finally took the chance and tested his hearing to see if the illusion was still present.

He heard nothing but the sound of his footsteps, his own heavy breathing, raspy from the smoke inhalation, and Grace's soft moans of pain. No crackles of flame, no sounds of smoke hissing around them.

He stopped running and allowed all his senses to flare back to life. It was too dark to see, a damn good sign that there was no firelight giving them romantic ambiance.

Grace was trembling violently against him. All the protective instincts of his Calydon heritage catapulted to the surface, and he enfolded her in his arms to shield her, to hold her tight against him, willing what was left of his strength into her body. "You with me, Grace?"

She let go of him suddenly, and he tightened his grip to keep her from falling to the rocky ground. He eased to his knees with her, his legs suddenly weak as well. He was more exhausted than he'd ever been, thanks to his little stint with death. He was not going through that die-and-recover thing again. It was too damned inconvenient to feel like a mortal. He needed a healing sleep, and he needed it soon. "It's over." He touched her hair, the brittle, burned ends flaking off in his fingers. "We're safe."

"No." Her protest was a harsh whisper as she slid out of his grip to the ground, curling into a ball, her face resting against the sharp rocks. "Go. You have to go."

"Go where?" As good as his night vision was, the total absence of light in the tunnel was more than even he could overcome, so he pulled out a small flashlight and turned it on. Then he shrugged off his jacket, lifted her head and tucked the jacket between her face and the rocks. Her skin was blistered and red, and he glanced at his own hands. His fingers were charred where he'd grabbed the steel door, and the burns stung as soon as he looked at them. He'd never heard of an Illusionist who was powerful enough to actually cause harm with an illusion. What the hell were they dealing with?

"Get away from me. I'm too dangerous." She scrunched her eyes shut, and a tear squeezed out from under her eyelid.

"Shit." He bent next to her and rubbed the pad of his thumb over her cheek, wiping away the tear that wrenched at his very soul. "We're out, Grace. It's okay. It's going to be okay."

She gave a shuddering sigh, then cracked her lids enough to look at him. "Thanks for getting me out of there, too. I...I would have stayed. It would have killed me."

He grinned. "I don't like having people die on my property. It drives up my home insurance rates." He brushed off a few small pebbles that had stuck to her cheek. Her face was slightly burned, her clothes singed, her eyes red from the smoke. He brushed her hair back from her face, his fingers drifting over her hair, pausing where it wasn't burned. Shit. He couldn't remember the last time he'd felt something so soft. "How did you know it was an illusion, even before it hit us?"

She opened her mouth, then sighed and looked up at the roof of the tunnel, shutting him out instead of answering him.

Quinn ground his jaw. "Grace. You have to let me in. I have to know what I'm dealing with, both with you and your sister." For Elijah's sake. For her sake. It was a hell of a lot harder to fix things if he didn't know what was broken, and he didn't have time to mess around.

The posse would be after him within hours, and it would be a race to find Elijah before they caught either of them, because he knew he would be declared a liability until they brought him in. He needed to know what the hell had happened back at his cabin, and he was damn sure Grace knew more than she was telling. "Grace, talk to me."

He let her feel the urgency of his request, needing her to understand that full disclosure had to come.

After a moment, she brought her gaze back down to his face. "Would you kill an Illusionist on sight? Because their illusions could someday kill an innocent?"

"No." He was well aware that many would have a different answer, however. Illusionists were hunted, and from that fire, he could see why people feared them. They were impressive as hell. "The Order does preemptive strikes only against rogue Calydons. Everyone else can do whatever they want as long as they don't threaten innocents in our presence. We're not a police force."

She nodded, and he felt some of her tension ease. "Okay, then."

Quinn almost smiled as he watched her summon her resolve. Her expression was so telling, so vivid, allowing him access to her emotions. Order members were trained not to feel. They'd learned that shutting down their emotions was the only way to deal with having to take out friends, family and innocents. After living with his stoic team for so long, it was fascinating to watch the play of emotions across Grace's expressive face. Her brows were furrowed in concentration, and the way she worried her lower lip with her teeth told him she was nervous.

He instinctively touched her hair to reassure her. "Whatever it is, you can tell me." Her hair was so soft, feminine, the thick curls tangling around his fingers as if they didn't want to let him go. "I'm an Order member. We're specifically chosen because we're so damned trustworthy. We're like Labradors."

Grace smiled faintly. "Labradors that attack at will."

"Yeah, true, but only in a way designed to save society from our own kind. You're not Calydon, so you're safe from me no matter what secrets you've got buried."

Grace's smile faded, and she looked at him. Her head tilted ever so slightly into his hand, a movement so faint he doubted she realized she'd done it. But he'd noticed that trusting move. Hell, yeah, he'd noticed. He damn well liked it. A lot. Too much.

He wasn't surprised when she finally nodded her willingness to share. "I'll tell you the truth, but no decisions until you hear the whole story."

"I always wait for full information before taking action. No other way to be."

She rolled her eyes. "You're such a badass warrior, aren't you?"

Quinn grinned. "Hell, yeah." Damn. When was the last time anyone had teased him? Yeah, his teammates did, but that was different from having some female give it to him. He liked it. It made him feel like he was connected to humanity, instead of severed from it and watching it from a distance. It reminded him of his family, of what it used to be like so long ago, before everything had changed. "You're not afraid of me, are you?"

"I'm too exhausted to summon up the terror I know I should be feeling." She wrapped her fingers around his wrist, as if to make sure he wouldn't leave her before she was finished.

Their gazes met as something sizzled between them at the contact, as the heat from her touch seemed to brand him. Her grip was strong, but her fingers looked so delicate against his thick wrist. Fragile. Vulnerable. Feminine. He liked it.

Neither of them pulled away. "I can sense an illusion when it's amassing power," she explained. "Someone was creating an illusion outside in your woods. It was a dark one, intending to do harm. That's why I stopped you from going outside."

Quinn raised his brows. "How do you sense illusions? What did you pick up?" Damn, it would be helpful if his instincts could see through illusions. Was that what had happened at the ridge? Had someone been working an illusion on him? Was that what they were dealing with?

Grace ignored his question. "The fire wasn't the illusion I had been sensing. That wasn't the one that was building in your woods." She looked at him, searching his gaze for his reaction. "There were two Illusionists at work."

He frowned. "Two?" How had he not sensed the approach of so many threats? Had it been his distraction with Grace? Or something else? That was not his style, and he didn't like it.

Her grip tightened on his wrist, and this time he noticed her fingers were trembling. Her hand was cold, and there was fear in her silver eyes. Not fear of him. Fear of... something else.

Tension rumbled deep inside him, and he had to concentrate to keep from calling out his weapon in defense of her. "Nothing can get through me," he said quietly, unable to keep the lethal tone out of his voice. "There's nothing to fear in this tunnel."

Her grip on his wrist didn't loosen. "I did it," she said.

"Did what?"

"I created the fire. It was my illusion. I did it. I tried to kill both of us."

Chapter 3

Quinn's body went rigid under her grasp, and Grace clutched his wrist tighter, as if she could call back that moment of intimacy when he'd touched her hair. "You swore you'd listen to the whole story before judging me."

"I'm listening." His voice was tight, reserved, utterly devoid of the concern she'd felt from him a minute ago. "You tried to kill me. I heard that."

"No. Not on purpose." She sat up, hating the look of distrust on Quinn's face, especially after they'd just connected. God, she was tired of being who she was. She was tired of not being trusted. And she was tired of the fact that everyone was right not to have faith in her.

When Quinn had agreed to help and whisked her away from the illusion, it had been the greatest relief to realize she wasn't alone in this battle anymore. She'd felt like someone had given her a ray of hope that maybe things were finally going to turn for the better.

After having been given the gift of his help, seeing the sudden look of distrust on his face stripped Grace of what little reserves of strength she still had left. She was too drained to pull herself together one more time. Too exhausted to lose hope and rebound one more time.

No. Giving up wasn't an option. She had to fight for this. For his help. Despite the distance he'd erected between them, she couldn't give up. "I would never hurt you, or anyone, on purpose. Never." Grace tightened her grip on him, willing him to understand. If anyone could, this man who saw death and evil on a daily basis was the one who would be able to see past the blood on her hands. "I have trouble controlling the illusions, especially under stress. It was a response to the threat I felt from the other illusion, and I couldn't stop it."

Quinn narrowed his eyes. "That's why it appeared? To protect you?"

"Yes."

"It protected you by burning you and nearly killing you?" He didn't hide his skepticism.

Yeah, okay, she could see how this was going to be tough to explain. Fine. She gave up trying to have any pride. He wanted the truth? He'd get the damn truth. "Okay, so you want the whole story?"

"That would be nice."

"Fine." Grace folded her arms over her chest. "The truth is that I'm the only Illusionist in history who's susceptible to her own illusions. I have no idea how to protect myself from them, and I can't control them. I don't know why they can actually cause physical damage when illusions by other people don't. I've tried everything to keep them from affecting me, but I can't do it."

She leaned her head back against the wall of the tunnel, not even bothering to hide the tears of frustration. "I know I'm a nightmare. I'm a threat to anyone unlucky enough to come near me. I've fought so hard to suppress them, but I knew I was slipping. I knew it was just a matter of time until I lost the battle, and I did." She closed her eyes, wondering what would happen now that they'd broken free once. Would they start coming more often now? Or would that explosion relieve the pressure? *Please, God, make them go away.*

Quinn said nothing for a moment, and she didn't

bother to open her eyes. She didn't say anything more. She had no more defenses.

"Who was supposed to teach you how to manage your powers?"

She squeezed her eyes shut against the sudden surge of loneliness. "My parents."

"Why didn't they?"

"They died."

"I'm sorry." He set his hand on her shoulder, the kind gesture making fresh tears want to fall.

"Don't be nice," she whispered, her voice raw with emotion. "I have no defenses against nice."

Quinn sighed and dropped his hand, and instantly Grace regretted her rejection of him. She wanted to crawl across that rocky ground, climb into his lap and stop fighting. Even for a minute or two, she wanted to stop fighting so hard to be strong.

"Why couldn't you get other Illusionists to teach you?" Quinn's voice was less cold, less hostile, and she opened her eyes to look at him. He was watching her intently, his dark eyes focused on her. His expression was sharp, as if he were rapidly evaluating all the information she was giving him, but at least he didn't look like he was facing down a would-be assassin anymore.

Hope flickered in her heart. Maybe she had a chance with him. "Illusionists are loners, and they're suspicious of others after being persecuted for so long. They don't play well together." Grace shrugged, not wanting to dwell on a past that she couldn't change, a childhood that had been stolen from her before she'd been ready. She'd been forced to figure out what she could on her own, sifting truth from fiction from the few facts she could find on the Internet and in her other research. It hadn't been enough, obviously. "It doesn't matter. Just please believe me that I didn't do it on purpose."

He rubbed her arm again, and this time she put her

hand over his, needing the contact with another person. His willingness to touch her felt like reassurance that she wasn't some monstrous freak undeserving of human touch. Not that Quinn was human, but close enough.

"I believe you that it wasn't on purpose," he said. "It doesn't bother me."

"It doesn't?" Relief rushed through her. "But I almost killed us."

"Not even close." He shrugged. "I can handle them."

She stared at him, at the calm confidence in his face, and some of her tension began to ease away. He didn't hate her, he didn't fear her, and he was still alive after having been attacked by her illusion.

"I can keep us both safe from you," he said.

He'd already proven he could.

"You really don't care that I'm an Illusionist?" she asked.

He shook his head. "Not a big deal."

Not a big deal. For a moment, Grace's guards fell away and she sagged against the wall, too exhausted to hold herself up. For the first time in years, she didn't have to fight it by herself. She didn't have to worry about hurting someone, or herself. By being able to protect both of them from her illusions, Quinn gave her that freedom. Just for now, while they were together and no one else was around that she could hurt, she didn't have to worry that she'd snap. If she did, it wouldn't matter. *It wouldn't matter.*

Her throat tightened at the thought of no longer having to fight every strong emotion for fear it would trigger an illusion... "You give me freedom," she whispered.

He raised his brows. "Freedom's good."

She stiffened at the levity in his eyes. "You're making fun of me."

"Hell, no." He gave her a reassuring smile that made her belly flutter, and then he brushed his knuckles over her cheek, leaving behind a trail of searing heat. "I'm just glad to hear that you weren't trying to kill me on purpose." He tangled his fingers in her hair and gave a gentle tug, before dropping his hand. "I was worried destiny had kicked into fast-forward before I had time to kick its ass, and I was damn glad to find out I was wrong."

She frowned, trying not to wish he was still touching her. "Destiny? What are you talking about?"

He ignored her question as his smile faded. His face became serious and thoughtful, and she knew he'd become a warrior again. "So, if you weren't trying to kill me, who was?"

"I don't know." She finally became aware of the rocks digging into her back, and she let go of Quinn's wrist to shift her position. His hands caught her and he helped her adjust, so she was leaning against the wall of the tunnel. "I don't know any other Illusionists well enough to identify them through their illusions. Well, except Ana, but that wasn't hers."

"Ana?" He laid his jacket over her lap and tucked it around her legs. "She's an Illusionist, as well? That's how she's murdering people?"

Seriously? He was tucking her in? Dammit. That felt much too delicious. She couldn't get weak or soft, or she'd crumble. But God, it felt good to have someone taking care of her. "She's an Illusionist, but she's not like other Illusionists. Hers aren't dark—"

He couldn't keep the surprise off his face. "Not dark? But all illusions are dark. Good illusions were selectively bred out of the race thousands of years ago, when Illusionists were used by leaders to torture people." He picked up her hand and ran his fingers over her burns, studying her already-healing injuries.

"Not Ana. She's an aberration." She'd started to tense when he'd mentioned the origins of her race, but he'd been so matter of fact and non-judgmental that she'd relaxed almost right away, realizing he wasn't going to judge her for what she was. He wasn't bothered by it, and he wasn't afraid of her. Somehow, she'd managed to stumble across the one being in existence that didn't care what she was. God, what a gift. "You're less bothered by what I am than I am."

He gave a soft snort. "Trust me, Grace, you're just fine."

She caught the undercurrent of his words. "You mean, you're far worse than I could ever be?"

His gaze went to hers. "I kill warriors who used to be my friends. Sometimes I even kill the women who love them. And I do it on purpose. You really think your history is going to bother me?"

"If you knew the details of it——"

"Screw that, Grace. It doesn't matter." He cupped her jaw and lifted her face to his. "It might bother you, but I don't care."

"You mean that." She swallowed hard, feeling her pulse beat under his index finger, heat suddenly pooling in her belly. Just the idea that someone could know the truth about her and not judge her...

"Yeah." His thumb began to stroke the column of her neck, his gaze went to her mouth, and hunger flared in his eyes.

God, yes, kiss me. The need to feel Quinn's mouth on hers pulsed through every cell of her body and she leaned into him, consumed by the intensity of him——

He dropped his hand and sat back, and she felt like screaming in frustration. Sexual longing burned through her veins from that short touch. What was wrong with her? That wasn't her. She wasn't some passionate vixen. She was the girl who sat in the corner at the party, too terrified to let go of her self-control long enough to risk going on a date, let alone being consumed by wild, crazy desire.

Except once. One man she'd trusted. Never, ever

going there again. *Ever.*

So, instead of chasing Quinn down, she sat back and folded her arms across her chest, struggling to contain the heat coursing through her body.

Quinn, however, didn't seem to be having any trouble concentrating. "If Ana's illusions aren't dark, how is she murdering people? Making them laugh themselves to death?" He grabbed Grace's hand and flipped it over to inspect her palm, his touch precise and clinical as he continued to catalogue her injuries.

She flinched slightly as his fingers probed a particularly severe burn, but she didn't pull away. She liked the fact he was checking on her. And she enjoyed the comforting feel of his hand wrapped so firmly around hers. "I don't think she can kill with them. How do puppy dogs and butterflies kill a Calydon? It might make them want to dance around a meadow and sing, but die? Not so much." She almost smiled at the thought of Quinn caught up in one of Ana's illusions. She wondered what his laugh would sound like, what it would be like to have him sweep her up in his arms and dance with her—

Quinn scowled as he shoved her charred sleeve up to inspect the burns on her forearm. He cursed softly. "Your illusion did some serious damage to you."

"It nearly killed me. I know." She glanced down at her forearm, then wished she hadn't. Just seeing it made it hurt even more, and the oozing, blackened skin looked horrible. "On the plus side, my body gets stronger after I generate an illusion, so I should heal quickly."

"The illusion heals you? Is that how it works?" He laid his hand over her arm, as if he could infuse her with his strength.

"It heals me and gives me energy, but most of its benefit will be used up healing the burns this time. My mom used to be able to heal me, but now I'm on my own." Her voice cracked slightly. "Even though she was a dark

Illusionist, she had a beautiful spirit. It's obvious where my sister gets her good side." God, she missed the brightness that her mother and Ana used to bring into her life. She missed her mother. It still made her so sad to know she would never see her again. If she lost Ana forever too…

Quinn's face softened, and his hand brushed against her cheek. "I'm sorry."

His voice was so full of sympathy and warmth that tears stung the back of her eyes and she leaned into his touch. Then she realized what she was doing and pulled back. She couldn't succumb to his comfort, the temptation to let him chase away her loneliness. She had to keep moving forward, focusing on her goal. She had no time to cry. "Yeah, well, it is what it is."

Quinn's eyebrows rose, and he dropped his hand, respect flashing in his eyes. "Do you need to do another illusion to finish your healing?" he asked.

Something about the tone in his voice caught her attention, and she realized he was going into protector mode. She stiffened. "You are *not* going to force an illusion on me just to get me to heal." Not that she could do another illusion so soon after that one, but she had to shut him down from that train of thought in a hurry.

His face hardened. "Sorry, darling, but it's far too late to ask me to step back and let you hurt yourself."

Darling? "Too late? What does that mean? And what business is it of yours what I do?"

His gaze was unwavering, drilling into Grace with an intensity that made her tremble in response. What the hell was *wrong* with her?

"I can't let you die if I can stop it." He scowled as he spoke. "Not my choice, trust me."

"What? You'd prefer I die? That's a lovely sentiment to be sharing when I'm trapped in some tunnel with you and can do nothing to save myself if you turn psycho killer on me." Grace yanked her arm free, wincing as his fingers dug into her burn for a split second before he could loosen his grip.

She turned her arm over to inspect the wound. The charred skin was flaking off, replaced by new fragile skin underneath. She showed it to Quinn. "I'll be in good shape in another hour, ready to find my sister. That's our focus, remember? Finding out who killed Elijah and is torturing my sister, instead of having you wax on about how my death would please you. Because that really wigs me out, if you want the truth."

"It's not that I *want* you to die," Quinn growled. "But I'm not turning rogue, not even for you. It would make my life a hell of a lot better if you weren't in it."

"Turning rogue?" Grace scooted to the side to put some space between them, her heart suddenly starting to beat faster. Quinn was emanating a dangerous energy, a vibration that made her want to crawl seductively across the rocks right into his arms. It also made her want to scramble to her feet and run back into the fire if that's what it took to get away from him. She'd never sensed that kind of sexual energy from someone, and she could feel it thrumming through her body, calling to her. "What are you talking about?"

He ground his teeth, then rose to his feet and paced down the tunnel. Her nerves jangled when he disappeared outside the range of the flashlight, then she scowled at herself for being stressed merely because Quinn had moved a short distance away from her. She should be *glad* he was giving her space.

Then Quinn was back, and he crouched in front of her. "Question."

He smelled good, she realized with a start. Sure, he smelled like smoke and dirt, but there was something else, too. Outdoors. Pine. *Freedom*.

There was a gleam of anticipation in his eyes. "Could an Illusionist screw with my battle instincts? Make me think a place was safe when it wasn't? Not by doing an external illusion that I see, but by doing something inside me?"

She wrinkled her nose while she thought about it. "You mean, like creating a feeling of anger when you're not actually angry?"

"Exactly."

Grace frowned. "Sure, I don't see why not. Instead of creating a false image, it would mean creating false emotions. I haven't heard of it, but I'm not exactly an expert, as you know."

He leaned forward, and she could see the pulse beating in his throat in anticipation of her answer. "Could an Illusionist sever friendship bonds of five hundred years and make one friend murder the other?" Quinn's voice was intense, tight. "Even if the two individuals were extremely powerful?"

She nodded. "With a strong enough Illusionist... probably."

He gave a small whoop of victory. "Hot damn. I *knew* it wasn't Elijah going rogue." He grabbed her shoulders and planted a quick kiss on her mouth.

They both froze, and then he kissed her again. Heat surged through her and the kiss instantly went from a shared victory to intense, scorching passion. He growled low in his chest, his hands went to her hips and he hauled her against him, never breaking their connection. Desire blasted through her, igniting every level of her soul.

His chest was searing against hers, her breasts crushed against him. He tasted of smoke and man, his muscles flexing as she grabbed his arms, desperate to hold onto him, to pull him closer, to kiss him deeper, to—

Quinn broke the kiss suddenly, pulling back but not releasing her. They stared at each other, the only sounds in the tunnel their heavy breathing and the thundering of her pulse.

"Another question," he said, his hands tight around her hips, his body still flush against hers.

"What's that?" She could barely get the words out, her whole body was vibrating so fiercely from the kiss.

His eyes darkened. "Did that kiss make you want to throw me down, rip off all my clothes and lose yourself in my body and soul until there was nothing left of either of us?"

She swallowed as her skin became so hot she felt like she was going to melt her clothing right off. "Um, yeah, actually it did."

His gaze went to her mouth, and desire pulsed in her belly. "I don't suppose that's an Illusionist thing? Increasing sexual desire and shit like that?"

"Not in my experience. I'd have been much more into sex if it had been." Grace knew full well she'd never experienced anything close to what she felt for Quinn. "Isn't this a Calydon effect? You guys are all about passion and lust, right?"

"Not like this. Never like this." He cursed, peeled his hands from her body and stood up, moving slowly, as if it took all of his willpower to force himself away from her.

She knew the feeling, because it was all she could do not to grab the waistband of his jeans and yank him back down to her.

Grace sat on her hands, while Quinn strode over to the other side of the tunnel and sat down, his back against the wall. Since the tunnel was narrow, that put his feet only inches from her. Too close. He pressed his palms to his forehead for a long minute, then draped his forearms over his knees and let his head clunk back against the wall, eyes closed.

She waited.

He said nothing.

Gradually, both their breathing returned to normal, and the raging desire released her from its grip, leaving her struggling to find her balance again. "Quinn? What's going on between us?"

Quinn didn't open his eyes, or even move. "We have a complication."

Her heart began to thump again. "The sex thing?"

"For starters." He ran his wrist over his forehead, the action of a man worn down. "Do you know what a *sheva* is?"

Grace frowned. "No." It sounded vaguely familiar, though. "It's bad?"

He opened his eyes and sighed. "To give you the short version, every Calydon warrior has a *sheva*. She's the woman who will call to his soul, and he to hers, until they fall so completely in love that the world revolves only around each other."

She swallowed, her mouth suddenly dry. "I had no idea there was anything that romantic about the Calydons."

He smiled grimly. "Will you still think it's romantic when I tell you that destiny commands that he will lose his woman, and it will drive him so mad with anger and rage and loss that he will turn on those he used to protect and save, destroying all those he cared about?"

She blinked. "Seriously?" Well, that wasn't quite so romantic.

Quinn nodded, his face deadly serious. "Once a Calydon goes rogue, his *sheva* will kill him to stop him, destroying the man she loves more than the world. His death will ruin her and she'll also die, a brutal, soul-wrenching death, forever haunted by the truth that she killed the one man who made her whole. But before they both die, if destiny is allowed to play out, he will kill every innocent in his life, even his own children, his neighbors, his friends... *everyone*." He looked at her. "Unless the Order reaches them first and kills one or both of them, depending on how far gone the situation is."

She hugged her knees to her chest against the cold

draft that had settled over her. "That's what the Order of the Blade does? You guys kill Calydons who fall in love?"

"Only if it's his *sheva.*"

"Well, gee, isn't that accommodating of you."

Quinn leaned forward. "Destiny commands that after they bond but before they die, whatever is closest to their hearts will be destroyed. Total devastation, insanity, and death."

She shuddered at the intensity in his gaze. "You believe this?"

Resistance flashed in his eyes. "It's the Calydon destiny," he said, not exactly answering her question. "I've seen it happen a thousand times. It has never failed to play out, not even once, but with the Order running interference, it rarely has a chance to get that far anymore. We kill one or both parties before the final destruction happens." Sudden sadness weighted his words, guilt that was personal and deep. "I've killed to stop destiny before innocents could be slaughtered. I'm the magic that keeps everyone protected from rogues."

"Why are you telling me this?" Her belly knotted up even as she asked. She knew the point of his story. She knew what he was telling her. But she asked anyway. "You don't actually think—"

"I know." He looked directly at her. "Grace Matthews, you're my *sheva.*"

※※※

Grace stared at Quinn, her eyes wide, then broke into a smile and started to laugh. "Oh, God. Just when I thought my life was already a mess..." She wiped the tears from her eyes. "Laugh or cry, Quinn. Sometimes you just have to laugh because you'll never stop crying if you start." She cocked her head to look at him, a stubborn twinkle in her eye. "You know, you're hot, you've got that badass manly man thing going, and I'm crazily attracted to you, but honestly, I suspect you're going to be a little too bossy for my tastes. Thanks for the offer on the whole love-me-die-for-me thing, but I'll pass."

"A manly man?" He was stunned by her reaction. "Did you not understand what I just told you? This is—"

She sat up and covered his mouth with her hand. "Don't even start, Quinn. I'm not a Calydon, and I don't have to believe your myths. I'm not going to die just because I have the hots for you. I might die because I accidentally kill myself, but that's totally different." She leaned close, amusement still crinkling her eyes. "You don't get to cause my death simply by being near me, so don't even suggest it." But her eyes were wary, and he knew she wasn't dismissing it as easily as she was pretending. He'd give her time to process before pushing it further.

But hell, just having her hand on his lips made him want to run his tongue over her palm and down her wrist, licking his way to her elbow... He grabbed her wrist, setting her hand back in her own lap. "Not a good idea to touch me like that."

She flushed. "Yeah, I was sort of hoping you'd suck my finger into your mouth and start doing magical things with your tongue."

Heat rushed through him and he glared at her. "Stop."

"Trying. Not so easy when all I can think about is—"

"I got it, okay?" He didn't need a reminder of all the thoughts and needs he was having every time he looked at her. They didn't have time for all this crap anyway. They both had people to save. "You feeling better now? Ready to move on?" Ignoring the fact that *he* still felt like he'd just risen from the grave—oh, wait, he had!— Quinn rose to his feet and grabbed his pack off the ground. "I have a truck stashed at the end of the tunnel. It's stocked with everything we need. All we have to do is get there."

He held out his hand to pull her to her feet, and she put her hand in his without hesitation, showing trust that made him feel too damn pleased. He tugged her up, and then dropped her hand before he could succumb to the urge to pull her closer against him. Her gaze lingered on his face for a minute, then she turned away, picked up her own pack and slung it over her shoulders.

He handed her the flashlight and fell in behind her as she made her way over the rocky terrain. Her feet squished in a pile of wet clay sitting on top of one of the rocks, mud that had clearly fallen from the roof of the tunnel.

"Quinn?"

"Yeah?" He eyed the ceiling, not liking the amount of moisture leaking through. He reached up and pressed his palm into the mud, frowning when his hand disappeared up to his wrist. A chunk of the clay fell to the ground when he pulled his hand back, and the other clay shifted, oozing into place where the clump had fallen out. *Shit.* Quinn peered ahead, inspecting the tunnel. More mud on the ground, and chunks of the ceiling were sliding down the sides of the tunnel.

"If I were your *sheva*...would we be able to stop our destiny from coming true?"

Wasn't that a loaded question? He glanced briefly at Grace, but she hadn't turned back to look at him. All he could see was the sway of her hair as she worked her way over the uneven terrain.

He was tempted to tell her the truth, that his life mission was to prove that destiny could be thwarted, but he was already having enough trouble getting her to take the damn thing seriously. "I've never heard of anyone managing to do it, not once they bond." But he'd tried to find that exception. He'd tried like hell, over and over again, to prove that a Calydon gone rogue over a *sheva* could be brought back. To prove that his uncle should not have died. To make good on his uncle's last request before Quinn had shoved his sword through his heart.

So far, Quinn had a one hundred percent failure rate. The grim reality was beginning to settle on him, that maybe he'd been chasing his damn tail all this time. He and Grace could not afford to be the final test of his theory. Not when so much was at stake for both of them.

Grace glanced back at him and promptly tripped on a rock. He jumped forward and caught her before she fell, and heat leapt between them as her breast brushed against his chest. She immediately twisted out of his grip and set her hands on her hips, but the flush in her cheeks told him that she'd reacted to his brief touch as much as he had.

"Listen, Quinn," she said. "I know you really buy into this destiny thing because it's your world and your lore, but I'm not going to go down in flames because of some Calydon mumbo jumbo. I'm just not." Her voice cracked and she spun away and started walking down the tunnel again, her boots making a sucking sound as she stomped through the mud.

He stared after her, a slow grin rising on his face. Hot damn. She really thought the *sheva* destiny was crap. If there was a woman he could have picked to get bonded with, it was a woman who refused to accept it, a woman who would fight their fate every step of the way. Of course, others had tried. Shit, he'd seen Calydons and their women bleed their hearts dry trying to stop the hell coming for them, and no one had made it. Not a damn one.

"I have things to do, dammit," she muttered as she yanked her foot out of a deep pocket of mud. "I don't have time for this shit. Destiny my ass."

Hell. Even her swearing made him hot. He started walking behind her, his amusement fading. No matter how resistant they both were to their destiny, neither of them had time to deal with it. Not right now. Not with the lives of so many people at stake.

He had time only to go after Elijah, not to throw Grace down, rip her clothes off, and cement their bond until they were both too exhausted to move…though hell, he liked that idea. Too damn much, actually. He grimly watched the tempting sway of her hips as she slogged across the wet ground. "Trust me, I have no interest in falling in love with you either, but if you don't stop swearing, I'm going to tackle you and take you right here in the mud."

She looked back at him and made a locking gesture across those decadent lips of hers. Not a word more, was her unspoken promise.

Not that he'd take her rejection of his offer personally, or anything, but damn. His *sheva* could resist him? He must not be as much of a stud as he'd always assumed he was.

Unfortunately, the fact that she'd shut him out so easily didn't help his own urges much.

A clump of mud dropped in front of him, landing with a squelch. He eyed the oozing ceiling with a growing foreboding that did wonders to curb his lust.

Turned out, the fact that he was taking his *sheva* deep into a collapsing tunnel was exactly the buzzkill he needed. See? He had everything totally under control.

⚎⚎⚎

Ana Matthews shivered in the dark woods, her wet tank top plastered to her body as she watched the flames finally burn themselves out, revealing the house she'd been brought here to work on. Her heart stuttered when she saw turquoise particles fall from the flames. She'd recognize that shade of dust anywhere: it was her sister's. "Grace?" she whispered, her heart leaping.

"Your sister?"

Ana recoiled as Nate Tipton walked up beside her, a long, serrated knife dangling from his fingers, his black eyes alight with interest. The Calydon warrior was wearing a stained brown T-shirt, still splattered with the blood from the last Calydon he'd killed. Similar stains covered his jeans.

It was the same outfit he'd worn the night he'd plucked Ana off a busy street. No one had noticed him take her. No one had heard her screams, even though there were people inches from her.

It was simply as if she hadn't existed.

Or as if they'd been covered by an illusion...but Nate wasn't an Illusionist. So how had he done it? Mind control? Calydons weren't capable of mind control. It made no sense, and she had to find out, so that if she escaped... no...*when* she escaped, he couldn't trap her the same way again.

Nate thoughtfully rubbed his palm over one of the bloodstains. "Your sister's here?"

Ana flinched as he trailed the edge of his blade down the back of her bare arm, even though she knew the threat of violence from him was over for the moment. The illusion had happened, so there was no more need to hurt her. For now.

She would never betray her sister's presence to him. Never. "No, she's not here," she lied. "I was just thinking that she'd be shocked if she saw the fire I'd made. She thinks I'm so innocent." And so had she. God, she never thought she could become the person Nate had turned her into.

Nate had made it very clear what he planned to do to Ana once he deemed her usefulness over, and she knew Nate would have no reason to keep from acting his fantasies out on her sister. He spoke of love and peace, but acted with violence. So creepy. So terrifying.

He'd brought Ana tonight so she would create an illusion that would draw yet another Calydon out into the open, distracted and injured, so Nate could kill him, if her illusion didn't kill him first.

But tonight Grace had created the fire before Ana's

illusion had manifested, and no one had come out of the house for Nate to kill. Why was Grace at a Calydon's house? But even as she asked the question, Ana knew the answer. *She's coming after me.*

Her knees trembled and her throat tightened with emotion, overwhelmed by the fact that Grace hadn't forgotten about her, hadn't condemned her for the string of bodies she'd left behind.

But as much as Ana wanted to get away from Nate, as desperate as she was for help, as much as she wanted to cry with relief at the thought of Grace coming to rescue her, the idea of Grace endangering herself to help Ana terrified her. No one else could die trying to help her. No one else. *Please, Grace, don't come after me,* she whispered silently, knowing her sister could never hear her, but needing to tell her anyway. *I can't bear the burden of your death if you get hurt trying to save me. Please, please, please just hide and take care of yourself.*

Ana could survive anything, as long as she knew Grace was safe. Her sister was all she had left in this world, all that had survived their terrible childhood, their curses. Her parents had died saving her life after she'd made a grievous mistake. No one else could die trying to protect her. *No one else.*

"I like the fire," Nate said. "Do it next time."

Ana closed her eyes as a shudder racked through her body. She had no control over the illusions Nate forced out of her, and she'd never created a fire. Now that he thought she could do it, he'd try to force it out of her like he'd done all the others.

God, that moment, that first moment when she'd seen that awful image fill the night sky, and she'd realized that she'd created it… A part of her soul had shattered right then.

Ana had always known emotional distress brought out Grace's illusions. She'd understood that darkness created darkness. But she'd always been spared. She'd always been able to stem her family's tide of hell with her own light. When Nate had taken her to that first Calydon's home and ordered her to generate something deadly, she'd been so happy with her inability to do so, so relieved that the only part of her that was good had somehow survived being thrust into Nate's world.

Then he'd brought out the knife and his fists, using them to show her exactly what she really was: a fraud whose happy illusions were a lie. They were nothing more than a façade to hide the truth that she was actually a monster who created images far more horrific than her sister's ever had been.

Ana was a monster who'd spent her life hiding behind butterflies.

The first time she'd seen a man die because of what she'd done, she'd been violently sick for days, horrified by who she was and what she'd done. She'd fought not to do it again, how she'd fought for rainbows and roses, but she'd been no match for Nate's persuasions.

She rubbed her hand over the newest bruise on her forearm, almost wishing she could create hell at will to avoid the beatings, but they still came out butterflies and roses until he tortured her so badly that her illusions would finally unleash their darkest evil to try to save her life.

Ana had tried repeatedly to turn her illusions onto Nate, but he'd never been affected by them, which she didn't understand. She was at the top of the food chain when it came to illusions. She'd never met anyone who was immune to hers when they were at full force, because she was so powerful. Before Grace had stopped doing illusions, Ana had been even more powerful than her big sister. But Nate wasn't affected. Why? Illusions were her only weapon, and they were useless against him.

It had been a terrible, disheartening moment of lost hope when she'd finally realized she had no way to protect herself against him.

"Come on." Nate took her arm, his fingers digging into her aching muscles as he lifted his blade in eager anticipation. She would heal slower tonight, because she hadn't done an illusion, which meant she would still be hurting the next time Nate dragged her along on one of his deadly hunts. "Quinn must be down from smoke inhalation. We'll clean up the mess Elijah failed to finish. I won't let Elijah screw up my plans."

"What plans?" As always, Nate ignored her inquiry, and she tensed as he dragged her through the woods, through the underbrush that was so green and vibrant that it made her want to cry. She trailed her fingers over the damp leaves, trying to focus on the beauty of nature, trying to tear her mind and her soul away from the horror she was becoming.

As long as she could still touch beauty, Ana had hope that she could still find her way back to who she used to be, who she wanted to be. Nate tugged her forward, and a leaf tore off in her fingers, the broken piece fluttering silently to the ground.

Her legs shaking from exhaustion, Ana stumbled, righting herself before Nate could use it as an excuse to grab at her again. *I can survive this. I know I can.*

She winced as he thumbed over her wrist, a tender, intimate gesture that made her stomach turn. "Oh, my little sweetness, I'm so glad to share this experience with you. I would have done my job anyway, but having you to play with while I do it..." Nate smiled. "You are the sunshine that the world deserves."

"Then let me be sunshine!" She jerked her hand free of his grasp, and his smile vanished.

He grabbed her and threw her up against a tree, pinning her against the wet bark. "You are not better than me," he snapped, his face cold, his eyes simmering with fury. "I'm tired of your attitude. You keep rejecting my kindness, and you'll get what you deserve when this is over." His upper lip sneered, showcasing perfect white teeth that had no business on a man with his tainted soul.

"Once this is over, you'll be dead," she shot back. She wasn't giving up. She'd find a way to get away from him, to kill him for what he'd done to her. She blanched at the thought. Oh, God, no, not *kill*. She couldn't kill. Not ever again. Those kinds of thoughts weren't hers. She was becoming a monster, the worst of her kind. Tears slid down her cheeks, tears at the loss of who she wanted to be, at the destruction of the self-image she'd carried of herself her whole life.

His brow went up. "Once this is over, I'll be far more powerful than you could ever imagine. You'll see exactly how worthy I am." He pulled her close, until his breath was hot on her face, making her stomach roil. "Do you think I'm doing this just to amuse myself? Because I get a thrill out of knocking you around and killing Calydons?" He grinned. "I admit, it's a hell of a high to take out these bastards who think they're better than I am, but that's not why I'm doing it. It's a bigger cause, one that you, of all people, should understand." He sneered at her as he stepped away and yanked her toward the house. "Unless you aren't the pure soul you keep claiming you are."

"What bigger cause? What do you want?" If Ana had some idea of what was driving him, maybe she could find a weakness and find a way to exploit it.

"A world where peace and harmony prevail, of course." Nate hauled her up the steps to the front door, not giving her any slack when she tripped and cracked her shin on the top step.

"Peace and harmony? You're going to get that by beating me and murdering people?" Ana challenged as she rubbed her shin, hoping to goad him into giving up something she could use against him. Now that she knew Grace was searching for her, she was infused with a new desperation. She had to escape before Grace was pulled into her mess and hurt, or even worse, killed. This wasn't just about her anymore. It was about keeping someone else she loved from dying for her.

"Peace and harmony are worth all the costs to achieve them." Nate placed his blade at her back and forced her through the door first, so she would take the first blow if their target was waiting for them.

Ana bit her lip, her heart racing as she stepped across the threshold. *Please, Grace, don't be here. Please tell me you got away.*

She walked into the small cabin, fear clogging her throat as she frantically scanned the area, praying with all her heart that she wouldn't see her sister. A bed was sprawled crookedly across the floor, a bottle of water was upended on a braided rug, and a fire was fading in the fireplace.

No one was there. *No Grace.* The house was empty. There was no one to die for her. No one to kill. No one to rescue her.

For a split second, the anguish of stark loneliness and terror welled up inside Ana. The emotional devastation of knowing she'd been so close to her sister and had lost her crashed down on her, and Ana staggered under the weight of what she was facing.

But as Nate swore in frustration and tore through the cabin searching for the prey that got away, Ana closed her eyes and fought back the anguish, forcing herself to be strong, to feel brave.

Grace and the warrior had gotten away. Without prey to kill, Nate would have no reason to beat Ana.

Tonight, no one else would die. This time, she would not have to cross that line into the person she was terrified of becoming. For one evening, she'd been given a respite.

Slowly, Ana sank to her knees, too exhausted to stand, knowing that the cycle would begin again, repeating itself unless she could find a way to stop it.

Chapter 4

"So, yeah, now I'm kind of thinking that going back into the fire was actually the better idea." Grace tried to keep her voice light, but it was a total lie. She was seconds away from a complete panic-induced meltdown. If she hadn't been so drained by her recent illusion and unable to generate a new one, she'd be ripping apart their world with hell right now.

Terror was a good word to describe what she was feeling.

The tunnel was less than a foot high now, and the ceiling was disintegrating in soppy globs of mud. Grace was inching along on her stomach. Quinn was on his hands and knees above her, using his strength to hold the roof of the tunnel up off both of them.

She could feel the mud oozing down over her legs as the tunnel collapsed behind them, its last remaining structure destroyed by their passage. Quinn had long ago given up on the flashlight, since he didn't need it to know where he was going, and Grace wasn't really feeling the need to watch her impending death.

"We're almost there," Quinn said. "We'll make it."

We'll make it. Yes, yes, that would be fantastic. Grace closed her eyes and tried to concentrate on the sensation of his chest brushing against her back as they inched forward. He was a Calydon warrior, for heaven's sake. Totally strong enough to hold up a cascading wall of earth long enough for them to get out, right? She certainly wasn't about to die a miserable death by aspirating wet clay, crushed under thousands of pounds of earth, never to be found...

"Your heart rate's going up," Quinn said, his voice strained with the effort of shoving his way through the mud, of forcing an opening for them to get through. "You holding up okay?"

"Yeah, sure—" Her voice cracked, and she knew there was simply no way to continue to uphold the confident woman façade. She was a trembling, sniveling, terrified wimp who was about two seconds away from curling up in a ball and crying until she was smothered to death. So what if this big, strong, Calydon warrior would be so unimpressed with how weak she was? She couldn't pull it off anymore. "Actually, I'm really not okay. I'm about to completely lose it." Grace's voice rose higher as panic set in. "I keep having visions of the clay filling my lungs until I can't breathe and—"

"What's your plan to stay out of my bed?" Quinn interrupted.

The query was so unexpected she had to actually replay the question twice before she could even grasp it. At first, she was shocked by his question. Then she was horrified by the fact that her body actually responded to it. Hello? On the brink of death was not the time for raging hormones to start dancing—

Then, being the brilliant numbnut that she was, Grace finally figured out what Quinn was doing. He wasn't attempting to seduce her. "You're trying to distract me?" Apparently, facing death impaired her cognitive abilities. Good to know.

"Yeah. Is it working? Go lower. There's a big rock ahead that I don't want to dislodge. I think it's holding up the ceiling."

"One little rock is holding up the entire ceiling? Didn't you consider steel beams when you were building this thing? I mean, this is Oregon, right? Land of rain and mud—" Her panicked rant ended when he dropped his body onto hers, shoving her down into the mud. She squeezed her eyes shut as her chin sank into the muck. "Quinn—"

"Turn your head to the side," he ordered. "Breathe."

She tucked her head into the pocket of air between his arm and his chest and inhaled cautiously. It was clean air. Clean enough to breathe, at least. Alive for another minute. Yay for that. The day was looking up.

He stretched his legs on either side of hers, his hips driving against hers. Was there no longer enough space for him to be on his knees anymore?

"The ceiling's too low now, isn't it?" She couldn't keep the tremor out of her voice. "There's no room."

"There's plenty of room. I just like grinding my pelvis into your sexy little bottom. Now keep moving forward. It's not much further."

Think of sexy little bottoms. Think of grinding pelvis action. Anything but dying. She dug her elbows into the slop, shoved herself forward another inch, and thought of drowning in mud again. "It's not working." Her chest was tightening up, her breathing was getting difficult. "I'm going to have a panic attack—"

His head dropped down next to hers, so his cheek was against hers. "We're going low only to go under the rock," he said, his voice rough in her ear. "It'll open back up. How are you going to stay out of my bed?" His hips drove against her butt, forcing her to move forward.

Grace tried desperately to concentrate on his question, on sex, on his bed. On anything but her situation. "It'll be easy to stay out of your bed. I'll just think about what an ass you are for taking me into a tunnel that collapsed." Whoops. The respite hadn't lasted long. She'd gone from his ass to collapsing tunnels in one breath.

He laughed softly, his whiskers scraping her cheek. "Nah. You'll be so appreciative of my ability to get us out alive that you'll throw yourself at me and shower me with hot, wet kisses that will drive us both insane with lust."

Heat ignited inside her belly, and she groaned with embarrassment when he chuckled, clearly sensing her arousal. "I must be your *sheva* if you can stir up sexual desire in me when I'm buried under a ton of dirt." She slid forward another inch.

"We're clear of the rock." Quinn lifted his upper body off hers slightly and her lungs expanded gratefully. "Maybe it's not the *sheva* thing. Maybe it's simply that mud's your aphrodisiac and I just happen to be the lucky guy who benefits."

"Entirely possible. I've always had this strange attraction to co-ed mud wrestling." Okay, this was good. The ridiculous craving she had for his body was coming in really handy. Fear of tunnels was fading fast, and hot desire was coming strong. Grace had never thought of herself as wanton before, but she was so taking that right now.

"So, is getting slimed up with mud and a hot guy all you thought it would be?"

A desperate giggle escaped at his playfully arrogant tone. Quinn was totally trying to work her over when they were about to die. Men were insane. That's all there was to it. "Actually, it seemed a little sexier in my dreams."

"Yeah? What's your wildest sex fantasy?"

She snorted. "Sex that was decent would be a good start." Embarrassment flooded her cheeks at the accidental over-sharing of information. "I mean, it's not like I'm bad at it or anything—"

"Hey." Quinn leaned down and grazed his teeth over her earlobe. "I've kissed you, Grace Matthews. I've tasted your lips and breathed your passion. Trust me when I tell you if you've had unsatisfactory sex in the past, the problem wasn't you." His voice was low, laced with sensual teasing. "You've simply been with the wrong men, sweetheart."

His body was so hot against her, his quads taut where he straddled her hips, making her body ache with awareness. "And you'd be the right man?" It had gone way past sexual banter now. Her whole body was vibrating with desire, and she was vividly aware of the way his body was so intimately pressed against hers from chest to calf.

He bit the side of her neck with a playful snarl. "I'd rock your world."

Laughter bubbled out of her, even while the cold mud oozed between her fingers as she pulled herself a little further along. "I can't believe you just said that. That's so cliché."

"Yeah, but I'm right, so who cares?" He shifted, and his weight pressed down on her again. "Hang on a sec."

"What's wrong?" She tucked her head to the side again, trying to find a place to breathe. Her lips hit mud and dirt oozed into her mouth. Terror seized her, then Quinn's hand cupped her chin and he turned her head until she found an air pocket.

Grace gulped the air gratefully, barely squeezing it into her lungs, trying to expand them under the pressure of his weight.

"I think this is it." His upper body tensed and jerked hard to the side, and there was a creak and a thud of something heavy smashing into the earth.

Light flooded over them, blinding her.

Her throat tightened and tears filled her eyes. "We're out?"

"Of course. Did you doubt me?" He shoved himself off her with a grunt, and she could feel him vibrating with the effort of lifting the mud up off both of them. "Go."

She squinted against the light and hoisted herself

up on her elbows, her arms trembling with fatigue. She scrambled out from under him, tumbled over a steel door, then pitched head-first off a shallow ledge into a bed of damp ferns. She rolled onto her back and stared up at the canopy of trees, inhaling the fresh air, drinking in the sounds of the forest, the breeze on her face, the feeling of being alive and free.

Quinn landed next to her with a groan. He rolled once until he came to a stop with his head on her stomach. He draped one arm across her legs and turned his head to the side so his cheek was resting on her belly, as if she were his favorite pillow. His breathing was labored, his body immobile, his eyes closed. "This is nice," he said finally.

Grace grinned, practically giddy with relief to be out of the tunnel. "Quite pleasant," she agreed.

"Aren't you going to jump me for saving your life?" Quinn asked, his eyes still closed. "You're going to have to do all the work. I'm too beat."

Something about the tone of his voice caught Grace's attention, and she propped herself up on one elbow to look at him more closely. He was caked in mud, as was she. His face was slack, his body heavy on hers. Concern lodged in her throat as she moved her leg to try to nudge him into opening his eyes.

He didn't.

"Aren't you supposed to be basically indestructible?" she asked.

"Did I tell you I died three days ago? Died and came back." Quinn groaned and wrapped his fingers around her ankle. "Apparently, it beats the crap out of a guy. I was planning to recoup for a few hours, but this chick showed up at my house, set it on fire and forced me to travel almost forty miles underground. It's been a hell of a week."

Grace tensed. "You're really hurting, aren't you?" It was surprisingly unnerving to see the warrior who'd been so strong for her suddenly seem vulnerable.

He opened his eyes, his steely gaze fastening on her face. "Grace. Don't worry. I'm fine." He squeezed her ankle with gentle reassurance. "I need to go into a healing sleep. A few hours is all I need."

"Then you'll be okay? You're sure?"

Quinn grunted in annoyance. "I'm a badass immortal warrior, remember? It insults my manhood that you can even doubt me. Clearly, I will have to prove my virility to you at a later date to restore my reputation."

She grinned, reassured by his relaxed humor. He really was okay. "You're such a guy."

"Yeah, thank the gods for that." He gave her a faint smile and planted a playful kiss on her belly. "Grace, I mean it. Don't worry about me. We have a date to buck destiny, remember? Getting all mushy about my well-being isn't going to help us keep our distance."

"I'm not getting mushy about you. I'm stuck in the middle of the woods with no jungle survival skills," she retorted as she looked around for the truck he'd said was there. She saw no truck, only trees and underbrush. "You're my ticket to freedom. That's why I'm concerned about you." It certainly wasn't because she was already having far too many personal thoughts about this man she barely even knew. Yes, granted, he'd saved her life, he'd accepted her dark side without judgment, he'd taken care of her when she'd been so cold at his house, and she'd seen enough pain in his eyes to know that he carried too much weight in his soul, but she was certainly too smart to let any of *that* sway her into connecting with him.

"Good. Screw the *sheva* thing. I like that." He closed his eyes. "You should sleep, too. We're at war. Rest when you can."

"I can't sleep. I'm too wired. You're really going to take a nap?"

"Have to. Gotta heal." Quinn tightened his grip on her ankle, and then flung his other arm up over her belly, anchoring her where she was. "'Night, darlin'. Wake me when breakfast is ready."

"Quinn—"

The even rhythm of his breathing told her he was already out.

Grace stared down at him, his face relaxed in sleep as he nuzzled against her belly. She hesitated, and then lightly traced her fingers over his jaw. Mud flaked off his whiskers, and she raked her fingernail through the coarse hairs to clear off more.

Quinn mumbled her name and nestled deeper against her, and she felt a swell of tenderness. Of protectiveness. Grace rested her hand on the back of his head, stroking gently.

Then she sighed, took her hand back, and stretched out on the bed of ferns. Grace clasped her hands behind her head while she stared up at the blue sky, all too aware of the comforting weight of Quinn on her stomach, of his fingers possessively clasping her ankle, as if he were afraid she'd sneak away while he slept.

If it wasn't for Ana, she would do exactly that, because this crazy *sheva* destiny wasn't something she wanted to take on. She'd laughed when Quinn had told her about it, but there was no denying the intensity of her physical reaction to him. Grace had been through too many horrors in her life to completely disregard his story.

She should run from him. Take off. Protect herself against the chance that what he'd told her had even an element of truth.

But Grace needed his help to save her sister, and that trumped everything.

So, instead of shrugging Quinn off and making a choice that might save her own life, Grace tangled her fingers in his hair, closed her eyes, and slept.

Grace woke up alone.

She sat up, straining to see into the darkness of the woods around her. She could hear the whisper of leaves in the wind, the rustle of animals in underbrush, and other sounds she couldn't identify. Fear rippled through her. Had he left her? "Quinn?"

"Over here."

Grace nearly sagged with relief. *He hadn't abandoned her.* She scrambled to her feet and turned around. Quinn was silhouetted in the moonlight as he vaulted over a huge fallen tree and landed soundlessly in front of her, carrying a small bundle of clothes bagged in plastic. He'd washed off the mud, shaved, and changed his clothes. His eyes were bright and energetic.

A man revived. Standing before her was the indomitable warrior who had dragged her to safety through a thousand tons of mud. He was tall, his shoulders were wide, and vibrant energy was rolling off him in thick waves. His sleeves were shoved up, revealing sinewy-forearms, one with the black brand of a sword, the other still covered in fresh scars. Standing in the forest like that, Quinn was elemental male, a part of nature, a force of his own.

Awareness surged through Grace. The part of her that was pure female came to life, responding to him as a man. As a lover. As a protector. As her destiny? *Please not that.*

"How are you feeling?" Quinn walked over to her, scowling as he got closer. "You have to stop looking so good when you get up. It's hell on my self-control."

Grace couldn't help feeling pleased at his frustration. Desire raged in his eyes, intense wanting just for her, even though she was covered in mud, days away from her last shower, and an emotional mess. He wanted her anyway, and it made her feel beautiful, sexy, hot. "Sorry. Next time I'll wash off the twenty pounds of dried clay and put on a negligee instead of my mud-caked clothes. Would that help?"

Quinn frowned. "No, probably not." He sighed and cupped his hand under her chin, lifting her face to his. "Do you have any idea of the erotic dreams I had because I was wrapped around you like that? Inhaling your scent with every breath? Listening to the cute little noises you make in your sleep? Do you have *any* concept what that shit did to me?"

She swallowed, her skin hot, her nerves on fire. "Um..."

His thumb traced over her lower lip, his eyes nearly glowing in the moonlight. "I want you, Grace. I don't know if it's the *sheva* thing, simply you being you, or some combination thereof. But I'm telling you right now that if you stay with me, it's just a matter of time until I peel off every last bit of your clothing and bury myself inside you until we're both too exhausted to move, think or feel." He lowered his head until his lips were hovering over hers. "It won't be now. Probably not tonight. But it *will* happen. Which means I'm dropping you off at the first gas station we pass."

And then he kissed her.

Something erupted inside Grace the instant Quinn's lips touched hers, something brilliant and scary and so uncontrollable she felt like she was spinning off a cliff, losing her direction, losing herself, losing everything she knew.

Being out of control was deadly for her, for anyone around her. Grace had spent a lifetime fighting the security of locking down who she was. Suddenly, with Quinn invading her senses and sweeping her into a world of sensual passion, spiraling desire and unrivaled sensation, everything that had kept her safe was slipping out of her grasp. She was freefalling into an unfamiliar and terrifying zone of recklessness, carnal instinct and uncontained fire.

Quinn's mouth was hot, his lips demanding, and she couldn't fight her need for *more*. She threw her arms around his neck, pulling him closer. She kissed him back desperately, not even understanding the raging need that drove her. Grace met his tongue the moment he invaded her mouth, drawing him in, basking in the taste of him, sweet and rough, like cinnamon and the pure freshness of the earth after a cleansing rain. Quinn was life, he was strength, and he was passion, melding together into a boiling cauldron of sensuality that was consuming her and shredding her tightly contained shields.

It felt amazing, as if she were alive for the first time in her life. It should have terrified Grace to feel this kind of intensity racing through her, but it didn't. With Quinn's strong arms wrapped around her, his deep kisses, and the way he'd handled her illusion before, she wasn't afraid of tapping into who she really was. He gave her the chance to live, truly live. For this moment, for this kiss, she was all his, and she belonged to the fire raging between them.

His fingers wrapped around her hair, gripping her so tightly that it almost hurt, but it felt good, exciting, like he was strong enough to handle all the horrors about who she was. Grace pressed herself against him, tugging him down toward her, frantically kissing him back, afraid it would end. Terrified she would lose the moment before she was ready. Before she'd gotten what she needed. Before she'd tasted what it felt like to truly breathe.

Quinn yanked her shirt up and slid his hands up her back, cupping her shoulder blades as he devoured her mouth. His hands were hot and rough against her skin, his touch tender but demanding. Possessing. Making her his. He dropped his head and his mouth was on her breasts, biting at her nipple through her bra. Uncontainable sensations tore through her, making her gasp at the shock of it. She trembled under the assault, her entire soul reaching out for him. For all that he was. For all that he could give her.

Quinn shuddered in her arms, then abruptly lifted his head from her breasts.

He stared at her, his eyes almost pulsing with desire. She didn't move, couldn't pull away, riveted by the intensity of his expression. His hands were still gripping her, holding her against him, his body hard and lean. The electricity between them almost audible, a metaphysical crackling in the air. "Holy crap," he finally said.

Grace burst out laughing, his comment breaking the tension between them. "Yes, you could say that," she agreed. "I'm glad it's not just me."

"Hell, no, woman. It's not just you." He brushed his lips over her forehead. "You make me forget everything else," he whispered. "At a time when I can't afford to do that." His hands found her shirt and gently tugged it back down to cover her stomach.

His eyes were dark, his face shadowed as his heavy breathing echoed in the night, and she knew he wanted her every bit as much as she burned for him. She'd never wanted a man like this. Never *needed* a man like this. It wasn't simply physical need. She wanted to bring him into her life, to snuggle up against him on a cold night, to tell him all her secrets and have him chase away her nightmares.

Grace wanted it so intensely that she couldn't stop herself from reaching out for him, from laying her hands on his chest, where she could feel the beat of his heart. She didn't get close to men. She didn't get close to anyone except Ana. She'd learned her lesson, God, had she learned it, and yet Quinn was reawakening the dreams she'd so carefully killed long ago. Here she was, tumbling recklessly into his arms while he worked his way so ruthlessly into her soul. "What's wrong with us?"

Quinn wrenched his hands off her and stepped back. "You're still denying you're my *sheva*?"

"I…" For a moment, the thought of being his *sheva* tempted her. If they really were bonded, he would always be connected to her. She wouldn't have to worry about it all unraveling like it had before, she wouldn't have to protect her heart from being eviscerated…

Until it all fell apart. Until he went rogue. Until they lost everything. As horrible as everything had turned out before, it would be even worse with Quinn. She couldn't go through that again. She'd learned her lesson, and she'd be a fool to forget it. She had to keep her heart and her mind protected from him, no matter how badly he called to her.

Quinn traced his finger over her jaw. "Grace," he said. "You are my *sheva*. Admit it, so we can deal with it."

"No." Denial dug deep. "I can't accept it." She turned away, trying to get space. "The only way I can get through each day is by believing that I'm in control, by holding onto who I want to be and by fighting off a fate I don't want to endure. I can't allow another terrible future into my life." She walked to the log he'd leapt over so effortlessly a few minutes ago and sank down onto the damp bark.

Quinn frowned. "Admitting you're my *sheva* isn't the same thing as giving up and accepting that crappy destiny. It's the first step toward beating it. You can't defeat what you don't acknowledge."

"Give me a break, Quinn. I am perfectly realistic about how crappy things are, but I need to believe my life is under my control, that I can do something to make it turn out okay. If I can't, if this horrible side of me is going to someday consume me…" She paused, trying to keep perspective on the enormity of the implications if he were speaking the truth. "If I accepted this whole *sheva* thing, it would mean I'm accepting that I don't even get to choose the man I give myself to, that a choice so personal doesn't even belong to me." She shook her head. "I can't live like that, Quinn. I can't be a victim to a force larger than I am."

Belief in her ability to fight for what she wanted was what had kept Grace going for the last fifteen years. It was why she believed she could still find Ana and everything would be all right again. She couldn't accept the fate he'd drawn out for them, couldn't live with the implication that the control she'd battled for in her life had been nothing but an illusion.

Empathy softened his face, and she wanted to cry. He understood how she felt. How could this stranger be so dialed in to who she was?

Sweetheart. His deep voice was suddenly in her mind, filling her head with his presence.

She jerked her gaze at him. "No," she whispered. "Don't do this."

He walked toward her. *If you aren't my* sheva, *how do you explain the fact you can hear me?*

"There are so many different reasons people can connect through their minds. A *sheva* is not the only possible explanation." She jumped to her feet as he approached, standing defiantly to meet him, but her voice was shaky. Cold fingers of dread laced around her spine.

It's different with my kind. He reached her, his eyes searching hers. *Only Calydons can hear the thoughts of other Calydons. There is only one exception: a* sheva *also has that ability.*

She felt the truth of his words reverberate through her, and she knew he wasn't lying. He was telling the truth. "Oh, God." Her legs suddenly gave out, and she sat down hard on the ground, her heart racing, her breath seizing in her chest. "I can't deal with this."

"Sure you can." He crouched in front of her and gently pushed her hair out of her face. "You've known it the whole time, Grace. We both have."

"This can't be happening. I can't afford for this to be true." She pulled her knees to her chest, wanting to crawl into his arms and let him comfort her. *Needing* him to comfort her. "I need a hug from you to make me feel better about the fact I need a hug from you. This is such a mess." She shoved at his knee, trying to get him away from her. "I won't die for you and your stupid traditions. I won't give up my power!"

"Screw that." His voice was fierce, his fist bunched. "I have no intention of becoming powerless. I'm not rolling over on this one yet, and neither are you. We may be stuck with this need for each other, but I refuse to let my world be destroyed because of it."

"My need for you terrifies me." Cold settled in her bones, and she hugged herself. She looked at him, realizing he was watching her intently, his dark eyes focused on her face as he continued to stroke her hair. "Until three years ago, I'd never dated a guy for longer than a month. I couldn't get that close. My emotions would get too involved, I'd become unstable, and I'd have to run before I snapped."

He smiled. "I'm not afraid of you—

"No! Listen!" She put her hand over his mouth. "Then I met a man. Victor Barrons. He was a good man, he had an amazing family, and I fell in love with him and his family. It was so easy, so safe that I never got scared, and I never had to worry about my emotions." She looked past him, remembering what it had felt like to belong. "He and his family welcomed me. His little sister was eight, and she and I became best friends. The way she looked at me, like I was some angel, was this most amazing gift. No one knew who I was, or what I'd done. They just loved me for me. It was the family I'd lost, a chance to have what I'd been wanting for so long. I stopped fighting my feelings for him. I thought it was safe." She looked at Quinn. "I just wanted to feel safe again. Loved. I wanted a home."

Quinn gave a grim smile. "You wanted the fairy tale."

She nodded. "A week before the wedding, I got stressed. I started to worry about what he might do if he found out who I really was. I felt like I was lying to this amazing family. It started getting me so upset that I started to lose control. Ana was there, and she did a beautiful illusion to stop me from snapping, but it was a battle to bring me back. Things got...ugly. When we turned around, his little sister was standing there. She'd seen the whole thing." Grace felt that same sense of anguish fill her. "The way she looked at me, like I was a monster. I'll never forget it."

He swore with disgust. "You're not a monster—"

"But I am! Two hours later, Victor and his father came to my room with guns." She shook her head. "They said we had five minutes to pack and leave or they'd kill us. They'd already shipped the rest of the family off the premises, afraid we'd kill everyone." She'd never forget that sense of utter betrayal. It had broken her when she'd seen the man she'd trusted with her heart and her dreams and everything she was, standing there with a gun trained on her, a look of such hatred and disgust on his face. "I lost them all that night, not just Victor, but everyone. I lost their trust, I lost it all."

"He's a stupid bastard," Quinn said.

"No." She had to make him understand. "Don't you get it? He's right. What if I'd started that fire when his little sister or his mother was there instead of you? They'd all have died. This wonderful, amazing family would all have died." She took a shuddering breath. "Victor was right, Quinn."

"No!" Quinn grabbed her upper arms, his face furious. "He's a spineless bastard who understood nothing about loyalty. You don't walk away when someone you care about murders someone or snaps and goes on a killing rampage. You stand by them, because you know their soul isn't black, and help them find their way back. You get that? Because that's my world, Grace, and as my *sheva* that's what you're getting from me."

She shook her head, biting her lip with the effort of not grabbing onto him and believing in everything he was saying, words that were so beautiful and so amazing, if only they would always be true. "Don't make promises, Quinn. If I am your *sheva* and all this destiny shit is true, then you're going to betray me anyway. Everyone betrays their *sheva*, right? Isn't that what you said?"

Quinn swore. "Yeah, it's what I said, but I think it's crap."

She almost laughed, laughed through her tears. "I agree, but—" She stopped when he lifted her hand and pressed his lips to her palm, an intimate gesture of trust and tenderness that brought tears to her eyes. "Kissing you is so out of my control," she whispered. "The way I feel about you? I don't even know you, but I feel like my life will be shredded if you're not in it. I can't let myself feel like that and then lose it all again. I've lost too much, Quinn. Ana's all I have left, and now she's gone, too. "

"You're not alone." His voice was matter-of-fact. Intense. "You have me."

She tugged her hand free, and he released her. "I don't want to need you for anything more than finding my sister. Getting close to you threatens my choices, my future, and my life, regardless of the *sheva* destiny." She rubbed her forehead, suddenly exhausted. "I need to get my life back together, not screw it up more."

His thumb rubbed against her jaw. "I know, Grace. I'm right there with you. This isn't my gig either, and I've got shit to take care of too." He leaned closer, and his eyes became intense. "But know one thing, sweetheart. As for trusting me, don't worry about it. I don't walk away." His hand slid to the back of her neck and he dropped his head, giving her the softest kiss she could ever have imagined. "I might have to have sex with you until you can't move, but I'm not going to hurt you."

Her body tightened in a traitorous response. "I can't

get involved with you. I can't trust you. And I really can't have sex with you. Didn't you hear anything I've said?"

"Yeah, I heard it all, and I have my own agenda that can't afford to be screwed up by a *sheva* destiny, but I suspect that's not going to be enough to stop us." His eyes darkened. "Sex between us will be a very big deal."

She swallowed, her skin getting hot. "I don't want to have sex with you."

He gave a soft laugh. "Oh, sweetheart, you won't have a choice. Neither of us will."

"You said we could resist the bond."

"Hell, yeah, we're going to fight like the devil not to crash and burn. But sex? That's different. Either we separate, or we're going to have sex eventually." His eyes were blazing. "And that has nothing to do with the bond. It is all about the fact I crave you with every fiber of my damn being, and it's getting stronger every single minute."

"So we separate." The words tumbled out of Grace's mouth before she could stop them. The thought of succumbing to Quinn was too much. She didn't want to lose herself in him, yet a part of her wanted to so desperately she could think of nothing else.

Quinn scowled and stood up. For a minute, she thought he was going to agree, and relief rushed through her. Relief and agony, at the same time. Then he shook his head and stood up. "I can't. If I let you go, he'll hunt you down."

"What?" She jumped up. "Who will hunt me down?" Hunt her down? She couldn't help it when she started to tremble.

"Gideon Roarke. He'll know the minute he sees me." Quinn cursed again and walked away a short distance, bracing himself on a tree trunk. "He'll find you wherever you go, and kill you."

"Why? Why would he kill me? Seriously?" What was *wrong* with these warriors? Could this situation get any worse? This was like a bad movie. "What did I do?"

Quinn turned his head. "I told you earlier. When a Calydon meets his *sheva*, he eventually goes rogue. It's the Order's job to stop that from happening, so we intervene before that happens, before destiny can play out. We pre-empt hell."

"By killing an innocent woman?" Because that sure sounded admirable and heroic.

"No. Not usually." He gave her a hard look, and she saw the warrior come to life. He was no longer the passionate lover, but the cold, disciplined fighter. "Usually, I kill the Calydon because our duty is to protect innocents."

"*You* do it?"

"I do it. I've killed hundreds of friends. I owe them the grace of dying by the hand of a friend."

She blinked. "That is so screwed up."

He narrowed his eyes. "It's all that keeps this world safe from rogues, until and unless someone can break that unbreakable cycle. Trust me when I say that you should be damn glad we do what we do."

"I should be glad you murder your friends?" She didn't understand how he could live with that. That was the same nightmare that haunted her daily, hurting someone she loved, and yet he did it willingly.

"That's not all we do." He walked over to her. "Rogue Calydons are so dangerous, that only the elite of our kind can stop them. That's me, and the rest of the Order. We're special."

She didn't miss the hint of sarcasm in his tone. "How special?"

He rested his hand on the front of her throat, his fingers lightly stroking her skin. "When it's an Order member who meets his *sheva*, the world can't afford to have him be the one to die. So, it's the woman who dies. Every time."

"Whoa." She stiffened. "So, it's already too late?

Your friends will hunt me down and kill me, even though nothing has happened? Seriously? Just because you claim I'm your *sheva*?" She shoved at him, trying to get his hand off her. God, she just wanted to get out of there. But where would she go? If the Order was after her, they'd find her wherever she went. "Damn you, Quinn! You knew this all along and didn't tell me!"

"Shit, Grace!" He didn't budge. "It wasn't like I had a plan in place to deal with you. I'm in a deadly race of my own right now, and I don't have time for this shit either. None of us do!" Quinn turned suddenly and threw his fist into the tree, splitting the trunk in half.

"Why don't you tell Gideon about Elijah being murdered, so he can worry about that instead?" *Yeah, yeah, good idea.* "You guys should be watching out for more illusions instead of worrying about killing me!"

Quinn went still, and he turned to look at her. "I forgot about the illusions. Dammit, I'm not even thinking clearly tonight." Quinn smacked his palm on the trunk again, then turned back toward her. "Here's the deal. This shit we're facing is big, much bigger than Elijah. I can't screw it up." He studied her face, and she could sense him falling into battle mode. The eyes that were looking at her were the cold, calculating eyes of a warrior, not the tortured eyes of a man. "You sensed your sister's illusion before it happened, right? You knew it was building before she even did it."

"Yeah—" Grace eyed him cautiously. Was this the mode he went into when he killed other Calydons? Was this how his friend would look when he came to kill her? His eyes were dark, his body rigid, his face impassive and cold. It freaked her out how he'd fallen into that role so quickly, as if he'd never kissed her so passionately.

"So, could you tell if someone was working an illusion on me? On my emotions?"

"Oh..." She bit her lip, trying to concentrate on his

question. "I could sense a typical illusion for sure, but I don't know about one that hits directly on your emotions. If it works the same as one of mine, yes. If not..." She shrugged. "I don't know. I'd guess I could, but I can't promise."

He grabbed her shoulders, his fingers digging in. "I'm down a weapon, my enemy has at least one talented Illusionist working for him, and someone's already tried to have me killed twice." Anger smoldered in his eyes. "I'd be screwed if I went in blind. I need you to tell me when someone's hitting me with an illusion. I need your help in battle, sweetheart, and I need you by my side where I can keep you safe from Gideon."

She stiffened. "So, we have to stay together?" Together meant sex, right? Together meant bonding. Together meant a fast track toward hell. But together also meant a better chance to save her sister.

"Oh, yeah." His expression was hard, the visage of a warrior focused on his job.

This wasn't the man who'd picked her up out of the mud and kissed her so passionately she'd melted into his arms. This was the man who'd killed thousands, and had been the one to walk away alive every time. Strategic, deadly and ruthless. She could see how being bound to this man could lead to death. Death followed him.

But she could also see in his eyes a man who would defend her life until the end. With him, she wouldn't be alone in her battles anymore. The thought scared her, but at the same time, she felt like he'd given her the most precious gift, a gift she didn't want, but had also yearned for her whole life. A gift that was dangerous because it would make her weak, if she let it. She had to be strong enough to stand on her own. "If we stay together, then what? What about the bond?"

He caught her wrist, flipped her hand over and pushed up her sleeve. "Look at your forearm."

She looked at the flush of the brand new skin that

had replaced the damage from the burns. "What about it?"

He ran his finger over it. "This is what we watch. When a Calydon warrior and his *sheva* complete their bond, a mirror image of his brand will appear on her forearms. They won't turn into weapons, but you'd be marked forever as mine."

She pressed her hand to her arm. "When it appears, it's too late?"

"It's gradual, because it takes time for a bond that strong to bind us." He dropped her hand. "All we have to do is keep the bond from fully binding us while we focus on finding Elijah and your sister. Then, after this shit is done, we'll split up and hope we can stay away from each other." His jaw was hard. "Destiny will not defeat us."

"But what about your friend who will track me down and kill me?"

He shrugged. "By then, I'll have something figured out."

She shoved her hands into her pockets. "Easy."

He gave her a grim smile. "Nothing is easy." He picked up the plastic bag that he'd been carrying earlier. Had he dropped it when he'd been kissing her? She hadn't even noticed. "Here are some dry clothes. They'll be big, but at least they don't have twenty pounds of mud on them. The clothes in your pack were damp. I'm drying them over the car heater now." He held it out to her. "There's a stream over the hill to wash in."

She was in over her head, but she had no choice. Her sister was all she had left, and she and Quinn had a better chance working together than going it alone. Her sister was worth every risk Grace had to take to save her. Ana had no one else on her side. The police were instructed to kill her. Bounty hunters the same. After a life on the run to protect Grace, Ana had never had the chance to make the friendships she'd craved so badly. She had no one to go after her, no one to believe in her, no one except Grace.

Ana had sacrificed everything for Grace, and she would not let her sister down.

Grace took the bag from Quinn. "Okay. I'm in." *Sheva* and all.

He nodded with grim satisfaction. "My truck's up and running. We'll head south to the bar where Elijah was murdered. I need to look around."

She nodded. As long as they focused on the search for her sister and Elijah, she'd be okay and could concentrate on something other than *him*. "I should be able to pick up some information about my sister there." She started to turn away, then stopped when Quinn caught her arm. "Don't touch me," she whispered, aching at the feel of his fingers on her.

He dropped his hand. "We leave in five minutes. Be prepared to listen to me, use your illusions, and hope to get a lead on Elijah and your sister."

She looked sharply at him. "Use my illusions? I thought you just wanted me to look for them—"

But he'd already disappeared into the woods, blending into the shadows and the sounds of the forest.

She bit her lip as she stared after him. It was one thing to use her talents to sense other illusions. It was something else entirely to call hers up. He'd seen what happened when she did that. He couldn't have intended it that way... But she had a bad feeling that's exactly what he'd meant.

Not that she had a choice. She had to find her sister, and teaming up with Quinn Masters was the way to do it. Gripping the bag of new clothes, Grace headed down toward the water to wash off, but she couldn't help looking over her shoulder, wondering when Gideon was going to appear and claim her life.

Chapter 5

"The Gun Rack is up around the corner," Quinn said, jarring Grace out of her restless nap. "We're almost there."

For a moment, Grace forgot where she was. Then she smelled the faint odor of mold and remembered too much. She sat up slowly, rubbing her neck as the musty scent of Quinn's truck itched her nose. The truck had been parked in the rainy woods for too long, and there was moss on the wheels and dampness inside. It had four-wheel drive, with huge treads on the tires and a coat of mottled gray and black paint on it, as if it had been patched up over the years. A truck that was understated, one that would blend into the world, unlike its overwhelming owner. One that would crush anything that got in its way, exactly like its owner.

Quinn looked over at her. "You doing okay?"

"Good." Nervous, scared, worried about her sister, but confident in the man beside her. The engine of his truck had purred along with powerful efficiency as Quinn had maneuvered up and down the steep mountain roads, and the tires had gripped the rain-drenched asphalt flawlessly. The drive had been slow due to a light fog and heavy rain that had rolled in. It had taken them almost four hours to get down out of the mountains to the place where Elijah had died.

Conversation had been minimal during the drive, which was fine with her. Talking was too intimate and best left alone. Right now, Grace needed to retreat back into herself and find her own strength. She had to focus on what she needed to do in this moment, instead of obsessing about her feelings for Quinn, or whether destiny would destroy them.

After spending the first twenty minutes checking her forearm every thirty seconds to see if Quinn's brand was appearing on her skin, Grace had finally shut her eyes and tried to meditate.

It had worked, sort of. It had kept her from checking her arm at least. A point for self-restraint…she pulled up her sleeve and checked again, relieved to see that there was no faint, shimmering outline of a sword taking shape on her arm. "All clear," she said.

"Of course it is," Quinn replied. "We haven't done any of the stages yet."

"There are stages?" God, there was something new to learn every minute she was with him. "What are they?"

"Don't worry. We're safe for the moment." He jerked his chin to the right. "This is the place," Quinn said, easing the truck to a stop along the edge of a dirt parking lot. He idled the engine without pulling into a spot as he carefully scanned the area.

Grace sat up and peered out the window, squinting past the high-speed wipers. It was too dark and rainy to see much besides the glow from his headlights on the ground and the reflection of taillights on all the trucks scattered along the edges of the lot. Suddenly, getting information about a bonding destiny that probably wasn't even true seemed to fade in comparison to their arrival at the last place anyone had reported seeing her sister alive.

Grace rolled down the window so she could see better. The sign to the bar hung at an angle, and most of the fluorescent red letters were burned out. A small "c" flickered, and a "Th" dangled at the front of the sign. The Gun Rack. A building left untended, designed to be ignored by all but those most intent on finding it.

The windows were blackened, rain was rattling off the metal roof, and a steady stream of water was pouring off the clogged gutters past the front door.

Quinn rolled down his window, then shut off the engine and leaned on the steering wheel, peering out into the night. No, not just peering...sensing. He was silent, and Grace suspected he was searching for smells or sounds that would whisper stories to him.

She let her vision soften ever so slightly, and she saw an iridescent violet dust coating the woods behind the bar. Excitement leapt through her and she gripped the door handle. "Ana's been here. She did a huge illusion in the woods."

Quinn peered in the direction she was looking. "How do you know?"

"Every Illusionist has a signature, a colored dust they leave behind after an illusion fades. Hers is violet. It's everywhere out there, but most heavily around the side of the bar and in the trees behind the bar." It glowed on the branches, bright light in a forest that was nothing but endless darkness, calling to her. Grace started to open the door, eager to get out—

"Wait." Quinn stopped her with a light touch to her arm. "Not yet. I want to get the lay of things first." He glanced at her. "I want to make sure it's safe before I let you go out there. No more deaths tonight."

Ah… he had a point. Reluctantly, Grace let go of the door. "So? Do you sense anything?"

"Still checking." Quinn leaned over her to peer out of her window. She felt a hum of energy from him, and she had to clench her fist against the urge to rest her hand on his back as he stretched past her. He shook his head and sat back. "I can't see your sister's dust."

She rolled her eyes impatiently. "Well, you're not an Illusionist."

"That, I am not, which is why you're here." Quinn drummed his fingers on the dash, echoing the pound of rain on the roof, as droplets splashed on his door through the open window. "Feels safe." He slanted a glance at her. "You sense anyone working an illusion on me right now?"

Grace frowned and studied him. "I don't feel any vibrations that would indicate an illusion, but..." She shrugged. "As I said before, if it's something inside you, I might not be able to sense it."

Quinn cursed, not pleased by her answer. "I need to know if I can trust my senses or not. It's critical." He worked his jaw. "Since you're my *sheva*, we're connected metaphysically, which is why you can hear my thoughts when I don't block them."

She eyed him warily. "So?"

"It'd be difficult because we haven't completed any of the bonding stages, but I might be able to build the connection between us enough for you to get a sense of what's inside me."

"Like reading your mind?"

"No. More than that." He rubbed his jaw. "It'd be more like a merging of our minds and spirits."

Her heart began to race, her belly tightening at the intimacy of what he was suggesting. "Won't that tighten the bond?"

"No. It's not one of the stages. Just a risk-free bonus of our plight." He took her hand and pressed it to his chest. "Close your eyes."

She grimaced. "I'm really not that good at trusting—"

"It's me, Grace." He gave her a crooked grin. "You're my *sheva*. I'd cut off my own hand before I could hurt you. You can trust me."

"Until you go rogue and lose your mind."

He shrugged. "Yeah, well, I never claimed to be perfect." He took her hand and folded it between his. "Let's do this, sweetheart. It's time."

His touch was warm and reassuring, his voice intense. He was the man who'd saved her life already. How much more did he have to do to prove himself? She had to learn to trust him enough to make this work, to save her sister. She nodded. "Okay."

He smiled and kissed her lightly. "Close your eyes, Grace."

Keeping her attention focused on the feel of his kiss, she let her eyes fall shut. *This is for you, Ana.*

"Relax your mind." Quinn's voice was calm and forceful, a warrior who expected those on his team to obey him. "Focus on the beat of my heart." He set her hand against his chest again. "Try to match your own rhythm to mine."

She focused on the thud of his heart under her palm. The steady rhythm was strong and reliable.

"That's right," he whispered. "Let your own patterns match mine. Don't force it, just feel them as they come together."

She allowed his even heartbeat into her mind. She let the pulse echo through her body, and she focused on relaxing all her muscles. But she was out of sync with him, beating irregularly. "I can't—"

"You can." He leaned forward and kissed her again. Not a kiss of wild passion. An intimate kiss of connection and unity. His lips moved against hers, seducing her, drawing her away from herself and into him. She felt her mind quiet, and her tension vanished. She felt his strong presence soothing her mind, tangling with her own thoughts, meshing as one.

Their patterns overlapped for a split second, creating a single heartbeat. Then another. Then a third, until her heart was beating in perfect synchronicity with his, so she couldn't tell there were two.

There was a whisper in her mind, and then she felt Quinn's presence, filling her with warmth, reassurance and a sense of power as he continued to kiss her, more deeply now, more connected. She realized he was infusing her with his warrior strength, the essence of his being.

Grace. His voice drifted through her mind, an intrusion that felt natural, not threatening. *Follow the thread that binds us.* His voice was compelling, luring her along, and she let her consciousness drift toward him, toward the dark pulsating energy that resonated with his essence.

It was as if she were traveling through a black tunnel, with safety on the other end...almost within her reach.

A heavy pressure settled around her spirit, wrapping her up tightly, and she knew she was connecting with the real Quinn, with the secrets he carried inside. Strength, power, energy, confidence. It was brilliant and heady, and she wanted to dance with the courage it gave her—

Then it went cold. Ice cold, like a frigid winter wind biting through her clothes. She recognized the energy around her as Quinn's, but it was so distant and bitter, almost dangerous.

You're in. His deep voice whispered in her mind. *Do you see an illusion?*

The warmth she'd felt from him earlier was gone. Instead, deep inside, in this hidden place in his soul, Quinn was stark and barren. Had he shut down all his emotions in order to do his job as an Order member, or had he never been truly alive? She reached out as if she were sweeping her hand through him, and the coldness was everywhere. The darkness of deaths, many, many deaths, grabbed at Grace, until it felt like something was pinning her chest with dozens of needles. There was isolation. A sense of being utterly alone. Connected with no one. A shadow lashing about in the wind with no roots, no anchor, nothing to hold it together. It made her want to cry for his pain, because she knew what it felt like. It was what she felt so often, an aching loneliness that was so hard to escape, and it was coating his soul, eating away at who he was. *This can't be all you are.*

His confusion tickled her, like a feather in her mind. *What are you talking about?*

She realized that he didn't even feel the barrenness inside him. He was so used to it that he didn't even notice it anymore. Tears filled her eyes for the burden he carried, and suddenly she didn't want to be lost in that void anymore.

She wanted out. She needed to breathe, to connect, to feel the warmth of humanity. Grace took over their connection, plunging past the place Quinn had brought her to. She burrowed deeper inside him, through the layers of darkness and isolation until she found what she'd known had to be there. A faint glowing light that she knew was honor. A warmth associated with Elijah and Gideon— friendship and loyalty.

This was the place inside him she wanted to be. It felt like home. It felt safe. She didn't want to leave this special hidden gem. This was what drove him, what he protected with his coldness so no one would be able to take it away from him.

Then her mind blurred and she was back on the surface, surrounded by the parts of himself he wanted her to see. There was an impenetrable barrier woven through his mind now, keeping her out of the place she'd just been.

Stay out of there, sweetheart. His voice was mild, but unyielding. *Focus on the illusion.*

Sorry. Embarrassed that she'd violated his privacy, Grace immediately opened her mind to search for the rising pressure of energy that went along with an illusion. She softened her mind's eye the same way she softened her vision when she looked for illusion dust. She went into that place more and more deeply until she was no longer seeing Quinn as a man, just a spirit made of energy vibrations.

That's when she saw it. Emerald-green dust fragments sparkling through his consciousness. Elation rippled through her. *I see illusion dust.* She paused, looking more closely. *It looks familiar. I know I've seen that shade before.*

He cursed. *So, I'm under an illusion?*

No. Dust is what remains after an illusion disappears. It means you had one before, but there's nothing active right now. She searched further and thought she caught the faint remnants of an illusion, but she couldn't be sure. Each time she tried to tap into it, it slithered out of her grasp, like an elusive thought.

The link between them broke and she slid back into her own mind and her own body, missing the connection with Quinn the minute she lost it. She opened her eyes, and then pulled her hand off his chest when she saw the shadowed expression on his face. "I'm sorry for invading your privacy."

His face was shuttered. "It's my fault for bringing you in. I should have realized I couldn't control you once you were connected to me." He took a breath. "I've never done that before. It was damn strange. I felt you inside me. Not just touching my mind, like Gideon and Elijah do. You were in there. I felt your breathing." His gaze brushed over hers. "I felt your loneliness."

"You did?" She froze, suddenly terrified. How much had he found out? What had he learned? "What else did you feel?"

His brows went up at her near panic. "I got a sense of your emotions. That's it. Nothing concrete." He studied her, his gaze knowing. "I didn't catch any secrets, Grace. Whatever you want to stay hidden from me is still hidden."

"Oh." She tried to relax, but she was still unnerved

by what Quinn could have discovered. She waited for him to ask questions, to demand she share what she was hiding, but he didn't.

He seemed to accept her need for privacy, and let it be. Maybe he needed to take back his own space himself. "What did you learn about the illusion?"

Grace tried to play off his cue and ignore the intimacy of what had just happened between them. "You were under an illusion at some point. The fact that the dust is inside you means that's where the illusion was. Someone was messing with your thoughts or emotions."

Quinn nodded in agreement. "It makes sense that I would have been under one the night I died. It's more reasonable than to think my instincts simply failed me." He looked relieved at the thought. "Is there anything currently working on me?"

She chewed her lower lip, trying to think of how to explain the illusion that had fluttered just out of her reach. "You've got this...*thing* inside you. It felt like an illusion, or the beginnings of one, but it was so faint or elusive that I couldn't pinpoint it and identify it for sure."

He frowned, his jaw cracking as he thought about what she'd said. "So, it's like a seed, waiting for a trigger? For someone to turn it on?"

"Maybe." She grimaced. "I'm not sure. I've never seen anything like it before."

"Can you get rid of it?"

"I'm not sure." Grace frowned, squinting as the bright headlights of an oncoming truck flashed across Quinn's face. It pulled into the lot, drove past them, then swung around and backed into a spot at the end of the row, just down from where Quinn had parked at the curb. Its front tire disappeared up to the tire rim as it sank into a rain-filled rut in the parking lot. It was a black truck like Quinn's, with a gun rack in the back window and a big steel toolbox in the bed. "I'll have to think on it."

"Well, figure it out quickly. I need to get clean." His face glowed bright in the headlights, and Grace could see his concentration in the tense lines around his eyes. Then the headlights turned off and he faded into the darkness again. "Do it soon, Grace."

She glared at him, chafing under his orders, not liking the pressure to delve into the side of her she'd tried to hide from for so long. "I said I would try."

He flashed a quick smile of apology. "Thanks." He squeezed her hand. "You did good, Grace. Really good."

Warmth filled her, and she realized that his orders weren't personal, they weren't an indication that he was trying to control her. It was simply his way of operating in battle mode.

His warrior side was why she'd sought him out, and she needed to get over her aversion to him directing her. She needed to trust him and allow him to do what he did best. But it was difficult when he was asking her to deal with illusions. She'd spent fifteen years fighting them off, and to suddenly embrace them...Grace took a deep breath, trying to steady the panic that was starting to build. It wasn't easy, even with Quinn by her side to protect them if she lost control. Her fear of what she was ran too deep.

Quinn drummed his fingers on the steering wheel again. "Okay, so I'm an unknown. We can't truly trust my instincts until you clear them." He glanced at her, then sympathy flickered across his face, an expression that was soft and human, and he brushed his fingers over her cheek. "You're not facing your illusions alone. We're a team, and teams go both ways. Ask me for help if you need it."

Her throat suddenly thickened. "Thanks."

He set his hand on her knee and rubbed gently. She immediately placed her hand on his and held on, not caring that she needed his touch, not even trying to resist it. Everything she was dealing with was so foreign to her, she needed to ground herself, and right now Quinn was what she had.

Two men got out of the truck that had just pulled into the parking lot. They stomped loudly through the mud and the puddles, talking about a hunt they'd recently been on. One of them glanced at Quinn's truck as they went inside, the door crashing behind them.

Quinn leaned forward as the door of the bar swung open, and a man in a denim jacket and a faded red baseball cap came outside to stand in the rain, facing their truck. Waiting. His challenge was obvious.

"That's our invitation to join the party, or to leave," Quinn said. "We sat here too long." He turned the truck back on so he could roll up the windows, then shut it down for good. "Let's go inside."

"Okay." Suddenly excited about taking action, about being where she knew her sister had been, Grace pulled on the oversized jacket Quinn had loaned her and tugged the hood up. It was her first real lead on her sister, and she was buzzing with energy.

Quinn opened his door. "Try not to look intimidated when we go in there. These men are the type who will try to take advantage of anyone weak. I'll have you covered, but—"

"Don't worry, Quinn." Grace kicked open her door, amused that he thought she couldn't handle herself with a bunch of rough locals. Yes, she was a pathetic wuss when it came to trust, illusions, bonding and pretty much anything else, but this was one situation she was confident about. It felt good to focus on something she knew she could handle. "Trust me, dealing with jerks in seedy bars is not a big deal. Illusions scare me. Places like this don't."

He raised his brows at her in surprise. "So, the lovely Ms. Grace has a side to her I don't know about? I'm impressed."

She grinned as they sprinted across the dirt parking lot. "There's a lot you don't know about me, Quinn." She leapt over a puddle, then landed ankle deep in the wet mud.

Quinn grabbed her around the waist and hauled her out of the muck, yanking her against him. "Tell me," he growled playfully. "I want to learn everything about you." He bit her chin lightly as he backed her toward the building. "I want to get inside you and crawl around until I know every inch of your body and soul."

She swallowed and set her hands on his forearms. "Quinn, this isn't the time—"

"Can't help it. Connecting with you got me all jacked up." He grabbed the back of her hair. "I want you, Grace Matthews. It's getting stronger by the minute."

Desire leapt inside her. "Quinn—"

He spun her around and tossed her up the steps to the front door. The man who'd come outside to check on them didn't move aside as they passed him, and they were forced to step around him to get inside. He didn't take his gaze off them, a lit cigarette dangling from his fingers, though she hadn't seen him take a drag.

Quinn nodded at the man, then set his hand on Grace's back and moved between her and the man. Quinn leaned over Grace's shoulder as he reached past her to pull the door open. "Later," he promised in a sensual whisper that was for her ears only. "Later tonight, sweetheart, we will finish this."

Grace didn't have to ask him what he meant. She knew it, in every quivering, trembling heated part of her body. "Damn you," she said as she walked past him.

He just grinned and followed her inside.

※※※※

Quinn was prepared when all eyes went to them as he and Grace stepped into the bar. There were about twenty-five people inside, mostly men, all of them wearing jeans, with grizzled faces and ragged hair. These were men who knew how to defend their territory and didn't like to share.

Quinn took Grace's elbow, grimly realizing he shouldn't have brought her inside with him. He needed to be focusing on looking for information about Elijah's death instead of worrying about keeping these men off her.

He glanced at her, and then raised his brows at the transformation.

She had her hands on her hips, her chin raised, and she was staring down every man in the bar. Her body language made it clear she was to be untouched, and the fire in her eyes said she'd kick the ass of anyone who disregarded her warning. With her dark hair tossed around her slim shoulders, and her silver eyes challenging anyone who looked too long at her, she looked like a siren ready to lure every man to his death.

Damn, woman. You're hotter than the fire that nearly took me down today. Toss some of that attitude over here, and you'll be in the backseat of my truck before you can take another breath. He was kidding, but not. He liked what he saw, and he wanted it. Now. All of it. *You're making me crazy, woman.*

Grace didn't look at him, but he saw the corner of her mouth twitch in response. Yeah, she was down with him. He was the only one who was going to get through those shields, and he liked it that way.

Quinn grinned, watching the testosterone junkies in the room gradually wither away under Grace's stare. One by one, the men stopped gawking at her, returning to their drinks, their game of darts or their game of pool or just pretending to suddenly find something interesting written on the table, daring only to sneak a well-disguised peek at the five-foot-two brunette who'd just taken over the joint.

Someone muttered the word "bitch," but before Quinn could whip out his sword and cut off the bastard's tongue, Grace grinned, looking very pleased, as if that kind of remark was exactly what she'd wanted to hear. Quinn frowned, studying his woman as she took a seat at the bar, next to a guy who looked about eighteen, pounding back a beer.

Quinn squeezed in between her and the kid, so his hip was against Grace's thigh. He leaned on one elbow so he could keep an eye on the room and still make it clear he was with her. "Where did you learn to put on that kind of attitude?" He kept his voice quiet so they wouldn't be easily overheard.

"Foster care."

He shot a sharp glance. "You were a foster kid?"

"For a little while. Not long, actually." She closed her mouth and turned her head away from him, clearly indicating the discussion was over. She bit her lower lip, as if regretting the slip.

The bartender leaned on the wood, the bill of his faded Yankees cap covered in something dark. Grease? Or blood? "Where you from?" It wasn't a casual question. It was the suspicious interrogation of outsiders.

Quinn answered for both of them. "The mountains. Up north about three hours."

The bartender looked at Grace. "You, too?"

She smiled at him, a radiant expression that made both Quinn and the bartender blink. *You're beautiful.*

Stop distracting me. I have an image to maintain here. Her cheeks flushed, and she shot Quinn a quick glare before returning her focus to the bartender. "I'm from nowhere. And everywhere." She nodded at Quinn. "For the moment, I'm where he is."

The bartender ignored Quinn, practically drowning in Grace's glow. "You get bored fast?"

Grace gave him a speculative look that made Quinn slide his arm around her waist and haul her across the bar stool, so her bent knees were on either side of his hips. *Mine.*

She raised an eyebrow at Quinn, but clearly realized

the futility of trying to escape his grasp. "I'm not bored," she told the bartender, "but if I am, I'll let you know."

"You do that." The bartender thudded two beers in front of them before he wandered off, his gaze lingering on Grace until he saw Quinn's hostile scowl, and then he quickly turned away.

Quinn eyed Grace as she took a drink of her beer, a pleased smile curving her lips. "You will not be getting bored of me, and if you did, you would not be letting him know."

She cocked her head at him, playfulness sparkling in those silver eyes of hers. "You're jealous."

"I've never been jealous in my life." He took a long drink of his beer, not liking the darkness rolling through him.

"You are now." She sounded entirely satisfied with that discovery, and she leaned over, pursing her lips inches from his. "You've never cared enough to be jealous, have you? Until you met me."

All right. That was it. A man could take only so much teasing when other men were checking out his woman. "Enough." He clasped the back of her neck. "You're messing with fire, Grace. It's dangerous."

Her eyes widened, and her lips softened in subconscious invitation.

That was all the encouragement he needed. He pulled her close and captured her mouth with his. Her lips were warm and welcoming beneath his, and she parted for him instantly. He growled and trapped her head where he wanted it, deepening the kiss. Harder, faster, owning her. Needing to show the whole damn place if they messed with Grace, it was him they were going to have to worry about, not her. He was her man, dammit, and everyone here needed to know that.

He tangled his fingers in her hair, nudging her mouth open, coaxing her response. She made a small noise of acquiescence in the back of her throat as she leaned into him, the tips of her breasts brushing across his chest, her knees flanking his hips. He swore as she slipped her arm around his neck, holding him tighter, deepening the kiss on her own—

"Peanuts?" The bartender slammed a wooden bowl on the counter next to Grace, and she jumped.

Quinn broke the kiss and turned his head to look at the bastard who'd dared to interrupt them. The guy grinned and doffed his hat, admitting defeat. Quinn jerked his chin in acknowledgement, and glanced at the room. No one would meet his gaze. He nodded, satisfied. The message had been sent.

"Are you going to pee on my barstool next?" Grace asked.

Quinn looked back at Grace, who was watching him with a mixture of amusement and annoyance. "It needed to be done."

"And why is that?"

"Because you're the only beautiful woman in a bar full of men who carry guns." He gripped the leg of her stool and pulled her closer, but this time it was for him, and not for any others. Screw the others. He didn't need to worry about them anymore. "You're a tough woman, Grace, and I admire that a hell of a lot." He lifted her hand and pressed his palm against hers, his hand dwarfing hers. "But I don't want you to have to fight more battles than necessary. If I can give you peace and a clear road to search for information about your sister, then that's what I'm going to do."

"Oh." Her face softened and the irritation dissolved. "Well, thanks, then."

"You're welcome." He leaned forward to nibble on her earlobe. "But just so you know, I'm also insanely possessive when it comes to you, and if I hadn't done that, I would have had to spend the night getting in brawls behind the bar with every man who looked your way."

She raised her eyebrows at him, but this time she was smiling. "I've never had a man get in fights over me."

"You've never had me." He cupped her hip. "But we're going to change that tonight."

Her eyes widened, and she slapped at his hands. "Stop it," she whispered. "We are not getting more involved! You know we can't."

"I know." Not that it was going to stop him when the moment presented itself. But now was not the time. He leaned back and picked up his beer again, trying to shift his mind to more neutral and productive topics. "How'd you learn how to handle the bartender like that? You deflected his question without him even noticing."

She grinned with obvious pride and scooted closer, as if she were sharing a secret. "When I was younger, I had trouble controlling my illusions, as you know." She rolled her eyes at herself and who she used to be in an expression that was disarmingly adorable. "People would always notice there was something different about me, so I had to learn how to distract them from the path their thoughts were on, without them realizing it."

"You're good at it."

She smiled, a liberated and confident smile that made his grip on her waist tighten. "Thanks." She wiped some frost off the bottle, and her face became more serious. "It was hard growing up, not being able to tell people about us. My parents had died and we'd, um, sort of skipped out on foster care without going through the appropriate channels, so there was always the risk that we'd be taken back, especially Ana, who was three years younger than I was."

He frowned. "How old were you?"

"I was fourteen and Ana was eleven."

"You were living on the street when you were kids?" At her nod, he swore. When he was fourteen, he'd been working his ass off on his family's farm and practicing his fighting skills out back every night with his uncle Felix, preparing to become a great Calydon warrior like his dad had been. He didn't like the idea of Grace being alone so young. "How'd you do it?"

She shrugged. "We had to lie and move around a lot, and we had to come up with answers when people asked us personal questions. We learned how to keep people at a distance without arousing their suspicions. Ana and I used to make it into a game."

Some of the light went out of her eyes at the mention of her sister, and he took her hand, holding it with an urgency he didn't quite comprehend. "Grace. We'll find her." And they would. Now that he understood more about Grace, he realized that her loyalty to Ana was the same as his commitment to Elijah. He admired the hell out of her for holding onto that faith despite all the crap she'd gone through, and he'd honor that.

"I know." She leaned into his touch for a moment and inhaled deeply, as if to shake off the moment. Then she took another drink of the beer, wrinkling her nose. "This is terrible."

He took one hand from her waist to take a chug of his beer. "Yeah, it is." But he kind of liked it, actually. There was something satisfying about crappy beer.

The boy next to them finished his drink and shoved off, leaving Quinn enough room to give Grace some space.

He didn't move. He damn well liked where he was.

"So, what's our plan now?" she asked.

"When Calydons die, our bodies are reclaimed by the earth, making it appear that our bodies have disappeared." He turned his head slightly to watch the room, searching for any signs Elijah had been there. *Elijah. You nearby?* He hadn't expected an answer, and he didn't get one, but he would keep reaching out on the chance it would work.

Most of the men weren't paying them any attention, but two men in the corner seemed to be working a little too hard not to notice Grace. Quinn settled his gaze on them, watching them carefully. "If I died, my body would disappear within a few hours because I'm so old, but a young one could take weeks."

She nodded. "I've heard of that."

"But we don't actually disappear. Not entirely."

She frowned. "What are you talking about?"

One of the men in the corner looked their way, so Quinn slid his hand so it rested on Grace's, giving the man an intimidating scowl. His sword began to tingle in his forearm and he sat up, staring more closely at the men. Was his weapon reacting to his caveman response with Grace, or something else? Were his instincts warning him about those men? "When we die," he continued, "a part of our spirit, our last moments on this earth, remains behind. It's the only physical thing that remains of us once our body is gone." The man paled and looked down at his drink, and Quinn nodded with satisfaction.

His sword continued to burn in his arm. Shit. What now?

Grace followed his stare to the corner, her eyes narrowing on the men, who were now bent over in deep discussion. Supposedly. "I don't understand," she said. "How does a spirit physically manifest itself?"

"It finds something of this earth and melds with it. The spirit itself is still intangible, but it's anchored to the object. Usually a rock that's nearby. It's called a *mjui*, and it carries with it an imprint of our death. Any Calydon can access that spirit if they find the *mjui*." He glanced at her, appreciating the intense look of concentration on her face as she listened to him. "If Elijah's dead—"

"If?" She looked surprised. "You don't think he's dead? But they found his body."

"Illusions are involved, Grace. Who knows what

they really found, and what they didn't. I'd know if he were dead...but I'd know if he were alive, too." If he were dead...No. Quinn wasn't going to go there. He was here to find evidence of Elijah's life, not proof of his death. If there was no *mjui*, then he would know Elijah was still alive and hopefully his search would turn up clues about what was going on. "If Elijah died, I'd be able to use his *mjui* to find out what happened in the moments leading up to his death."

"Oh...so, you'd know if Ana killed him?" Hope flared in Grace's eyes. "Or, you'd know if someone else did it?"

He nodded. "I'd know."

"Then we find the *mjui*." She looked around the room. "So, if he was killed in the bar, the stone would be in here, right?"

"Yeah." He caught her arm as she started to slide off the chair to search the bar. "The *mjui* is difficult to find, unless you know what you're looking for. I'm blood bonded with Elijah, so I'll sense it if I get close enough to it."

She wrapped her hand around his and squeezed. "I'm sorry you have to wonder if he's dead. I know how much it sucks to lose someone you care about."

He saw the sadness in her expression, and he suspected she was talking about her parents. He had a sudden urge to pull her into his arms and take away her pain. He had an insane urge to tell her how much it had sucked to be betrayed by a man he'd long considered his brother, that he got what she'd gone through. He got her, and he knew she'd get him. And—

Shit. *Get a grip, man. Toughen up for hell's sake.*

He pulled his hand out of hers and gave a quick inspection around the bar. The men in the corner were gone, and his sword had quieted. He could feel no threats, caught no scents that were out of the ordinary. "I'm going to do a walk-through of the bar to see if Elijah's *mjui* is in here. If it's not, then I'll need to check the woods where you saw Ana's illusion dust." He held out his hand again. "Come on."

"No." She shook her head. "I saw a bit of Ana's dust near the ladies room, so I want to sift through it first. If it's uncontaminated enough, I might be able to figure out what her illusion was. Since she's my sister, I can often get a hit off her dust and can see whatever illusion left the residue."

He frowned. "What would that tell you?"

"Illusions are often based on whatever is going on with the Illusionist at the time, either strong emotions they are dealing with, or something in their physical environment. Like at your house, I'd been standing by the fire and feeling the heat from it, so when my illusion came forth, it was fire. Ana's illusion might have some clues about her current situation." She stood up. "I'll meet you back here, okay? If you're outside already, I'll come out because I want to check the woods, too."

Quinn scowled. "I don't like separating. Stay with me. Just because I can't sense any threats in the area doesn't mean it's safe."

Her wary gaze scanned the room again, but she shook her head. "It's more efficient to split up. I can't help you find Elijah's *mjui* and you can't help me read Ana's dust."

He ground his teeth, realizing she was right, but hating the thought of walking away from her. *Get over it, Quinn. Treat her as a partner, not a mate. Get in, get the information, and get out. Stay focused on the goal.* What the hell was wrong with him? Elijah was his priority, not defending Grace against some threat that might not even exist.

Not to mention, she could pretty much kick the shit out of anyone who messed with her. The fire illusion had been some serious weaponry. He scowled at her, not liking the decision but knowing it made sense. "Fine. You check the ladies room and meet me back here. Don't leave. Don't go outside. Don't talk to anyone, and keep your mind open to me. If we're close enough, I'll be able to connect with you." He started to turn away, then spun back, grabbing her wrist and hauling her against him, so he was in her space. "I will be extremely pissed if you get yourself killed. If you get in trouble, throw up an illusion. I'll get us out safely."

She tensed, but didn't pull away. "I don't need an illusion. I'll be fine."

"Promise me, Grace," he ordered.

"No, I won't. You don't have the right to order me around just because you'd fall apart if I die."

"I didn't say I'd fall apart. I said I'd be pissed."

She gave him a steady look. "It's the same thing, Quinn. I know because I feel the same way about you. The thought of you dying makes me so crazy I can't concentrate. So I get it. But we can't let that control us. Right now, we make the right choices, and that's for me to go find my sister and you to look for Elijah's *mjui*...or whatever you can learn about him that will give you answers."

The thought of him dying made her crazy? Stunned by Grace's admission, Quinn released his grip on her without another word. No one worried about him dying. That wasn't how his life worked. He was always in danger of dying. It was who he was, and it was his way of life. The way of life for the Order. It simply was.

But the way Grace had said it, with so much emotion in her voice, rocked Quinn back on his ass. It made him feel something. What, he didn't know. He couldn't know, because he couldn't go there.

She touched his arm. "Quinn. No one's after me. It's just the Calydons who are being murdered. I'm not the one in danger."

He ground his jaw. "Gideon could be after you by

now. If my team shows up—"

"Don't they have to see you first before they'll know you're bonded?"

He scowled. "Yeah," he admitted.

"So, now's the time. I can actually manage to walk down the hall to the bathroom without being in danger of being attacked, okay?" She shook her head at his protest. "I have to do this, Quinn. I'll meet you back here in a few minutes. Go do your thing, I'll do mine, and we'll be on track to find the people we care about that much sooner."

He gripped her arm. "Grace, there's shit going down and I don't have answers. I don't know what the hell's up, but since your sister is involved, I wouldn't be so quick to assume you're not of interest to someone as well. Be careful."

Acknowledgment flickered across her face. "You have a point."

"Thank you."

"I'll be careful." Her expression determined, Grace turned away and walked down the hall.

"Screw that." Quinn sprinted past and intercepted her before she reached the bathroom door. He motioned for her to stay back and opened the door. He stepped inside and did a careful scan with all his senses. No one was in there, and he sensed no threat.

"Are we good?" Grace was standing in the doorway, an indulgent expression on her face. "All clear?"

"Yeah." Quinn strode over to her, grabbed her around the waist and pulled her up against him. "Be careful."

She nodded, her amusement fading. "I will."

He kissed her hard, once, and then stepped back before the lust could take over. "I'll be in the main bar and then out in the woods. The minute you're done, you go to the bar, and if I'm not there, go out the back door. I'll be right out there."

She raised her brows. "Can't I just call you in your mind?"

"No. Not until we've done the blood bond. For now, we have to be within close range."

She blinked. "Blood bond? Like vampire stuff?"

Arousal pulsed through him at the idea of bonding with her and he swore. "Later. Now's not the time to get involved with that topic." His instincts were calm, his sword not burning, his mind knew it was the most efficient choice to part, but he was not happy about it.

"Or not." She shook her head. "No blood bonding, thanks so much."

For now.

She glared at him and walked past him into the bathroom, giving him a gentle shove into the hall and shutting the door behind him.

Quinn stood where he was and watched the door, waiting to make sure no one went in after her.

No one did. No one even came out in the hall.

She's safe, man. Do your thing. She's not going anywhere.

"You good?" he called through the door.

"I need to concentrate. Go away."

Quinn laughed softly, then he forced himself to turn away and focus on what he'd come there to do: track Elijah. As he strode back into the bar, he knew that he had to find a way to stay away from Grace and focus solely on his mission, or else the *sheva* destiny would commence the slow death spiral of everything that mattered to them both.

CHAPTER 6

Grace grimaced at the stale odor of cigarettes and dirty toilets in the small restroom. There were two stalls, and the wooden doors were barely covered with chipped black paint. Metal fish-eye hooks hung loosely to keep them closed.

There was only one sink, with a cloudy mirror and porcelain stained with rust from years under a dripping faucet.

Grace tried to ignore the stench and the depressing sense of abandonment of the room, and instead focused on her sister. She softened her mind and took another look around the room using her Illusionist senses. The moment she shifted awareness, the room literally glowed with violet dust. It was all over the floors, kicked up more thickly against the walls. "Ana." Grace whispered her name, as if she could bring Ana to life right there in that moment, simply by connecting with her.

Grace walked over to the corner, crouched down, and brushed her fingers through the dust. The pads of her fingers tingled, and she smiled with relief. The dust was still active. It hadn't been that long since Ana had stood right there, living and breathing. Alive.

"I'm coming for you, Ana. I promise." Excited by her progress, Grace cupped her hands and scooped up a handful of dust. She lifted it to her face and breathed deeply, letting the dust float into her nose, throat and lungs, dispersing through her body and spirit. A tingling began to spread over her body, and she felt a pulsing deep within her as her own Illusionist spirit rose to meet her sister's, recognizing Ana's presence.

Grace closed her eyes, opening herself to experience the joy of Ana's illusions, then suddenly darkness ripped into her. Images of death, blood, and tortured bodies burned in her mind. Grace stumbled to her feet, horrified by the torment flooding her senses. Dear God, she was going to do an illusion! "Quinn!" She backed toward the door, gripping her head… and then realized her head didn't hurt. There was no pressure building inside her. The poison wasn't coming from within her. As she stood there, it faded away, like a gentle wave on a beach at low tide.

She frowned and looked around the small bathroom. What had she just felt? There was no shift in pressure indicating an illusion building nearby, but she'd definitely felt the brutality of a dark illusion. *Quinn?*

I'm going outside, sweetheart. I'll be out of range when I'm in back. You all right?

She rubbed her forehead. *Fine. Is everything okay? Do you sense anything wrong?*

Quinn was quiet for a moment, and she knew he was double-checking. *I'm not picking up anything.* His voice became more urgent. *What's wrong? I'm coming in there.*

No, no. Everything's okay. Keep looking. I want to get out of here as soon as we can. Chills slithered down her arms as Grace looked around the unkempt bathroom. Had that darkness been her imagination?

You're sure? Quinn didn't sound convinced.

She felt better simply connecting with Quinn and hearing his voice. His immediate focus on her made her feel not so alone, more empowered to take a risk. *I'm sure.*

Let's just both hurry. This place is giving me the creeps.

Okay. But be careful.

You, too. They cut off communication, and Grace felt a little tense realizing that Quinn was moving out of range. Yes, he was close, and it wouldn't take much for her to get his attention, but she still felt increasingly nervous. Something deadly had just brushed against her, and she didn't know what it was.

She cleared her throat, facing the room again. "Okay, Grace, focus. Read Ana's dust and then get out. That's all you need to do." She walked back across the room and scooped up another handful. Her skin began to tingle right away, and she bent her head and breathed it in again—

Darkness swirled through her. Pain. Fear. Death. Blood. She saw the flash of a blade and stumbled back. The dust fell from her hands and the deadly images stopped.

She stared in growing horror at the dust floating so gently back to the dirty floor. "Ana?" No, no, it couldn't be. Ana wasn't like that. She hadn't been cursed. Numbly, Grace dropped to her knees and ran her hand through the dust. "Please God, don't do this to her. Don't give her my nightmare."

Grace scooped up the dust and tried a third time. This time, she was prepared. This time, when hell came again, she was ready. She closed her eyes as the nightmares took over, grief for her sister welling in her chest. It was Ana's dust that was so tainted. It was her sister who had created such terrors. "Oh, Ana," Grace whispered, "I'm so sorry."

The pain, the fear, the horror pervading the illusion was what Ana had been feeling at the time she'd created it. Ana wasn't just creating darkness, she was living it. "Ana." Grace's heart ached for the anguish she knew her sister was facing, the terror she'd tried so hard to protect her from all these years.

Grace pressed her lips tighter, fighting against the tears. It wouldn't help Ana to cry for her. She didn't have time to grieve for her sister. It was now even more urgent that she find Ana, before things became worse. Jutting out her jaw, Grace opened her senses more, trying desperately not to think about how much Ana must have been suffering in order to generate such a dark illusion. What must have happened to her to make her cross that line? What was happening to her right now?

Grace shook her head, knowing that she couldn't afford to go there. She had to focus. She clenched her fists, reaching with her inner eye through Ana's tortured emotions, past her fears...and then Grace saw the face of a man. A long, narrow face, haunted eyes, dark hair and a smile so evil it made her skin crawl. That was who was hurting Ana. The man who had killed Elijah. It hadn't been her sister. It was him. "You bastard—"

"Excuse me?"

The image vanished and Grace jumped to her feet, startled. A man stood in the doorway...the man from the corner table who Quinn had stared down. It wasn't the man in her vision. This intruder was grinning, his teeth yellowed and crooked, his hair greasy, his clothes smelling like he hadn't washed in far too long. Ignoring the racing of her heart, she set her hands on her hips and gave him her hard look, the one that always set men back at the distance she felt comfortable with. "This is the women's bathroom."

"My name's Red." He didn't move away. "I was here that night."

She had no idea what night he was talking about, and she didn't want to know. He was blocking the door, but at least it was still open. She could see into the hall. She could see freedom behind him, if only she could get past him. "Not interested."

A woman with a brown ponytail and a black rain jacket tapped his shoulder. "Hey. This is the women's room.

Out."

Red stepped back to allow passage, and Grace bolted instantly for the door, keeping the woman between her and Red as she darted out. As she ducked past him, Red flashed a grin at her, still looking far too comfortable. "You look like the girl who was here that night."

A trickle of nervous sweat dripped down Grace's back, and she glanced over her shoulder at him as she kept walking down the hall, back toward the bar. "What night?"

"The night the Illusionist made the sky fall. You look like the girl who did it."

A low undercurrent in Red's tone caught her attention and she tensed. *He was hunting her.* Holding out bait she'd be unable to resist.

But he was right. There was no way she'd ignore even the smallest chance that he had information that might help her find Ana. Ever so slowly, she turned to face him, even as she kept moving toward the bar area.

Red leaned against the wall, propping his shoulder against the knotted pine, his eyes narrowed as he watched her sidle away. His body was tensed and ready, waiting for her to make a quick move, but he seemed perfectly content to allow her to ease away from him.

"I have no idea what you're talking about." She gave him her coldest stare. *Quinn? Can you hear me? I have a problem here.*

Silence.

Red dangled the lure a little further. "She said you'd have silver eyes, like hers."

"She said...what?" Grace stopped walking. He'd really met Ana? "You talked to her?"

Red nodded, his eyes gleaming with triumph. He'd snared Grace, and he knew it. "She told me a girl with dark hair and silver eyes might come looking for her. She said you'd know to go into the bathroom. Grace, right? That's your name?"

Grace's heart began to race. Had Ana left the dust behind on purpose? "What did she say? Is she okay? Was she hurt?"

Red shrugged. "She looked fine. Kind of quiet, but a sweet kid. She asked me to give you a message if I saw you."

She gave him her full attention. "What message? What did she say?"

"She said she didn't do it."

Grace's legs began to tremble. *Ana hadn't killed those men.* She'd been present, but she hadn't done it. Grace sagged against the wall, too shaken to hold herself up. Ana hadn't killed anyone. She didn't have to live with the nightmare that haunted Grace every day, at least not yet. God knew what would happen if she stayed with the man in her vision much longer. "What else did she say?" Grace knew she was playing into his trap, but she didn't care. She had to find out everything she could about her sister.

"The guy came back before she could tell me anything more."

A cold draft shivered over Grace as the image she'd caught from Ana's dust shimmered in her mind. "Can you describe him? Did you get a name? What kind of car was he driving? Did she try to get away from him? Did he have a weapon? How was he keeping her from leaving him?"

He looked past her. "Hey, Vaughn. Nice of you to join us."

There was a movement to her right, and she jumped to the side as the other man from the table walked up beside her. Unlike his greasy, unwashed compatriot, Vaughn exuded a dangerous, predatory energy. He had defined cheekbones, short blond hair and clear hazel eyes. His clothes matched the rough décor of the bar; the man wearing them didn't. He was intelligent, refined, an enemy worth fearing. He was the man she needed to worry about—

There was a loud snap and pain shot through her wrist as Red grabbed her arm. "Gotcha," he said.

She jerked her arm out of his grasp, but it was too late. A thick copper band was molded to her wrist, already embedding itself in her skin. She recognized it instantly as an illusion band, because she'd experimented with them in the past to suppress her illusions, but stopped because they made her violently ill. With it on her wrist, she wouldn't be able to call up anything to save herself, no matter how hard she tried.

Dammit! How could she have been so stupid? Nausea churned through her belly, and her head began to ache from the band, as it suppressed the illusion that had naturally started to rise in response to her stress.

Red grabbed her arm and spun her toward the outside door before she could gather her thoughts. "The guy the Illusionist was with said that if you showed up, he'd pay a nice reward to have you delivered alive. He provided the band. Said it would keep you from doing that weird shit the other girl did."

They were right. The bands did work. *Quinn! I need your help!* Her head began to throb and she started to sweat. Grace took a deep breath, trying to fight off the nausea from the band.

Again, silence from Quinn.

She shouted for help as they passed by the open door of the bar, and a few heads turned in their direction. Vaughn made a slicing motion across his throat, and people quickly looked away, pretending they hadn't seen them. *Oh, crap.* Quinn was nowhere in sight, and she realized he must have already headed out to the woods where Elijah's body had been found.

"Hey!" She shouted. "He's kidnapping me—"

Red slapped his hand over her mouth and yanked her against his chest, his fleshy body crushing her, his arms tight around her. Her heart pounding, she forced herself not to struggle as they shoved her out the front door, and his arms loosened in response to her acquiescence. *One chance. She'd have one chance.*

The water was pouring off the roof even more fiercely than before, and there was no way around it. With Vaughn still a few steps behind them, Red stepped under the cascade of water, and for a split second, she sensed his attention go to the water.

She reacted instantly to the opportunity, ripping out of his distracted grasp and bolting for the woods. "Quinn! Help!" She screamed his name as she ran, her feet sloshing in the mud, the rain coming down so hard she couldn't see anything in the darkness except the pulsing glow of Ana's dust. She ran in the direction of the violet dust, knowing it would show her the way around the back of the bar, to the woods where Quinn had to be.

She could hear her pursuers' boots pounding through the puddles, and she skidded around a truck, nearly falling in the mud before she caught her balance. She ran to the edge of the parking lot, and half-slid in a frantic flight down the side of the hill toward the woods. "Quinn!" she screamed.

Something hit her in the back and she fell forward, landing on a dead log covered in moss.

The impact jarred her for a second. As she fought to regain her breath, Red screamed and suddenly sailed through the air, crashing headfirst into the trunk of a tree. He slithered down the trunk into a motionless lump in the mud.

"Quinn!" She whirled around, her body weak with relief. Then she froze when she saw Vaughn standing about twenty yards behind her, water pouring down his face, mud caking his clothes. He was silhouetted between two pine trees, his width dwarfing them. He was the one who'd thrown her other captor fifty feet into a tree? Holy crap.

What was he? *Quinn? I'm really in trouble here.*

No Quinn in sight. Damn the man. Where was he? Seriously, it wasn't like she made a habit of relying on others for help. The one time she finally did, and he was off doing his man thing when she needed him? Not okay, thanks so much.

"Stop running," Vaughn ordered her. "I'm not going to hurt you."

She held up her wrist. "No?"

He nodded in acknowledgment. "Sorry about that. If I'd taken that shithead out in the bar, it would have created questions I don't have time for. I was using Red to find you and Quinn, because I didn't know what you two looked like. I need to talk to Quinn. Where is he?"

Go left. She felt Quinn's soft push in the back of her mind, and she obeyed immediately, whipping to her left and sprinting toward the trees. Vaughn cursed and took off after her, shouting at her to stop so he could explain. Yeah, uh-huh, she was so going to listen to that request.

She'd gone only about one hundred yards into the woods, when Quinn sprang up soundlessly in front of her, as if he'd come out of the ground, wrapped his arms around her and leapt straight up into the trees above their heads, all in one fluid move. "Silence," he breathed into her ear.

He caught the trunk with one hand while he settled them both on a thick branch. She wrapped her arms around him, trembling at the sight of him, at the feel of his warm bulk enveloping hers.

You okay? Quinn's arm tightened around her and he pressed his lips to the top of her head.

Warmth flared to life deep inside her, comfort that chased away the residual horrors of experiencing Ana's illusion and being caught by the men. The nausea from the band began to subside, as it always did when there was no illusion trying to break through it. *Yes. I'm fine.*

Grace. At his whispered sigh, she glanced up at

him, his face barely visible in the dark night. He touched her cheek, then kissed her. It wasn't a tender, soft kiss. It was a kiss of fury, of needing to feel that she was alive and safe, of needing to connect with her. She hung onto him, needing the same: the connection to her foundation, the one thing in her life that she could actually grasp and believe in.

He tightened his grip around her, then pulled back. He smiled briefly, brushed her hair off her forehead, and kissed her nose. *Don't get in trouble like that again.*

Quinn sounded tense and agitated, and his concern made Grace feel good. What woman wouldn't want a badass immortal warrior keeping an eye on her well-being? *I'll do my best.*

That's not an answer, woman.

She laughed, and he put his hand over her mouth. Her laughter died in her throat, and she followed his glance down toward the forest floor. Vaughn was walking through the clearing that Quinn had snatched her from. He made it about halfway across then stopped. He was at least forty feet beneath them, yet he'd stopped exactly below their spot, as if he sensed where they were, even though he couldn't quite locate them.

He's got talent. Quinn sounded impressed.

That's not a good thing, Quinn. Having a worthy opponent is not always the goal, you know. The bark was slippery under her feet, and she dug her fingers into Quinn's jacket.

I love it when you give me attitude. Quinn gave her earlobe a playful nip that made her jump. Before she had time to smack him for nearly unseating her, he was back in battle mode, his face serious. *Am I under an illusion now?*

Oh, who was she kidding? He'd probably never been out of battle mode. Flirting and fighting were probably not mutually exclusive for a warrior like Quinn. He was probably always aware of everything around him, always ready to react no matter what else he seemed to be doing.

So, yeah, time to focus then. Grace set her hand on his chest and called upon her Illusionist heritage to search for any vibrations within him, the same way she'd done in the truck. It was easier this time. Now that they'd already done it once, she seemed to slide right into his being. Her mind began to hum with energy, and then pain shot through her head and spiked through her stomach. She doubled over instantly, and only Quinn's grip kept her from tumbling out of the tree.

"Shit, Grace." He anchored her against his chest. *What's wrong?*

She held up her wrist, showing him the band. *Get it off!* It was all she could do to keep from shouting, with the raw pain clawing at her, her stomach churning, her head pounding. Yeah, okay, so clearly it should have occurred to her that the band would react to any use of her powers, like searching the hot warrior guy for illusions.

Quinn grabbed her wrist and tugged it in front of his face so he could get a better look. *What the hell's that?*

It shuts down my powers. It makes me violently sick when I try to use them. Sweat trickled down her temples and her head throbbed. *I triggered it when I tried to search you for illusions.*

Stay calm. I'll take care of it. He ran his fingers over the edge of it, his touch deft and confident as he assessed it. *It's embedded in your skin.*

Yeah, I know that. Get it off! She could feel it digging deeper, burrowing into her flesh. She frantically tried to shove her illusions and her Illusionist spirit back into the box inside her soul where she'd kept it for the last fifteen years. *Quinn, please.*

He wrapped his hand around it and squeezed experimentally. Pressure built in her wrist, and he stopped before she could protest. *If I try to shatter it, I'll break your wrist. I need my sword to cut it off, but our friend downstairs will notice if I call it out. Can you hold off?*

She rubbed her hand over the band and tried to dig her fingernails under the edge of it, but it was already sunk too far. *Yes, but I can't check you for illusions until it's off.* She closed her eyes and concentrated on suppressing her illusions. The nausea began to subside somewhat, and the pain in her head started to abate enough that she could think.

Quinn's frustration pulsed at her, but he said nothing. Instead, he set his hand on the top of her head as if to reassure her, then leaned past her and peered down at the clearing again. Vaughn was perfectly still, immobile, his chin raised as if he were scenting the air for them.

Quinn cursed, then leaned back against the trunk, pulling her against him, wedging her between his knees.

His name's Vaughn. She rubbed her forehead, wiping away the tendrils of perspiration that were mixing with the rain. *What is he?*

I don't know. He sounded thoughtful, but when she tried to twist around to look at him, he pulled her back against his chest. *Don't move. One mistake and he'll know we're up here.*

She forced herself to remain still, grateful that Quinn's reassuring presence had made it possible for her to keep the illusions at bay, so she was no longer feeling so ill. *So, what do we do?*

We wait.

For what?

To see what he does. To see if he reveals what he is or why he's looking for me. Or if anyone is with him. His arms wrapped around her more securely. *Patience.*

She settled back against him, angling herself so she could watch Vaughn. He still hadn't moved. *How long do we wait?*

Depends on what he does. I won't let him get away, don't worry. The cold, calm confidence in Quinn's voice made her shiver, and she knew she was now in the arms of a warrior ready to kill.

They waited. The rain continued to come down, dripping between the branches and saturating her jacket. But Quinn was warm, his body emanating heat where he had her bundled against his chest and between his muscular thighs. She was aware of his arm locked under her ribs, brushing against the underside of her breasts. Her heart pounded with each breath he took, his chest moving against hers so intimately. She couldn't stop noticing the strength of his body as he kept them both balanced on the branch. Dammit. Why couldn't she stop responding to him as a man? But she couldn't. She simply couldn't.

She leaned against him, and he shifted so his cheek was against hers as they watched the scene below. They didn't move again, their body heat mingling, their scents mixing, his flawless balance keeping them both secure. It was an intimate moment, one where there was no need for conversation. It would almost be romantic, if they weren't perched high up in a tree, in the rain, waiting for some bad guy to play his hand.

Then again, romance hadn't exactly been a part of her life. Maybe, in her world, this was all there was. Maybe this was the holy grail of romance for someone like her. She looked up at Quinn, at his hard jaw, at his dark eyes, and she almost smiled. Maybe this could be enough. It wasn't like she had lofty goals. A moment of connection. A kiss to remember. A man to help her up when she fell in the mud.

Quinn glanced at her, flashed a quick smile, then resumed his vigilant watch. She nestled deeper against him and peered below just as Vaughn suddenly looked down at the soggy ground. He stared at it for a long moment, then nudged the decaying leaves aside with the toe of his boot.

Quinn hissed. "Shit."

Vaughn dropped to his knees and started digging.

I sensed Elijah's presence there. He left something

behind. I was just digging it up when you arrived.

Grace looked at him, sudden disappointment weighing heavily. *His* mjui? *Is that what you found?* She realized she'd adopted Quinn's thinking, hoping that Elijah wasn't dead, that there was some answer that could give them all a happy ending.

Quinn's face was impassive. *I won't know until I have a chance to examine it. All I know at this point is that something in the ground there has Elijah's energy wrapped around it. I have to get it.* He unpeeled her hand from his waist and wrapped her hands around the branch above their heads. *Try not to fall off while I'm gone.*

Grace dug her fingers into the rough bark, too aware of the slippery moss lining the branches and the rain-drenched bark under her feet. Somehow, she wasn't feeling quite as stable on her own. Note to self: stay out of trees when solo. *Try not to get killed. You're my ride back down.*

He grinned at her, clearly fired up to go confront Vaughn. *Sweetheart, you can ride me all night long.*

Quinn! She rolled her eyes at him, but the incorrigible bastard simply winked at her then dropped out of sight.

※※※

Quinn stood in the bushes, not three feet from Vaughn, yet his quarry had no idea he was there.

He was itching to stop Vaughn before the bastard found Elijah's object and learned its secrets, but instead, Quinn searched the branches above until he found Grace. She was exactly as he'd left her, firmly holding onto the branch, her face gritted in determination. Reassured that she was safe, he pulled his thoughts away from her and concentrated on the night around him.

He sifted through the sounds of the forest, assessing the smells, then stiffened as he caught the scent of another man, just off to his left. No sound, no breathing, nothing but the faintest hint of...Calydon.

Quinn eased back into the woods, circling around behind where he thought the second man was standing. It took several minutes to pinpoint his quarry, he was so well hidden in the shadows, and he was so still.

The kind of still only an Otherworld being could maintain.

Quinn paused to let his eyes adjust until he could discern the Calydon, all the while listening to the sound of Vaughn digging in the clearing, waiting for the brush of his fingers against the object.

The shoulders of the shadowed man were narrow. His waist was lean. Quinn realized it was the youth who had been sitting next to Grace when they'd first arrived at the bar. The one who didn't even look eighteen. What was he doing out here? For a second, Quinn wished he had both swords, but it was a useless wish, not worth the energy it took to think it.

Instead, he slipped forward until he was directly behind the kid, listening to him breathe. Hearing the flutter of his eyelashes the one time he blinked. Rookie.

When Quinn finally moved, it was so fast that even a seasoned Calydon wouldn't have had time to react before being face down in the mud, his arms behind his back and Quinn's knee in his kidney.

And all in total silence.

Quinn kept the kid's face pressed into the mud, hoping the boy at least knew enough to stop breathing until Quinn let him up. Quinn extended his left arm and called out his sword. It ripped out of his forearm in a loud crack of black light, and he hurled it. It whistled through the air and the handle bashed into Vaughn's head just as he was turning toward the sound. Vaughn dropped to the earth, motionless. Quinn held out his hand and his sword shot back to him, returning into his palm with a satisfying thud.

He rolled off the kid, jerked the youth to his feet and pinned him up against a tree with the sword at his throat. "Who are you?"

The youth's eyes were so wide Quinn could see white all the way around the corneas, and his freckles were standing out, even in the darkness of night. "Did you...did you kill my uncle?"

"I have no idea. Who's your uncle?"

The kid lifted a shaky finger toward the clearing, toward the man Quinn had just knocked out.

"Vaughn? No, I didn't kill him. Want me to?"

The youth shook his head quickly. "No. Don't hurt him. Don't hurt me. Please?"

Quinn's gut told him this kid was all right, not a danger, but damned if he'd let down his guard. He'd also thought Grace was safe in the bar and she'd wound up with a neutralizing band of some sort on her wrist. "In five words or less, who the hell are you?"

In an impressive summoning of courage, the kid pulled his shoulders back and looked him in the eye. "Sir?"

Quinn narrowed his eyes. "Yeah?"

"My name is Drew Cartland. I'm Dante's son."

Quinn's senses went on high alert. "Dante's son?" The Order leader didn't have a son, or a family, or anything else that would have made him vulnerable. He had no time for split loyalties. All he cared about was following the Order's mission, at the expense of all else. "Dante would not have a son." Quinn pressed the blade into the boy's neck, not breaking the skin but letting the boy feel a hint of pain. "Try again."

"I'd never met my dad until a month ago. He just found out about me, I guess." Drew's voice cracked. "Now he's missing."

"Missing? What are you talking about?" Quinn studied Drew's face, looking for tells that he was lying, but all he was getting was a sense of gritty truth from the kid. "Dante doesn't 'go missing.' He makes others go missing."

Drew's mouth tightened. "I think he's dead."

"Dead?" Quinn frowned. He hadn't felt Dante's death, but they weren't blood bonded, so he wouldn't necessarily have sensed it the way Gideon had detected his. The way he should have felt Elijah's if Elijah really had died... Shit. If Dante was dead, they were all toast.

"Dante told me that if anything happened to him, I should go to you," Drew continued, the words tumbling out in a hurry, as if he were trying to plead his case before Quinn chopped his head off. "The last time I saw him, he said you were the only one he'd trust if he couldn't trust anyone else. After Dante disappeared, I went back to my uncle. But when we saw the report that Elijah had died, we knew something was wrong. I promised Dante I'd come find you, so we've been waiting here for you, figuring you'd come to find out what happened to Elijah. We were headed to your house next."

Shit. If this rookie and his uncle had accurately guessed he'd come here in search of Elijah, so would others. Since when had he become predictable? Why hadn't he been prepared for that?

Quinn didn't even have to look up into the tree for the answer to that question. Grace was his distraction, and he'd been thinking about her safety, and her concern for Ana, instead of focusing on his mission. She was making him vulnerable.

Drew fastened his brown eyes on him. "There's someone hunting me. I can feel it. I need your help. I don't know who else to ask for help."

Quinn cursed. "I don't have time—"

"Dante said you'd help me," Drew burst out. "I don't know what else to do!" He reached into his pocket, pulled out something and tossed it at Quinn. "He said to give you this when I found you."

Quinn didn't recognize the small black zippered case, so he handed it back. "Open it."

Drew quickly unzipped it and dumped the contents out on his hand. He held it out without a word.

Quinn glanced at the object in Drew's hand, then he cursed and grabbed it, holding it up to look at it more closely. It was the ring belonging to Quinn's uncle Felix, the man whose death had haunted Quinn since the day he'd thrust his sword through Felix's heart and killed him.

Dante had taken the ring after Quinn had killed Felix, ostensibly to give Felix an honored burial as an Order member, but he'd never returned it to Quinn…until now.

Felix had been Quinn's mentor growing up, taking over after Quinn's dad had been killed in battle. Felix had trained him as a Calydon even before Quinn had come into his powers. Felix had been one of the most powerful, most deadly Order members, a man of honor…until he'd met his *sheva* and gone rogue.

Dante had forced Quinn to honor his uncle by being the one to kill him. Murdering Felix had been Quinn's first assignment as an Order member. To this day, Quinn still saw the look in his uncle's eyes as life bled from him. The look of sanity, of sadness, of understanding that he'd just lost. The words that slipped from his dying mouth, "Make my death worthwhile, son."

Rogues had no humanity, which meant that those words proved his uncle had come back from the edge just before he'd died. It meant his uncle hadn't had to die. Dante had refused to alter the Order's standing order to assassinate all rogue Calydons on sight. He'd claimed it was too risky to play "wait and see" based on some unproven claim by Quinn that he'd seen sanity in his uncle's eyes just before he'd died.

Hell, yeah, he'd prove it. Quinn had spent the next five hundred years doing his best to prove that he hadn't imagined his uncle's words and the sanity gleaming in his eyes, that a Calydon turned rogue from the *sheva* bond could be redeemed.

He had failed every time. No rogue had been turned. Every last one had needed to be killed. But Quinn hadn't given up. It was what drove him, what haunted his every thought and every choice, his mission to make his uncle's death worthwhile.

And now, Dante had given the ring back. Why now? Quinn turned the ring over in his fingers so he could read the inscription in the band. *Honor shall prevail.* Honor hadn't prevailed for Felix, not once his *sheva* had come into his life.

He ground his teeth as he thought of Grace, the ring a reminder of what was at stake for both of them. He recalled how it had ripped him apart to sink his blade into his own uncle, watching the life flow from the man who'd basically been his father and best friend. He closed his eyes against the swell of grief, an emotion he hadn't felt since that day, when he'd learned how to shut down and do his job.

By simply showing up on his doorstep, Grace had made him feel again, and now things were crashing hard and fast. Felix, Dante, Drew, Grace, Elijah... Shit. He couldn't afford empathy and regret. No warrior could. He had to get it back under control. Shut it down again.

Quinn closed his fingers around his uncle's ring and returned his gaze to Drew. "Where did you get this?"

"My dad. Dante. He gave it to me a week ago. Told me I might need to come to you for aid soon."

"A week ago?" That would have been four days before Elijah had gone rogue. Had Dante known something was going to happen? "What did he say—"

A pulse of awareness shot through Quinn and he lifted his head, scenting the air for Grace. He located her behind a large fir tree, about twenty yards off to the right. Of course she would have found her way out of the tree and come down to check on him. "Grace. Come on out." There was no point in her hiding. He had no doubt Drew was who he said he was. The ring proved it.

She stepped out from behind the tree.

"This is Drew."

Grace looked over at Drew, and Quinn was gut punched by the sadness on her face. He realized she'd heard Drew talk about his father's death, and it was bringing up her own grief at losing her parents.

He held out his arm to her, keeping his weapon at Drew's throat. Even though he believed Drew was Dante's son, that didn't mean Quinn could trust him, not after what happened with Elijah. He would wait until Grace confirmed there were no illusions working them over.

Stepping carefully through the mud, she walked toward him, giving Drew a considerable berth. She stopped next to Quinn and held out her wrist, the one with the band. He ignored the band, threw his arm around her and hauled her up against his side. He pressed his lips to her head. *I'm sorry for your pain, Grace. I'm sorry being with me is making your losses haunt you.*

Her hand went to his chest, and she let herself lean into his body for a moment. "The losses haunt me anyway," she whispered. "At least with you around, I'm not alone."

Desire pulsed through him at the feel of her breath against his neck, and he held her for another minute, keeping his eye on Drew, but needing to feel her body against his. She slid one arm around his waist and held up her wrist. "Take it off, please."

He gave Drew a threatening look, then dropped the sword from Drew long enough to slice through the band. He immediately returned his blade to the kid's throat, not daring to take any chances with Grace by his side, even though he was pretty damn certain the rookie wasn't a threat.

The band fell off into the dirt, leaving behind a

brutal red channel on her wrist. Anger roared to life inside him at the sight of her injury, but before he could react, she put her hand on his chest. "We don't have time for that right now. It's enough that you care." She smiled and touched his cheek, making his body tighten.

Growling softly, he threaded his free hand through her silky hair, cupping the back of her neck as she faced Drew. He couldn't stop his fingers from sliding through her curls, feeling the softness of her skin under his rough hand. She was feminine and soft, but she was strength and comfort as well.

She shifted, leaning into his touch, and he caught a scent of her arousal in the air, making his groin tighten instantly. "Stop distracting me," she whispered.

"Sorry." But he didn't remove his hand. He couldn't. He needed to touch her. She was grounding him after his slide into the past, into the memories that unraveled his focus.

She set her hand on his. He felt a faint vibration in the air, as if she were sending out energy, and he knew she was checking for illusions.

Drew's eyes were wide with astonishment, sweeping over Grace as if she were an angel. She smiled at him, then turned to Quinn as he let his hand slide down to her shoulder. "There are no illusions around us."

He turned his attention to the environment to do one last check to make sure nothing was amiss. Satisfied, he sheathed his sword.

Drew's legs buckled with relief and he fell to his knees.

Quinn stopped Grace as she started to walk toward Drew, lifting her wrist to his face for closer inspection. It was raw and bleeding, with jagged red marks extending up her arm. His brand burned with the need to unleash the sword and kill the man responsible for hurting her. "Did Drew's uncle put this on you?"

"No. The other man did."

"Red's dead," Drew said, barely holding himself up on trembling arms as he leaned over. He looked like a kid who had been through too much in the last few days. "My uncle had to kill him. No path can lead back to us. Plus, the guy hurt Grace. That kind of thing really pisses him off."

"I like him already." Quinn clenched his jaw, trying to keep his emotions under control. He needed to think logically, not obsess over Grace's wrist. If Drew was telling the truth, and the ring indicated he was, then he couldn't leave the kid behind. But they had to vacate fast. Others would come looking, and soon. "You guys have a truck here?"

Drew nodded, still kneeling in the mud.

"You'll follow me." No. He needed to have them under his control. "No. You'll ride with us. Wait here." Quinn jogged into the clearing, brushed off the last of the dirt covering Elijah's object, pausing when his fingers hit a small, moss-gray stone. He knew instantly that was what he'd been looking for. Round and smooth, it looked like it had been softened by years in the ocean. He picked it up, and closed it in his palm. It was warm, sending a vibrating heat up his arm, heating up to a painful level almost instantly, and he knew he was feeling death, Elijah's death.

It was a *mjui*.

Elijah was dead.

◉◉◉◉

Quinn closed his eyes against a crash of grief. Anger roared through him and his body vibrated with rage. He lunged to his feet and punched his fist through a tree, a loud roar ripping from his throat. *Elijah!* He screamed for his teammate, and there was no response. Nothing. Just emptiness, like a black void cutting at his soul, leaving him barren and stripped.

The night was dark. Fury and violence billowed through him. Quinn fought for control. He battled to suppress the emotions like he did every time he faced death, but this time was different. This time, it was Elijah. This time, it was Quinn's failure to make good on the promise he'd made five hundred years ago, that he would never let another warrior close to him go rogue and not come back.

Blackness streamed across his vision, his sword sprang unbidden into his hand—

Soft hands touched his back. "Quinn?"

"Grace!" He whirled around and hauled her up against him. Her arms went around him, holding tight as he buried his face in her hair. The warmth of her body was like a whisper of sanity in the raging mess of his mind, and he gripped her even tighter. He breathed her scent and concentrated on the beat of her heart, using her to bring himself back to the present. To sanity. To a place where the loss didn't shatter him, where the failure couldn't reach him. To their mission.

It was no longer about finding Elijah. It was to avenge his death and bring justice. Again, like he'd done with Felix: avenge the death, not stop it. Because he hadn't stopped it. He hadn't fucking stopped it—

"Quinn!" Grace touched his cheek. "Come back to me."

He stared into those silver eyes and the world began to solidify beneath his feet again. His mind calmed, his shields rebuilt, his focus resumed.

He took a deep breath as he compartmentalized himself, burying his grief so deeply he couldn't feel it, then he released Grace.

She didn't move away. Her forehead was furrowed with concern, her hands still tight around him. "What can I do?"

He kept his mind quiet and focused, refusing to acknowledge the tangled mess trying to derail him. "Go to Drew. Keep an eye on him while I get his uncle. We're leaving."

She nodded, squeezed his hand, then turned and walked back across the clearing toward the boy. Quinn watched her kneel next to the youth and begin talking to him. He appreciated that she hadn't asked if he was all right. Or what was wrong. Or told him it would all be better. She'd somehow known he wouldn't want to talk about it, yet she'd been there to ground him. She'd given him exactly what he'd needed, and she'd done it on instinct. A good woman.

His grief under control, he turned his focus back to their mission. *Gideon. You up yet?*

No response.

Gideon should be up by now. Dark foreboding skittered through Quinn. *Gideon. Wake the hell up.*

Still nothing.

Where was he? What if their enemy had returned to the site and taken Gideon out while he was unconscious from Quinn's blow? Alarm began to creep in as Quinn recalled the disturbances in the air they'd both experienced at the site of the carnage, the malevolence. At the time, Quinn had thought it was residue from the attack. What if there'd been a current and active threat lurking, and he'd left Gideon there defenseless? Quinn's adrenaline spiked and his fist closed around the handle of his sword. *Gideon!*

No response.

Quinn opened his mind, thrusting all his mental power into his blood link with Gideon, injecting his own life force into their connection, trying to wake the bastard up himself. Come on! Then he felt it. A faint pulse of life he recognized as Gideon. Still unconscious, but alive. He groaned and dropped his head to his hands. *Damn, man. You scared the hell out of me.*

Quinn swallowed his relief and forced himself to return to the emotionless state required of a warrior.

Gideon was still alive. For now, Quinn was going to assume Gideon had a soft head and was still getting some beauty sleep in Quinn's woods, and not wonder whether Gideon had actually been captured by whatever dark threat they'd detected.

It was his only option. There was nothing he could do about Gideon right now. He had to accept that and keep moving forward. Gideon was alive, and that was all he needed to know at this point.

Quinn shoved the *mjui* into the front pocket of his jeans, then swung Drew's uncle over his shoulder. Drew was talking with Grace, watching her intently while she knelt next to him. He said something to her, and she smiled. For a second time, Quinn felt waves of sadness from her and he saw the weary hunch of Drew's shoulders. Tough times for everyone, and it was going to get worse if Dante really was dead.

Quinn strode back over to them. "Come on," he said gruffly. "Let's move."

Grace stood and helped Drew to his feet. A part of Quinn chafed at the sight of her hands on another male, then she flashed him a tired look, and all he could think about was getting her dry and warm and safe. Screw the sex right now. He just wanted to take care of her, which was completely insane. He didn't even take care of himself, for hell's sake.

On their way back to the parking lot, they passed by the dead man who'd cuffed Grace. Quinn was grimly unsettled by his desire to shove his sword through the man's heart just to ensure he really was dead, to revel in the satisfaction of marking the man even in death.

Because he'd slapped a bracelet on Grace? That was an extreme reaction for any Order member, but especially for him. He was a master at staying cool and logical, but he was losing his shit at everything right now. He wasn't right. He wasn't himself. He was off-kilter and couldn't pull himself back… He frowned, a sudden thought coming to him. "How's your arm, Grace?"

She frowned. "My wrist?"

"No, your forearm. Is my mark starting to form?" If the bond was affecting him, it would explain a lot.

Her eyes widened, and she quickly pulled back her sleeve as Drew trudged beside her, glancing nervously around them. "It's too dark for me to see." She held it out and Quinn caught her forearm to steady it as he looked at it. Shit, her skin was soft.

The arm was clear. Nothing on it. Not even the faintest hint of a brand. "You're still good." But he didn't feel relief.

What he felt was a consuming need to grab her and haul her against him, crushing her body against his, kissing her, *devouring* her, stripping her and taking her right there in the woods. He wanted to fill her with his body and his seed until he ripped through both their barriers, until the first signs of his brand blossomed to life on her body, beginning the process of sealing her as his, for now and forever, until death destroyed them both.

Well, shit. That was a thought he hadn't seen coming.

Grace's eyes widened and she stopped walking. "The look on your face right now—" Desire flared into her eyes, and his body hardened instantly.

He started toward her, thinking of nothing but her body against his, how her breasts would taste, how her body would writhe under his touch.

She watched him approach, and he felt her calling to him, reaching for him—

He suddenly noticed Drew backing away from him. He felt the rain pounding onto his face. He became aware of Drew's uncle over his shoulder. He saw the mud streaks on Grace's face and the raw red mark on her wrist. What the hell was he doing?

He forced himself to stop, willed his body to go no further toward her.

Grace's features wrinkled in confusion, in frustration, then he saw her become aware of their surroundings as well. Her face flushed with the self-conscious realization that they'd both been seconds away from going at it in front of other people, in a zone that could become unsafe at any moment.

She jerked her sleeve down over her arm. "Don't *ever* look at me like that again." She whirled around and started slogging up the embankment toward the parking lot, her boots sliding in the mud, as if she could run from him and what was building between them.

He palmed her hips to help her up, and she shot him a hard glare. "Don't touch me," she said. "I can't deal with it right now." She smacked his hand away with a fierceness that told him exactly how badly she was burning for him, and it sent lust roaring so fiercely through him that he had to stop walking just to keep himself from taking her right there.

Drew warily skirted around him, then hurried after Grace.

Quinn let the rain pound into him for nearly a minute before following, his gut actually shaking from the need pulsing through his body. Tonight wasn't just going to be about interrogating Drew about Dante, or finding out who killed Elijah.

Tonight was going to be about finding a way to get Grace the hell out of his system so he could do his damned job. He couldn't wait any longer. Tonight he was going to take her.

CHAPTER 7

By the time Quinn and Grace had put enough distance between themselves and The Gun Rack, the rain had eased off, but the fog was getting heavier. The headlights were reflecting off the water droplets, and Quinn could barely see the lines on the road through the drifting mist.

Drew was quiet in the back seat, next to his unconscious uncle. Quinn was busy thinking, trying to decide how to handle the situation. Dante couldn't be dead. He simply couldn't be. He'd been the Order leader for almost seven hundred years. He was, literally, unstoppable. He *was* the Order. He was only the second leader the Order had ever had, the first one leading for twelve hundred years. It had taken all of Dante's strength to keep control of the warriors who worked for him. Without Dante... Quinn rubbed his forehead.

Grace twisted around in her seat to face Drew. "So, where's your mom? Is she okay?"

It was telling that her first question was about the safety of Drew's family. Grace didn't belong in this world, this crappy, brutal world of his.

"I don't have a mom," Drew replied. "She died a long time ago." He nodded at the unconscious man. "Vaughn raised me."

Grace shot a sharp glance at Quinn, and he could

tell what she was thinking from the stricken expression on her face. He shook his head. "I didn't kill Drew's mother. Dante never met his *sheva*."

Her lips pressed together, and her cheeks flushed with embarrassment at her quick judgment of him. "Sorry. I didn't mean to judge you."

He shrugged. "It is what it is."

There was a sudden movement in the backseat, and Quinn slammed on the brakes as Vaughn lunged over the headrest at Quinn, his eyes glowing bright green. The truck skidded to a stop, as Vaughn wrapped his arms around Quinn's neck and tried to snap it with a fierce growl.

Nice try with that one, but yeah, not so much.

Quinn grabbed Vaughn's shoulders and threw him into the windshield, shattering the glass as Vaughn burst through it. Vaughn skidded across the hood and landed on the pavement with a thud that made Grace gasp, then he rolled out of sight, devoured by the fog.

"Stay there," Quinn ordered Grace, as he slammed open his door and leapt out onto the pavement, adrenaline pulsing. He called out his sword, searching the night for Vaughn, ready for another attack. Even with his preternatural vision, the fog was too thick to penetrate, so he relied on hearing and scent to find him.

The metallic scent of fresh blood drifted up to Quinn and he knew Vaughn was hurt.

"Quinn's helping us!" Drew jumped out of the truck. "Don't hurt him, Vaughn."

"Get back in the truck," Quinn snapped. He could hear Vaughn's heavy breathing, but the sound was bouncing off the droplets of water in the fog, and he couldn't pinpoint it. "Or I'll make you."

Drew hesitated, but Dante had trained him well, because he silently climbed back in the truck, following orders despite his personal stake. That kind of mentality would make a good potential Order member, but a man who would forego personal loyalty for duty would make a crappy teammate to Vaughn, with his willingness to follow orders instead of protecting him. Quinn wouldn't have gotten back in the truck. Not anymore.

"I don't think it's Quinn you need to worry about, Drew." Grace's tense voice drifted toward him, and he swore, realizing Grace was unprotected in the front seat behind the broken windshield.

He vaulted onto the hood of the truck and crouched in front of her, facing the night. Ready to protect her if Vaughn tried to use her for leverage. "Grace," he said quietly. "Lock your door."

He didn't turn, but he heard the soft click of the doors locking. He went predator-still. He could hear the rapid thud of Grace's heart, he could smell Drew's nervous sweat, and he could feel the heat from Vaughn rippling over his skin—

A faint breeze drifted over his right shoulder, a displacement of air so subtle he almost missed it. He swore and threw up his right arm in a block a split second before Vaughn exploded out of the fog, his eyes glowing green like a demon possessed.

Quinn grunted as Vaughn hit him from the side with unbelievable force, sending them both careening off the truck and into the road. Quinn grabbed Vaughn and threw him to the side as they hit the pavement and skidded across the asphalt. The friction burned Quinn's jeans and tore his jacket before he was able to stop the slide.

Vaughn spun around and leapt onto Quinn like a wild demon beast, those freaking eyes like windows into hell. Quinn jammed his elbow into Vaughn's throat, throwing all his strength into the move. Vaughn gagged and grabbed his throat. Quinn threw him off, leapt to his feet and jammed his sword against Vaughn's neck as the man fought for air. "What the hell was that about?"

There was the thud of feet hitting the asphalt as

Drew sprinted up, shouting at Quinn to leave his uncle alone. So much for following orders, but Quinn was glad to see the kid had enough loyalty to his uncle to get in there and stand the enemy down. If Quinn were hiring for the Order, that's the shit he'd be looking for.

"Don't kill him," Drew demanded.

Quinn kept his sword where it was. "He'd already be dead if that was my goal. Now move or I'll go through you to get to him."

Black light flashed, two loud cracks filled the air, and then Drew was holding a polearm in each hand, long staffs with impressive blades on the end. He backed toward his uncle, who was still struggling on the asphalt. "No," he said. "Sheathe your sword, Quinn."

"Sheathe *my* sword?" Was the kid serious? Quinn would have grinned at the show of attitude, but he didn't have time for that crap right now. Vaughn's breathing was already getting better, and the bastard would be up in two seconds. "Use your head, kid."

Drew stared at him, and he saw the youth's brain kick in, trumping the Calydon instinctual reaction of resorting to violence. After a moment, he lowered his weapons. "Dante trusted you."

"Damn right he did. Now back off." *Now* he was impressed with the kid. He was able to follow orders, but he also knew when to disregard them to protect his teammate. And then showing the ability to stand down and assess the situation accurately even when his adrenaline was rushing. Good stuff. Great instincts.

Quinn detected Grace's presence nearby, but he couldn't see her in the fog. What was with all these people who refused to stay out of the crossfire? He couldn't concentrate on the situation with Grace out of the truck and vulnerable in the woods. "Grace," he barked. "Get back in the truck."

"No." She walked up, staying out of range but

within his sightline.

He glared at her, but the moment he saw her strained face in the glare of the headlights, his hostility vanished. "You okay?"

She nodded, her silver eyes meeting his. "Are you?"

He almost laughed at the question. She was worried about him? "Sweetheart, this is what I do—"

Vaughn shifted, and Quinn jerked his attention back to the fallen man as Vaughn coughed again, his breath wheezing into his lungs. Drew crouched beside his uncle. "Vaughn—"

The older man shoved Drew aside and staggered to his feet, putting himself between the sword and his nephew. Again, impressive. Quinn appreciated the man's priorities, not letting a boy take a hit for him. His respect for them went up a notch. They had the right values, both of them. Quinn surveyed Vaughn as strength visibly returned to his body. His muscles tensed, his eyes began to simmer with aggression, and energy began to roll off him as he prepared to attack.

Quinn moved into an answering stance, ready to meet the threat. Vaughn would be a formidable opponent, different than the rogue Calydons because his mind was clear and focused. Vaughn was good, whatever he was, and neither of them had time for a battle. But Quinn would do it if he needed to. "Friend or foe? Make the right choice."

"Vaughn, he's a friend," Drew urged. "Let him help us."

Vaughn's eyes were still glowing that weird emerald color, and Quinn sensed power amassing within him. What the hell was he? Something impressively strong and quick. He'd moved faster than Quinn twice, and that was unheard of. Damned if he didn't want to sit the guy down with a beer and get to know him.

But things being what they were, he had to content himself with poking the man in the chest with his sword instead.

The green finally began to fade from Vaughn's eyes, and he seemed to suck the power back into his body. "Instinct," he said to Quinn. "You knocked me out. I woke up on the offensive."

"Understood." Quinn still didn't sheathe his sword. "And now?"

"Drew needs you." There was acceptance in that statement, an unspoken vow that he'd step back and allow Quinn to help. But Quinn knew the truce would be broken the moment Vaughn thought Drew was in danger from him.

"I don't think he needs my help," Quinn said. "Not with you around."

A smile flashed on Vaughn's face, and then was gone. "Drew needs more protection than I can give him," he said. "Anyone who can kill Dante can kill me."

"Now *that*, I agree with." Quinn finally lowered his sword, but kept it out and ready.

Grace let out a sigh of relief behind him, and Drew came to stand beside his uncle, his face reflecting the white of the headlights. Fog was drifting through the air between them, a misty gulf separating the two groups.

Quinn studied the man, noting his wide shoulders and athletic stance. The hard lines of his jaw. Vaughn had been in battles, and he'd seen death. "What are you?"

Vaughn smiled faintly. "This isn't about me."

"Sure it is. You, Drew, Dante. It's about all of you." There was a rustle in the woods off to his right, and Quinn paused to identify it. Small animal with claws. Not a danger. "I need to know everything you guys know."

"Now?" Vaughn asked.

"Sure." It was always smarter to move forward with information than to run blind. He looked at Drew. "Tell me about Dante. How'd you meet him? Why do you think he's dead?"

Drew didn't hesitate, as if he'd been waiting too long to unburden himself. "A month ago I had my dream. My dad showed up the next day."

Grace walked over to Quinn, and he instinctively wrapped his fingers around her wrist to settle her in the spot he could defend with the most ease, just off his left side and slightly behind him.

His adrenaline began to settle at their contact, but he didn't want to think about the implications of the fact that touching her grounded him. Instead, he focused on the situation at hand. "Let me see your brand," he said to Drew.

Drew tugged up his sleeves and held out his arms. On each of his forearms was a dark black brand in the shape of a polearm, with a long staff, a speared metal tip, and sharp spikes circling the base of the tip. The lines were still thin, not fully developed, but there were weapons in there already, fully functional. New brands, not more than a month old.

Grace shifted to peer around him at Drew's arms. "What dream are you talking about?"

Drew pulled his sleeves back down as Quinn answered. "When a Calydon is eighteen years old, he has a dream that he's in the middle of a violent battle, but it's not actually a dream. It's another world, or another dimension or something. We don't know exactly what. If he survives the dream battle, he wakes up with his brands. If he doesn't, he dies in his sleep. Many don't survive." He gave Drew an appraising look. "Congratulations."

Drew flashed him a nervous smile. "Thanks, sir."

Yeah, okay, enough touchy-feely. "So, tell me about Dante."

Drew nodded. "He walked into my room an hour after I woke up and said he'd sensed me the minute I'd had my dream. He took me to this fishing shack in the woods, where we've been for the last month." Drew's chest puffed with teenage pride. "He's been training me to use my weapons, and he's been teaching me about the Calydons."

Quinn had been to Dante's shack. It was Dante's personal oasis, open only to Order members on special invite. Dante had taken Quinn there after Quinn had killed his uncle. It was there that Dante had taught Quinn how to suppress his emotions so he could do his job, so he could kill without having his actions destroy him. Dante had given Quinn the tools to succeed, had stepped in and become Quinn's mentor after Felix had died. Without Dante there to guide him and to help him direct his rage and guilt at killing his own uncle, Quinn was absolutely certain he would have gone rogue.

If Dante had indeed taken Drew to the fishing shack, it was a significant statement by Dante about how important this kid was.

Vaughn paced behind Drew, his hands clasped behind his back, his gaze warily settled on Quinn.

Quinn ignored him. "What happened at the shack?"

"At first, it was cool, you know? This total bonding thing and all. He's a brilliant warrior, and a great instructor." Drew grinned. "I can hit a target on the run from almost twenty yards now."

Quinn almost smiled, remembering the heady rush of power after he'd had his dream and had first started eviscerating the physical limitations that had bound him as a youth. "Dante," he reminded Drew.

"Right. So, after a couple weeks, he started to change. Got really quiet and moody. Distracted. He'd take off for days at a time, and he'd come back all silent and angry."

Moody? Quinn had never known Dante to be moody. Dante was the ultimate warrior, brutal and deadly, killing without remorse, always focused on his goal, never rattled by any situation. Dante brought a sense of control to everyone around him, enabling them to focus and stand down from the intense emotions that were so dangerous to Order members. Moody? Never. Quinn glanced at Vaughn for confirmation of Drew's story. "Did you see Dante?"

"I stopped by a couple times, and the guy was an ass," Vaughn said.

Quinn grinned, knowing full well how Dante would have reacted to Vaughn's interference in Drew's training. "Well, an ass is different than moody. Which was it?"

"Moody," Drew said. "Irritated and short with me. Annoyed when I made a mistake."

Quinn's smile faded. Dante would never waste time being annoyed at a rookie mistake. He'd simply train them to be better. For him to become irritated with Drew, something extraordinary had to have been bothering him. "Did he tell you what was wrong?"

"The last night, before he disappeared, he said Ezekiel's prison walls were weakening. He's getting out."

"Ezekiel?" Quinn stiffened. Ezekiel was the forebear who had created their race, a warrior who had bled evil into the land like a demon who had taken over the earth. He was what the Order had been created to contain. He was the doom that haunted them all.

And now he was back?

※※※

Quinn's adrenaline fired on at the idea of Ezekiel hunting them. Swearing, he pulled Grace against his side where he could defend her, fisting his sword as he carefully spun around, assessing the messages the dark forest offered him. Searching for that same malevolent presence he'd felt at his house.

Grace stiffened against him. "Who's Ezekiel? What's wrong?"

Quinn squeezed her once, ignoring the wary stares

from Vaughn and Drew as he continued to search their surroundings. He sifted through every sound, every scent, everything he could see, but there was nothing there.

For this moment, in this spot, they were safe.

But he didn't lower his sword. He couldn't. Not if Ezekiel was out. "Stay with me, Grace. Whatever you do, stay with me." As if he could keep her safe against Ezekiel by himself. *Gideon. We might have a major problem.*

No response.

He growled in frustration. *Wake up, pretty boy. There's no time for beauty naps.* There was no time to breathe.

Again, nothing. *Come on!*

"Quinn." Grace's voice was urgent, her silver eyes wide. "What's going on? Who's Ezekiel?"

Vaughn shifted into a battle stance, his feet spread wide, hands flexing, eyes beginning to glow a faint green. "Yeah, who's Ezekiel?"

"He's one of the two original Calydons. He created our race. He's the source of evil, death and everything deadly and destructive about the Calydons. If he gets out, he'll bring it down on everyone, not just us." Quinn flexed his grip on his sword, scanning their surroundings again, twitching at every sound, every shadow. "The entire damn world."

Vaughn snorted with skepticism, relaxing slightly. "No one man can bring down all life."

"Ezekiel almost did it two thousand years ago, and the only man who could stop him is dead." Everything made sense now. The taint at his place. Elijah getting sucked into going rogue. Dante going AWOL. Ezekiel could make all that happen, and so much more.

"Wait." Grace pulled away from Quinn. "What happened two thousand years ago that was so bad?"

"I can answer that." Drew faced Grace and his uncle, clearly feeling important to be able to share the information. "According to what Dante told me, Ezekiel and his twin brother Caleb were these poor kids who were beat up by their dad. Their king was this total bastard. He used to send his troops to kill people and abuse women, just because it was fun. Totally messed up situation, you know?"

Grace pressed her lips together. "Sometimes it sucks to be a kid."

Quinn thought of her being homeless at fourteen, and he brushed his fingers against hers. The past could never be changed, and they both knew that. But when she flashed a small smile at him, it made him wonder whether its grip could ever be loosened.

"Ezekiel was this badass," Drew continued, "and it pissed him off to not be able to fight back, you know? The only good thing in his life was this girl who lived near him, Evangeline. He fell in love with her, see, but then the king's men took her. Ezekiel went crazy looking for her, but he couldn't get to her in the king's castle. It sent him over the edge."

Quinn watched Grace as she bit her lip, her expressive face showing her worry for those kids from two thousand years ago, and the young man who lost the only good thing in his life to something made of pure evil.

Quinn thought of what it would be like if something happened to her, if some bastard took her and hurt her. Something dark rolled through him. He had a sudden vision of calling out his sword, of eviscerating anyone that hurt her, of doing whatever it took to pry her free… and then for the first time in his life, Quinn understood Ezekiel and his willingness to do whatever it took to save Evangeline.

"Ezekiel had heard rumors of a stream in the mountains that would create warriors of mythical strength," Quinn explained. "He and his brother went in search of the river because they knew they couldn't defeat the king on their own."

Grace looked at him. "The stories were true? The magic really existed?" He saw the question she wasn't asking, whether there was truth to the powerful destiny of his kind.

"Yeah. They drank." Quinn held up his arm, showcasing his brand. "And they became us."

"Dude, yeah, so cool." Drew interrupted, trying to get Grace's attention. "They were total badasses, see? They went back and killed the king."

"And Evangeline?" she asked. "What happened with her?"

Quinn met her gaze. "By the time Ezekiel got to her, she was dying from the king's abuse. She died in his arms. Ezekiel went mad and cut down everyone associated with the king. Women, children, animals, everything the king had ever blessed with his poisoned hand." Quinn thought of the dead man by The Gun Rack, and his desire to plunge his sword into the bastard's chest for hurting Grace. It had been a small slight, with no lasting impact, yet Quinn had wanted to kill for it. It was an extreme response, out of character for him, and he wasn't even bonded with Grace.

How much had it taken to make Ezekiel cross that line from a heroic rescue to deranged insanity? Even his brief contact with Grace made Quinn realize that the potential to go rogue to protect his female was already inside him, inside every warrior, just as the legends stated. For the first time, Quinn began to understand the true power of the *sheva* bond they were facing. For two thousand years, no warrior had triumphed over it, not even the strongest, most powerful, and most honorable men he'd known.

They were warriors who had started like Quinn: strong, determined, faithful. Men who had begun with the honor and courage of his uncle. Men who had lost, men who had somehow, unbelievably, utterly abandoned who they were simply because of a woman.

Quinn had always figured they weren't strong enough. He'd assumed Ezekiel started off with a poisoned mind. But now, after Grace, his brief interaction with her, it made him wonder. Had the men been too weak, like he'd always claimed? Or was the bond and the Calydon dark side simply too strong, like history had proven?

"When Ezekiel tried to kill the king's young daughters, Caleb restrained him," Drew said, picking up the tale with a curious look at Quinn for stopping the story. "Caleb wouldn't condemn his brother, but he wouldn't join him in his insane quest, either. So he took their mother and sisters and left, starting a new life away from all the misery they'd grown up with."

Grace nodded in understanding. "A new start," she said softly. "I understand that."

"But that's when the shit went down," Drew continued, his eyes glowing with the excitement of a youth who didn't understand the significance of the story he was telling.

Quinn got it. As he absorbed Grace's tense expression, saw the moonlight flicker across her cheeks, watched the wind lightly toss her hair, and felt his body respond even though he knew damn well what a bad idea it was. Yeah, he was starting to get it in a way he never had.

He sensed Vaughn watching him, and he glanced at the other man. Vaughn's eyes were mostly brown, only the faintest hint of green, but his stare was intense, as if he were analyzing every breath Quinn took and cataloguing his weaknesses. Vaughn's attention drifted toward Grace, then back again as he raised one dark eyebrow in question.

Shit. Vaughn already realized that Grace was Quinn's vulnerability.

"Ezekiel went crazy," Drew continued. "He got this idea that if he could just get rid of all the bad people in the world, then no one would have to suffer like he had, like his family had, like Evangeline had."

Quinn walked away slightly, listening to Drew's enthusiastic rendition of a tale that was always told with a veil of doom in official circles. With Drew's phrasing, for the first time, it made sense to him what Ezekiel had wanted to accomplish by cleansing the world of what he considered to be evil. It was what the Order did, in a way. Ridding the world of taint before it could destroy others, before it could hurt innocents. The Order's mission was based on exactly that which had driven Ezekiel to insanity, what the world had condemned him for. Was the Order so different from the man who'd been vilified as the enemy of all creation?

Quinn looked back at Grace, at the soft curls drying on her shoulders, at the delicate curve of her nose. She seemed small and vulnerable. If he knew she was going to suffer, would he do whatever it took to cut that threat down before it could come after her? Yeah. He would. He'd break the damn rules, and he'd do whatever it took to make it happen. "Ezekiel knew he wasn't strong enough to take down the whole damn world," Quinn said, "so he recruited some other malcontents and took them back to the stream. Again and again he went back there, drinking with his team. Each time he created more demonic warriors."

Grace looked over at him, her face troubled. "Their strength came at a cost, didn't it? The river was tainted."

"Demon magic. He got stronger, yeah, but so did the darkness inside him."

"The darkness that continues to haunt you all to this day," she said. "The side that makes you all turn rogue."

Quinn flashed his sword. "You got it, babe. We're no angels."

"Wow." Grace leaned back against the bumper of the truck, as if she was overwhelmed by the story, by the truth of what he was. "So, what happened?"

"Ezekiel bled evil," Drew said. "Literally. He could walk down the street and living things would just keel over on the spot. He was contagious, like poison, and people started turning on each other, like he'd gotten into their heads, you know?" He shrugged. "He became paranoid, seeing evil in everything. He'd wipe out anything that he thought dripped of taint. No one could stop him because, seriously, he was stoked up on demon power, right? What could stop that?"

"His brother." Vaughn spoke for the first time, having been silent until now. He was standing in the shadows, out of range of the headlights. "As twins, they are the light and dark of the same coin. His brother had to become as powerful as Ezekiel was."

Quinn looked in surprise at Vaughn, the edge to Vaughn's voice suggesting that he understood far too deeply about the conflict between brothers. "You have a brother," he observed.

Vaughn looked at him. "I *had* a brother."

Dead? Killed? Or exiled? Vaughn was more than what he seemed. Quinn would watch him carefully. Being screwed over by family could mess up a guy.

"Caleb came back," Grace guessed. "To stop his brother."

Quinn paced the road, on edge as he recalled the rest of the story. "Caleb understood the dangers of that stream, so he took with him his insurance policy, the one thing he could count on to keep him sane." He looked at Grace. "His wife. The woman he loved."

Grace met his gaze. Something hung in the air between them, and he understood why Caleb had taken his woman with him. He'd always thought Caleb was a fool to have brought his wife into that situation, but now Quinn understood the need to keep something pure in his life when the shit was poisoning everything else. Grace was changing things for him, changing everything.

"Did it work?" she asked.

"It did until Ezekiel showed up to get more water

and saw them," Drew said, oblivious to the rising tension between Grace and Quinn. "The dude fell in love with his brother's wife on the spot, kicked Caleb's ass and took his wife."

"Oh." Grace's hand went to her chest. "It's like the *sheva* destiny. Once he finds her, he will lose her and it will drive him mad," she said, repeating the words Quinn had told her in the tunnel.

"Yeah." All this talk of losing women was making him crazy. Quinn strode across the asphalt toward Grace and pulled her against him, needing to touch her. "Ezekiel drew first blood when he took his brother's wife. After that, all that mattered to Caleb was getting his wife back."

"Caleb selected twenty soldiers. They drank from the stream, then destroyed it so no one else could become tainted by it," Drew said. "His team took out Ezekiel's army, but it was one on one between the brothers. It shook the whole earth, the battle they had."

"He didn't kill him," Vaughn said suddenly. "Caleb wouldn't have killed his brother."

Loyalty again. Quinn narrowed his eyes at Vaughn. "No, he didn't. He got some magical assistance and locked him up in a prison. Ezekiel has been stewing in there ever since." He looked around at the dark woods. Until now?

Grace looked at him. "Did Caleb get his wife back?"

Quinn shook his head. "No happy endings, sweetheart. She got killed in the battle. Caleb lost his shit, and his team had to take him out."

And he understood. For the first time in the hundreds of years that he'd heard the tale of their origins, Quinn grasped Ezekiel's need to fix the world to atone for failing his woman, and he got why Caleb couldn't hold his shit together after he lost his wife.

The fact Quinn actually understood where they were coming from was unnerving as hell. If he could empathize with their choices simply because Grace had knocked aside some of his shields, what was next? Was he truly destined to follow that same path? Did the holy grail Quinn had been pursuing for so long really exist, or if he bonded with Grace and then she got hurt, would he be exactly like his ancestors, and all the Calydons since?

"And there, the legacy begins," Grace said quietly as she pulled out of his grasp. She walked away from him, hugging herself, and he let her go. Distance between them felt like the right choice right now.

Quinn turned and strode away from the group to keep himself from going to her. From being distracted by her. He faced the woods and listened to the night, opened his mind to the dark energy that was Ezekiel, but all seemed safe. Illusion?

Vaughn was pacing restlessly, his body almost seeming to overflow with an energy Quinn didn't recognize. His eyes were glowing again, and he carried the dangerous aura of a protector whose charge had been threatened. "Tell him the rest, Drew."

Quinn turned to Drew as the kid answered. "He said someone's helping Ezekiel get free." He looked at Quinn. "He thought it was someone from the Order. Betrayal from within."

Quinn closed his eyes. Elijah? Someone else? "Did he give you a name?"

"Dante didn't know who it was," Drew said. "But you were the only one he felt certain about. He said you would know what to do."

"Do you?" Vaughn's challenge was harsh in the night, and Quinn opened his eyes. "Do you know who it is?"

Vaughn had stopped pacing and was staring at him. "No. I don't." Why the hell would Dante have put this on him? Quinn's driving motivation for the last five hundred years had been to invalidate Dante's edict to kill rogue Calydons on sight, to shred the hold that the *sheva* destiny had on his people. If there was anyone who wouldn't stand by the Order, it would have been Quinn, yet he was the one Dante had chosen to trust.

Vaughn came to a stop beside Drew, his fists bunched by his hips. "Who's hunting Drew? You know who the traitor is. I can see it in your eyes."

"I don't know who it is." Suddenly, Drew's earlier comment that someone was after him took on much larger significance. The youth was wanted. Why? For his weapons like the trainee? As a tool to kill others, like Elijah? Quinn knew suddenly that Dante had sent Drew to him for a reason.

Drew wasn't simply a kid who needed help. He was the clue Quinn had been searching for. He was the screw that everything turned on. "What happened when Dante disappeared?"

Drew's gaze settled on Grace. "It was the night that the girl with silver eyes like yours made the night scream."

※※

Grace stiffened, shocked by Drew's comment about the girl with silver eyes. She'd been so immersed in making not-so-feel-good comparisons between Calydon history and her own future that she hadn't been considering whether Ana had been a part of Dante's death. "Ana?" She grabbed Drew's arm. "My sister was there? What happened?"

Vaughn growled and Quinn pulled her back from Drew. *I don't trust Vaughn. Stay behind me.*

She saw the pulsing emerald shine of Vaughn's eyes, and she reluctantly moved back to a spot beside Quinn's shoulder. Vaughn and Quinn exchanged glances, and she knew they were bonding over their common need to protect their charges. Great for the manly men, but dammit! She wanted to find out about her sister. "Tell me about Ana," she urged Drew. "What happened?"

"I was at the river working out with the boulders,"

Drew said, "when my dad warned me to stay away from the camp, you know, with that mind thing."

Quinn laughed softly, as if he knew exactly what Drew's response to that order had been. "As soon as you got that message, you hauled ass to get over to camp as fast as you could, right?"

Drew flushed, his reaction reminding Grace how young he was, even though he had his weapons and the emerging muscles of a Calydon warrior: deadly, but still a child. Just as she had been that night she'd heard the screams of her parents dying. Like Drew, how fast she'd run toward them, praying she could get there in time, praying she could save them. She knew all about how time could stand still during that run, how the heart could break into a thousand pieces from sheer, raw terror.

"Yeah," Drew acknowledged. "I had to go get him."

Quinn nodded. "I would have gone, too. Screw orders."

A smile flashed across Drew's young face, and then it faded. "I reached the ridge and saw there were three men, and one of them was holding the girl by the arm." He glanced at Grace. "Then there was this horrible noise, like the screams of thousands of people being tortured. I thought my head was going to split open from the pain."

Grace pressed her lips together. "An illusion," she guessed. "From my sister." Torture and screams so real that they caused physical pain, like hers did. Ana was all Grace was, and more.

Quinn set his hand on the back of her neck and squeezed gently. *We'll find her.*

Grace nodded, but couldn't bring herself to answer. What if they didn't? What if they got there too late?

"It hit my dad, too, because I saw him stumble." Drew's voice shook for a brief second, and Grace saw his vulnerability: a boy who'd finally been given the gift of his father, of belonging, and he'd lost it too soon, so violently.

She knew what that was like. Losing your world in a single moment of violence was brutal, awful, agonizing. What was this world that asked boys to be warriors? She looked at Quinn, with his stoic face and his hard expression, and her heart softened for him, too, for whatever had brought him onto a path where he had to slay friends and innocent women without hesitation.

"Dante called out both his weapons," Drew continued, drawing her attention back to him. He had pulled back his shoulders, and his voice was stronger, as if he was already learning how to be tougher than grief. "And he hurled them at the guy standing in front, the one closest to my dad. The other two jumped in front to protect him, and Dante killed them both." He grimaced with embarrassment. "Then I sort of passed out. I couldn't take the pain in my head anymore," he admitted, scuffing his boot on the asphalt. "When I woke up, everyone was gone, but I could smell death. It was in the ground, where Dante had been standing. I think he died on that spot, and then he faded."

"And the girl?" Grace's fists clenched. "What about her?"

"I didn't see what happened to her." Drew's gaze became sympathetic as he looked at Grace, the first hint of the young Calydon warrior feeling protective over a female. "But she was on her knees during the fight," he said. "She was pretty beat up. Bleeding. Bruised. She didn't look good."

A sob welled up in Grace's throat, and she put her hand over her mouth. "Oh, God."

Quinn pulled her against him, but she didn't want to be held. She wanted to take action, go somewhere, do something. "No." She tried to shove him away. "We have to get her. We have to find her. Now!" Her hands were shaking. Her fingers ice cold. With all the horrors around her, the heart-wrenching Calydon history, Drew's burdens, her worry about her future and Ana… she couldn't take it anymore. She had to do something to change it, to make it stop, to fix it. "Let's go." She shoved past Quinn, stumbling toward the truck. "Give me your keys. I'll drive."

"Grace." Quinn caught her arm and turned her toward him. His face was gentle, his dark eyes understanding. "We will go after her. I promise you. But in order to do that, we need answers first."

His expression was intense, his words fierce, and Grace realized he meant it. He wouldn't give up. She wasn't alone. "Okay," she whispered.

"Okay." He pulled her close, and this time she let him. She squeezed her eyes shut and fought not to cry, to hold herself together, but it was hard. God, it was hard. There was just too much to deal with. She just wanted peace. She wanted to sit beside her sister and lose herself in some beautiful illusion for five minutes. It wouldn't be real, but she didn't care. When was goodness ever real?

"Why do you think someone is after you?" Quinn asked Drew, his voice clear and focused, the way Grace should be.

How would she help her sister if she fell apart? She was stronger than this. She forced herself to lift her head and look at Drew while he glanced around into the thick fog.

"Ever since we left Dante's camp, I've felt someone following me. Hunting me." He ran his hand over his hair, near the base of his skull. "There's this pressure in my head, like someone's trying to get inside."

"That sounds like a Calydon attempting to access your thoughts." Quinn squeezed Grace and then set her gently to the side. "I can track him back." He set his hands on Drew's shoulders. "You haven't learned how to touch my mind, but I can build a bridge to connect us. Just relax, and let me in. I'll see if I can tap into whoever is trying to access your thoughts. Okay?"

Grace stood back and hugged herself while she watched Quinn work on Drew the same way she'd connected with him earlier. *Can you do this, Quinn?*

He waited too long to answer. Did that mean he didn't actually think he could?

You bet your sweet little ass I can do this. Quinn chuckled when he felt Grace's surprise at his comment. He'd paused before replying, trying to decide the right approach to take with her. He couldn't stand seeing all that pain on her face, and he needed to pull her out of it. He'd decided to try sex, humor and attitude, always good options. He knew that emotions were destructive. The only safe option was to keep them buried deep inside, and it was important to help Grace get back into her equilibrium. They had too much at stake.

Plus, her curves were just a damn good thing to think about.

You're incorrigible, she finally replied, sounding annoyed.

I know, babe. Don't you just love me? He could already feel her panic easing. Good.

Quinn! Just find my sister!

Working on it, babe. What's my reward when I do? An endless night of hot sex? Even as he said the words, Quinn connected with Drew's mind. The kid was open to him, trusting him completely. The youth had no defenses. No one should trust that much. No one.

What is wrong with you? Grace still sounded aggravated, but she was focused now. Good. *This isn't about sex.*

Actually, you're wrong. Everything in this whole damn affair is about sex, starting with Ezekiel and Evangeline. That's all it was, this whole screwed up thing: sex. The entire foundation of their race was built on the connection between a warrior and his woman. Now that he'd met Grace, Quinn understood the power of sex and the intensity of a male-female connection in a way he never had.

Oh. Grace was quiet for a moment. *You have a point.*

I know. It's sex, babe, from two thousand years ago right up to the way the earth shifts when your body melts against mine. He got it, hell yes, he got it. He was living it and breathing it. In fact, all the talk about the past and Ezekiel's need for his woman had stirred up Quinn's lust for Grace even more. Yeah, he was on edge about Ezekiel getting free, and he was going to stop that hell from going down, but that didn't change the fact that the history lesson had reminded him exactly how strong a Calydon's need for his woman was.

He wanted Grace, and there was no way to deny it.

Quinn. Sensual heat laced Grace's words, desire ignited by the mere thought of their bodies meshing together. *Do you think Ezekiel and Evangeline started like us?*

Maybe.

Fear and determination flicked through their connection. *Well, we're not ending like them.*

But Quinn shook his head, finally grasping, for the first time in his life, the magnitude of what they were up against with the *sheva* bond. He wasn't going to capitulate, but there was one thing he knew he wasn't going to be able to stop from happening. *You're going to end up in my bed, sweetheart. The rest we'll just have to deal with.*

He felt her sudden swell of desire mixed with a cold twist of fear, but before she could respond, Quinn caught a hum of energy vibrating inside Drew's mind and he jumped on it, trying to track and identify it. It was definitely another Calydon. It felt like tentacles pulsing into Drew's energy, trying to pinpoint his location, calling to him, trying to draw him in.

It was a cold energy. Dark. Hostile. Whoever was tracking Drew meant him harm. It wasn't an energy Quinn recognized, which meant it wasn't Order. Well, yeah, booyah for that. No traitor today.

Quinn sped along the connection, but the Calydon drew back quickly, no doubt sensing Quinn's presence and realizing he was a threat. The intruder severed the link, and Quinn lost him, but he was satisfied. Next time, he'd get him. He knew what to look for now, and he would be able to move faster. Round one to the good guys.

Quinn wove some protections inside Drew's head so his pursuer would have more difficulty pinpointing his location, then he broke the connection.

"It's gone." Drew rubbed the back of his head with visible relief. "How'd you do that?"

"He felt me and left. He'll be back."

Drew's face fell, and Quinn was glad he'd taken the time to erect some protections for the kid. "But you're correct. You're being hunted, and whoever it is knows you're here right now. Until I know who's after you, and I have everything in place to deal with it, I don't want to be standing around waiting to get caught, so let's keep moving." Until Quinn had a better sense of who was after Drew, he was going to honor Dante's legacy by protecting his son. If Dante had thought the kid was important, then he was. "Into the truck. Now."

For a moment, no one moved, then Drew broke his stance and sprinted back to the truck in a clear statement of faith. Vaughn gave Quinn a steady look. "Where are we going?"

"I haven't decided." He checked the night and caught a hint of the energy that was after Drew. Now that he knew what to look for, he could feel it. "But they're getting closer."

Vaughn turned and strode back to the truck as he

urged Drew back into the vehicle.

"Is it my sister?" Grace made no move to leave. "If it's her, we should wait here for her."

Quinn took her hand and heat leapt between them. She jerked in surprise and tried to pull her hand away. He didn't release her. "It's a Calydon," he said as he walked her toward the truck. "It could be the one who has your sister, but until I know more, we're keeping ahead of it." He practically shoved her into the truck, then climbed in after her and yanked his door shut. He wouldn't risk Drew and Grace by staying to fight an enemy he couldn't identify.

Not with Ezekiel's walls falling.

CHAPTER 8

You're an asshole. Gideon's voice burst into Quinn's mind with sudden force. *You knocked me out, left me in a pile of dead bodies and then woke me up while I was having a dream that I'd been taken prisoner by a bunch of lust-ridden fairies with a thing for Calydon warriors.*

Gideon. Hot damn. Quinn grinned as he turned off the main road and shot up over a dirt-caked hill that would cut twenty miles off their route. He'd decided to head toward Dante's shack, with a brief stop to read Elijah's *mjui*, and he knew exactly which place would be safe enough for their stopover. *Hell, man. Wear a helmet next time. You're getting soft.*

I took an extended nap to give you extra lead time. Gideon got right to the point. *You find Elijah? Straighten him out?*

Quinn's grip tightened on the steering wheel. *I found his* mjui.

For a split second, there was no response, just the icy cold of disbelief and shock emanating from Gideon. Then his blast of grief hit Quinn so hard he doubled over and had to hit the brakes. He swore, grimacing as Gideon's pain pummeled him, like millions of daggers stabbing his brain. *Hell, Gideon. Get control.*

Quinn felt Grace's hands on his shoulder, but he couldn't lift his head against the agony ripping through him. His chest was burning, and his stomach churned, tearing at his insides like acid. *Gideon!* Quinn's own grief for Elijah swelled up inside him in response to Gideon's pain, and he had to cut off the connection with Gideon.

The relief was instant, like he'd been delivered from a dance with demons into sunshine and roses.

Quinn let his head fall back against the seat as the anguish vanished, leaving behind nothing but a lingering numbness. He forced his own grief back down, barely holding control of his emotions. He had not been prepared for that level of response from Gideon. Gideon was the ultimate warrior, hard and cold, never standing down from what he had to do. Quinn had not expected his shields to crack. Not Gideon's.

"Quinn?" Grace's forehead was furrowed, her dark hair tousled carelessly around her face. "What's wrong?"

He caught sight of the stunned faces of Drew and Vaughn in the back seat, and he gave a quick shake of his head. "I'm fine."

She frowned. "You're not fine."

He caught her hand as she went to touch his face. *Let it go, Grace. For God's sake, just let it go.*

She studied him for a moment, those silver eyes searching for his truth, and he thought she wasn't going to let it go. Then she gave him a brief smile and retreated to her side of the vehicle. He wanted to apologize, but he couldn't. He was barely hanging on, and he couldn't take a show of sympathy from her.

Gideon initiated contact again. *You tell anyone about what just happened and I'll kick your ass.* His energy was tightly controlled, and there was no emotion in his voice. Like Quinn, he'd pulled his grief back inside and shut it down.

I get it. Quinn admitted. *I'm with you.*

There was a soft laugh from Gideon. *Elijah would laugh his ass off if he could see us falling apart over his death.*

He'd appreciate it.

Yeah, he would.

They were both silent for a minute, then Quinn tried to focus on their situation. *Have you talked to Dante?*

Haven't had a chance. You knocked me out and I just woke up, remember.

You have a phone on you?

Yeah.

Try calling his cell.

Gideon didn't ask why, he simply did it. *No. It's off. Why?*

Quinn glanced in his rearview mirror at Drew, who had his forehead pressed against the window as he watched the dark woods. Looking for whoever was stalking him?

Quinn released the brake and resumed driving. He quickly filled Gideon in on everything, including the part about a traitor inside the Order. As Dante had trusted him, he trusted Gideon.

When he finished, there was a stunned silence from Gideon. *That's the shit that's in your woods? Ezekiel?* Gideon's voice became grittier. *I'm looking around now, and I can see that some of your ferns are dying. Were they turning brown before?*

No.

Hell. If Ezekiel's already killing vegetation, we've got a major problem.

Quinn nodded. *I need to stash Drew, read Elijah's* mjui *and then I'll meet you at the fishing shack. Be careful.*

I'm on it.

He shut off communication, satisfied that they were finally taking action, and then he noticed Grace studying him thoughtfully."You trusted Gideon with the truth," she said. "You don't think he's the traitor?"

Shock rippled through him. "You heard that?" No one could have broken through their closed connection, no one except a fully bonded *sheva*. He grabbed her arm and shoved up her sleeve. Not even the faintest hint of a brand.

"Yes. It's getting easier." She bit her lip. "That's not good, is it?"

"You shouldn't be able to. Not without us having done any of the bonding stages." He frowned and laid his palm over her forearm, to see if he could feel building heat from the brand beneath the surface. Still nothing, which both relieved him and created a pulsing urge within him to mark her. Instead of doing the animalistic male thing and branding her, he managed a grim shrug. "Seems our bond is stronger than normal. Figures. Makes it more interesting, right?"

She gave him a resigned look. "'Interesting' isn't the word that comes to mind right now."

No. It wasn't. "How about damned inconvenient, then?"

The hint of a smile teased her mouth. "That'll do."

He held out his hand and she set hers in it.

This time, it wasn't about sex.

It was about joining forces to beat the hell out of this thing.

<hr />

The sky was just beginning to lighten when Grace shoved the rusted key into the motel cabin lock and used her hip to force the door open. They'd been driving all night in the general direction of Dante's property, but they'd avoided the direct route. The heavy fog and winding roads had kept them going slow, and Quinn had pulled the truck off into a riverside motel shortly after dawn. He was sure he'd shaken the Calydon stalking Drew, and the motel was secluded enough in the heavy woods to hide Vaughn and Drew while he read Elijah's *mjui*.

Quinn had put himself and Grace in the cabin next to the others, so he could keep everyone close enough to protect. He'd gone next door with Vaughn and Drew to set up some safety precautions, while Grace carried her pack into the cabin. The fog wasn't lifting with the dawn, and the cabins were shrouded in heavy mist that would keep them hidden even if someone was looking for them.

During the drive, Grace had filled Quinn in on what she'd learned about Ana from tapping into her illusion dust at The Gun Rack. When he'd learned she had an image of the man who'd kidnapped Ana, he'd spent a couple hours teaching her how to place that image in his mind, until she'd finally been able to do it. It had been a total rush to succeed, but by then, Grace had been exhausted, and all she wanted to do was crash.

Neither of them had mentioned the fact that the *sheva* bond was the reason she'd been able to give the image. They'd needed to do it, so they'd done it and not discussed the consequences.

They hadn't been as successful with Drew, however. He'd apparently blocked the image of his dad's death too deeply in his mind. Quinn couldn't access it, even though he'd tried for several hours. Frustrating, because Quinn really wanted to know the faces of the Calydons who'd gone after Dante, and Grace wanted to see what had happened with her sister. Partial victory was better than none, though, so she tried to stay positive. They would get more answers when they reached Dante's home.

Grace kicked off her boots inside the door and tossed the heavy coat she'd borrowed from Quinn on a large nail sticking out of the wall. The place was smaller than Quinn's home, with barely enough room for the double bed and one floor lamp. God, the bed looked inviting. Sudden exhaustion flooded her, and she wanted nothing more than to crawl onto that faded comforter and give herself up to sleep.

She rubbed her hand over her forehead, and dried mud came off. She was still filthy from the hunt at The Gun Rack, and she had never really cleaned up after the trip through the mud tunnel. A shower first. Then sleep.

She glanced around the room and saw a door at the other end of the room. A bathroom? *Please don't let there only be an outhouse here.* Her thick socks padded silently on the wood floor as she crossed the cabin. The bare wood door swung open under her touch. Bathroom! Relief rushed through as she stepped into the tiny room. A single chain hung from a light bulb in the ceiling, and a ten-inch sink was tucked in the corner, beside a small toilet.

But glory be, most of the space was taken up by a narrow, standing-room-only shower. The drain was rusted, the showerhead antique, and there was no tile, just a stained vinyl curtain to keep the water out of the rest of the room. Not much, but it was a shower, and she'd take it. Grace's skin tingled at the idea of the wet, hot warmth cascading over her. She immediately yanked her shirt off, desperate to get out of her muddy clothes and to feel clean again—

There was a thud from the bedroom and she turned as Quinn kicked the door shut and dropped two bags on the floor, effectively eliminating what little floor space there was in the room. He started unbuttoning his mud-caked coat and strode toward her, muttering to himself.

She clutched her shirt to her chest as Quinn looked up. He went still, his gaze dropping to her bare shoulders. Heat simmered in her stomach, and her muscles trembled as she hugged the shirt more tightly. Slowly, Quinn pulled his attention off her body and met her gaze.

The fire blazing in his eyes made every nerve in her body jump. He looked behind her, at the bathroom, then back at her. "You're taking a shower."

Grace swallowed. "You can go first." The obvious answer, the one hanging in the air between them, wouldn't come. The offer for them to shower at the same time. She couldn't say it, even though every part of her was calling for him to resume his walk across the floor. To see his expression intensify as he neared her, as he backed her into the bathroom, as he shut the door behind them and—

"No." Quinn peeled off his jacket and tossed it in the corner. Without his jacket, she could see the breadth of his shoulders and the way his jeans sat low on his hips. He was all male, pure strength, dominating energy, and he was looking at her as if he wanted to throw her up against the wall and make love to her until there was nothing left of either one of them.

"No, what?" she whispered, instinctively taking a step back. Inviting him in or running away? She didn't even know. Didn't care.

"No, you can go first." He turned away, crouched beside a large, black duffel and unzipped it. "I need to get organized."

She stared at him in agonized disbelief, her body aching with need for him. "What?" He wasn't going to come after her? Yes, good. No, awful. God, she didn't even know what she wanted from him.

Quinn looked up then, and she saw his eyes had gone almost black. He slowly rose to his feet and walked toward her, his boots thudding with each step on the wood floor. He didn't stop until he was inches from her, forcing her to crane her neck to look up at him. Silently, he picked up a lock of her hair and wrapped it around his finger.

Her heart was racing now, utterly out of control, her breath tight in her chest. "Quinn?"

He traced his finger down the side of her neck, along her shoulder, and then down, across her collarbone and over the swell of her breast. His skin was hot, and goose bumps shivered over her at the sensual, teasing contact. She couldn't break away from his spell, couldn't stop the tide of desire building inside her, the awareness of how close they were.

"Where's your protest?" he asked as he lowered his head, his mouth almost touching hers. "Aren't you going to stop me?"

She scrunched her eyes shut, fighting against the swirl of desire inside her, the need to reach out for him, to pull him against her. "I can't," she whispered.

"Can't what?" He brushed his lips over the side of her neck, a hot tease, a dangerous seduction. "Say no? Say yes?"

She opened her eyes, staring into his turbulent ones. "I don't know," she whispered. "I've never felt like this. I want you so desperately it hurts."

He growled, a deep, carnal sound that sent spirals shooting down her spine, then he grabbed her around the waist and hauled her up against him. His mouth descended with an almost violent force and a primal passion that invaded her deepest protections and shredded her defenses. The kiss was hot and wet, aggressive and dominant, taking, sucking, consuming her, and it was amazing. She wanted more, needed more, burned for more.

Quinn. She dropped her shirt and threw her arms around his neck, kissing him as desperately as he was kissing her. He lifted her up, and then her back was against the wall. The bare wood dug into her skin as he continued his assault, his body burning with heat as he pinned her there, his hands on her hips, her stomach, her ribs—

"Jesus." He pulled back suddenly, and she nearly fell at his sudden departure. He caught her arm, holding her up, while the sound of their heavy breathing filled the small room. She leaned against the wall, bracing herself to keep upright.

Quinn lifted his hand and she jumped when he touched her arm. Her skin was on fire, so sensitive as he hooked his index finger over her bra strap and ever so slowly teased it off her shoulder, letting it fall over her arm.

She didn't move, couldn't move. All she could do was watch the expression of awe and desire on his face as his gaze roamed over her body, drinking her in. It was now. It was going to happen, whatever the consequences—

A loud knock on the door of the cabin made them both start. "Quinn!" Vaughn yelled. "You ready? Let's go."

Quinn swore and dropped his hand. "I need to set up security."

She nodded, her mouth too dry to speak.

"I'll be back."

She nodded again. "Okay."

Neither of them moved, the tension tight between them. Finally, Grace spoke. "It would have been a mistake. Too dangerous."

"Dangerous, yes." He raised his brows. "Mistake, maybe, but perhaps that doesn't matter."

Vaughn pounded on the door. "Quinn! Let's go!"

"Coming." Quinn gave her one last look, then he turned away and grabbed his bag off the floor, reverting into the warrior again.

Respite granted.

Grace slammed the bathroom door shut and leaned back against the wall, trying to catch her breath. What was she doing? Since when had she become some lust-driven hussy unable to control herself? Seriously? After hearing the story about Ezekiel and Caleb, hadn't that been enough to curb her desire to have Quinn sweaty and naked on top of her?

Grace heard the low murmur of men's voices from the cabin, giving her relief from having to make an immediate decision. Quinn wasn't going to walk back into the bathroom with Vaughn out there. The moment was over. She'd been given her respite. By the time he came back, she'd be back to her sexless, in-control self.

Groaning, Grace peeled off the rest of her muddy clothes, set them on the sink, stepped behind the nearly-transparent shower curtain and turned on the shower.

She yelped when the cold water hit her, jumping to the side until it finally warmed up. Then she sighed and turned her face up into the wet heat, letting it sink into her body and wash away the mud. Her wrist stung where the copper band had been, reminding her how dangerous this whole world was that she was involved in. All she wanted was to rescue her sister. That was it. One simple goal, but so complicated, and getting more entangled by the minute.

She rested her head against the wall as the hot water pounded at her, loosening her muscles, bringing warmth to a body that felt too cold, too exhausted, too weary—

"Grace."

She snapped her eyes open and jerked upright at the sound of Quinn's voice right outside the bathroom door. He was so close, separated from her only by a flimsy wooden door. She was suddenly aware of how naked she was, how completely vulnerable. If he opened that door and came in, she would have nothing to hide behind. Nothing to put between them. No way to stay safe from the way he made her feel. "What?" Her voice was breathless and throaty, too shaky and vulnerable for the self-assured image she wanted to project to herself, to Quinn and to the world.

"I'm going to do a run-through of the woods around this place with Vaughn and Drew." His voice was serious and focused, all warrior, no lover. "I need to make sure everything's as I want it to be before I shut down to read Elijah's *mjui*. If I'm not back when you finish showering, go ahead and go to bed. Rest while you can. I want to be at the fishing shack by midnight. Gideon's going to meet us there."

"You're leaving?" She couldn't keep the disappointment out of her voice. The anguish of unfulfilled passion laced with giddy relief.

He laughed, a low guttural sound that pulsed low

in her belly. *Don't worry, sweetheart. With that kiss, and the image of you naked in that shower burning in my mind, I will definitely be back soon. You can count on it.*

※※※

It took less than an hour.

Quinn had been so amped up by the kiss with Grace that he'd completed his circuit of the woods in a fraction of the time it usually would have taken him. He'd been impressed with Drew's ability to keep up, but Vaughn had been the one who had really made him take notice. Vaughn had kept up easily despite Quinn's adrenaline-charged pace, and he'd had some insightful suggestions about security. Vaughn had refused to give up any information about himself, but he was clearly a warrior. A man who'd been around and made it back more than a few times. A good man to have on your side. A man who would complicate things if he was working against you.

Vaughn made it clear that he was ready to go from friend to foe in a minute to protect Drew. A truce had been drawn between the two warriors, but neither man was naïve enough to trust it blindly.

Quinn was looking forward to having Gideon at his back again, a man he didn't have to watch. He'd touched base with his teammate, but Gideon hadn't arrived at the fishing shack, and hadn't been able to rouse Dante either. They both agreed it was looking grim.

After Quinn had parted ways with Vaughn and Drew, he'd taken time to try to reach Dante again, but he'd gotten nothing. He'd managed to pick up the faint pulse of Drew's hunter again, though, and he spent some time trying to pinpoint it or identify the source. He was successful at neither. In the end, he'd simply erected a block to interfere with it. He didn't know if it was coming closer or going in the other direction, but he was certain he'd set up enough safeguards that Drew was safe there, safe enough that he could leave him while he went up to Dante's shack.

Until Quinn was certain no more Order members were going to go rogue, he wasn't going to risk exposing Drew to the rest of the Order. Vaughn had been in agreement, and the two of them had spent some time double-checking safeguards until they were both certain Drew would be unfindable as long as he stayed in the cabin.

While Quinn had been working, he'd been trying to assimilate all the info he'd acquired and figure out what was going on, but he'd been unable to get the image of Grace in the shower out of his damn mind. Every time he tried to focus, his mind would wander to those bare shoulders, to the taste of her mouth, to the swell of her breasts beneath her folded arms.

He needed a calm mind to read the *mjui*, but he hadn't been able to stop thinking about Grace long enough to concentrate. Quinn finally decided that distance wasn't going to help the situation. It was time to deal with it straight on, so he could read the *mjui* and get focused on finding Ana, avenging Elijah's death and figuring out what else was going on before Ezekiel's walls fell.

Frustration was roiling through him as he threw open the front door of the cabin. "We're going to deal with this now."

Grace bolted straight up in bed, her eyes wide with the shock of someone abruptly woken out of a sound sleep. "What's wrong?"

Her hair was still damp, in tight curls around her shoulders, and she was wearing his T-shirt, one she'd apparently pilfered from his bag. Damn. He liked the fact she was wearing his shirt. It was almost as good as being wrapped around her himself. Her face was scrubbed clean, her hands clenching the worn quilt as she tried to regroup from being startled awake.

He cursed and quietly shut the door behind him. "I didn't think you'd be asleep yet. Sorry. No crisis."

"Oh, good." She collapsed back to the bed with a soft sigh, falling limply onto the mattress. She looked so innocent and fragile, snuggled down in the bed with her wet hair. "I was more tired than I thought." She yawned. "I have a major headache from that image-transfer thing."

"You up for talking?"

She rubbed her palm over her eyes. "Yeah, sure. What's up?"

He sat next to her on the bed, sitting close enough that her hip was pressed against his, his hand braced across her on the bed. She'd kicked her leg out from under the covers, showcasing a long expanse of skin and a pair of his boxers. He flicked his finger over her waistband, brushing over the bare skin of her belly. "You're wearing my shorts?"

"Seemed smarter than going commando." She wrapped her fingers around his wrist and tried to move his hand away. "After that kiss, I figured it wouldn't be a good idea to climb into bed half-naked. You know."

"Yeah, I know." He resisted her hint to give her space when he felt her stomach quiver beneath his hand. Instead, he spread his fingers, palming her belly. "That's what I wanted to talk about. We need to figure out how to deal with this attraction between us."

She wiggled to the side so her hip was no longer touching his, but there was a faint flush rising in her cheeks. "Sex is a bad idea."

"Yeah. It is. It's one of the stages of the bond." He had a sudden vision of crawling under the sheets and nestling up tight to her, wrapping his fingers in the silky dampness of her hair. Shit, no, that was what he was here to stop! He swore and pulled his hand back—

"No, don't go." Grace instinctively grabbed his arm. The instant her hand closed around his arm, the moment he felt her desperation not to lose physical contact with him, an answering need roared to life inside him and his willpower shattered.

He grabbed her and hauled her against his chest as he kissed her. Hard. Deep. Wet. Exactly how he'd imagined. Precisely as he'd wanted.

Her arms went around him and she kissed him back, frantically kicking her way out from under the covers, until her legs were free. She crawled into his lap, sliding those long, bare legs around his hips in a move that elicited a growl from him that was too carnal and too primal. As she settled into his lap, her thighs tight around his waist, he knew he was going to have her. She wasn't going to push him away. Nothing was going to stop them. Not this time.

The moment he realized that, his desperation eased. His kisses slowed to savor the feel of her mouth under his. He slipped his hands beneath the hem of her shirt and groaned at the feel of her bare back beneath his fingers.

Reveling in the feel of her skin under his, Quinn ran his hands up and down her spine, tracing every curve of her body, every bone, every muscle, everything that made her who she was, until he could stand it no longer. "I have to see you," he whispered into her mouth. "I have to know every inch of your body, memorize it, and make it mine." He grabbed the hem of her shirt as he spoke, sliding with tantalizing slowness up her hips.

Quinn wasn't a man of delicate sensibilities. He wasn't a lover who basked in sensation. He was a ruthless warrior who took what he needed and moved on before the situation could spiral, never staying present long enough to risk any kind of connection or bond. He was not a man who was fascinated with the play of light across a woman's body, or the sensual curve of her mouth as she caught her lower lip with her teeth. He had never noticed the sinfully decadent sensation of a slow, erotic undressing.

Until now. Until Grace. Until this moment, when his world seemed to suddenly come to a screeching halt until there was only her, only him, only the sizzling electricity crackling between them.

Grace sat back on her hips and stretched her arms over her head, her gaze anchored to his. The look of sensual anticipation on her face made him groan as his gaze slid over the swell of her nipples barely visible through the T-shirt and down to the flat expanse of her belly. He was riveted by the tiny quivers in her belly as she waited for his touch. "That is the sexiest damn belly button I've ever seen."

She let out her breath in a nervous giggle, and he bent his head and lightly kissed her navel. Her skin was still damp from the shower, dusted with the fragrance of fresh soap. Natural beauty, sinfully tempting, pure woman. His woman. *His woman.* He clasped her hips, holding her still as he kissed it again, swirling his tongue with a torturous slowness that made her shift restlessly. Then he hooked his thumbs under the hem of the shirt and dragged it upward, sliding it over her ribs.

He kissed his way along each rib, nipping lightly, sweeping his tongue across her skin. With each movement, with each kiss, Grace reacted. A sharp intake of breath. A light touch to his hair. A small noise of pleasure. The subtle shift of her hips to move closer to him. All signs that reached inside him and thrummed his desire higher and higher.

With tantalizing slowness, he slid his hands up her body, taking the shirt with him. Up her sides, to her shoulders. He caught her arms and continued his ascent along her triceps, sliding that cotton shirt up over her chest, his thumbs brushing against her nipples.

Quinn caught her surprised gasp with a kiss. The feel of her mouth under his unleashed a sudden fierceness he could barely contain, a desire to become the raw beast that history had made him, to take her, to make her his—

But he didn't want that. Not this first time. Not with Grace. He pulled back, nearly undone by the heated look in her eyes, by the fullness of her lips, by the way she looked at him with such raw longing on her face. He knew he was seeing the real Grace, not the shield she tried to put up. Her vulnerability, her passion, her need for him was vivid and evident, and it was perfect. This was how he wanted her: true, raw, unguarded, for him alone.

He kissed her again, a slow, tantalizing kiss designed to seduce and tempt. Only when he felt her lean into him did he pause, pulling back just enough to slide her shirt over her head and inch it over her wrists, letting it drop from the tips of her fingers.

And there she was. For him. For only him. He pulled back from her, letting his gaze travel over her body. Over the elegant lines of her neck, the curve of her collarbone, the deep rose of her nipples, taut and ready for him. Tentatively, almost reverently, he cupped her breast with his hand, its petite curves like a gift in his palm. "You make me see beauty in places I never did before," he said, his voice raw with uncertainty for this unfamiliar territory of sensuality and temptation. "You're like all the sunshine and heavens I've missed, all brought to me in this one moment."

"Quinn," she whispered, her silver eyes softening.

He kissed her again as he moved onto his knees, edging her back until she was beneath him. He lowered himself onto her, groaning as her body shifted beneath him, as her legs parted to accommodate him. "What, sweetheart?"

"The way you look at me, makes me feel..." she hesitated.

He kissed her tenderly as his hands slid up her ribs and cupped her breasts, his thumbs brushing lightly over her nipples. "Feel what?"

"Beautiful."

He smiled at the awe in her voice. "You are." Then he bent his head and kissed each breast. She arched her back with a soft moan, and he grazed his teeth over each nipple. Her body tightened beneath him, her hips moving restlessly.

He needed more. She needed more. So much more. Pressure built inside him, and he kissed her again, more aggressively this time. She grabbed onto his hair, diving into the kiss with desperate passion. He moved to her breast, nipping harder now, licking at the puckered peak, as he slid his hand down her hip under her shorts.

He hooked his hand around the back of her bare thigh, pulling it around his hip. She hooked her leg behind his back, and he shifted so he could reach her mouth again. The kiss was carnal and hot, deep and wet, taking control of them both. She writhed beneath him. Her hands were in his hair, on his shoulders, her nails digging in as she arched under him, her body calling to him as he moved his hand again, to her inner thigh, to skin so soft he felt like he'd been gifted with an angel in his arms.

The world began to swirl and his body pulsed at him, needing more, needing her. He crushed her with his kiss, losing himself in the taste of her, in the heat of her mouth as his hips pressed between her legs, his hardness driving against her, blocked only by his jeans and her boxers.

Unable to break the kiss, unwilling to tear his mouth away from hers, he shifted his weight and slid his hand beneath her shorts again, this time finding the heat that was hers, sinking deep into her. She gasped and her body shuddered beneath him, ready for him, so ready. Her knees fell apart as she twisted her feet around his legs, arching to meet him as he sank his fingers into her depths.

"Quinn." Her voice was a soft moan of such pure hot desire that he forgot to think. Forgot to breathe. Forgot everything but the feel of her body everywhere he touched, the taste of her mouth, the delicate scent that was hers.

He rolled to the side for a split second, yanked off her boxers, ditched all his clothes, and then he was back. Gone was the slow seduction, the sensual build, the sinful temptation. All that was left was a fierce, dangerous, unyielding need for connection, for her, to bury himself so deeply that they would never recover.

He groaned as he lowered himself onto her, as the first feel of her belly against the raging heat of his erection roared through him. Hot energy suddenly leapt between them with violent force, so intense it felt as if it were burning through his soul like a violent electrical shock. He paused, his body rigid with the effort of not dropping his hips and plunging inside her, his nerves screaming from the pain of their metaphysical connection. "Grace?" He bit the question out, barely able to restrain himself. "Too much?"

"No, no, no." Her fingers dug into his shoulders and she wrapped her legs around his hips, positioning herself beneath him. She lifted her hips to him. "Please, Quinn, don't stop." She grabbed onto him and kissed him, so hard, so deep. She dropped her hand between them and clasped his swollen member. "Now," she whispered.

"*Grace.*" The moment her hand closed on him, his control snapped, and he drove into her, so hard and so fast that their bodies smacked together with a crack that reverberated down to his soul.

Grace rose to meet him, her hips undulating as he pulled back and drove even deeper, and again, both of them moving and meeting, faster and faster, his need for her escalating, spinning around him, twisting around every cell in his body, every corner of his spirit until he was burning with such need, such desperation for her, his body coiling tighter and tighter until he knew it could take no more. He kissed her fiercely as he dropped his hand between them, finding her most sensitive spot as he drove into her again, as far as he could, reaching even deeper with his spirit, and his mind, letting her feel his desire, his desperation.

Their minds touched, and the true depths of her need for him hit him so hard his world shattered around him, sucking Grace with him into the vortex as it spun him ruthlessly, ripping his foundation, until all he could do was anchor his mind to Grace's and hold her against him, promising her over and over again that he'd keep her safe.

He hoped his promise wouldn't turn out to be a lie.

Chapter 9

Grace burrowed into Quinn's body as she slowly regained her breath and her equilibrium, as the trembling faded from her limbs. He was draped over her, his whiskered face buried in her neck, his leg flung over hers, his arm snagged around her belly, trapping her in the curve of his body. His fingers were loosely clasping her wrists where they rested against her chest. "Quinn?"

"Still with you." He inhaled deeply and swore quietly. "I've marked you. Your scent has changed."

Grace waited for tension to hit her, but it didn't. It was more like resignation. How could what they had just shared *not* have marked her? It had been far more than sex, and they both knew it. "I smell different?"

"To me." He released her wrists and wrapped his palm around her forearm. "Your skin's hot."

He flipped her arm over and raised it up so they could both inspect it.

Up by her elbow, on the top side of her arm, were some faint silver marks on her skin. Her breath caught. "Is that it?"

He laid his arm next to hers, showing her his brand, the thick, dark lines woven into his skin. The brand was in the shape of a beautifully intricate sword, with a long blade and a carved handle.

The designs on the handle of his sword matched up perfectly with the lines on her skin. An exact replica, except hers was faint silver and his was an angry, black brand. Her stomach thudded, the mark on her skin dealing the final blow to the shred of hope that had remained coiled inside her that the legend had no truth.

Gone was the steady, hopeful conviction that she had remained above some all-powerful metaphysical destiny, that a horrific fate hadn't clawed its way into her life to try to catapult her toward a future it had pre-selected for her. "So, that's it then. It's real."

"It's always been real."

Grace extricated herself from Quinn's arms and sat up, drawing her knees to her chest under the quilt and wrapping her arms around her legs. Her chest ached, and she almost rolled her eyes with the irony of how much she wanted to crawl into his arms and feel the beat of his heart against hers while they figured out how to resist that which drew them together.

Now was not the time to turn to Quinn for strength or comfort. She needed to feel her independence. She needed to prove to herself that she could survive without him, even while she was yearning for his touch. "So, what now?" She kept her voice cool and reserved. Strong.

His eyes were stormy. Unsettled. "Even though I know it's screwed up, it feels damned good to see my brand on your arm." His gaze went to her mark. "It makes you mine, and I like it."

She tensed at the possessiveness in his voice and body language as he leaned over her, his bulk dwarfing her in the bed that suddenly felt too small. "I'll never be yours," she said.

"You're mine already."

She kicked off the covers and jumped out of the bed, her bare feet slapping against the floor. "Dammit, Quinn! I'm not! Stop talking like you've already given in!"

He didn't move, but his body was vibrating with a dark energy. The muscles in his shoulders were taut, his abs like steel across his lean torso. "I said you're mine. You are. I'm yours. It's the way it is. But that doesn't mean we let it rule us."

"How can we not?" Grace gestured at the covers that were torn askew from their lovemaking. "Look at what we just did! That wasn't just sex. That was some major metaphysical stuff going on, and you know it. Neither of us wants this future. We knew sex would take us closer, but we did it anyway. Dammit. It's already controlling us."

"Oh, Grace, you are so wrong." Quinn rolled onto his back and lightly clasped his hands over his head, the muscles in his arms flexing with the force of his action. His eyes were lighter now, almost peaceful. He almost looked like he was laughing at her. "We didn't have sex *because* of the bond. The bond just intensified what we already feel for each other. We had sex because we wanted to, because we belong together and we both know it." He raised his brows in a challenging gesture, daring her to step up and admit the truth. "The attraction is us, Grace. Just us. There are no excuses."

"There's no way it's just us." She couldn't accept that. She just couldn't. "I want you so much it hurts. That's not me. That's something else. *That's not me.*"

"You're right. It's not you. It's *us*. Part of the reason you're responding to me is because you can feel my need for you. We feed on each other."

"Like parasites?" Because that sounded so romantic.

He laughed aloud this time. "No, not like parasites. Like soul mates who have been hunting for each other for centuries. Isn't that what women want? Romance? Soul mates? Forever love?"

Grace folded her arms across her chest, refusing to acknowledge the female side of her that wanted to agree with him. Why? Because she lived in the grittiness of the real world, and she knew there was no happy romance down the road for them, not just because of the *sheva* destiny, but because she'd had so many dreams broken that she'd learned not to have them. "You just finished telling me how Ezekiel's love for Evangeline caused the breakdown of the world. Call me cynical, but I just don't see the romance in that. Do you?"

Quinn's smile faded, and he gestured to the bed for her to sit. "Being soul mates is not a bad thing, Grace. The problem comes when we fall victim to it."

Grace chewed her lip. Trusting the soul mate thing seemed like the fast track toward emotional devastation. "We already succumbed once."

He grinned. "Grace, sweetheart, you are the most sensual, most courageous, most achingly beautiful woman I've ever met in my life. That's why I couldn't stop myself. You need to give yourself credit for who you are. That was you I was making love to, not the bond."

"Stop." She held up her hands. "Don't say things that make me want to go all weak, Quinn. I can't do that. I can't fall for you. It's too much, so you have to stop trying to get me to believe in you. I know it was the bond. I don't respond to men and sex like that, and men don't want me like you do. If the *sheva* thing can make me do that, what chance do we have?"

"Grace. Sit." He flipped the covers aside to make room for her. "Not all the stages are like sex, which was driven by so many other factors. We need to talk about them, and get control of this thing going forward."

"Control? God, I'd like some of that." She grabbed his abandoned T-shirt from the floor, perched on the end of the bed, and crossed her legs. "Talk." She wanted to crawl up the bedspread and tuck herself under his chin, run her hand over the muscles in his chest, breathe his air. "Dammit!" She pulled the shirt on, hiding behind the thick cotton. "What are the other stages? Don't tell me they're like if I eat food in the same square mile as you, or drink out of the same cup? Accidentally brush against you? Because those will be difficult to avoid."

He laughed softly. "No, they're more significant than that. We can't do them by accident. There are five stages to the bond. They can go in any order. Sex, of course. Then the blood exchange."

"A blood exchange." Her stomach roiled. "It sounds disgusting, so no worries there. It's not going to happen."

"We might want it to happen."

Oh, God, really? "Why?" Did she really want to know? The nightmare was getting worse.

"A blood exchange will let us communicate mind-to-mind across any distance. I would be able to find you anywhere, and you, me."

"Good to remember if I decide to get kidnapped like my sister." Her forearm began to itch and she rubbed it. "A cell phone with a tracking device would work great, as well."

He almost smiled. "Not the same thing, darling. You know it's not."

Her heart skipped at the endearment, and her response made her uncomfortable. How was she supposed to hold onto who she was if she got all weepy whenever he made her feel special? "Don't call me darling."

He met her gaze, and she saw the resignation in his eyes. "I'll try."

She sighed. This whole romance thing was so not her comfort zone. It was too dangerous for her. She couldn't afford to break down and forget how to protect herself. "What else do I need to know?"

Quinn raised his brows, clearly telling her that the sex/romance topic wasn't over, but he granted her the respite by answering her question. "The Death Ritual is another stage. Taking a life to save mine. And I take one to save yours. Or we risk our lives to save the other. Either one works."

Her stomach balled up in a knot. Killing someone? *Please, no. Not that.*

His gaze narrowed. "What's wrong?"

She shook her head, her throat too tight to talk.

Quinn sat up, all amusement gone from his handsome face. "Grace? You look like you're going to be sick."

The concern in his voice made her chest ache, fraying her composure. "No." She pulled back from him, her body starting to shake. "I don't want to kill. I just don't want to."

He leaned forward and caught her shoulders. "Hey." His voice was quiet. Soothing. "You don't have to kill anyone. That's why we're talking about it. I'm the one who knocks people around, remember? It's what I do. The whole point of this discussion is that I *don't* want you to kill because that will tighten the bond, okay?"

She clung to his wrists, no longer able to fight the support he offered. She was too vulnerable when it came to killing someone else, too raw, too terrified of who she was. "What if the bond makes me kill someone? Like it made us have sex?" Her fingers dug into his skin.

"It didn't make us have sex," he said again, for what seemed like the thousandth time, as if repeating it would make her finally hear it. "We both wanted to. That's why we did it."

"Do you really believe that?" God, she wanted to believe that. She wanted to believe that she had some control over her actions, and that those silver lines on her arms weren't dictating her future. But the intensity of how she responded to Quinn wasn't natural. It wasn't her. She wasn't like that. She didn't see how she could ever convince herself that the coupling they'd just had was not influenced by some magical bond drawing them together. Frustrated, she released him, trying to take back her own space. "Could we have said no? Truly? Could you have walked away from me?"

His face darkened. "There was no chance in hell I was going to walk away, and that had nothing to do with the bond, Grace."

The intensity of his stare was unnerving, but also reassuring. It was awful to think that all those attentions he lavished on her had been against his will. "You're so sure about that?"

"Yeah, I am." His thumbs rubbed small circles on her shoulders. "I like using my sword, Grace. I'm not going to let you kill anyone and steal my thunder, okay?"

"Yeah, okay." He did have a point about him being talented when it came to knocking people off, and he'd already shut down her illusion once. He could deliver on that promise, he really could, and she had to believe that. She needed to relax. Stressing about a future that might never come wouldn't solve anything. All that ever worked was taking it slow and having a plan. "What about the other stages?"

Quinn gave her a look like he knew she wasn't fine. "Transference occurs when my weapon recognizes you as my mate, and you'll be able to call it to serve you." He began to massage her neck muscles, and she realized she'd coiled herself up into a wad of tension. "The last one is trust, which involves an act that reveals our ultimate trust in the other one. Often it takes the form of revealing your darkest secret. Sometimes it's giving your mate the power to kill you." He shrugged. "Trust comes in a lot of different forms."

"Trust?" She had learned not to trust anyone, not with what really mattered. And secrets? She shuddered at the thought of telling Quinn what she'd never told anyone, what no one would ever know except Ana. "Well, that's safe, then. I'm not that kind of girl."

"That's too bad." His eyes glittered with challenge.

"I think trusting your team is the most important weapon you can have in battle. That's the one thing I'd want us to have before we take on this hell we're facing."

Grace lifted her chin. "Don't start with me, Quinn. I'm not one of your Order members. I'm just me, and I can't do this your way, okay?"

"Trust has to come, or we fail." Looking aggravatingly confident with his declaration, Quinn leaned back, propping himself up against the pillows, continuing before she could argue. "So, that's what we're dealing with. Blood Exchange. Death. Transference. Trust. And sex."

Grace rubbed her forearm, realizing the futility of arguing with him. She'd survived just fine on her own, and she didn't believe him that they had to be intimate confidants in order to be effective. There were many paths to survival, and for her, it was all about understanding the threats so she could deal with them. "So, as long as there's one stage left undone, we're okay, right?"

Quinn's hand slid down her arm and began kneading the marks in her forearm, almost absently, like he didn't realize he was doing it. She liked his touch; she liked the comfort from their connection. Was that the bond, or just the truth that it felt better not to be alone? She sighed, too drained to push him away. She wanted his touch, and she would take it.

"As long as we don't complete the bond," Quinn agreed, "destiny won't be triggered."

"Okay, so we can do this." She took a deep breath, then crawled back across the bed and climbed in next to him. She needed the comfort of his body against hers, of his arms around her. "We'll stop and pick up some Band-Aids and gauze pads in case we get into a bleeder situation, so there's no accidental blood exchange, and we'll be good."

He chuckled and the bed shifted as he eased down beside her. "We save the world by having an ample supply of gauze pads. Sounds like the birth of a new legend to me."

"I think bucking the *sheva* destiny would be a good legend to initiate." She stared at the ceiling, too tense to relax. Her forearms were throbbing. Her imagination or real? Not that it mattered. The marks on them were very real.

She was his. There was no denying how much better it felt to be snuggled against him than separated from him. It was terrifying beyond words, but at the same time...she had a place. For the first time since her parents had died, she had a place in this world she could count on. She had a foundation that couldn't go anywhere. Granted, it was a tenuous place with a real potential downside, but that didn't change the fact that in the moment, for the first time in too long, she belonged. She was connected to someone who would stand by her no matter what. It was like a gift she'd long ago given up ever having again.

"Yeah, it would be a good one to start." Quinn took her hand and leaned over her. His dark hair was tousled, his brown eyes serious, his shoulders powerful and strong. "You need to understand something, Grace. I'm hardwired to protect. It's why I was selected for the Order, because I'm willing to kill friends to save innocents." He laid his hand over her heart. "You fall under my protection." He tapped the mark on her arm. "You're number one, now. Keeping people safe is what I do, and you get all of me. Got it? Count on me. It's okay. I'm tough as shit, and I believe I'm tougher than destiny."

Grace pressed her lips together as her throat tightened with emotions she had tried so hard not to feel. She knew he meant it. She wasn't alone anymore. She really wasn't. He was there for her.

"Grace? I'm not moving until you tell me that you understand." He managed to look slightly annoyed. "I'm one of the most deadly badasses who has ever walked the earth, and as your mate, I will take it as a personal insult if you refuse to believe how well I can protect you."

She burst out laughing then, the tension rushing out of her at the affronted look on his face. "You're so insane."

He grinned, a smile that made his eyes crinkle. "But tough, right?"

She held out her hands in capitulation. "Fine. So tough. Unstoppable."

"Perfect. That's all I needed to hear. I need to know that my woman isn't afraid." He kissed her quickly and then tossed back the covers and hopped out of bed. Just the sight of his bare backside as he stepped over the stack of bags was enough to make delicious fantasies swirl through her mind…. Oy. She was turning into a lust-craved maniac. Was Quinn right that it wasn't the bond? That it was just her? Maybe she really was some sort of sexual goddess of desire, and she'd just never met the right guy before. That was always a possibility, right?

Would it be a good thing or a bad thing if her mind-boggling attraction to him was all her own doing? Grace wasn't sure. "How is it that you manage to make me laugh when I'm about to cry?"

"Habit." Quinn flipped aside his jacket and found his jeans. "I do it with my team all the time. Tension relief always helps with focus." He picked up his pants, shoved his hand in the pocket and pulled out what appeared to be a small, round rock. "Never had to have sex to clear my head though. That's a first."

She propped herself up on her elbows, thoroughly enjoying his shameless nakedness. His muscles were taut and strong, his wide back angling down to strong buttocks and thighs that were sheer bulk and strength. She sighed, a totally girly moan of appreciation. She had to admit, she had good taste in choosing him as the man to awaken the wanton hussy she was apparently always meant to be. "Yeah, well, I've never let a guy I just met rip my clothes off. Firsts all around." Her gaze settled on the stone he held.

"That's Elijah's *mjui*?"

"That's it." His right arm flashed with black light, and his sword appeared in his hand with a loud crack that made her cover her ears. "Only a Calydon weapon can access a *mjui*. We're a very elitist bunch when we die."

She scooted forward, curious. "How do you read it?"

"With violence, of course. What else?" Quinn set the stone on the floor, then raised the sword. It cut through the air with a swish as he brought it down, the blade easily piercing the stone. Blue smoke began to emanate from the rock. "It's like magic."

"It's beautiful." Grace edged closer to watch. The smoke was a vibrant, swirling miasma of blues and greens as it spiraled toward the ceiling. The faint scent of pine and woods filled the air, as if they were back at The Gun Rack again. "Did it absorb the smell of the woods?"

"Yeah." Quinn crouched beside it, watching it intently. "It came from the earth at that spot, so that's what it's made of." The stone began to turn blue, the same color as the smoke. "It's ready." Quinn lifted his sword and plunged it into his thigh.

"Quinn!" Grace gasped as he twisted the blade in his thigh with a grunt of pain, and then yanked it out of his leg. "What are you doing?"

"I told you, sweetheart. Violence. It's our way." He winked at her, as if he didn't have a gaping sword wound in his thigh. "Blame Ezekiel. The bastard condemned us." With a nonchalance she couldn't imagine, Quinn picked up the glowing stone and placed it on his leg where the wound was pulsating with a weird, black glow. It wasn't bleeding, not quite, but it was raw and ragged. He placed his palm on the stone, then shoved hard with a grunt, forcing it into the hole he'd made in his leg.

"Oh." She sat up, holding her hand to her chest. "That hurts."

"Nah. It's all good." Sweat beaded on Quinn's brow as he wedged it into his body, and his jaw twitched, but he made no other indication of how much it had to hurt.

The rock pulsed in his thigh, the blue making his entire quad glow as if it were on fire with turquoise flames. There was a faint humming noise, and Quinn's jaw flexed with pain as he pressed his palm to his quad. "Come on," he muttered. "Accept me."

"What are you waiting for?"

"The *mjui* has to choose whether to release the truth. It's fighting me, which it shouldn't because I have Elijah's blood in my system—" The light suddenly faded, and his leg returned to a normal flesh color as the injury sealed itself up with a soft whooshing sound. "Done." He stood up, showing no indication of what had happened, other than a jagged red scar on his thigh. He palmed his sword, and it vanished from sight.

Her own forearm burned as his sword returned to his body, and she rubbed her skin restlessly. "I can't believe you stabbed yourself."

Quinn gave her a flippant look. "And to think you doubted how tough I was."

She managed a strangled noise that couldn't quite qualify as a laugh. "Seriously, Quinn, you didn't need to do that to convince me."

"I always need to impress my woman. It's a guy thing." He gave her a grim smile, showing his resignation about the monster he was. "And now you fear me."

"No." Grace would never judge Quinn for what he had to do. She knew all too well that a tough situation could force someone into brutal actions just to survive. She realized her hands were clenched and she quickly relaxed them. "I just wasn't expecting you to shove your own sword in your leg. What happens now?"

"I dream." Quinn walked over to the bed, still naked, and clearly not caring. His face was hard and focused, concentrating on the battle they were facing. No passionate lover now. Just warrior. "I dream of Elijah's death."

Grace scrambled out of the way as Quinn climbed into the bed and stretched out. "I'll be out for a few hours. When I wake, we'll head out to meet Gideon at the fishing cabin." He stretched his long legs over the comforter, like a predator easing off for an afternoon siesta. "My instincts are telling me it's safe for me to sleep. Illusion check?"

Grace did a quick scan. "Same as always. You've got a hitchhiker but nothing that seems to be active."

Quinn nodded, closed his eyes, clasped his hands over his abdomen and relaxed. His breathing slowed almost immediately and she realized he was already asleep. She studied him as he slept, inspecting the new scar on his thigh and the brand on his forearms, realizing the truth of what he was.

He wasn't simply a man who had saved her from an illusion and agreed to help find her sister. He was a Calydon who lived by his sword, whose destiny was to kill. A man who had been briefly murdered by his best friend. He knew betrayal. He knew isolation. His fate as a Calydon was to die by violence, to spend his life fighting until it destroyed him, whether death came by his *sheva's* hand or in battle. He was violence, he was a warrior, and he brought into her world everything she didn't want. Sex with a stranger. Blood exchanges. Turning her into a killer? Into his *sheva*? Into a woman who thrust herself into his bed without a thought for protection, for sanity or for her future?

God, what was she doing with him?

Grace hugged her knees against her chest, knowing full well why she was with him. She was saving her sister, and the cost didn't matter. Quinn was her last resort, and she had nothing left to lose. Without him, her sister was dead, and if that happened, nothing else mattered.

But as her gaze dropped to Quinn's face, and she studied his dark eyelashes resting against his cheeks as he slept, Grace knew that the longer she stayed with him, the more personal it would become. Already, she knew it was a lie to try to claim it was only about her sister. It wasn't any more.

Would the bond eventually trump her goal of saving her sister? Would her need for Quinn tear her away from that which mattered most to her? Was the very man who was the answer to her prayers actually going to be the cause of her losing everything?

Grace rubbed her hand over her new marks and knew she could no longer convince herself to believe that everything would work out. She didn't know what would happen. She didn't have the answers. Not anymore.

All she could do was try, but would that be enough?

She bowed her head and thought of Ana, praying she would somehow be strong enough to survive it all and save her sister.

⬥⬥⬥

Quinn concentrated on Grace's familiar scent as he drifted off into the sleep of the *mjui*, setting her as his anchor to find his way back out of the dream. Consciousness began to fade, and then he was in Elijah's body, becoming the man whose death he was about to live through.

He was back in The Gun Rack, sitting across from a man who looked exactly like the image Grace had pulled from Ana's illusions. Quinn instantly knew he was a Calydon.

The moment Quinn took up residence in Elijah's mind, he felt Elijah's stress. His head was pounding, his heart was racing and he was sweating. Even the room seemed to blur.

Quinn hadn't expected that response from the man who was as cool in battle as any Order member. It had to be bad shit for Elijah to be that rattled.

"Elijah," the man said.

Elijah nodded, tension rippling through him. "Nate."

Nate. They had a name now. Anticipation rushed through Quinn. Minutes into the dream, and they already had more information. *I'll avenge your death, Elijah. I give you my word.*

Nate gave a thin smile. "Give me the weapons you retrieved."

Elijah grabbed a duffel bag off the floor, where he'd had it stashed between his feet. He tossed the bag on the table, and it landed with a loud clunk. Quinn sensed Elijah's frustration, and his anger, his reluctance to hand over the bag and his inability to stop himself from doing it.

"Is this all of them?" Nate asked.

"Yeah." Elijah folded his arms over his chest and leaned back in his chair. A relaxed pose, but inside, he was a miasma of tormented stress and anxiety.

Nate unzipped the bag and rifled through it. Elijah didn't lean forward, so Quinn couldn't tell how many weapons were in there, but he could hear metal against metal, which meant there were at least two. Weapons again. Why would Nate need Calydon weapons? They wouldn't perform for him. What other use could he have for them?

Nate looked up sharply, his green eyes suspicious. "Quinn's weapon isn't here. Where is it?"

Quinn frowned. If Elijah didn't have it, who did?

Elijah didn't so much as flinch on the outside, but Quinn felt a stab of pain inside Elijah. Of grief. Of regret. "He got away." A lie.

Quinn grinned, realizing that even though Elijah had been unable to stop from handing over the weapons, he was still protecting Quinn. A traitor? No chance.

Nate narrowed his eyes. "Quinn got away?" He didn't sound like he believed it.

"Yes." Like Quinn, Elijah had been trained to lie perfectly, and now was no exception. But as Elijah spoke the words, the pain in his head increased and he had to grip the table to keep from losing his balance. Punishment for the lie? Resistance to whatever hold was compelling him?

Nate folded his arms and leaned back in his chair, his eyes studying Elijah with an intensity that made Quinn's brands tingle in warning. "You're lying," Nate said.

Elijah said nothing, but the throbbing in his head began to intensify even more, pressing so hard that Elijah finally cursed and pressed his palms to his forehead.

"Elijah, Elijah, Elijah." Nate leaned forward. "Tell me how you feel about Quinn. Your best friend, no?" There was a deep curiosity underlying his question, as if he wasn't sure what Elijah's answer would be. "You wouldn't really kill him, would you? I can't imagine—"

"Stop it!" Elijah jumped to his feet as rage exploded inside him, a hatred so strong that Quinn could feel it blackening his heart. "I don't hate Quinn," he growled. "I *won't* hate him." He hurled the bag of weapons at Nate so hard that Nate went over backwards with a grunt of pain.

Elijah lunged for Nate, but before he could reach him, pain hammered at his head. He fell to his knees, digging his fingers into his head as he bellowed with agony.

What was going on? Elijah's pain was a brutal torment, searing agony in his head. What was it? An illusion? Dammit. Quinn couldn't tell. *Grace! I need your help.* He injected urgency into his request and felt her awareness the moment she heard him.

Her response was instant. *What's wrong? Are you okay?*

Come in with me. Even as he made the request, Quinn pulled her into the dream, steeling himself as Elijah's torment continued to pummel him.

Quinn felt Grace's presence in his dream immediately, a gentle warmth that put a silver hue on everything. He was distantly aware of her nestling up next to him in the bed, as she reached out to him for an understanding of what she was experiencing.

We're in Elijah's body as if we were living what he experienced. Quinn didn't have time for a slow intro, because the dream was still progressing. *Is he under an illusion?*

There was a sharp stab of pain in Elijah's neck and he looked up. Nate was standing above him, a dagger at the warrior's throat.

That's the man who has Ana! Grace sounded shocked.

I know. His name is Nate.

Is Ana there?

I haven't seen her, but we can only see what Elijah notices. She could be right behind him and we wouldn't notice unless he turned around.

Nate's eyes were glittering with anger and... amusement? "It pisses me off when people throw things at me," Nate said, standing over Elijah, who was still down on his knees, gripping his pounding head. "Now, what the hell's going on with you and Quinn? Did you kill him? Do you hate the bastard or what? Because that's what I heard was supposed to happen, but all I'm getting from you is a bunch of loyalty for him. What's the deal?"

There was a sudden assault of hatred in every level of Elijah's soul, a brutal abhorrence that was pulsing and alive. Quinn was shocked by the intensity of Elijah's emotions, by the sheer force of his hate. It was nothing like the Elijah he knew. *Grace. What's going on with him?*

Grace quickly turned her focus onto Elijah, taking Quinn with her as she traveled metaphysically through Elijah's body. At first, there was nothing but a neutral gray, and then they got to his stomach. It was glowing with a deep iridescent orange, nearly pulsating with energy, wrapped around his core so tightly.

That's an extremely powerful illusion. Grace probed softly at it.

Can you tell me what the illusion is?

Hatred. True and relentless hatred. For you. I think he's been fighting it, and he finally succumbed.

Quinn felt like punching the air in victory. Elijah hadn't betrayed him voluntarily. Not on any level. *That's what I needed to know.*

Elijah reached behind him, pulled something from a strap across his back, and then he held out Quinn's sword. "Is this what you want?"

Nate couldn't mask his surprise. "You actually killed him?"

Elijah's fist closed around the blade of the sword until blood dripped from his palm, then he dropped it with a clatter. "He's dead."

Nate's eyes followed the sword, and so did Elijah's. They both reacted in surprise when the weapon shimmered and began to fade.

"Shit!" Nate grabbed the weapon off the floor. "You lied! If you harvested his weapon at the moment of death, it wouldn't fade!"

Quinn felt Elijah's shock and his staggering relief. "I didn't kill him." There was awe in his voice as he fell to his knees, his palms pressing against his eyes. "I didn't kill him," he repeated.

The illusion's gone, Grace whispered. *He just broke through it. The news that you survived pulled him through.*

Elijah's head snapped up and he eyed Nate. Quinn was hit with the new rage building inside Elijah, directed at Nate this time. This was different than the tormented, anguished hate for Quinn. This was the cold, hard anger of a warrior on a mission. "You messed with me." Elijah's voice was low, laced with such lethal violence that Quinn knew Elijah wasn't in control of his rage. He almost sounded... rogue? Shit!

Nate grabbed the bag of weapons and sprinted out

the back door.

Elijah stared after him for a long minute, then he stood up, dusted his knees off, and took a quick scan around the bar, not giving chase.

Everyone was staring at him, beers frozen in people's hands, darts hanging limply from fingertips. He growled, and everyone jerked their gazes off him and pretended not to have been staring.

Elijah searched for another moment, clearly looking for someone.

I don't see Ana, Grace said. *Where is she?*

Keep watching. Maybe we'll see what's going on. Why hadn't Elijah gone after Nate immediately? What or who could he be looking for that would be worth losing Nate, especially after Nate had forced him to kill Quinn?

Elijah didn't find whatever he was seeking and abandoned the hunt almost immediately. Instead, he sprinted after Nate, calling his throwing star out of his right arm as he went into hunting mode.

Quinn felt Elijah gather his thoughts, ratchet down his emotions and retreat into the cold, emotionless state of an Order member before he killed. Nate was going to die.

Elijah threw open the back door and stepped out into the dark night. There was no sign of Nate, so he eased to a stop to ferret out his quarry before taking action.

The night was quiet, the earth making crackling noises as the rain earlier in the day settled into the moist ground, the steady drips as the trees released the raindrops off the tips of their leaves. The scrabble of rodent feet, the hoot of an owl.

There was a scuffle from the left, and Elijah spun in that direction, his throwing star in his palm. Ready.

A woman stumbled into view around the corner of the bar.

Ana! Grace's anguish hit Quinn hard as Ana stumbled and went down on her knees. Her legs and arms were bleeding. Her shirt was torn. She had dark hair like Grace's, but it was tangled around her shoulders, stuck to the blood on the side of her face.

Oh, God. Grace's voice was full of horror, and Quinn felt that same sense of disbelieving shock ripple through Elijah when he saw the battered woman.

The warrior didn't hesitate. He strode immediately to Ana's side and scooped her up in his arms, even as he kept his throwing star ready. Quinn could feel the trembling of Ana's body against Elijah's and he knew Grace could, too. Their minds were so merged that her tears wet his own cheeks, her anger made his own body vibrate.

"No, no, no." Ana shoved at Elijah's shoulder, trying to get him to let her go. "Put me down! I'm a trap! You have to run. Save yourself."

"Screw that." Elijah tucked her against his left hip to free his right hand. "Who did this?"

"Let me go!" She fought against him, her body twisting in panic. "He's going to kill you!"

"Let him try." Elijah tightened his grip around her, holding her snugly against his chest despite her struggles. "Nate did this to you, didn't he?" There was a calmness in his voice that hadn't been there before, a clarity to his thoughts, as if touching Ana had grounded him. Before, he'd been a violent killer on the edge of going rogue. Now, he was clear, focused, and far more deadly.

Ana shook her head and pushed at his shoulder. "No, don't. He'll kill you. You have to go!"

"No." Elijah gently wrestled her until she was pinned against him, his arms bulging with the effort of immobilizing her. "I'm not leaving you behind."

She froze, staring at him with silver eyes that looked exactly like Grace's. "But I'm going to kill you," she whispered. "You have to leave me."

"No chance."

Her eyes widened with the realization that Elijah

wasn't going to abandon her, and Quinn saw such hope on her face that his own heart tightened for her. "What's your name?" Ana whispered.

"Elijah Ross."

"I'm Ana Matthews—" She suddenly groaned, and sadness filled her bruised face. "Oh, no."

She's about to do an illusion. Grace's voice whispered through Quinn's mind. *It's a dark one.*

Ana sagged against Elijah. "It's coming. I'm so sorry. I can't stop it."

"What's coming?" Elijah tucked Ana closer against him as he raised his star, searching the night for whatever impending threat Ana had sensed.

"An illusion," she whispered. "I'm what's going to kill you."

"An illusion?" Elijah shuddered and lost his grip on Ana. He barely caught her before she hit the ground, his body shaking so hard he could barely pull her back up to his hip. "You're an *Illusionist*?" There was such anger, such hate and such deep-seated terror in his voice that Ana jerked her head up to look at him.

Her eyes filled with tears at whatever she saw on his face. "Oh, Elijah," she whispered. "What did my kind do to you?"

But before Elijah could answer, the sky thundered and rain began pouring. Elijah held out his hand, then made a noise of shock when he realized it wasn't rain.

It was the crimson red of blood. Drenching him. Cascading out of the heavens. Still hot as it ran down his arm.

Elijah cursed and pulled Ana tight against him, trying to shield her with his body, his Calydon instincts forcing him to protect her despite his clear horror at her revelation that she was an Illusionist. His body was shaking, his mind was a blurred mess, and he was talking in an old language Quinn didn't recognize.

Anger, hatred, terror, violence whirled through Elijah and he staggered even as he tried to wipe the blood off Ana, his hands shaking as he continued to rant in some undecipherable language.

"Stop!" Ana was crying now, her tears mixing with the blood on her face. "For God's sake, stop helping me! The illusion is a distraction so he can kill you, if I don't do it first. Please, please, let me go!"

Wetness sloshed around Elijah's ankles and he looked down at the ground. Quinn felt Elijah's rising horror when he realized the blood pooled around his feet was rising fast and hard. Certainty rushed through Elijah that he was going to drown, an illusion-triggered response that wasn't how the real Elijah would react to a threat. His emotions and perception of reality were being manipulated by the illusion, exactly how Quinn had first feared the fire in his house. Difference was, Quinn had shaken it almost instantly. Elijah was getting sucked in with no way out, and his pulse skyrocketed as he hauled Ana higher up on his body, desperately trying to get her to safety instead of trying to protect himself from what he thought was certain death.

Saving her instead of saving himself.

"Let me go." Ana pulled back and tried to twist out of his grasp again. She accidentally grabbed his throwing star, and the point pierced her skin.

Elijah swore and jerked his weapon back. "Are you all right?"

"Please don't die for me. I'm not worth it." Ignoring his question, she grabbed his shoulders, her face desperate. "Run while you can."

"Nate's the one who hurt you, isn't he? If I let you go, he'll do it again." Fierce protectiveness laced Elijah's words and he tightened his grip on her.

She shook her head. "It doesn't matter—"

"It does." Elijah's voice was strained, his muscles

tense as he spun around and started sprinting through the woods, away from the battle, away from his chance to kill the man who'd manipulated him. He cradled Ana tightly against his chest. "I'm not leaving you behind."

She pummeled her fists against his shoulder, desperation making her frantic. "It's a trap," she said. "I'm just bait so he can hurt you—"

"No, Ana." He looked down at her, and in his tormented mind was the clarity of a man who knew exactly what he was doing, who knew precisely the choice he was making. "I'm the man who is meant to save you."

She stared at him, tears filling her silver eyes, as hope gave life to her streaked face. "Okay, Elijah," she whispered, her voice raw with emotion as she slipped her bruised arms around his neck, a tentative gesture of acceptance and desperate faith. "Thank you—"

There was a flash of movement, and they both looked up as Nate lunged at them, a dagger gleaming in his hand. Ana screamed as Elijah twisted, tucking her against him as he dove to the side, hurling his throwing star at their assailant—

Nate's blade plunged into Elijah's throat. *Ana.* Her name tore through Elijah's anguished mind, and then the dream went black.

CHAPTER 10

Ana winced as the throbbing ache in her palm pried her from restless sleep. Reluctantly, not wanting to see the reality of her circumstances, she opened her eyes. Cement walls, iron bars on the windows, everything painted steel gray. A toilet in the corner. She was back in her cell, Ana realized with a crush of despair. Again.

She didn't even remember how she'd gotten here this time. She couldn't recall what nightmare Nate had thrust her into on their latest trip. It was a blessing to forget. A respite she knew wouldn't last.

Ana rolled over with a groan. Every muscle, every bone, every inch of her hurt.

The memory of Nate's last beating hit her, and too soon the last few days came tumbling back. The fire in the woods. The uplifting realization that Grace was searching for her, and then the subsequent terror that her sister would be hurt trying to help her. She grimly remembered the hell of being dragged through the Oregon woods by Nate, her body so beaten and exhausted she'd been unconscious half the time. The bar...*Elijah.*

Ana's heart leapt into her throat at the memory of his strong arms, and the intensity of his expression when he'd said those words that had been haunting her sleep ever since. *I'm the man who is meant to save you.*

Had it been real? Had *he* been real? Had there really been someone with a good heart, the soul of an angel, who had believed she was still worth rescuing after all she'd done? Afraid to look, afraid to find out it was all an illusion, Ana stole a peek at her palm.

Her heart tightened when she saw the puncture wound from Elijah's throwing star. There it was. Truth. Reality. The injury she'd gotten while trying to persuade Elijah to abandon her to save himself, when he'd refused. She'd been marked by his death. Tears filled her eyes and she pressed her hand to her chest as the rest of the memory vividly tore away at the gift of being held by someone who treasured her.

Elijah's death. His voice calling for her so desperately as he'd died. The weight of his body as he'd fallen to the earth, Nate's knife in his throat.

Ana dropped her hand back to the cot with a moan, as despair overwhelmed her in a crushing flood. She'd clung to Elijah as he'd fallen, as life had bled from his body. She'd fought to hold on to him, to give him a link to life to hang onto, but he'd slipped away, dying in her arms just as she'd lost consciousness, unable to hang on any longer.

A courageous warrior had died for her. He'd died because he'd tried to save her, instead of saving himself. How was it possible that he'd made that choice? Elijah Ross was a stranger, a man who had no reason to give up his life for hers, and yet he'd done it anyway.

Ana had felt him recoil when she'd told him she was an Illusionist, and yet he'd stayed. He'd planted his stubborn feet and claimed her life as more valuable than his. Why would he do that?

Guilt pressed down on Ana, guilt and shame for all the people who had died trying to protect her. Her parents. Elijah. Grace's suffering and sacrifices on her behalf. If Ana was stronger, if she was smarter, if she was better, no one would have had to make those choices. "Dammit, Elijah" she shouted. "Why did you do that?"A man with that sense of honor and that kind of beauty in his soul should still be alive, not dead because he'd chosen her life over his.

Of all the warriors who'd died because of her over the last few months, Ana could think only of Elijah. She would never forget the way he'd looked at her as he'd picked her up, as if she were an angel of light brought into his life. The fierceness of his expression when he'd seen her bruises—in that one second, she'd thought her nightmare was over: the torment, the beatings, the killings, and the hell of what she had become. She'd finally believed that she'd found her path to safety and freedom. She'd thought she was free.

And then… God… to have it all end like that, with such violence, with Elijah's death… Ana's heart swelled with pain, and all the loneliness and isolation and fear she'd been holding back crashed down on her, crushing her—

The door creaked and Ana sucked in her sobs, trying to catch her breath so Nate wouldn't see her cry. She couldn't let him know how much Elijah's death had affected her. Somehow, he'd use it against her. The connection she and Elijah had made in that terrible moment had been private, something special that she would never tarnish by allowing Nate to touch it.

Elijah was dead, yes. But he'd died for her, and that would bind them forever. Ana rolled onto her side, away from the door, and she wiped her cheeks, trying to pull herself together. She braced herself for the sound of Nate's voice, for the nauseating feel of his hand on her arm.

But there was no smug laughter about who they'd killed.

There was no claustrophobic touch to her body.

There was simply the quiet shuffle of gentle footsteps, not the forceful sound of Nate's boots hitting the cracked cement floor. It sounded like a woman, like kindness, like hope. But how was that possible? Was Ana imagining it? She was too tired to believe. Too drained to face one more disappointment.

But Ana rolled over to face the room anyway, because hope was all she had left. Once she gave up on that, she knew she would die. So she opened her eyes a slit to inspect the room, and then blinked in surprise.

It was a woman with a tray of food. A woman about her age. A woman with a gentle sway to her hips and a kindness to her face. Not a danger. A friend?

Hoping against hope, fighting against disbelief, Ana watched silently as the woman crossed the room and set the tray next to the cot. The newcomer was wearing a flowing white skirt that drifted around her legs, and a white cotton camisole. She was barefoot, and her pale blond hair hung limply around her shoulders, tucked behind her ears. Her clothes were slightly tattered and dirty, but she held her chin at an angle that spoke of courage and strength.

She met Ana's gaze and smiled, her moss-green eyes full of warmth and empathy. "I brought food."

"I see that." Ana flinched at her guarded tone. "Thank you," she added, trying to find her way back to the person she used to be. Someone who was pleasant, who found joy in the small things in life. Like having food and someone to talk with who wasn't wielding a knife. "Who are you?" Her voice sounded raspy, and she took the glass of water from the tray, letting the cool liquid soothe her parched throat.

"My name is Lily." The woman sat back on her heels, glancing at Ana's legs. Sadness filled her eyes, and Ana followed her gaze. Her legs were covered in bruises, black, purple, yellow. Not an inch of unmarred skin remained. Cuts everywhere, some of them oozing, others freshly cleaned. By Lily?

"Nate got to me," Ana said.

Lily met her gaze. "When he brought you in last night, I thought you wouldn't recover."

Defiance flashed through Ana, and she made herself sit up. "I'm not ready to die. I have to kill him first." She cringed at the sentiment, at the violent words that seemed to tumble so freely from her mouth now. She wouldn't let him turn her into that kind of person, no matter what. "I mean, I need to get away from him. I need to go home."

Something flashed in Lily's eyes, but it was gone before Ana could identify it. Anger? Empathy? Longing? She wasn't sure. "I know how you feel."

"Do you work for him?" Ana asked tentatively. Was it really possible Lily was on her side? That she wasn't alone here anymore?

"No. I'm his prisoner, like you." Lily glanced at the door, as if half-expecting Nate to walk in. "I talked him into letting me bring you food and check on your injuries. I wanted to make sure you were healing." Anger simmered in those gentle eyes. "He's resting up."

"Resting up for what?" The room began to spin as pain took over, and Ana scrunched her eyes closed against a wave of dizziness.

"I'll kill you if you want," Lily said. Her beautiful green eyes were hard with reality. "Spare you what's to come." There was a gritty realization in Lily's face that said she knew what Nate would do to her if she killed his precious toy, but she was willing to do it anyway. For Ana.

"Thanks, but I'm not willing to give up yet." Ana eyed her thoughtfully, rejuvenated by the camaraderie with this stranger. For the first time since she had been stolen, she had a connection to someone. Her first real break. "How long have you been here?"

"Two years."

Ana's stomach turned, and all her newfound energy dissipated. "*Two years?* You've been his prisoner for two years?"

"Yes." Lily's eyes were haunted. "My elegant lodgings are just down the hall from you. Same décor. So lovely, aren't they?"

Ana was startled by Lily's humor, so out of place in this nightmare. But at the same time, it felt like a breath of normalcy to quip lightly. It felt good, and she understood why Lily had done it. How else was she still sane after two years here? "I hear crumbling cement is quite the rage in New York these days," Ana managed to reply, trying to follow Lily's lead and find some kind of relief from this hell they were trapped in.

"I'm sure it is." Lily winked, then she leaned forward and lowered her voice, her amusement gone. "I heard Nate talking. He has plans that will require an extremely powerful illusion from you. Very deadly. He'll do whatever it takes to make you do it."

Ana couldn't help but shudder. More blood? More death? Murdering another innocent man? She thought of Lily's offer to kill her. Was Ana being selfish by wanting to stay alive? Her existence was causing more people to die. Was it fair of her to turn down an offer to rid the world of the threat she brought? Maybe not. Maybe she should accept it.

But dammit! She didn't want to die! She wasn't brave enough to sacrifice her own life to save all those Calydons, but the warriors she'd helped kill would haunt her forever.

Especially Elijah. She shuddered as she remembered the visceral hatred burning in his eyes once he'd realized she was an Illusionist. That hadn't been simple prejudice. It had been personal, and she ached for him, for whatever had been done to cause that kind of response in him.

"Ana? Would you like me to kill you?" The pleasant tone in Lily's voice was in such sharp contrast to the words rolling so easily off her tongue. Lily's eyes were hard, but at the same time, they were so laden with exhaustion and fear that Ana's heart tightened for her. They were the same, she and Lily. Caught in Nate's trap without any way out.

Surviving from breath to breath, praying that the next one would bring the freedom they were living for.

"No." She met Lily's gaze, wondering how exactly Lily had planned to kill her. She didn't look strong enough. "But I appreciate the offer." She hesitated, suddenly afraid of losing her. "Can you come again? Will I see you?"

"Probably not. It was difficult enough to get in to see you this time, but I had to talk to you. I needed to let you know you weren't alone." She smiled. "No matter how hard it gets, remember that I'm here too." She pointed to the right. "I'm just down the hall, and I'm always here. He doesn't let me outdoors. It helps to know you're not alone."

Ana nodded. "It does," she agreed.

"I have to go." Lily rose from her knees, her movements slow as if she, too, were hurting. "Nate's vulnerability is the stone. Take it from him."

"The what?"

"The stone. I heard him talking about it, and I know it's critical, but I haven't found it and I don't know what it's for. But it's clear that it's a source of great power. If you find it, take it. Use it against him." She pushed her hair out of her face. "That's your only chance."

Ana nodded, her fists clenching in determination. For the first time, she had a goal, a target, a possible way out. "I'll find it."

Lily smiled, a sad smile that burned with the same will to live that Ana had. "Good."

The door opened and a heavily muscled Calydon leaned into the room. "Time's up."

"I'm coming." Lily pulled her shoulders back and walked across the floor with staunch pride, showing none of the exhaustion she'd let Ana see. As she reached the door, she glanced back at Ana one last time, her green eyes seeming to urge Ana not to give up.

Then the door closed, cutting their connection. Lily's soft footsteps faded down the hall, leaving only silence behind, a silence that seemed to loom so much larger and thicker than it had before Lily had brightened the room with her friendship and empathy.

Loneliness overwhelmed Ana as the one kind voice she'd heard in the last six weeks walked away. She groaned and buried her face in her pillow, trying to suppress her tears. *I won't let him make me cry.*

She thought of Elijah, and how he'd stood his ground until the last second. She remembered the strength of his body, the determination in his gaze as he'd held her tight, the honor and courage he'd offered in the face of death. She clung to that image, to the memory of what it had felt like to have his arms wrapped around her, holding her up, protecting her. Slowly the urge to cry retreated, as if Elijah's power as a warrior was seeping into her and giving her the courage to fight a little longer.

Ana hugged herself and stared at the ceiling. She thought about the lead Lily had given her by telling her about the stone. Her key to escaping. The nebulous chance for a miracle escape that Ana had no information about, that somehow she would have to find.

The stone.

What was it? Could she find it? And if she did, then what? Would it really help her get away from Nate?

Ana rubbed her thumb over her injured palm, over the wound left from Elijah's weapon, and knew there was only one answer she could accept if she were to have the strength to keep on fighting.

The answer was yes.

※※※

Elijah hadn't betrayed him.

Quinn hadn't been able to stop thinking about Elijah's death the whole drive to the fishing shack. Elijah hadn't gone rogue. Not truly. He'd been manipulated into it, and then he'd shaken the compulsion and reclaimed his sanity. He didn't have to die. Quinn wouldn't have had to kill him, which meant that he'd gotten there too late. Again. He'd failed Elijah just like he'd failed his uncle. He might as well have wielded the blade the second time, as well as the first.

Quinn cursed and slammed his fist into the steering wheel.

Grace looked up from typing into Quinn's satellite computer, which she'd been using to try to find information on the type of illusion they were dealing with. "That's the seventh time you've punched the truck. Are you going to tell me what's wrong, or do I need to invade your privacy and find out for myself?"

He shot a surprised glance at her. "You were counting?" She'd been subdued since the *mjui* dream, and he knew she was worried about Ana. He hadn't thought she was paying attention to him.

"Of course I was." She closed the lid of the computer and faced him. "I feel your torment without even trying. Elijah didn't betray you. That's good, right?"

"Yeah, but since he wasn't rogue, I wouldn't have had to kill him. He didn't have to die." The truck tires spun in the mud as Quinn navigated up a steep embankment that was practically invisible in the thick fog, which still hadn't lifted. It was almost midnight, and they were right on time to meet up with Gideon. "If I'd found Elijah sooner—"

"You couldn't have found him sooner. You were still out cold when he got killed." Her voice was soft and non-judgmental. "And don't lie to yourself that you should have sensed you were under an illusion when you took the trainees to the river. Whoever is doing this is strong enough to make a Calydon murder his best friend. So you had no chance."

He shook his head. "It's my job to be better. That's what I do."

"I'm so sorry he died, Quinn." Grace touched his arm. "But you can't blame yourself."

"I don't—" He cut himself off as her hand folded around his. The touch was full of kindness, forgiveness, gentleness; things that hadn't been a part of his life for so long that he'd forgotten what they felt like.

Without a word, Quinn flipped his hand over and entwined his fingers in hers, as they reached the end of the access road to Dante's shack.

Quinn slammed the truck into park, tossed the computer onto the dashboard and pulled Grace across the seat toward him. He was immensely pleased when she came willingly and climbed onto his lap. He folded his arms around her and buried his face in the soft strands of her hair.

She wrapped her arms around his head, holding him close. "It's awful when people die," she said. "You don't have to lie about how much it hurts. Not with me. I know."

He didn't answer. He simply breathed in her scent, felt the heat of her body against his, and felt something deep inside him snap as she wrapped her arms around him and held him against her. "He wasn't supposed to die," he finally said, his voice gruff. He couldn't hold it back anymore. Couldn't turn down her offer of comfort.

"I know." She held him tight and pressed her lips to his head.

His eyes began to sting, and he pressed his face deeper into the curve of her neck, his throat raw, his chest aching. "I can't believe he's gone."

Her fingers stroked his hair, holding him close as his body began to shake.

"There are supposed to be three of us. It's always been the three of us." His voice was raw. "Now, there's just Gideon, and he's an asshole most of the time."

"I'm the asshole?" Gideon's amused voice shattered their intimacy.

Quinn jerked his head up out of Grace's hair. The fog was so thick he couldn't see even the hood of the truck, let alone Gideon. Quinn hauled his grief back in its cage and peeled his hands off Grace as she scooted back to her side of the truck.

Quinn opened his door, and Gideon materialized out of the darkness and fog. He hooked one arm over the frame and leaned down, his bulk filling up most of the doorway as he peered into the interior of the truck, his face unshaven and his blond hair damp from the moist night. His blue eyes settled immediately on Grace. "Hey."

She lifted her chin and gave him an unflinching inspection, even though Quinn could hear the pounding of her heart. "Hey, yourself."

"And you are?"

"Grace Matthews."

Gideon sniffed the air and tensed, a reaction so subtle Quinn wouldn't have noticed if he hadn't been waiting for it. Ever so casually, Gideon leaned further into the truck and inhaled again. Then Gideon's eyes narrowed, and he looked at Quinn. "You marked her."

The sword in Quinn's forearm tingled. "Yeah."

Gideon's eyes slid toward Grace again, then he held out his arm to call out his weapon. Quinn grabbed Gideon's forearm and threw him back onto his ass, moving with lightning speed.

Quinn jumped out of the truck and kicked the door shut behind him. "You hurt her, and I'll kill you." His sword was straining under the skin, desperate to leap out and sink itself into Gideon's chest.

Gideon vaulted back to his feet, dripping mud, a glistening double-bladed throwing axe with a spiked handle clenched in his hand. "Listen to yourself, Quinn. You're defending your *sheva*. The bond's changing you. I already lost Elijah." His voice was hard and lethal. "I'm not losing you. Step aside and let me kill her."

Quinn heard Gideon's words, and somewhere deep in his mind they registered as a truth. It wasn't his way to openly threaten his blood brother. He knew Gideon was right, that he was changing for Grace. But it didn't matter. He would not back down from protecting her, and if he had to kill Gideon to make her safe, he would.

The thought rocked Quinn back on his heels. Son of a bitch. He was ready to take out the one man still standing that mattered to him?

He saw Gideon's determination to save him, to cut down Quinn's *sheva* before Quinn went rogue, fulfilling the promise they'd all made to each other five hundred years ago. Quinn knew he would battle for Grace's safety every bit as hard as Gideon would strive to kill her. Hell. He had to defuse the situation quickly and come up with a reason for Gideon to back down. "Grace needs to live if we're going to defeat Ezekiel," he said evenly, keeping his voice cold and reserved, as if he had no personal stake in whether she lived or died.

Gideon paused, his blue eyes alert, ever the loyal Order member. "Why?"

"We're taking on at least one, maybe two Illusionists who are strong enough to force Elijah to kill me. Grace is an Illusionist, and she can help us deal with it. The Order needs her." He opened their link and showed him Elijah's death.

When he finished, Gideon was staring at him. "He didn't need to die."

"And she doesn't either."

Gideon's eyes narrowed. "How far along is the bond?"

"One stage. It's under control." Quinn shot his friend an arrogant grin, just to show him exactly how sane he still was. "You already know I think it's all a crock of shit anyway, this destiny thing. I'm not going rogue, my friend. You can count on it."

Gideon's jaw flexed, and for a long moment, tension hung in the air between the two warriors. Quinn's sword burned in his arm, but he didn't call it out. He waited, knowing that any sign that he was becoming overly aggressive would trigger Gideon into a pre-emptive strike.

Gideon finally gave a quick nod of his head. "I agree that she might be able to help us, and you aren't rogue." He sheathed his axe. "She's safe from me for now, but if I get any hint you're going rogue—"

"Enough of this crap."

They both turned around to find Grace standing about ten feet away from them with a gun aimed at Gideon. Quinn recognized it as one he kept stashed in the back of his truck, just in case he ever needed to fight a battle when he was out of swords. Desire rushed through him at the sight of her with his weapon. Yeah, that was his woman, facing down against one of the most deadly Order members in existence. *Nice, Grace. You know I want you more now.*

"Shut up, Quinn." Refusing to accept the intimacy of their mind-to-mind connection, Grace gave them both a grim stare. "While you guys have been wasting time discussing whether I get to live for another day, whoever it is that's been tracking Drew is getting closer and my sister is possibly being forced to murder someone else. Stop with the macho positioning, admit you're glad to see each other still alive, and help me find my damn sister!" Her voice cracked at the end, and Quinn felt her courage falter at the thought of her sister, but she didn't lower the gun or stop scowling.

I haven't forgotten about her, Grace. I'll find her.

"Oh, come on, Quinn," she glared at him with exasperation, and he tensed at her emotional withdrawal from him, the way she refused their mental connection. "You guys were talking about killing me. For real. Call me overly sensitive, but that kind of takes the romance out of a relationship pretty damn fast." She scowled at them both, frustration evident in her voice. "How could some stupid legend from two thousand years ago compel otherwise sane and powerful warriors to make such idiotic choices and waste time in such asinine discussions when there's so much at stake?"

Grace. He waited until she looked at him. *I will not let you down. I promise.*

Weariness flickered in her eyes, and he knew the moment she stopped fighting him. "I swear to God, Quinn, sometimes I want to shoot you."

He smiled. "I know. Most people do. It means you like me. I'll take it as a compliment."

His beautiful woman rolled her eyes, but the tension was past. "Of course you would. That's a guy thing, right, to think it's great when someone wants to kill you? No wonder 'asinine' was the word that came to mind to describe you guys. Seriously."

Gideon grinned and slapped Quinn on the shoulder. "Damn, man, I can see why you don't want her killed. She's not even my *sheva* and I like her."

"You were the one who wanted to kill me." She turned her hostility onto Gideon. "I hate it when men don't take me seriously." She raised the gun and shot the axe out of Gideon's hand, barely missing his fingertips.

The smile dropped off his face. "Where'd you learn how to do that?"

"Girl Scouts." She blinked as the axe dissolved into the forest floor, then pointed the gun at Gideon's heart.

He raised his brows and glanced at Quinn, who couldn't keep the shit-eating grin off his face. "Does she know she can't kill me with a simple bullet to the heart?"

"Yeah, probably. But I'm sure she has a follow-up plan, don't you, sweetheart?"

"Always." But instead of confidence, Quinn felt Grace's sudden drop in body temperature, and her rush of fear at the idea of killing someone. Her hands started to shake and a sheen of perspiration broke out on her forehead. "I just want to find my sister," she said. "I promise not to suck Quinn's blood, okay, Gideon? I don't do the blood bond, you don't sever my head from my body. Deal?"

Gideon's eyes narrowed. "You won't have a choice. The bond will compel you."

Oh, for heaven's sake! Did none of the men understand the power of a determined female? "Don't underestimate me, Gideon. And *don't* underestimate my commitment to my sister." She lowered the gun, clicked the safety on, and set the weapon onto the ground. Then she stalked off into the fog, completely unable to see where she was going.

"The shack's off to your right," Gideon called out.

"Right next to the steep cliff you're hoping I walk off of, I'm sure," she snapped, but she turned right and kept walking.

Grace.

She didn't turn around.

I won't let you die.

Not yet, at least. Her voice was resigned. *I'm glad I understand the truth now about this world you're from. I can never trust you, can I?*

Dammit, Grace. You can. Restlessness haunted him at the distance she was putting between them. He was going after her—

"Dante's dead." Gideon's words stopped Quinn in his tracks. "I could sense his death as soon as I got up to the cabin."

Quinn turned back to Gideon. "You're sure?"

"Yeah."

"Hell." Quinn let out his breath and stared into the woods in the direction of Dante's shack, absorbing the news. "How are we going to take down Ezekiel without Dante? He's what keeps half the team on this side of rogue."

"I'm sure that's why Dante had to die." Gideon sounded equally grim. "Ezekiel's laying the foundation for his escape. We're all that's standing in his way, so he has to weaken us. He's clearly got someone on the outside helping him." He met Quinn's gaze. "Someone besides Elijah."

"We can't let him get out," Quinn said, his sword burning in his forearm again, this time with a fierce intensity that was almost painful. He frowned, pausing to assess the woods. His instincts didn't usually react to distant threats, just immediate ones. What danger was he sensing? "We have to find out how he's bringing down the walls and stop it before he does."

Gideon nodded. "Agreed. I sent out a call to the others. They're all here, up at the shack. We were waiting on you, but so far everyone's keeping it together. The threat of Ezekiel is enough to keep them focused for now—"

Son of a bitch. "They're here? Now? With my *sheva?*" That was why his instincts had been triggered. Because *Grace* was in danger. Not him.

"They're up at the campsite. We'll catch up to Grace before—" Gideon was cut off by a yelp from Grace and the loud crack of a Calydon's weapon being called into action.

Quinn was in a full sprint before the sound faded, Gideon right on his tail.

⚜

Grace stumbled backwards as a three-bladed sai appeared in the palm of the dark-haired warrior. The triple blade flashed in his hand as he whirled on her, his eyes black with deadly intent.

He thrust the sai toward her heart and she instinctively jerked her arm up to block it. A loud crack split the night, then Quinn's sword appeared in her hand and thrust deep into the warrior's gut.

The sai fell from his hand as he dropped to his knees, clutching his stomach, blood pouring from between his fingers.

"Oh, God." Grace scrambled to her feet, bile rising in her throat as the handle of Quinn's sword disappeared into the stream of blood. "I didn't mean to." She fell to the ground next to the warrior, holding his heavy shoulders as he crumpled to the soggy earth. "Please, God, no. Not again. Please—"

"Gabe! Don't!" Quinn's shout broke through the night, and she looked up to see another warrior standing above her, the blade of his hook sword glistening in the moonlight as he brought it down toward her.

She froze, realizing she had no time to get away.

There was another crack and a throwing axe careened past Grace's head. The flat of the handle bludgeoned Gabe's hand with a bone-crushing thud, less than an inch from Grace's head. He howled as his hand shattered under the blow and his hook sword went flying.

Grace scrambled back, stumbling over the warrior she'd stabbed as Gabe called out his other hook sword. Then hands grabbed her and flung her to the side as Quinn charged past her and threw his shoulder into Gabe's stomach. Grace's knee landed on a rock and she hit the dirt with a dizzying flash of pain as Quinn tackled her assailant.

Gideon dropped to his knees beside her victim and yanked Quinn's sword out of his gut. "Hang on, Zach," he ordered. "Stay with us."

Quinn flung Gabe onto his back and crushed his hands around his throat. "She is not to be touched," Quinn growled. "Do you understand?"

"She's your *sheva!*" Gabe fought against Quinn's grip. "We can't let her live. You know that."

The muscles in Quinn's arms bulged as he tightened his grip on Gabe's throat relentlessly, until the warrior began to gasp.

"Quinn!" Gideon ripped his shirt off and bunched it into the gaping hole in the downed warrior's gut.

"Enough! Let him go."

"He tried to kill her." Quinn's voice was ragged and fierce, nothing like she'd heard from him before.

"Oh, no. Quinn's going to kill him." Grace stumbled to her feet, slipping on the blood from her victim's wound, her knee screaming as it faltered under her. "Quinn, *stop*." She tripped in the underbrush as Gabe's face contorted with the effort of staving off death. She heard the crack of other warriors calling out their weapons, and she knew they were coming for Quinn.

"Let him go!" She fell into Quinn's shoulder, his muscles rock hard beneath her hands. "Quinn!" She pounded at his arm, her fingernails clawing at his wrists as she fought to get his hands off Gabe, but his fingers kept tightening, and trickles of blood began to slide down Gabe's neck.

"Dammit, Quinn!" She grabbed his hair and yanked his head back so she could see into his face. His eyes were glowing red, contorted with a deadly rage that was so violent she almost released him. She faltered for a second, horrified by the demon staring back at her. *No. This was Quinn. Not a demon.* "Quinn." She forced her voice to be calm, even as fear fought to overtake her. "Don't let the bond win."

There was no recognition in his eyes, just lethal rage consuming him, and Gabe's body began to convulse as death sank its fingers into him.

"No!" She threw her arms around Quinn's neck and slammed her mouth onto his, plunging her tongue past his clenched teeth, wincing as she sliced her tongue on them. The coppery taste of her blood was sharp on her tongue.

Quinn's body shuddered. His arms snapped around her like steel bands, and he threw her to the ground, covering her with his body. The heat of his erection pressed into her belly, and she trembled with sudden desire as he plundered her mouth. He thrust his tongue ruthlessly and drove his hips into hers, whipping her hormones into a rage even through their jeans.

His hand slipped beneath her waistband and his fingers plunged inside her. She gasped at the invasion as he razed his teeth over her tongue again. Pain echoed somewhere in her mind as he sliced her tongue with his teeth, clamped his lips over the cut and sucked on the wound, his hand still moving within her. He thrust his tongue again, raking it over the edges of her teeth as he drove deeper inside her with his fingers, stretching her with a decadent twist that sent delicious spirals through her. Desire built inside her until her body coiled, and still his mouth demanded her response, his hips driving against her until her body shook with a desire and a need so strong she couldn't think.

Then his tongue was between her teeth again, and she couldn't resist his offer any longer. She grazed her teeth over his tongue, and the coppery taste of his blood slid through her mouth, a delicious and amazing sensation that felt like the heavens had just swept her up into the skies and gifted her with the seeds of life. A sense of utter rightness blossomed through her as his fingers brought her over the edge into the whirling place where her body and soul were striving to go, as his voice filled her mind.

Mine to you. Yours to me. Bonded by blood, by spirit and by soul, we are one. No distance too far, no enemy too powerful, no sacrifice too great. I'll always find you. I'll always protect you. No matter what the cost. I am yours as you are mine.

She whispered the words back to him, the unfamiliar promise tumbling out on its own, as if she'd always held it in her spirit, waiting for it to be called to life. *Mine to you. Yours to me. Bonded by blood, by spirit and by soul, we are one. No distance too far, no enemy too powerful, no sacrifice too great. I'll always find you. I'll always keep you safe. No matter what the cost. I am yours as you are mine.*

Yes. His guttural sigh of triumph trumpeted through her as his fingers brought her body screaming into completion. The orgasm crashed into her, thrusting itself through every inch of her body. Her orgasm swept him up, and he came with her, his hips driving fiercely, his mouth locked down on hers with a passion that made her body rage with a wildness so far out of her control she knew she'd never return, never come back, never be the same.

CHAPTER 11

Quinn sagged into Grace's warmth. He pressed his face into the curve of her neck as he tried to regain his breath. His muscles were spent. His energy was drained, as if he'd thrust every last bit of his soul into Grace and left nothing for himself.

But Quinn didn't feel depleted. Intense satisfaction was like a bright light burning with fresh energy. Even as he lay there, his nerves tingled, and fresh strength surged into his muscles, rebuilding him with astonishing speed.

Quinn was so aware of Grace, tucked beneath his body. The steady beat of her heart was like an echo of his. The sated sensuality easing through her body soothed his own muscles. Each breath of air into her lungs filled his own with the crisp freshness of the mountain air. They were so connected, it was as if their souls were still tangled and wrapped in desire.

Grace's fingers were still clenching the front of his jacket as microscopic tremors rippled through her. Quinn loved the feel of her holding onto him, as if he were her anchor, the only thing keeping her grounded.

"Oh, wow." Grace let her head drop back against the ground, strands of her dark hair falling raggedly to the earth. "I thought you were gone," she said. "Your eyes were red."

Quinn tangled his fingers in her hair. "Nah. I was fine." But he wasn't sure he was telling the truth. He could still recall with vivid clarity how focused he'd been on making Gabe pay for threatening Grace. How far would he have taken it? Would he have killed his own teammate?

He would never know, because Grace had intervened. His courageous, insane, daring mate had thrown herself into the mix-up against all common sense. It had been foolhardy and dangerous, and yet she'd done it anyway. "Grace."

Her eyes slanted open, half-mast with exhaustion and relief. She managed a faint smile that resonated deep inside him. "Yes?"

Quinn kissed the tip of her nose. "You are too brave, woman. You should not have been jumping in the middle of that battle. Don't take charge of my safety. It's *my* job to look after *you*."

"Really?" Grace laughed softly and laid her hand on his face, her touch so soft and gentle, a sensation so foreign to him. "When are you going to learn that you don't get to boss me around, Quinn?"

He set his hand over hers, holding her palm to his face. "Never. I need to be in charge."

"I need to control my own life." Grace shook her head, but the denial was subdued and weary, a woman who had used up all the resources she had. "I knew I should have shot you back at the truck."

"Never. You think I'm fantastic."

She raised her brows. "And you think I'm fantastic, sexy, brilliant and amazing."

His smiled faded. "Yeah. I do." When her eyes widened with surprise, he knew his *sheva* really didn't get how much she brought to the table. "Damn, you're amazing, Grace." He leaned down and kissed her.

She sighed with pleasure and kissed him back, her hands going around his neck. Her mouth parted for his, and he deepened the kiss. His tongue brushed against hers, and he caught a faint coppery taste still lingering—

Oh, hell. Her blood. *Holy crap—*

Gideon invaded his mind. *Quinn.*

Shit. He'd forgotten the Order was all around them. Quinn wrapped his arm around Grace, sliding her more tightly beneath him as he lifted his head and took quick stock of their surroundings.

A rapid assessment of the dark forest told him that he and Grace were alone, but he could sense the Order standing just out of sight behind the nearest trees. Energy hummed through the air, and he knew they were all armed, ready to take him down the instant they thought he'd gone rogue. Their lust was thick in the air, crowding too close to Quinn's woman. Adrenaline rushed through Quinn and he went to his knees, still covering Grace, but ready to protect, prepared to defend.

Take it easy, Quinn, Gideon said. *They're already on edge and looking for a reason.*

Tell them to back off. Quinn shifted his weight to free his sword hand as Grace's eyes opened wide. She went still beneath him, suddenly alert. She eased her hand to the collar of his shirt and lightly grasped it, as if she could stop him from leaping up by that simple action.

Except it worked. The moment Quinn felt her tug on him, something inside him quieted. *Leave us alone, Gideon,* he said.

After that? I can't. I need to check in with you.

I'm not rogue. I won't jump anyone as long as they don't try to kill her. I may not be rogue, but I'm not dead either. If anyone messes with her, I will protect her. The effort of keeping his voice calm ground deep, when all Quinn wanted to do was jump up and do some macho shit to them for lusting after his woman. Yeah, not rogue, but not quite himself either.

Gideon laughed. *Point taken. Get your ass off her.*

We have a bad guy to catch.

Grace released his shirt and touched his lips, pressing her finger to them, worry creating a pucker between her eyebrows. Quinn looked down at her, and their gazes met with silent intensity. *We need a minute.*

Quinn felt Gideon touch his mind. He allowed him access the way he'd brought Grace in, so Gideon could see for himself that he wasn't rogue. Satisfied, Gideon agreed. *I'll take the men back to the fire. Make it quick. They're restless.*

How are Zach and Gabe?

They're both pissed at you. Zach was impressed with her, though. Said she's almost tough enough to beat your ass.

She is. Quinn agreed, relieved that both men would survive. *We'll be up there in five.*

They shut off the connection, and Quinn heard the whisper of movement through the woods as Order members vacated the area. He knew the moment he and Grace were truly alone. "Grace," Quinn whispered, shifting his position so he could see her face. She looked even more concerned, and her fingers were pressed to her own lips now. "You okay?"

She shook her head once. "Did we—" She stopped, uncertain.

"The blood exchange? Yeah, but we're still good. Got a few stages to go."

She closed her eyes and rested her palm on her forehead. "This is happening faster than we intended. It's taking us, Quinn—"

"No." He cut her off with more fierceness than he had intended. Now was not the time to doubt. Now was the time to get tougher. "We're stronger than it. For hell's sake, you took down an Order member when he was trying to kill you. You're motivated by your love for your sister, and there's nothing more powerful than that. My uncle broke through it, and so can we."

Grace chewed her lower lip as she searched his face, then she slowly nodded. "Okay."

He nodded. "Okay." Yeah, maybe in two thousand years, there'd been only one man who'd broken through the rogue state caused by a *sheva*, but where there was one, there could be others. Grace was gifted with an inordinate amount of strength, and she was driven by such intense love for her sister. He was putting his money on Grace, and since he was descended from the one man who'd done it… yeah. They could do it. "You ready to go take on a bunch of old-school warriors?"

"Wait." She grabbed his wrist. "Did I kill…" She stumbled over the question, but he knew what she was going to ask.

"Nah. Zach's a tough old bastard. He'll be fine, but I think he has a crush on you now."

Oblivious to his joke, she searched his face, and he was surprised by the depth of desperation in her eyes. "Really? You swear he's not dead? Or dying?"

Quinn took her hand and kissed her palm. "He's fine, sweetheart. We get more damage than that on a daily basis. It won't even leave a scratch."

"Oh, thank God," she whispered. She let her head drop back to the ground and scrunched her eyes shut, but not before the tears trickled free, sliding down her cheeks. She pressed her hand over her eyes, and her body started to shake.

"Hey, hey, hey." He rolled to his side, so he could pull her into his arms and hold her against his chest. "It's okay, *sheva*. It's over." He kissed her hair.

She shook her head, her hand still over her eyes, her body shaking even harder. "It won't be over. It will never be over."

"Grace. Listen to me. You didn't hurt him."

"I killed a man once. A boy. I killed a boy." Her

voice was ragged, her breathing raspy.

"Oh..." Quinn cupped her face as the tears started to fall for real, as her anguish pervaded his mind. He felt the truth of her words, and he finally understood her. Killing his uncle had changed him forever, forced him to harden himself, to find meaning and honor in his actions, or else it would have broken him. Quinn had trained his whole life to become an Order member. He'd been indoctrinated since birth on the need to slay the chosen few in order to save the rest, and yet killing his uncle had still been a brutal shock.

For Grace, with her tremendous capacity for love and loyalty, with her deep sensitivity toward hurting others, he knew it had to have rocked her to her core. Quinn wanted to tell her it was okay, that it didn't matter, but he knew those words were empty. Nothing could erase the magnitude of taking a life. So, instead of trying to comfort his woman with meaningless words, he took her hand, pressed his lips to her palm, and offered himself to carry her burden. "Tell me what happened," he said, letting her know through his voice that he didn't judge her. "I want to know."

Tears streaked down her cheeks and she looked past him at the night sky, as if she were remembering a past long forgotten. "I was fourteen and in foster care. One of the boys came into my room, thinking it was the bathroom. I panicked when I saw him fumbling with his fly, thinking he was coming after me. I didn't mean to, but I called out an illusion." Her voice thickened, heavy with tears and a lifetime of guilt. "It was knives." Her gaze flicked to his, so full of self-recrimination and horror. "Knives, Quinn. They were stabbing him, and he believed it was real."

Quinn frowned. "Did the knives actually hurt him?" At her nod, his respect for her grew. Grace was a force to be reckoned with. For her illusions to be so powerful that a person's skin actually split itself open in response to a knife wound that the mind had imagined… shit. It was almost incomprehensible, the power the mind had over the body. Yeah, he knew all about stress causing heart attacks, but this was a whole different level.

"He was screaming," Grace said, the words tumbling out now, as if she couldn't contain them anymore. "He was holding his arms over his face to try to protect himself, and the knives kept coming, slicing him to bits. There was blood everywhere. I tried to stop the illusion, but I couldn't. I ran over and tried to protect him, and I couldn't stop it."

"Shit, Grace." Quinn had a vision of her at fourteen, this young girl generating such violence and such horror, so beyond what she was capable of coping with.

"The other kids all came running, and there was so much blood and so much screaming…" Grace held her hands to her ears, as if she were trying to block the shrieks of death and terror and revulsion. "He died in my lap. I still hear his screams. I see the flash of metal as those blades flew across the room and sank into him." She held up her hands, her arms shaking. "I still feel his blood, trickling down my arms. I can still feel his fingers digging into my arms as he begged me to save him—"

"Okay." Enough. Quinn couldn't stand to see her torment herself anymore. It had been too long, too many years, and it was time for it to end. She didn't deserve this hell she'd been putting herself through, and he knew her well enough to know that her spirit was innocent, regardless of what had happened. He gently clasped her arms and tucked them against his chest. "Listen to me, Grace. It was an accident. Do you understand?"

She shook her head, tears streaming down her cheeks. "That's not an excuse—"

"You were fourteen, burdened with a power that you had no idea how to control. You were alone and terrified, and your survival instinct kicked in to save you." Quinn kissed away her protest. "You have to stop blaming yourself. It ends now."

"It never ends, Quinn. I relive it all the time." Grace's eyes were glistening and desperate. "I still see his face, right before he died. The terror, the unbearable pain, the confusion about why this was happening to him." She closed her eyes. "Ana and I ran away that night, and we've been on the run ever since. I still look over my shoulder, waiting for someone to grab me and take me back there to make me pay for what I did—"

"Hey." He tugged on a lock of her hair. "Did it ever occur to you that maybe your illusions were right?"

Grace blinked in confusion. "What?"

"My instincts always tell me when there's a threat, and my sword responds. How can you be so sure that kid was there to use the bathroom? How do you know he wasn't there to hurt you or someone else?" Quinn put his finger over her lips before she could respond. "Maybe that kid was pure evil and you knew it and you saved a hell of a lot of lives by what you did that night. Did you ever think of that?"

She started to protest. "Quinn—"

"No." He cut her off. "Look into your heart, Grace. You're all good in there, and there's no chance in hell you would ever have killed an innocent in cold blood. You don't have it in you."

Hope flashed in her eyes, hope that he was right, that she wasn't the monster she'd always believed, but she quickly crushed it. "I don't? What makes you so sure?"

"Because I've done it, and I know what it takes."

She rolled her eyes. "You kill for honor—"

"I killed my uncle Felix when I was nineteen," he interrupted. "Felix was my best friend, my dad, for all practical purposes. He was Order, and he was my hero. He was married with three daughters. Best damn guy I've ever known. Then he met his *sheva* and went rogue. Dante told me I owed it to my uncle to be the one to kill him."

Quinn stared up at the pine trees as he remembered that day. "I looked into his eyes as I took his life. As Felix died, the rogue-red glow faded from his eyes and he told me to make his death worthwhile." Quinn rubbed his hand over Grace's arm. "I realized he'd come back from being rogue, but it was too late to save him. There was no going back for me. He was my first kill, and he'll be with me forever."

Grace propped herself on her elbow, watching him. "How did you forgive yourself? How do you move on from doing something like that?"

"At the time, I thought it was a choice between his life, or that of my aunt and my cousins. He had to die. The innocents could not. There was nothing else to consider. It was easy." Quinn sifted through her dark curls, watching the silky strands tumble off his hands. "Although I used to blame Dante for making me kill him, the truth is that I made the choice to wield the blade against the man who'd raised me as his own son. That's what I live with every day, the truth that if I had fought harder for him, if I had waited longer to kill him, we would have realized he didn't need to die."

Quinn entwined his fingers with Grace's, her fingers cold. "You're different than I am, Grace. You didn't choose to kill that boy. It was an accident." He traced his thumb over her lips. "No matter what, you can always hold that in your heart as the truth." He set his hand on her chest and tapped his fingers over her heart. "In here, you're pure, and that's what matters."

She stared at him, her eyes glistening with unshed tears. "Thank you. Thank you for sharing. Thank you for listening and not judging me. What you said...it makes sense in a way nothing has before. You gave me something to think about."

He'd done good by his *sheva*? Damn. That felt good. "Yeah?"

"Yes." Grace lifted her arm so she could see his

mark on her skin. "It's hot right now. It almost hurts."

Quinn flattened his palm over her arm, trapping her fingers underneath his, feeling the heat from her mark rising into his skin. "We have to be careful now. We're halfway there."

"Halfway?" She caught her breath as she remembered. "I called your sword. How did that happen?"

He kissed the mark on her arm, damned pleased that his weapon had saved her life. "You were about to die, and it wouldn't allow that to happen. You needed it, and it was there. It will always be there for you now."

She wrinkled her nose. "What if I don't want it?"

He chuckled. "You'll have to take that up with my sword. It's between the two of you." His laughter faded as her arm became even hotter under his touch. He frowned and moved their hands to the side so he could look at the mark.

Grace leaned her head against his. As they watched, another line appeared, traveling down her arm toward her wrist as if someone was drawing it with a marker. It stopped at the tip of the blade, pulsed once, then was set.

Half the outline of the blade finished.

"Oh, no." Grace let her breath out. "*Trust*."

Quinn realized what had happened. "The boy. That was your secret?"

She nodded. "Only Ana knows."

"And me."

"And you."

Something twisted in Quinn's gut, something deep and powerful. Grace had trusted him with everything in her heart. He was nothing but a bitter, cynical warrior with nothing to offer but a dead uncle and a lifetime of violence, and yet this amazing, vibrant woman had opened her very soul to him and entrusted everything to his safekeeping. "I won't let you down, Grace. I swear it."

She gripped his wrists, her beautiful silver eyes

aching with an emotion that turned the very depths of his soul in a way he didn't even understand. "Thank you, Quinn."

"Thank you?" He laughed softly as he bent to kiss her. "Sweetheart, there are no thanks necessary, trust me—"

"Quinn!" Gideon's voice echoed through the woods. "Get over here." *The men need to hear from you soon.*

Quinn ignored his teammate and kissed his *sheva*, needing to connect with her, to bring them together, and he wasn't satisfied until she finally started to kiss him back. The desire surged instantly between them, and he broke the kiss. "I swear to God, Grace, I would take you right here even with the guys waiting. You get to me, woman."

Grace managed a small smile, the first real one he'd seen in far too long. "Yeah, well, it's mutual." She pulled her sleeve over her mark as Quinn stood up.

"Glad to hear that. One-sided uncontrollable sexual desire is not a good thing from a guy's perspective."

"Quinn!" Gideon's voice echoed through the night. "You coming?"

"Yeah, we're on our way," Quinn shouted back as he took Grace's hand and pulled her to her feet.

"It's me that's making them restless, isn't it?" she asked.

"It's *us.*" He brushed some of the dirt and pine needles off Grace's back and legs. "It's unheard of for an Order member to allow a *sheva* to live, and it's against everything that our organization is about to bring one into a mission."

Her expression was serious, showcasing full understanding of what they were about to face. "But you're about to ask them to do both of those, aren't you?"

"Yep." Quinn turned her to face him and set his hands on her shoulders. "You up for it?"

She lifted her chin, and he was glad to see the

determined glint back in her face. Her eyes were dry, her cheeks clear of tears. "I'm in."

He smiled. "Sometimes, it's entirely clear to me why I didn't walk away from you when I still had the chance."

"Because of my great rack?"

He took her hand to lead her through the woods. "Because you're tough enough to survive in my world. And because of your great rack."

She smiled, her fingers tightening on his.

Then they fell silent as they approached a flickering campfire and the circle of warriors who were bound by oath to kill her at first sight.

※※※

All amusement faded, replaced by a sudden urge to bolt, when Grace emerged from the woods and saw seven huge Calydons glaring at her, their expressions ranging from hatred to distrust, contempt, and lust. One warrior lurking in the shadows had a hint of envy on his face. Even Gideon looked wary.

The campfire was roaring, a huge blaze that lit up the clearing, practically up to the sky. The fog had burned off near the fire, but it still hung thick in the woods, like an ominous threat circling the cozy gathering and waiting for a chance to consume them.

Every warrior had a weapon in his hand. The orange flames from the fire danced in the steel blades, drawing her attention to the seven sharp implements being grasped oh-so-casually by the Order.

Gideon was the only one who didn't have his weapon out. He was standing in the middle of the circle, arms over his chest. He was rigid and intense, and she sensed he was doing everything in his power to keep the men seated.

They were waiting for a signal, ready to move on her.

Um…yeah… Grace decided that maybe it would be smartest to give Quinn a chance to talk to them before forcing her way into their circle. She slowed down. "Quinn—"

Quinn clamped his hand tighter around hers and pulled her into the middle of the circle so there were weapons on all sides. There was no way to watch them all, or guard against them. It was a statement of faith by Quinn to the men.

Great for Quinn that he was feeling such love and trust for his team, but she had no basis for deciding it made sense to put her life into their overly-aggressive hands. Her palms began to sweat as she looked around, hoping Quinn was right to put his faith in a team that had been trained to kill her no matter what.

"This is Grace Matthews," he said, his voice booming with authority. "As you know, she is my *sheva*."

Oh, man. He had to come right out and start off with that? Really?

Seven weapons shifted into ready positions, a move that really wasn't all that subtle.

Quinn gripped her hand more solidly. "We haven't completed the bonding, and we don't plan to," he announced with an astounding degree of confidence, given the intricacy of the brand that was already decorating her arm.

Grace swallowed as cold skepticism filled the air and the warrior's faces hardened. Of course they would be cynical. They'd just witnessed a completely out-of-control bonding ritual right in front of them. *Quinn. I think you need to come up with a different angle.*

Have a little faith, sweetheart. "Grace is an Illusionist. Her talents are critical for the mission we are facing, and she must be allowed to live." Quinn raised their clasped palms for everyone to see. "I speak as an Order member, and as Dante's man, not as her mate."

No cheers of joy answered his statement. In fact, a few of the men clenched their weapons more firmly, and a warrior to the right rose to his feet from the log he'd been sitting on.

Grace's mouth became dry. This was not going well. If she got killed before she could rescue Ana, she was going to be seriously upset. *Quinn, let me talk to them—*

They need to hear from me, so they know I'm not rogue. He didn't even look at her, instead making intentional, precise eye contact with each warrior. "The Order of the Blade was created to protect the world from Ezekiel, and everything we do must further that goal. That means Grace stays alive. There is no other way."

Huh. Well, okay then. Grace had to admit that was a pretty compelling argument. But when she looked around, not a single warrior had softened his stance, and her heart started a slow thud of fear. What else did they need to hear?

"I concur." Gideon moved to stand beside Grace. He didn't look at her as he took her other hand and raised it up, his grip tight on hers. She was a little startled by the show of support, by having these two powerful warriors by her side, standing up for her. She was so used to being on her own, to hiding who and what she was. Her life was about finding acceptance by hiding who she was, not by announcing it to the world.

"Quinn is telling the truth," Gideon said. "I've seen it in his mind. I'll let Grace live until we find out who killed Elijah and figure out what's going on."

Until then? So, there'd be a quick axe to the head once they didn't need her? All Grace's good feelings evaporated, jolting right back to what she was used to: being hated for who she was. Now she wasn't just an Illusionist, she had the added stigma of being a *sheva*. Yay, good day for the girl. Not.

One step at a time, sweetheart. Quinn's voice

brushed through her mind. *We must be smart.* Unwavering in their support, Quinn and Gideon kept her clasped hands raised, waiting.

For the longest time, no one moved, and Grace's last remnants of hope ebbed away. What would happen if someone came after her? If a blade came whistling through the night straight toward her heart? Could Quinn really stop them? Or would everyone die—

There was sudden movement to their right. Grace jumped and quickly looked over as the warrior she had stabbed stood up and began walking toward her. He was moving slowly, as if he were in great pain, which would make sense, you know, given that she'd just stabbed him. "I'm sorry," she blurted out. "I didn't mean to."

He came to a stop in front of her, studying her intently. He was wearing all black with metal rivets on his coat. Metal rivets stained with his blood. A long scar cut down the side of his face, almost hidden under his thick, dark hair. "Never apologize for acting in self-defense," he said. "It's the mark of a true warrior to be able to defend yourself."

Grace was startled by his genuine admiration. "You're not mad?"

His brown eyes flashed. "If you are going to be on this mission, it's a damn good thing you can fight."

Grace blinked at his words, at the rush of victory she felt emanating from Quinn. "I'm going on this mission?"

"Yes." He lifted his weapon so it was level with her face. It was the same sai that had been headed for her throat such a short time ago. "My name is Zach Roderick, and I accept you on this mission." He went down on one knee before her with a small grunt of pain and set his sai at her feet. He bowed his head and didn't move until his weapon shimmered and disappeared into the ground. Then he stood up and walked slowly back to the log he'd been sitting on.

Is that it? Are we good, Quinn? Grace realized now that everyone had been waiting for Zach. Since she'd stabbed him, he was the one who had to make the first move.

Not yet. There is one more. No one else moved, and there was a slight rise in tension from both Quinn and Gideon. The attention of the entire team seemed to be centered on one man, someone standing in the shadows.

Finally, he moved and walked into the circle of firelight, the bright flames flickering over his face, illuminating his bruised neck. She realized it was Gabe, the one Quinn had almost killed.

He was wearing jeans and shitkickers, and his black T-shirt was torn around the neckline. His bruises were beginning to fade, but there were still streaks of blood on his skin. He stopped in front of Grace. "Why are you here?"

She lifted her chin at his aggressive stance. "The man who killed Elijah and Dante has my sister. I won't let her die." She let her feelings be reflected on her face, let him see the truth that drove her.

"You aren't here to help us?"

"No." Grace didn't hesitate, somehow knowing that a lie, any lie, would condemn her instantly. The truth might as well, but she at least had a chance with it. "My sister's my life. I'm here to save her."

Gabe nodded with approval. "Your loyalty is evident. You'll do what it takes to save her." He looked over at Gideon, not Quinn. "You're sure saving the *sheva's* sister helps us?"

"It's the same mission," Gideon said. "Grace has skills to deal with it that none of us possess."

Gabe returned his attention to her. "I believe you care enough about your sister to fight off the bond until she's safe. You're not a danger right now, and we need you, so I'm cool with you joining us. But then—" He raised his hook sword to her face and rotated the blade so the light from the fire caught it, reflecting the glare into her eyes. "It will be my honor and duty to preserve the Order as it was meant to be, and to honor the death of a woman who has the courage and loyalty of a warrior."

Well…that compliment was good at least, right? Grace swallowed hard, but forced herself to meet the threat, the promise in his gaze. She didn't even allow herself to blink. She couldn't think that far ahead. Right now, in this moment, she had to take every opening she could get. "I will save my sister, but I won't let you kill me."

Respect flashed in Gabe's eyes, and he lifted his hook sword until it brushed the tip of her nose. "My name is Gabe Watson, and I accept you on this mission." He lowered himself to one knee, gave her a final look that promised he would never abandon his commitment to the Order, then bowed his head and set his weapon down. He didn't move until it vanished into the earth.

Once it was gone, Gabe stood and strode back across the clearing to stand in the shadows of the fire, fastening his dark gaze on her once again.

It's done. Gideon's voice was relieved as he spoke to her and Quinn. *The others will follow now.*

And they did.

This is Ian Fitzgerald, Quinn whispered into her mind as one of the men stepped forward. *Elijah had to kill Ian's* sheva *about six months ago, and it was rough. I don't know how he'll react to you.*

Ian's face was gaunt, his cheeks sunken, his eyes hollow. His dark hair was shaggy and disheveled, his brown eyes tired. His black leather coat and jeans hung off him as if he'd lost a significant amount of weight. Though he still walked with the grace and power of a warrior, there was something missing in his energy. A flatness. A resignation. As if he simply didn't care anymore.

Ian stopped in front of her, such grief and pain on his face that she wanted to hug him. "I'm so sorry you were brought into this, *sheva*," he said.

"Quinn didn't bring me into this. I invited myself," Grace said. "He explained the risks and I came anyway."

Ian's gaze went to Quinn, then back to her. "You two have no concept of what you've gotten yourselves into." He raised his hand to her hair, his fingers drifting over the ends. "It's too late for you both." Ian took Grace's hand, pressing a kiss to the back of it. "My heart bleeds for you, *sheva*."

Her throat tightened at the bleakness in his voice. "I'm not giving up."

Ian's eyes met hers. "There's no choice left to make. You're already dead. The only question is whether you take Quinn with you." He looked at Quinn. "I suggest you go with her when she dies. It's not worth it to be left behind."

Foreboding shivered through Grace, but she mustered a smile and stood on her tiptoes to kiss Ian's cheek, startled at how cold his skin was when her lips brushed it. "Thank you for caring if I die. No one else seems to."

He brushed his knuckles over her jaw. "You are mistaken, *sheva*. Quinn cares. He cares more than either of you have any concept." The regret on Ian's face made her knees tremble, but he raised his flange mace on his two palms as an offering. "My name is Ian Fitzgerald, and if this is what you wish, I accept you on this mission. May the angels ease your pain when it comes for you."

Ian knelt before Grace and laid his weapon on the ground, bowing his head as he waited for it to disappear. Ian's shoulders were hunched and he pressed his hand over his eyes while he waited.

There was such silence around the fire that she could hear the crackling of the sparks and the echo of the night.

After a long moment, Quinn set his hand on Ian's shoulder. Ian lifted his head and exchanged glances with Quinn. Then he rose to his feet. Quinn dropped his hand as Ian turned and walked back to his seat on the log without another word.

Gideon called out his throwing axe and pointed it toward the sky. "The spirit of Catherine Taylor shall forever be under my protection and that of the Order."

All the men raised their weapons and repeated those words. Ian sat up straighter, his voice ringing out louder than the rest. When the chant faded into the night, Ian stood up and walked out of the light, disappearing into the woods.

Catherine Taylor was Ian's sheva. Quinn's voice was quiet in her mind. *We honor her for her death.*

Grace grimaced. *I'm sure she appreciates such kindness, you know, after you guys killed her.*

I won't let her fate become yours.

She looked at him, Ian's grief making her believe that he had done everything in his power to save his own *sheva* from his team, and he'd still failed. *No, Quinn. We won't let her fate become mine. I'm fighting it, too.*

Quinn nodded. *Good.* Then he looked past Grace. *Thano Savakis is next.*

She turned back toward the fire as another warrior approached. He had short dark hair, green eyes that sparkled in the firelight, and the vibrant energy of a man who hadn't lost his optimism. He grinned at her. "Bunch of depressing old men around here, aren't there?"

She was surprised by his cheerful tone. "You look the same age as the rest of them."

"Ah, yes, it looks that way but I really *am* thirty-five. They've been mucking about this world for centuries, decrepit, old and bitter."

Quinn coughed and Thano grinned at him, then pointed his halberd, a long spear with an assortment of hooks and blades on the end, at Gabe. "Unlike my cynical brethren here, I'll be wearing my short skirt and raising my pompoms, cheering you on until the very last minute when you guys crash and burn."

Gabe snorted, the marks on his neck from Quinn's assault almost gone. "You'd look like shit in a short skirt. Your legs suck."

Thano grinned, then raised his halberd. "My name is Thano Savakis and I accept you on this mission." He kneeled before her and laid his weapon on the ground, whistling softly as it disappeared. Then he hopped up, sauntered across the clearing and plopped down next to Gabe. Thano was smiling, but there was a shadow in his eyes.

Another warrior stood up and walked over, wearing only a pair of black pants and boots. No shirt covered his torso and Grace gasped as her eyes fell on his chest. He was covered in scars. They were intricate designs, as if someone had taken a knife and dug deep, using him as a canvas for their art. His chest, arms and neck were all decorated, the scars disappearing under the waistband of his pants, as if he was marked on every inch of his body.

His skin glowed in the firelight, making the scars look as if they were alive, dancing. He raised a double spiked flail, clenching the steel bar with the two chains on one end in his hand. The spiked balls on the ends of the chains dangled loosely. "My name is Kane Santiago and I accept you on this mission."

Kane knelt to lay his weapon at her feet, and she could see the scars across his back, not an inch of skin left unmarked. The design was beautiful and horrific at the same time. *What happened to him?*

No one knows. He bares his body in hopes that someone he meets will know what the design means and have answers for him. He's the only Calydon we know of who can teleport, and he believes it's somehow connected to his scars.

Really? She glanced at Quinn as Kane rose to his feet, but Quinn wasn't watching her. He was focused on the one Order member who hadn't come forward yet.

The warrior was standing in the shadows of the trees. He was wearing all black, as were the rest of them, but the way he wore his clothes was different. More ominous. She couldn't articulate exactly what was different about him, but when the men all sat up, their instincts on alert, their remaining weapons readied, Grace realized she wasn't the only one who sensed it.

He shot a disdainful look at all the weapons that had come to life when he moved, then strode arrogantly across the clearing to stand in front of her. Gideon and Quinn adjusted their positions, moving slightly in front of her.

The warrior's eyes narrowed. They were almost black, brimming with anger and rage. She tensed, expecting him to voice a dark threat to her life, or to whip out his weapon and kill her before she could move.

But he simply raised his machete to her face, ignoring Quinn and Gideon when they moved even closer to her, as if they were fully expecting him to attack. Danger was practically seeping from his pores, and his body vibrated with violence.

She couldn't keep herself from taking a step back.

A deep bitterness tightened the lines around his eyes at her retreat. "My name is Ryland Samuels," he snapped out. "I accept you on this mission." He jammed his machete into the ground and inclined his head in a quick move. Ryland didn't even wait for his weapon to vanish before stalking back to the shadows, where he folded his arms over his chest and leaned against a tree, alone.

Only when he was back in his spot was there a shift around the campfire, and the weapons lowered.

Gideon stepped in front of Grace. He was wearing the focused expression of a warrior who was making the choice for the good of the mission, and for no other reason. "My name is Gideon Roarke, and I accept you on this mission."

His throwing axe remained at her feet for far longer than the others had before it disappeared, causing a murmur of approval among the warriors.

Quinn was the last one to stand before her. He called out his sword and held it before her, balanced on both palms. His eyes met hers, and she saw his duty reflected in them. He wasn't distracted by lust, or the bond or anything else. He was a warrior with a mission, not her lover, not her mate. A deadly warrior with one goal. "My name is Quinn Masters, and I accept you on this mission."

Then he knelt before her, laid his weapon on the damp earth and bowed his head.

His weapon remained on the ground, and it didn't fade. It simply stayed.

The men got restless, and Ryland spoke up from his solitary spot in the shadows. "The weapon lies. He can't be our leader on this mission. He has broken our oath by teaming up with his *sheva*. Gideon was marked as second in command. It's he who must replace Dante on this mission."

Quinn swept his sword off the ground and turned to face the warriors. "The weapons don't lie. I accept."

Gabe called out his other hook sword, the bruises on his neck pulsing with hostility as he angled his blade at Quinn. "Ryland's right. You're a liability right now."

Quinn's eyes narrowed. "The weapons don't lie. You know that." He laid his sword at Gabe's throat. "Make the right choice, Gabe."

"Yo' big guys, let's all chill out here." Thano walked up and set his hand on Gabe's shoulder. "With Elijah and Dante dead, we're running lean already, and we need all eight of us to win this thing. We can have a 'Kill Quinn and his chick' party later if we need to, but right now I'm more worried about the bad guy coming out to play than I am about whether we might have to knock off Quinn and his girlfriend later." He winked at Grace, as if to lighten his words. "In the absence of our leader, we have to follow the weapons." He glanced around, his face becoming serious. "I know you guys were all really tight with Dante, but we can do it without him."

Kane gave him a hard look, the scars on his body reflecting the firelight like a maze of carvings. "Fuck off, rookie. You have no idea what Dante was for us."

"No? I listen." Thano looked around the fire. "I know most of you owe your life to him." He looked at Ryland. "Yeah, maybe *you'll* go insane without him around to keep you under control—" Ryland growled, but Thano didn't back down. "—but the rest of you have been preaching honor and oath to me since I joined the Order. Dante's gone, so someone else has to step up now. The weapons picked Quinn, so obviously they know something we don't. Let him lead, for hell's sake. It's just for this mission, right? The real leader has yet to emerge." He grinned. "Who knows? Maybe it'll be me."

Grace saw the seriousness in Thano's eyes that belied his smile and light tone. Thano might act casual, but he was every bit the warrior that the rest of them were, and he understood the tenuous thread of control hovering over the gathering. "We have to put our faith in the weapons," he said. "It's our way."

Gabe stood his ground for a moment longer, then nodded once and sheathed his hook sword. "We good?" he said to Quinn.

"We're good."

Gabe nodded and walked away. Thano followed him, slugging him lightly in the back of the shoulder. There was a ripple of relief, and the men finally relaxed. Greetings were exchanged, shoulders slugged in acknowledgement as the men finally got a chance to bond.

The danger was over. For now.

Quinn caught Grace's arm as her legs began to

tremble. "You did great," he whispered.

"I need to sit."

He helped her over to a fallen tree near the fire, and she sank down gratefully onto the damp wood, her body starting to shake. Quinn stood next to her, his hand on her shoulder, his muscular thigh pressed against her for reassurance while he did his male-bonding thing with his team.

As Grace watched the warriors bonding around her, she realized how alone she was. She'd been grudgingly allowed onto the team because she could help them, but that was it. They didn't want her. They didn't trust her. And they didn't care if she lived or died.

Quinn was her only link into this world that was so foreign and unwelcome. God help her, Grace didn't want to rely on the support of a man whose closest friends were counting the minutes until they could kill her. She wished she could fight her battle alone and not have to put herself and her sister into the hands of this team of warriors who were so grounded in violence and so committed to their mission that both her life and her sister's meant nothing to them.

But she had no choice. Right now, Grace needed the Order, and she needed Quinn.

Long gone was the fairy tale she'd held onto for so long, a dream of a happy life, of being loved, of waking up in the morning with peace in her heart. In its place was a rising sense of doom, and a race against the clock to save Ana before this house of cards came crashing down around her.

CHAPTER 12

Nate was coming.

Not for Ana. This time, he was coming for her.

Lily swallowed nervously as the lock to Nate's office creaked, but she stood up and set her hands on her hips, as she'd done every time she'd faced him in the last two years.

She tried to hide her trembling as the lock slid open. He'd stashed her in here hours ago, and she was starving, exhausted and strung out from waiting for him, which was his plan, she was sure. Lately, he'd upped his efforts to break her mentally, and it was starting to work.

She fisted her hands. *No, Lily. He's not going to win. You're still in control.* It was getting difficult to believe that, but she had no choice. If she gave up... No. She wasn't going to give up. *He won't win.*

Lily forced herself to think of Ana down in that cell in the basement. She'd gone to visit Ana to offer some support, but in the end, Lily felt that connecting with Ana had ended up helping herself even more.

For two years, Lily had been locked in Nate's remote house in the Oregon high desert. She hadn't spoken to anyone except Nate and a couple of his bodyguards. She'd felt like the world had been lost to her, like no one even knew she existed. But now Ana knew she was alive. Ana had looked at her, spoken to her, and given Lily validation of her existence.

Unlike Lily, Ana got to leave the house with Nate. Yes, it was horrible what she had to go through, but every time Ana got outside, there was a chance that she'd get away. If Ana were eventually able to escape, then there would be someone on the outside who knew Lily was here, trapped, unable to get any kind of message to the world.

Ana was Lily's thread of hope, a shot of adrenaline to revitalize her spirit, which had been growing more and more devoid of optimism. She'd seen Ana's determination to break free, and Lily clung to the faith that Ana would succeed. Once Ana was free, then maybe she could send someone to help Lily. She just had to hang on until that happened.

Lily had survived two years. She could take another minute. And then another. One minute at a time. That was all she had to do to make it through.

The heavy oak door opened, and Nate strode in. He'd changed out of his bloody clothes. He was now sporting a pair of black leather pants and a red silk shirt open at the neck to reveal several gold chains. With his diamond stud earring and designer loafers, he looked like a fraud, like a nobody who was wearing someone else's fancy clothes and donning the arrogant airs of the powerful man he would never be.

Underneath, Nate was weak. He wasn't smart. He was pathetic and needy, and she knew he wasn't the intelligence fueling his operation, but she'd been utterly stymied in her attempts to glean more information. What kind of academic was she? Two years of research and she had come up with no answers.

"Lily. So nice of you to wait for us." There was still blood under Nate's fingernails from the Calydons he'd murdered, and his eyes had that eerie glow they always had after he'd taken a life. "I'd like you to meet my associate, Frank Tully."

An associate? Her mind leapt into alertness as Lily looked past Nate, hoping for her first chance to learn more about her captor and what his plans were. Information was her greatest weapon, and she had uncovered shockingly little of it since Nate had kidnapped her.

The man Nate had called Frank Tully walked in. His stride was long and powerful, but his body was lean and wiry, almost underweight, with shoulders that were too narrow and a waist that was too thin.

He was dressed with understated power, the kind that he didn't need to show because it pulsed so thickly from within. His gray sport coat was perfectly tailored to his underfed build, his white button down shirt was starched to perfection, and the pleat on his black dress pants was crisp. Simple dress shoes were polished to a radiant shine, and his silver-tinted hair was carefully trimmed and styled. Nothing was overdone. No designer labels. No gaudy or expensive watch. Just raw, pulsating presence.

Unlike Nate and everyone else she'd met here, Frank wasn't a Calydon. He had no violent energy emanating from him at all. She didn't think he was from a race of aggressive beings, but he was oozing with power. Ultimate, deadly power that needed no violence to destroy.

Lily looked into Frank's eyes, and she froze, certain she had just met the man who would be able to destroy her.

His eyes were the palest blue, like ice, and utterly ruthless. Lethally calculating and intelligent. The kind of eyes that belonged to a monster who would stand over her and carve the skin right off her body without flinching. The kind of creature who would get off on the pain he could cause others. A man who would spend hours torturing, carefully and precisely, merely because he could. Because he had the power. Because it gave him power.

Two Calydons followed him inside and stood behind him, like bodyguards. To protect him from Nate? Or to protect Nate from him?

Frank's cold gaze settled on her, and she couldn't stop herself from shuddering at the speculation in his eyes. His eyes roamed over her body as if he already owned her, as if he was already making plans. This man was about domination, about hoarding power, about crushing for the sake of doing so. No remorse. No compunction. No mercy.

"Lily's afraid of you," Nate observed, his voice tinged with jealousy. "She never looks at me like that. How the hell did you get that kind of response within five seconds, when I can't get it after two years?"

Frank's gaze slithered to Nate, disdain dripping from his features. "Because you are you, and I'm me." He glanced over at Lily again, a thoughtful expression in those intelligent eyes. "You said she was difficult. I don't think she'll be much of a problem." His voice was smooth, gliding over her like the sharp edge of a knife. "Hello, Professor Davenport. My name is Frank Tully. I've been looking forward to meeting you."

She swallowed. "You're here for me?" That wasn't a good thing. Nate, she was able to manage. Frank? She knew he was different.

He didn't deign to answer her, a move she knew was all about establishing the balance of power between them. Okay, so she would take that as a good sign. He considered her formidable enough to take the time to try to intimidate her. He certainly wasn't bothering to do that with Nate.

"So, she's Satinka." Frank walked around her, inspecting her like some object in a porn museum. "A rare magical dancer."

Lily stiffened at his comment, shooting a sharp glance at Nate. That was why he was here for her? Because she was Satinka? But why would Frank care? Her powers were valuable only to Calydons. Nate had tried to access her magic before, but he'd been no match for how thoroughly she had learned to shut herself down.

She'd learned her lesson all those years ago. God, how she'd learned her lesson. Sudden fear flickered through her at the memories of a past long suppressed, and she quickly shoved it aside.

She didn't have time to be pathetic. She had to focus on ferreting out every bit of information she could, like the fact Frank was interested in her magic. Other than his occasional moments of egoistic experiments with trying to awaken her magic, Nate had never made a big deal of her being a Satinka, and she hadn't clued in on that as being important. *Come on, Lily. Be smarter than they are. That's your only weapon.*

"No sex with her," Nate snapped. "I'm saving her. She can't be touched."

Tension Lily hadn't even realized she'd been holding released at Nate's words. The mere thought of combining Calydons, sex, and her magic brought back memories she knew would debilitate her in an instant if she gave them any power. *No sex, Lily. It's okay. Focus on the situation.*

Frank laughed. "She's no virgin, Nate."

"Doesn't matter. No sex. He'd be furious."

Lily looked sharply at Nate. Who would be furious? Who was he saving her for? Despite his affinity for using his Calydon weapon on poor Ana, Nate had never once called it out in Lily's presence. He'd done his share of other nasties to her, but he'd never used the knife she could see branded on his forearm. *Why?* There had to be an answer there, something significant that she wasn't getting.

"Make her dance," Frank said. "I want to see it."

She sucked in her breath. Frank wanted her magic? But why? Her power enhanced Calydons only, and he wasn't Calydon.

"She won't dance. I've tried." Nate paced the room, his eyes black with anger. "I have to figure out how to force her to dance. Beating it out of her doesn't work."

"Of course it wouldn't work," Frank said. He

came to a stop in front of her and his gaze went to her breasts. "Satinka magic is about a sexual connection with a Calydon. She won't feel that if you're beating her."

Lily shuddered, unable to stop herself from doing so. As much as Nate had knocked her around, he'd never touched her sexually. She didn't like the direction of this conversation. Oh, God, she didn't like it. "My magic can't be forced," she said quickly. "It will only come with the Calydon who's meant to be my mate." True, but also not true. God, how horrifically, awfully not true.

"As long as you *feel* like it's the right man, it'll come." Frank jerked his chin toward Nate. "Turn on the music I brought, Nate. I want to see her feed your power. I'll take care of her need to be attracted to you. All you have to do is get her turned on with dancing."

Nate took the CD and set it in the sound system. What did Frank have in mind? Was there really a way he could make her body respond sexually to Nate?

She recoiled as Nate hit play on the CD player, his lecherous eyes roaming over her too eagerly. *No, no, Lily, it's okay. They can't bring your earth magic without fresh soil. It won't happen.* It was a well-guarded secret that Satinka magic could not be brought unless there was contact with the earth, her people's defense against Calydons who would steal her magic and drain her until she died. Some Calydons got lucky, like those men—

God, no, Lily! Don't think of it!

She watched Nate as he approached, her heart racing frantically. If he touched her sexually... How much more could she take at Nate's hands? How much longer could she summon the strength not to shrivel up and die? *Think of Ana. She's your chance. You have to hang on until she can get away.*

The music began to fill the room, an eerie, aching sound that made Lily's body want to sway to the rhythm. She froze, shocked by the response inside her. How was that possible?

No. She wouldn't let that happen. Lily made her body rigid, locking her muscles against the instinct to move to the music.

"Touch her," Frank ordered. "I need to see if she really has the magic."

Nate strode across the room to her, slid his fingers around her wrist and yanked her hard. She fought against his touch, but his move knocked her off balance and she fell into him. The moment his Calydon skin brushed against hers, her magic awakened deep inside her, recognizing him as a Calydon, testing him to see if he was her mate. Her magic began to swirl to life inside her, wanting to tap into his power, but not able to find release without having the power of the earth to feed on.

Oh, God. Not this. Please not this. Tears burned in Lily's eyes as she fought to hold herself rigid, to cut him off from her magic.

Nate grabbed her hips and ground his erection into her stomach. Bile churned inside her, even as her magic tingled in response, a muddy, reluctant tingle, as if it didn't like Nate's energy any more than she did, but was unable to resist the touch of a Calydon.

Then suddenly, her body leaned into his, even as her mind screamed in resistance. Her head was thick and murky, and she couldn't think clearly. She couldn't remember what she was supposed to be fighting. Nate's hands slid down her back, and somewhere in the recesses of her mind, she knew it was wrong, but she couldn't process the situation fully enough to react. It was like her mind wasn't hers anymore. The music seeped into her soul and her body began to move—

No, Lily! He's doing something to your mind. You have to stop!

Nate bent his head and licked her neck.

Lily! Break out of it! Don't let him do this to you!

But her body followed his lead, her hips moving with his as he gyrated against her.

"It's working," Nate said, his voice bright with excitement. "She's dancing!"

"There's no magic," Frank said, his voice distant through the fog surrounding her brain. "Where's the magic?"

"It'll come." Nate's hands slid over her breasts, and his erection pressed into her, sliding between her thighs, her flimsy skirt no protection against the heat of his thrust.

Revulsion swelled, breaking through the mist holding her mind captive. "Stop!" She jerked back and pounded her knee into his crotch. He swore with fury and swung his hand to strike her—

Frank grabbed Nate's arm and flung him to the floor, the gaunt man easily besting a Calydon. "Never hit a woman in front of me," Frank snarled. "Your kind disgusts me how they think it's their right. I'm the only one who can make that decision." His fingers flexed, as if he were trying to stop himself from killing Nate right then.

Even Nate went still, not daring to antagonize this skinny, understated geek.

Lily froze, the hairs on her arms standing up at the venom pouring from Frank. His defense of her was terrifying, the way hate and rage were spewing from him, held so tightly, like an explosive he was waiting until the right moment to unleash.

Frank turned his head to look at her, those icy eyes ruthless and cold. "You *will* call your magic for me, Lily. I'll find out how to make it come, and you'll learn that you're not more powerful than I am just because of your connection to these pieces of shit Calydons." He ground his boot into Nate's back, pinning him to the floor. "The moment we're ready for you, Lily, I will bring you down and enjoy every minute of it." His voice was laced with venom and deadly promise. "You'll wish for death, and you won't get it until there's nothing left of you but a shriveled shell of pain and misery. You may be a woman, but you no longer fall under my protection, not after you scorned what I asked for."

Lily shuddered at the threat in his eyes and knew her time had run out. She had to get away from Nate before Frank came back for her. She'd never survive him. *Never.* But God, how could she get away?

She had to find a way. *She had to.*

Frank turned toward the door. "Get up, Nate. I'll tell you how to break her. You need to get started now."

Nate's grin was so full of malevolence she could practically feel it eating away at her skin. "Yeah, I'm looking forward to that." He strode up to Lily and yanked her over to him, his fetid breath wafting over her face. "I'll be back for you, Lily. Make sure you wait up for me."

Then he shoved her back and followed Frank out. The door banged shut and she heard the click of the lock.

Lily sank down right where she was, hugging herself as she finally lost the battle to hold back her tears. *Don't you dare give up, Lily.* She bit her lip, fighting to keep her sobs silent, knowing Nate was probably standing outside the door, hoping for an indication he'd finally broken her.

She had to keep believing.

Believing in what? That someday she'd be standing in her living room again? Visiting her parents for Sunday dinner? Sleeping in her own bed, without lying awake at night wondering if Nate was going to come for her?

This time, the sobs caught at her throat and a whimper leaked out of her mouth.

Dammit, Lily! Be strong! Lily dug her fingernails into her palms, and scrunched her eyes shut, fighting for control, to reclaim some semblance of the person she had worked so hard to become after she'd nearly died all those years ago. Strong. Confident. Successful. Resourceful.

She was still all that. She had to remember who

she was. She could survive this. With Ana in the basement, things had finally shifted. The end was almost here. Now was the time to get stronger, not weaker.

At some point, Nate and Frank would make a mistake. They would allow Lily to get near dirt, and the right Calydon would finally be within reach. She could find the Calydon her magic recognized as a partner, a Calydon who would infuse her magic with a power that would bring down both Nate and Frank.

She sighed and a faint smile touched her lips at the idea of finally getting free. All she had to do was stay alive until she had her chance. She had to keep them from figuring out how to drain her magic, but she knew Frank would figure out the earth element soon. She had to be gone before then, before Frank had the chance to inflict on her the demons he carried inside himself.

***

Zach plopped himself down on the log next to Grace as everyone took their places around the campfire. His shirt was still darkened with blood from where she'd impaled him, but he didn't seem to care. "Nice move with Quinn's sword."

She was surprised when he handed her a beer. "I really didn't mean to stab you. It just happened—"

"No worries." He leaned back and stretched his long legs out in front of him with a groan. His dark hair was messy and casual, his jeans were well-worn, and his boots were heavy-duty and creased. A man who dressed for function, not fashion. "Dante taught us how to build mental connections with our weapons, until they're able to act on the same battle instincts that we, as warriors, have," Zach continued. "When we're in battle, we don't have to think about our next move. It just happens." He shot her an appraising look. "That ability gets transferred to our mates. It wasn't your fault. It was Quinn's." He winked at her. "You're forgiven."

"Thanks." Uncertain whether to trust his overture, Grace managed only a small smile. She was an outsider here, and Zach's friendship was unexpected. Not sure what to say, she averted her gaze from him, watching Thano erect a makeshift spit over the fire and string up some animal she couldn't identify. The smell of dinner cooking made her stomach growl, and she realized she hadn't eaten in a long time. Quinn walked around the fire, filling everyone in on what had happened and what he knew so far.

Gabe called out a question and she jumped at the sound of his voice, unable to forget his promise to kill her when there was no longer a need for her.

Zach leaned into her. "You can relax, you know. Gabe has given you his oath. He'll protect you with his life during the mission. It's how we are."

"But he hates me—"

Zach shook his head. "It's not about you. It's that you've shifted the loyalties of the warrior who's been the most ruthless bastard of us all for the last five hundred years. Quinn was always the one to volunteer to hunt down the rogues and their *shevas*, and he's slain more *shevas* than anyone else has, by a long shot. Now he's asking us not only to let you live, but to bring you into the mission..." He slanted a look at her. "It's not like him."

Grace's stomach tightened as she involuntarily glanced at Quinn as he answered Gabe's question. The light from the fire had turned Quinn's black clothes orange and red, the flames dancing in his dark eyes. Why had he hunted down so many *shevas?* Was it because he'd wanted to give the men a final chance to reclaim sanity before killing them? And if so, why hadn't he told the others, instead of letting them believe he was some *sheva*-killing aficionado? Or had he not told her the whole truth about who he was?

Zach gave her an appraising look. "So, we're all

wondering whether Quinn isn't the warrior we believed he was, or whether you're something special, a *sheva* far more dangerous than any we've encountered before. Or more powerful, perhaps?"

She bit her lip, unsure what to say, what was true, what to reveal. "I don't have the answer to that."

Zach shrugged. "We'll have it figured out before the end of this mission." He held up his beer. "In the meantime, enjoy it. It's going to be a hell of a ride."

He continued to talk, but she stopped listening as the night began to pulse with an energy rhythm that was all too familiar. Grace sat up as pressure began to build in her head, similar to the pressure that preceded a powerful illusion. Ana? Or someone else? Or…herself?

Quinn scowled, keeping his back to Zach and Grace. It was grating on him to see another warrior whispering so intimately with her, and he wanted to stalk over there and knock Zach on his ass for getting too close to her.

But Gabe had been watching him, so Quinn turned away before he could give away his thoughts. Gabe had been right to question his sanity. Gabe was the only one in the circle who truly understood how close Quinn had been to rogue, but Quinn didn't want the others to realize it. He'd almost killed Gabe tonight, and the other man knew it.

If Grace hadn't stopped him, both he and Gabe might be dead.

Quinn had truly gone rogue for a brief moment, and the bond was only at half-strength. What would it be like if they completed more stages? He couldn't allow it to happen.

But a part of him, that stupidly male side, made him want to beat his chest like some dumb-ass Tarzan wannabe, just at the thought of his mark on Grace's arms. He wanted to lock her down so she could never deny she was his.

Instinctively, his gaze slid toward Grace. She was pale, staring intently into the woods, her body rigid. Immediately, he forgot about all the other warriors and focused only on his woman. *Grace? What's wrong?*

Grace's gaze jerked toward him. Her eyes were a darker shade of silver, almost steel gray, heavy with shadows. *I feel energy amassing in the woods.*

Quinn instantly focused on the woods, on the scents and sounds, but caught nothing. *An illusion?*

I don't know. At first I thought it was, but it seems to have dissipated. I'm not sure what it is... Her attention wandered back to the forest, her brow furrowed in concentration. *Maybe it was nothing.*

Quinn had too much faith in her Illusionist talents to believe that. *Keep searching. I'll keep an eye out as well.*

He turned back toward his men. "Grace picked up a threat. Anyone catch anything?"

The circle of Calydons fell silent and the night practically hummed with energy as the warriors concentrated. One by one, they shook their heads.

But Grace was still frowning. *Grace?*

It feels like the illusion that was affecting Elijah. She was studying Zach, who was still next to her on the log. She casually leaned toward him and set her hand on his back.

Quinn stiffened. *Is it affecting Zach?*

I'm not sure.

"Quinn," Gabe interrupted. "What's the plan?"

Quinn wrenched his gaze off Grace and looked at Gabe. "You and Kane will go to Ezekiel's prison and assess it. If the magical protections are weakening, get some answers."

Kane and Gabe nodded, and the atmosphere around the campfire became heavy with the reminder of the deadliness of the issue they were facing.

"Gideon will stay and read Dante's *mjui*," Quinn continued, "and Zach will retrieve Dante's son and—"

"Quinn." Grace's voice cut through the night, interrupting him.

All the warriors turned to look at her, and he felt their surprise and annoyance that she would be bold enough to interrupt. A few of them looked at him, clearly expecting him to ignore her, or to tell her that she wasn't permitted to speak up during their meeting.

He turned to face her. "What's up?"

"Zach's under an illusion. The same thing I saw in Elijah before he turned your weapon over to Nate. I can't see it clearly because I'm not connected to him, but there's something there."

Zach rose to his feet instantly. "What are you talking about? No one's messing with me."

Quinn's brands began to burn, and he knew Grace was right. "Anyone else?"

She studied him, and he felt her reach out along their connection. "You."

"Me?" He swore. "Who else?"

Gideon set his hand on Quinn's shoulder. *You feel like killing anyone, big guy?*

Grace's gaze snapped to Gideon the moment he touched minds with Quinn, building a connection that gave her access to Gideon. "Gideon is, too."

Gideon dropped his hand. "Me?"

The men were all on their feet now, moving restlessly. Weapons were out, and their bodies were primed for battle. Muscles flexed, senses on alert. They watched each other carefully, waiting to see who was going to turn on whom.

"Test everyone," Quinn commanded. "In line.

Now!" He grabbed Grace and hauled her over to Kane. "Drop your shields," he snapped at Kane as he set her hand on Kane's scarred shoulder. He dove ruthlessly into Kane's mind using the mental connection they shared as Calydons.

By touching them both, he connected Kane to Grace, so she could see inside him easily. Kane bristled at the intrusion, but Grace was already shaking her head. "He's clean." Kane relaxed visibility, and then Thano was in front of her, holding out his arm. Grace touched him and Quinn held the connection for her. "Clean."

The others fell quickly in line, even Ryland and Gabe. It was a sign of how efficient they were as warriors: once they'd accepted Grace into their mission, they gave her full credit for her powers. No hesitation at all to rely on her. Warriors to the end.

Grace checked them all, then shook her head. "Everyone else is clean. It's just Quinn, Zach and Gideon."

Zach was pacing outside the light of the campfire, his weapon clasped restlessly in his hands. "She's wrong. She's lying. I'm fine."

Quinn narrowed his eyes at Zach's uncharacteristic disengagement from the team. That alone was enough to convince him that something was wrong. He'd be willing to wager that the illusion was turning Zach against the rest of the Order, exactly how Elijah had been manipulated to hate Quinn.

Quinn looked around at the forest. "If someone's holding an illusion on us, how close does he or she have to be?"

"Close," Grace said. "A few hundred yards."

"Find him!" Quinn snapped.

Ryland spun so he faced north, his head cocked slightly as he listened. "Got it." He sprinted straight through the clearing and into the woods, four other warriors on his heels.

Quinn grabbed Zach's arm as the warrior turned to

follow them. "Not you. You stay."

Zach wrenched his arm out of Quinn's and fisted his weapon. "How can you trust her? She's an Illusionist, and illusions killed Elijah and Dante. She's trying to mess with us now. Don't you see, Quinn? She's the enemy, infiltrating our ranks. What better weapon for Ezekiel than to bring down the Order from the inside? Spin us into confusion by making us not trust each other or our instincts."

Quinn scowled. "She's not the enemy." But even as he said it, doubt flickered though his mind. Doubt that wasn't his. Doubt he couldn't stop.

※※※

Grace saw the instant that the illusion took root in Quinn. Gone was the look of steadfast loyalty, the eyes that saw only the good in her. Instead, there was that slithering hesitation, as if he wasn't sure anymore. *Quinn. It's an illusion. You know you can trust me. I'm your* sheva. *I couldn't betray you even if I wanted to.* She connected with him through their minds, and saw the angry orange illusion glowing inside him. It was directing hate and distrust toward her. She took a step back as Zach stalked toward Quinn, still shouting about her. *Quinn. You need to block it—*

Gideon grabbed her and spun her toward him. "What's the illusion that's on me? Talk to me, Grace." He glanced at Quinn and Zach, who were circling each other, weapons out. "I can feel their hostility toward you and each other, and I have a bad feeling about this. Where do I stand?"

She hesitated. "I don't know if I can read you that clearly without Quinn building a bridge for us—"

"I have his blood inside me. We can do it." He shot another wary look at Quinn and Zach, who were arguing now, their voices heated, their muscles tense in aggressive stances. His gaze returned to her. "Now."

Grace set her hand on Gideon's chest and concentrated on the rhythm of his heart, searching for a pathway into his mind. He met her almost instantly, and she let her consciousness fly down their connection, surprised at how easy it was now that she knew how to do it. She felt Quinn's energy inside Gideon...the same, but different. It was tinged with a hardness Quinn didn't have... and a sadness. But she didn't waste time prying. She found the illusion almost instantly. It was pulsing orange, nearly vibrating with the power of it. "Distrust. Your loyalty is being shredded."

"Loyalty to whom?"

"Someone you trust completely. A man you admire."

"Quinn? My only thoughts about him right now are that I'm afraid he's gone rogue for real this time."

"No..." She searched harder. "A leader. Dante? Is it Dante?"

Gideon cursed and pulled away from her. "Shit. You nailed it. Now that you pointed it out, I can tell I'm pumped Quinn chose me to look at his *mjui* so I can prove Dante was betraying us." He raked his hand through his hair. "Jesus. How could I possibly believe Dante would betray us?"

There was a clash of weapons, and both she and Gideon spun around. Quinn and Zach were fighting now, and Zach was shouting at him for trusting Grace, accusing Quinn of being a traitor to the Order.

"Quinn," Gideon shouted. "Connect with Zach's mind! We need to use you as a bridge!"

Quinn obeyed instantly, and Grace was able to read the illusion working over Zach. "Someone is trying to get Zach to deliver Drew to him. I can feel Zach's loyalty building even now to this guy, and he's making Zach not trust any of us."

"You lie," Zach shouted. "I would never betray the

Order." He leveled his sai at Gideon. "All of you are trusting the wrong person. She's the enemy. She's trapping us all."

Quinn whirled around to look at her, his eyes dark. She saw his conflict, his confusion, and she realized he was succumbing to the illusion. He was going to kill her.

Um, yeah. Uh, oh, anyone? Grace stumbled back from his lethal coldness. "Quinn! Someone's trying to keep you from trusting me. From listening to what I say."

"She's trying to poison us." Zach set his hands on his hips, his fists shoving aside his jacket to reveal the hole in his shirt from where Grace stabbed him. "The *sheva* is trying to destroy us. She killed Dante. She killed Elijah."

"No, I didn't. Dammit! Come on, you guys! Have some resistance!" She glanced desperately at Gideon. "I don't know how to free them, Gideon."

Quinn turned toward her, his sword clenched in his hand. "No Order member would betray us. Only an outsider. Someone like you." Anger flared in his eyes, a dark, lethal anger that made her heart stutter.

Gideon stepped in front of her. "Quinn. Stand down. This isn't you."

Quinn. Come back to yourself. She threw all her mental energy into her thoughts and shoved them at Quinn, but the instant she opened their connection, she could feel Quinn's loyalty to his Order pulsing strong within him... entwined around a deep-seated distrust of all *shevas*. A hatred born of centuries of refinement. She instinctively began to back up. "You *know* I'm not a threat."

His eyes narrowed, and she saw his resentment for what she'd brought into his life. Gideon grabbed her and shoved her behind him. "Watch yourself, Grace. I've never seen him like this."

"No." She pushed Gideon out of the way and faced Quinn, knowing she had to reach through the illusion and find him before Zach and Gideon succumbed to theirs. Quinn was the only one she had a connection with. He was her only chance to stop everything from blowing up, destroying all hope of finding her sister. "Know the truth."

Zach turned toward her, standing behind Quinn. His face was cold, his three-pronged sai held high above his head, his gaze fixed on Quinn. "Quinn," she warned. "Zach's behind you!"

Zach thrust his weapon toward Quinn's head, but Gideon lunged past her and tackled Zach. They slammed to the ground with a crash that made the trees shudder. Zach threw Gideon off him and leapt to his feet, and the two went to battle. She knew Gideon was distracting Zach so she could work on Quinn, who was currently pointing his sword at her.

Um, yeah. How could she stop an illusion that was strong enough to make Elijah kill his best friend? What was stronger than the blood bond these men shared? Her forearm pulsed. *The* sheva *bond was stronger.*

Quinn lunged toward her, and she dove to the right, calling his sword, praying it would work. Just as she'd hoped, the weapon flew out of his hand and smacked into her palm. She rolled to her feet, holding the sword out with both hands.

Quinn stopped dead, staring in surprise at his empty hand.

Listen to your gut, Quinn. I'm not the enemy. I'm your sheva *and I'm hardwired to be loyal to you.* Not that she was going to run around kowtowing to the damn bond, but it seemed like a good time to at least pretend she was.

Grace felt Quinn's internal struggle as he tried to fight down the illusion, as he battled to access the part of him that was connected to her, that could never hurt her. *Quinn!* She screamed his name into his mind, concentrating all her thoughts, emotions and energy on him and their bond. *The illusion is screwing with your emotions. Shut your emotions down and concentrate only on the facts. Focus only on the truth as it is.*

Quinn stopped and closed his eyes, and there was a surge of power from deep within him, a power she'd never felt before. Electric and dangerous. It crashed through him and the illusion screamed with pain as if it were being eviscerated. Grace yelped and covered her head as pain exploded in her mind, Quinn's sword falling to the ground as she went down under the onslaught.

"Grace!" Quinn was suddenly on his knees beside her, his arms around her. "Are you all right?" His hands were flying over her, as if checking her for injuries. "Jesus, baby, I'm so sorry."

She lifted her head as the pain began to fade. Quinn's eyes were soft brown, aching with regret and pain. "You're back." She threw her arms around his neck and fell against him, utterly drained. His strong arms wrapped around her, supporting her, giving her back the sense of security that she'd lived without for so long.

Quinn hugged her tightly, burying his face in her hair, his hands clenching her tightly against him. "I knew what I was doing the whole time. I knew it was wrong, and I couldn't stop myself." He pulled back and kissed her hard. His kiss was aggressive and desperate, as if he needed to taste her just to be sure she was there, safe and in his arms.

God, it felt good to be kissed by him. "I thought you were going to kill me. You're way too violent for me," she said as she gripped his shoulders, kissing him back. "You have to stop that. I don't like violence. You know that."

He swore under his breath, laughing softly as he tunneled his hands through her hair. "I've never been so helpless in my life." He pulled back searching her face. "I thought I was going to hurt you," he said. "I was terrified watching what I was doing and not being able to stop it." His body was shaking, his lips frantic as they found hers again.

"But you didn't hurt me. You wouldn't let yourself." Grace sagged into him, kissing him back with a desperation she'd never before experienced. Relief, exhaustion, exhilaration. She needed to touch him, needed him to ground her. *I can't do this without you. I can't navigate this world of yours and find my sister alone.*

I know, babe. I know. He rested his forehead against hers, still holding her tightly, while they both breathed in the relief of surviving the moment. *We'll get there.*

She nodded. *We have to.*

I agree.

There was a shout and they broke apart, whirling around in time to see Zach sink his blade into Gideon's thigh and send the warrior to his knees. "Gideon!" Quinn leapt to his feet as Zach raised his sai and plunged it toward Gideon's heart. Quinn reared back to throw his sword, but Grace knew it was too late. He'd never stop him in time.

A machete flew through the air and crashed into the sai, knocking it out of Zach's hand. Zach howled and grabbed his sai off the ground as Ryland burst out of the woods, He charged toward Zach as he called his machete back to his hand.

"Don't kill Zach," Quinn shouted. "He's not rogue!"

Ryland leapt over Gideon's hunched body and smashed both feet into Zach's chest. Zach flew backwards, hit a tree, then bounded to his feet, weapons up and ready in both hands. Ryland landed several yards from him, machetes glistening.

"Just keep Zach contained," Quinn ordered as he sprinted across the clearing to Gideon. "Don't kill him."

"Just keep him contained? He's trying to kill me." Ryland blocked a deathblow from Zach, barely getting out of the way. "I could use some help if I'm not allowed to bring him down."

Gabe charged up, brandishing a hook sword with a lethal blade that had a spike and a hook on the end. He swung it at Zach as the warrior thrust his sai toward

Ryland's heart, connecting with the back of Zach's head. Zach pitched forward, crumpling to the dirt, a brutal wound on his crown.

He didn't get up.

There was silence for a long moment, no sound except the heavy breathing of Ryland and Gabe, and the sound of Gideon's clothing rustling as he struggled to his feet, his right leg useless, his jeans stained with blood.

Gabe took a breath, then sheathed both his swords. Ryland stripped off his shirt and handed it to Gabe as he knelt beside Zach. Gabe pressed the shirt to Zach's injury, then rolled him onto his back. The warrior's muscled body was limp, his jaw slack, a stream of blood sliding from the corner of his mouth. Gabe pressed his fingers to the warrior's throat, then nodded, and Grace felt the men shift with relief.

Gabe rested his forearm on his thigh and pressed his bloody palm to his head for a long moment. "What the hell's going on? In all my four hundred years, I've never seen the Order fall apart like this. Dante's dead. Elijah's dead." He looked at Quinn. "You attack me, and now Zach breaks his mission oath and tries to kill us all? His eyes aren't red, which means he broke his oath when he was sane. And then we don't find anyone in the woods, even though we all felt someone." His gaze drifted to Grace, and other warriors did the same. It wasn't friendly. "What the hell's going on?"

At that moment Thano, Ian and Kane sprinted out of the woods, weapons raised. They coasted to a stop in the middle of the clearing, and it wasn't until Gabe, who was kneeling beside Zach, nodded that they finally lowered their weapons.

"I hate it when you guys party and don't invite us," Kane said, but his eyes were alert and ready. "What happened to Zach and Gideon?"

Quinn walked over to Grace and put his arm

around her shoulders, pulling her tight against him. "Our enemy has finally made a mistake. We have a plan."

"Seriously? A mistake? I must have missed it while I was fighting off one of my own team members who was trying to *kill* me." Ryland had paced away from the group, and was facing the woods. His body was rigid, his weapons clenched tight in each fist. His voice was quiet, laced with lethal intent, strained with the effort of keeping control. The loner of the group, Ryland lifted his face toward the sky, and let out his breath with a shudder that vibrated through his whole body.

Quinn squeezed Grace's shoulder. "It's your floor, *sheva*. Bring 'em up to speed."

She blinked. "Me?"

He nodded. *The men need to hear from an Illusionist right now. They need answers only you can provide.*

Grace looked around at the battered team. So many injured. Distrust. Anger. Confusion. The Order was starting to fragment. They were losing control of the situation, and they needed to regain it fast if they were to recover in time to find Nate and Ana before it was too late. And it was up to her to help them?

Grace could see by the aggressive body language of the men that the answer was yes, and there was no room for a mistake. Which was fantastic, because jumping into this world of violence, death, and deadly warriors who didn't believe in her was *so* her forte.

It wasn't like her sister's life was hanging in the balance if she screwed this up or anything.

"Grace?" Quinn looked down at her, his dark eyes full of questions. "You up for this?"

She had to be. There was no other option. As she looked around at the circle of warriors, she realized that they were all looking at her expectantly, as if they thought she would have the answers, the clues they needed to go forward. Gone were the distrust and the hostility from when she'd first met them. True to Zach's word, they were looking at her with full acceptance, ready for her to deliver the information they needed to succeed on their mission.

Excitement pulsed through her. Right now, in this moment, they believed in what she had to offer, and that felt incredible. She grinned at Quinn. "Yes, I've got it." And she knew she did.

CHAPTER 13

This was it. Their last chance. Lily knew it.

Her mind frantically working out the last details of what she wanted Ana to do, Lily clenched Ana's tray of food tightly to keep the plate from rattling in her shaking hands.

The Calydon standing guard outside Ana's cell unlocked the steel door and shoved it open. Ana was asleep on her cot, one hand wrapped around her other forearm. Her face was at peace, her body relaxed, as if somewhere in her dream, she had found what she wanted.

"Ana!" Lily hurried inside, knowing she had little time until Nate showed up. "Wake up!"

Ana bolted upright, the confusion of sleep still on her face. She saw Lily and smiled. "Lily! You came back!"

"Yes, but he doesn't know I'm here." Lily limped over to the cot and set the food down. "Listen, Ana—"

"He hit you?"

At the empathy and kindness in Ana's voice, Lily's tough façade slipped for a split second. She couldn't hide her sudden swell of tears when Ana touched her arm, the first kind touch Lily had felt in two years.

She grabbed Ana's hand and sat beside her, clinging to the first sign of humanity she'd had in so long. "I'm fine," she said firmly, refusing to think about how much her body hurt, about what Nate had done to her after he'd come back from his meeting with Frank. "But things are happening fast. Tonight's your chance."

Ana became alert, and she leaned forward, her silver eyes glistening with anticipation. "Tell me," she urged. "What's the plan?"

"Nate's taking you out for another run tonight."

Ana's mouth tightened almost imperceptibly, but she nodded. "Okay. I'm ready."

Lily smiled at Ana's determination. "You give me hope, Ana."

Ana laughed. "You have no idea what you do for me, Lily." There were footsteps in the hall and they both leaned forward, huddling together.

Lily's forehead bumped against Ana's. "I think this is his final run," she whispered. "Whatever Nate's planning is coming together, so this is your last chance. You have to get away tonight."

Eagerness gleamed in Ana's eyes. "I'm all over it. Tell me what to do."

Footsteps paused outside the door, and Lily heard the low murmur of conversation. "Do you remember I told you about that stone he has?"

Ana nodded fiercely. "Did you find anything else out?"

"Not yet, but I think we'll have our chance." She held Ana's bruised hands, squeezing gently, refusing to think about what would happen if Ana didn't get away. She couldn't survive much more of what Nate had done tonight, and she knew Frank would push him even further.

Ignoring how much her body ached, Lily focused on their opportunity, on their chance to get out. Nate might hurt her, but she would not let him break her. "Nate's on his way down here with another man named Frank Tully. They've been arguing violently about the stone for hours. Frank wants it, and Nate won't give it to him. I'm almost positive Nate has it on him. You have to get it from him tonight. Whatever it is he's planning, he needs to use the stone."

Ana nodded. "If Nate has it with him, I'll find it."

"Good." Lily smiled, and sudden exhaustion overtook her now that she'd accomplished her goal. Everything was in Ana's hands now. She bowed her head to her knees, too drained to hold herself up anymore. "When you get out, send someone for me. Will you do that?" With a groan, she let herself roll to her side, resting on the cot. Just for a minute. Her eyes fell closed, and it felt like too much effort to keep them open. To think.

"Lily." Ana crouched beside her, worry creasing her forehead. "You have to hang in there."

"You have to figure out how to get away," Lily mumbled, still not opening her eyes. "How are you going to do that?"

Silence.

Lily pried her eyes open and saw Ana chewing her lower lip. Fear coursed through her. "You have to get away," she said. "This is your last chance."

"I know, but I'm not sure how to do it—"

"Ana!" Lily grabbed her hand. "You're one of the most powerful Illusionists in existence! Use your illusions against him. You have the best weapon available!"

"I can't," Ana protested. "They don't work on him."

Lily groaned. "Oh, come on, he's just a Calydon, and he's not even a powerful one. He's probably been trained to resist them, but that's not infallible." She took Ana's hand and squeezed fiercely. "I can't go out there. You have to do it. Be the murderous Illusionist you have to be and stop holding back!"

Ana stiffened. "I don't want to murder—"

"Then it's over. Then he wins." Lily flopped onto her back, grief consuming her. It was too hard to keep hoping. Too difficult to keep fighting. She couldn't do it anymore. "I give up," she whispered as she closed her eyes and stopped fighting her injuries, the hopelessness and the despair. "It's done." She realized that it felt good to finally stop fighting. To just be. To let fate fall where it will.

"Oh, come on, Lily! Don't give up on me." Ana grabbed her under the arms and pulled her into an upright sitting position, leaning her against the wall. She held Lily's shoulders, keeping her upright. "You're my strength."

Lily wrenched her eyes open, fighting the overwhelming urge to lie down and simply give up. "Can you do it, Ana? Can you do an illusion that will break Nate?"

Ana looked down at her forearm, and rubbed her palm over the skin, as if there was some message there for her. When she looked up, there was a new determination in her eyes. "I'll do it."

Lily knew she would. "Okay, then." She let her head flop back against the wall. "Then I'll hang on a little longer."

Ana nodded. "You'd better. I'll be really mad if I come back for you and you're dead."

"Well, I wouldn't want to make you mad." Lily had a sudden image of her cell door opening, of that feeling of disbelief when she saw someone besides Nate walk through that door, someone who held the door wide open for her, of that moment when she realized she was free, that the nightmare was over. Truly, blessedly, over. The triumph. The relief. The gift of a second chance at life. It would be worth everything she'd suffered to reach that moment. "I'll be here," she whispered. "I'll be waiting."

Then the door clicked, and Lily's stomach rolled with the grim reality of what she was facing. *Okay, girlfriend, time to take this one home.* "They're here."

Ana's gaze jumped to the door as she stood up with determined strength. Gone was the victim. In its place was a woman ready to finally win.

And that's when Lily knew they really had a chance. Adrenaline and excitement raced through her, chasing away the pain and the fear. "Help me up. I can't let him think he's won. "

Ana grabbed Lily's arm and helped her stand as the door began to open.

Lily braced herself against the cold cement wall and lifted her chin, willing strength into her body. "Okay, Ana, let's do it."

Ana squeezed her hand. "You got it, sister."

Sister. Lily smiled to herself. "I like the sound of that."

A smile flickered briefly across Ana's face. "Me, too."

Then the door opened, and in walked Nate and Frank.

Quinn saw the tension in Grace's body as she surveyed the circle of unsmiling warriors, preparing to lecture them on illusions.

He gave a reassuring touch to her mind. *You'll be fine. They're not going to kill you in the next five minutes.*

Gee, that's so reassuring, especially when I have one of their teammates bleeding out at my feet.

Zach's not bleeding out. He's taking a nap.

She snorted, then pulled back her shoulders and faced his men. "I saw the illusion that's inside Zach. He no longer trusts Quinn, or even the rest of the Order, to do what's right. His loyalty to someone else is being strengthened." She walked across the clearing, her hands gesticulating with passion as she talked.

Quinn folded his arms over his chest as he watched her. With the firelight dancing in her dark hair, she looked like a powerful force as she strode past his men.

Damn, she was impressive.

"The illusion appeared in Zach as soon as Quinn put him in charge of keeping Drew safe," Grace explained. "I think he was selected because he's the one who will have access to Drew. This guy wants Zach to hand Drew over to him."

"Who is the man?" Ryland asked. He was still pacing at the edge of the woods, restless and moody. Thano stood near him, watching him, but the other men had moved away to sit on the far side of the clearing.

"I'm not positive, but I got a sense of him." She looked at Quinn. "I think it was Nate."

"Nate again? I can't wait to find that bastard," Kane growled. "Where's Zach supposed to meet him?"

"It wasn't part of the illusion. The illusion was to make Zach not trust the Order, and to trust Nate, so that's all I could see. The illusion was about changing Zach's emotions, not specifics like where to do a handoff. He'll have to make contact with Zach to arrange it."

"What about Gideon?" Kane asked.

Grace quickly explained the illusion being played on Gideon. There was a rumble of disbelief when she said he was questioning Dante's loyalty, but when Gideon stepped in and admitted it was true, there was a distinct increase in their respect for Grace.

Any force powerful enough to make Gideon distrust Dante was a hell of an opponent, and with Gideon's confirmation that Grace had been correct, they all knew they needed what she could offer.

The men stopped resisting, and there was a universal shift as they all leaned forward, listening intently, the same as they would have to any chosen leader. They had now truly accepted Grace's value to their mission.

Pride surged in Quinn. How in the hell had she managed to do it? He'd forced their agreement, but Grace had won them over. Hot damn. She was good. He studied her as she walked, watching the gentle sway of her hips, the soft tangle of her hair over her delicate shoulders, the way her shirt cupped her breasts. She was all woman, all sensual heat, and at the same time, she was a warrior.

He became hard, and he laughed softly to himself. For a man who'd been celibate for more centuries than he'd been active, he was one raging inferno of lust when Grace was around. He liked it. He liked what she ignited in him.

"Gideon was put under the illusion after Quinn had put him in charge of reading the *mjui*," she explained. "Nate, or whoever it is, wants the Order not to trust Dante."

"If Gideon read the *mjui* while under the illusion, he would have misinterpreted it. That means there's information we need in that stone." Thano was standing in the back, balancing his halberd horizontally on the tip of his index finger, and spinning it. The triple damage end, with a hook, a spear, and a knife, caught the glow from the fire as it spun, making it look like it was on fire. "We all would have thought Dante betrayed us." He raised his brows. "I don't know about you fellas, but I'm impressed as hell. That's some damn fine card playing he's got going on."

Quinn nodded. "But now that we know what he's doing, we can use it to our advantage. We can—"

"What about you?" Ryland interrupted. "She said you were under an illusion, too."

"He shook it off." Grace said. "It's gone." She met Quinn's gaze, mischief flirting in her eyes. "We used the *sheva* bond to do it." She glanced at the men. "Who knew a *sheva* could come in so handy, eh?"

Thano barked with laughter. "Well, isn't that a kick? The bond you all were so worried about actually strengthened Quinn and enabled him to shake off the illusion. Guess the weapons were right to pick him, eh?"

"Shut up, rookie," Kane snapped.

But a few of the warriors were chuckling now, and Grace grinned.

Oh, yeah, one woman was changing history all by

herself.

Quinn gestured to get everyone's attention. It was time for him to step up now that Grace had, by some miracle, pulled the team back together. "Even though he's under an illusion, we'll still allow Zach to go after Drew. But we'll track him and be there when he makes the drop. We'll take out Nate at the same time, but not until he's given us answers about Ana and Ezekiel. Everyone clear on that?" He gave Ryland and Kane long looks. "You will *not* kill him until we get answers."

Kane's shoulders flexed, making his scars dance, but he nodded.

Ryland cursed. "He's mine."

"And mine." Kane met his gaze, the two men who had been most connected to Dante, who owed him the most. "We kill him together."

After a tense moment, Ryland nodded.

Quinn looked around. "Who wants to go with Zach and make sure we don't lose him?"

Gabe stood up, his hands still covered in Zach's blood. "I will. I owe him after almost killing him."

"You're prepared to convince him you don't trust us?"

Gabe snorted. "Of course. You're a slippery bastard with an ego and a *sheva*. What's there to trust?"

Quinn grinned. "Watch it or I'll have to cut off your head."

"See? Slippery bastard. As I said."

Quinn nodded. "Ian, you still go to Ezekiel's prison and check it out, but I'm keeping Ryland here to read Dante's *mjui* instead of Gideon." He looked around. "Thano, Kane, Gideon and I will stand guard while Ryland enters the sleep of the *mjui*. Once he awakes, we'll make decisions based on what we've learned."

"That's it?" Kane swung his double-spiked flail restlessly, the spiked balls at the end of the metal chains whizzing though the air. "You want us to sit around for eight hours while Ryland reads the *mjui*? Screw that. I'm going with Ian. We'll hit Ezekiel's prison and find out what's going on."

"Good." Quinn liked the efficiency of Kane using his teleporting abilities to get Ian to the prison more quickly. "That way you guys can get back fast if you find anything."

There was no hesitation as the warriors got to their feet, all except Zach, who continued to lie in the mud, unconscious. Weapons were sheathed and the night began to hum as they all opened their senses to search for Dante's *mjui*.

Grace walked over and sat down next to Zach as Gabe headed over toward them to guard Zach. "I'll watch him and let you know when he starts waking up."

Quinn frowned. "I don't want you close to him when he wakes up. He'll be coming for you again if the illusion is still active."

Grace pulled her knees to her chest and rested her chin on them. "I'll call you in plenty of time, but I can't help find Dante's *mjui*." She nodded at Gabe. "He can." She looked at Quinn. "I can't stand sitting around doing nothing while Ana's in danger. It's a waste of time to have Gabe guarding Zach. I'll do it so he can be productive. I'll be fine."

Quinn cursed at the thought of leaving her, but he knew she was right. The clock was ticking, and they had to be efficient. He crouched before her and cupped her chin. "Be safe, *sheva*."

There was a weariness in her gaze he didn't like, but she smiled. "I'll do my best."

"Not enough. Promise me."

Her eyebrows went up. "I can't promise that. Being

safe isn't my priority right now. You know that."

"Even for me?"

She hesitated. "Yes."

"Damn you, woman. Just when I was starting to like you." He sighed and kissed her softly. Then he stood up and turned to Gabe. "Let's go."

Quinn made it all the way to the edge of the woods before he succumbed to the need to look back and check on her. She was already leaning over Zach, using the hem of her shirt to wash the blood from his face.

"Come on, man. Let her go. She's just a woman." Gabe nudged his shoulder.

Quinn scowled at Gabe, clenching his fists against the urge to lay Gabe out for dismissing her. "Just a woman? She's a woman taking care of Zach even though he tried to kill her. She's a warrior and she deserves a chance to live."

Gabe raised his brows in surprise, a thoughtful look on his face. "That's your only response? No call to arms?"

Quinn gritted his teeth. "The bond is under control."

"Glad to hear it man. She's awfully damn sexy to have to kill." Gabe slugged Quinn on the shoulder then headed off into the woods.

Quinn glanced at Grace one last time, his heart tightening as she smiled up at him, her eyes tired but determined. Then he turned away, breaking into an easy lope as he followed Gabe into the woods, his stomach burning as he left his *sheva* behind with a man who wanted her dead.

Ana was surprised by how much Lily jumped when the door slammed open. Where was the calm, focused woman she'd met the first time? Now, Lily was on edge and stressed, making Ana feel like the one who had it all together. Given Ana's state of mind these days, it was just not a good thing if they had to resort to relying on her, was it?

Nate walked in, his eyes smug and satisfied when he saw both women in the cell. "Lily, what a pleasant surprise. I thought you'd be in bed by now."

Lily lifted her chin. "I'm fine, Nate, thanks for asking." But Ana could feel Lily trembling. With fatigue? With fear? With pain? Anger began to build inside Ana, fury at these men who thought it was all right to hurt Lily. "Though I must admit," Lily added, "I'll feel that much better when you're dead."

The man Ana assumed was Frank laughed softly. "Enjoy your spirit, Lily. It won't last."

Lily tensed, and fear rippled over Ana. Beneath the pleasant tone of his voice was a promise of his willingness to do terrible things to get what he wanted.

"Step aside, Lily," Nate said, "Frank wants to meet Ana."

Lily squeezed Ana's hand, then moved to sit on the cot. She sat regally, giving no indication of the traumatized state she'd been in when she'd walked in. How could she give off such a powerful aura when she was hurting so much inside? Ana admired her for that courage, and it renewed her determination to find a way for both of them to get free.

"Anastasia Matthews," said Nate's cohort thoughtfully. "My name is Frank Tully." He had hard lines on his face, too much weight in his jaw. He looked like he was in his early fifties, but it was difficult to tell. He was studying Ana intensely, as if he were dissecting her, tabulating her weaknesses and strengths, preparing his plan for her. Thoughtful and calculating.

Ana stiffened, bunching her fists. She'd had enough of men making plans for her. "What do you want?" She shoved her hair out of her face and gave her haughtiest glare, trying to mimic Lily's confident stance.

Frank's thoughtful visage turned deadly, and his mouth twisted in an enraged line as his gaze settled on Ana's temple. "You're hurt?"

Ana touched the bruise he was looking at, wondering how purple it was. "Of course I am. Nate beats me up to get me to do dark illusions."

"What?" Enraged, Frank strode across the cell toward her as Nate slithered back toward the door. She recoiled from Frank as he reached for her.

He held his hands up in a sign of peace. "I want to see your injuries."

"I'm fine." Ana glanced at Nate, and her gaze went to the gold chain around his neck. Was the stone on his necklace? She hadn't seen him fancied up like that before. What an ass, to be dressed in elegance when they were suffering. She knew it was to mess with them, but it disgusted her.

Lily followed her glance at the necklace, then shook her head. She'd already checked the chain. There was no stone on it.

"You're not fine." Frank grabbed her wrist and Ana couldn't stop from yelping in pain. Frank shoved her sleeve up and looked at her arm, ran his fingers over the bruises. "Nate did this?" His voice was low, boiling with anger. "Nate *hurt* you?"

Did this man have control over Nate? "Yes, he hurts me all the time," she said, intentionally goading him, wanting to see his response. Was he her secret ally? Was he the one who could help her? "Lily, too."

Nate's eyes narrowed and he tapped the brand on his forearm in a silent threat to tell her to stop talking. Her gaze involuntarily went to the image of the knife...the knife with a stone handle.

Her heart caught. Was that it? Was that what Lily was talking about? The stone was his knife?

Frank glared at Nate. "You were supposed to help

Ana develop her dark illusions, not beat her."

Nate shrugged. "That's what it takes."

"You should have told me. We would have found another way." Frank frowned at Ana's bruised arm. "I'm sorry, Ana—" Then he stopped and peered more closely at her arm. "What's this?" He ran his finger over her skin.

Ana frowned when she saw what he was looking at. On her forearm was the faintest hint of several silver lines, thin and delicate. They were barely visible through the bruises, but there was no mistaking them. What were they? "I have no idea. I've never noticed it before." They looked familiar, though. Where had she seen them before?

Frank grabbed her other arm and yanked up her sleeve. The identical image was on that forearm.

"She's been marked?" Nate moved up to stand beside Frank, peering at her arms. "They're not mine."

Marked? Marked by what? Ana looked at Lily, whose eyes were wide as she, too, looked at Ana's arms. Wide in a "holy shit" kind of way that made Ana tense. "What are you talking about?"

"Calydon brands. You've bonded with a warrior. One of the ones you killed?" Frank gave Ana a speculative look that made her skin crawl. "They look familiar," he mused. "I've seen them before, but where?"

Calydon brands? Ana knew instantly who they were from. The marks on her arms matched part of the design of Elijah's throwing star. The brands on his forearms were now on hers? She had no idea why, but Elijah was her private memory, not to be tainted by men like Frank and Nate. She'd rather stay in the dark than engage them in discussions about it.

She yanked her arm back, not wanting Frank to figure out who the marks belonged to. "What do you want from me?"

He gave her a speculative look, displeasure wrinkling his brow. "I wanted to make sure you were all right." He glowered at Nate. "I'm not pleased."

Nate shrugged. "It's not your problem, is it?"

Ana watched as Frank slowly turned and faced Nate. He was smaller than Nate, but he carried an aura of power. Of utter and complete confidence.

A faint feeling of recognition fluttered through Ana. She recognized that stance. The way he leaned slightly to the left, as if he was trying to keep his weight off his right side. She'd seen it before. She *knew* him. But how?

Frank's eyes narrowed at Nate. "I gave her to you because I wanted her trained, not beaten."

Gave her to Nate? What? Nate had been the one to abduct Ana off the street when she'd been going for a morning run. She'd never seen Frank Tully before in her life. Or had she?

She had. She *knew* she had. But where?

He must have sensed her watching him, because he smiled at her.

She knew that smile. It felt...familiar. Scary. And comfortable. Right. And wrong. "Who are you?"

"In due time, my dear." He turned back to Nate. "They're bringing the young Calydon to you. I'll provide enough men that you won't need Ana's illusions. No more beatings. Now that you've gotten the dark illusions out of her, I can help her develop them." There was distinct pride in his voice as he glanced at Ana. "You've always been special, Ana, even if you didn't believe it."

Ana frowned at him. "What are you talking about? How do you know me?"

"Beating is the only way," Nate interrupted. "I need to do it for this last illusion—"

Frank's hand moved so fast Ana didn't even see it change position. One minute Nate was standing there looking smug, and the next minute he was flying across the room. He crashed into the wall so hard the cement cracked.

Ana scrambled backwards as Nate slid down the

wall, blood trickling down his cheek. *God, please let them kill each other.*

Nate called out his knife with a crack and hurled it across the room. It sank deep into Frank's shoulder, and Ana gasped as he dropped to his knees with a groan.

"Don't challenge me," Nate snarled. "Bring your men with you and do what I tell you to do, or you get nothing. We both get nothing. How many times do I need to remind you what we're dealing with? The ultimate power doesn't come without risk, and we can't afford to displease him. He deserves our loyalty and our commitment."

Frank yanked the knife out of his shoulder and tossed it behind him. It landed with a clatter on the floor of the cell. Lily lunged for it and swept it up as Frank faced Nate, who'd called out his other knife and was twirling it around on his finger. "You underestimate me," he told Nate. "With Ana properly trained, I'm strong enough to—"

"No. You underestimate who I'm working for. Big difference."

Trained for what? While the men continued to argue, Ana glanced at Lily, who was studying the knife. Ana hurried over to Lily, who held it out to her. The blade was metal, but the handle was stone. There was writing inscribed on it in an old language Ana had no hope of deciphering. Ana knew instantly that this was the stone they'd been looking for. "I can't read it," she whispered to Lily.

"I can. I just need a few minutes—"

There was a hum and the knife snapped out of Ana's hand and slapped back into Nate's palm. Lily groaned in frustration.

Frank was staring at the knife, a look of surprise on his face. "You had the tablet inscribed on your *weapon?*"

Nate sheathed the knife inside his arm. "And poof, it's gone." He spread his hands. "You'll never get it from me, so don't bother to try. Just play nice and we'll all get what we want." He jerked his head toward Ana. "I assume we're finished here."

Frank glanced at Ana, and his face softened. "For now." He crouched in front of her and touched her forearm where the marks were. "I'll be back for you, Ana."

She knew that would be a really bad thing, but something deeper inside her yearned for him to do exactly that. "Who *are* you?"

He patted her cheek, then stood up and strode out of the room.

Nate walked over to Lily and grabbed for her, but she ducked out of his grasp. Displeasure darkened his features. "Come on, darling. It's time to go back in your play pen." He strode to the door as Lily strode after him, her gait regal and poised, a woman to be reckoned with despite how Ana knew she was crumbling inside. Just seeing Lily's courage made Ana stand a little straighter.

Lily glanced back at Ana as she walked out. "You can do it," she whispered. "I'll be waiting."

Then the door shut behind them, leaving Ana alone in her cell once again.

Ana's forearms began to burn, and she pushed her sleeves back to study the marks. Somehow, just having the marks on her arms gave her confidence. They made her feel stronger because they were her connection to a warrior who had lived and fought for centuries. She knew she could do it. She'd find a way. *She would.* Elijah might have fallen to Nate's blade, but he was still with her. A part of her. Giving her his warrior strength. With him, she could do it. After having too many people dying to save her, it was finally time for her to repay the favor. This time, she would do the saving. This time, no one would suffer to keep her safe. "I'll get free, Lily," she said. "And I'll come back for you."

Adrenaline and fire rushed through her, and Ana grinned. For the first time since Nate had taken her, she was looking forward to their next outing. This time, she wasn't going as the victim. This time, she was going to be the victor.

Ana tucked her arms against her chest, and curled into a ball on the cot, knowing she needed to sleep, to gather her strength. With the marks on her arms pulsing with reassurance, she fell into a true sleep for the first time since Nate had kidnapped her and thrust her into this nightmare.

She dreamed of a warrior in black leather. One who hated her, but saved her anyway.

◆◆◆◆

After successfully concluding the search for Dante's *mjui*, Quinn wearily strode back into the clearing just as the sun was beginning to peek through the trees, burning off the fog that had been surrounding them for days.

Grace was sleeping, curled up next to Zach, her hand on the warrior's heart as she held his jacket closed over his chest. She was muddy, Zach's blood was on her hands and face, yet she was still holding tight to him.

"Look at how she put that coat over him, as if a little damp chill could hurt Zach?" Gabe's voice was quiet beside him. "Does she think we're a bunch of pansies or what?" But there was respect in his tone, an appreciation that hadn't been there when they'd left her hours before.

"Probably." Quinn walked into the clearing and kneeled beside Grace. "Come on, *sheva*," he whispered. "It's time for Gabe to take over."

She mumbled something about watching out for Zach, and Gabe crouched next to Quinn. He lifted his hand as if to touch her hair, but let it drop without touching her. "I'll watch him now," he told her. "You did well."

Quinn slid his arms around Grace and gently lifted her against his chest, absurdly pleased when she leaned into him and let her head fall against him. "You keep your mind open to me," he reminded Gabe. They'd done a blood exchange earlier in the night so they'd be able to keep in touch over a long distance.

It would create a life-long bond between them that was tighter than most warriors felt comfortable with, but it had been necessary. Once Gabe and Zach were on their way to retrieve Drew, it would be the only way for Gabe to contact Quinn without Zach realizing it.

Gabe nodded and sat in the mud beside Zach, forearms draped over his knees. "You'll know when we're on the move. Just don't forget to show up when I give you the word."

"It'll be the party of the year. We'd never miss it." Quinn gave a few final instructions to Gabe, then he carried Grace back toward where Ryland was just entering the sleep of the *mjui*. Thano was standing guard. The others were already sleeping, catching a few winks before their rotation as guards. Quinn had the last shift, so he had several hours until he was on duty.

He had to try to sleep. He knew he needed to, but he couldn't slow his mind down enough to do so. He was too haunted by what had happened earlier, by how close he'd come to going rogue, and by the power of the *sheva* bond to bring him back not once, but twice.

Quinn found a spot in the woods that was hidden from the others, but close enough to provide immediate assistance with his sword if he were needed. He kicked a bunch of sticks and rocks out of the way, then he stretched out on the damp earth, settling Grace on top of him so she wouldn't have to sleep on the ground. He wrapped his arms around her as she nestled her head under his chin. "I'm sorry," he whispered.

She stirred. "Mmm..."

"I'm sorry I almost killed you tonight." He grimaced as the moment came crashing back: that terrifying moment when he'd turned toward her with his sword in his palm and deadly intent in his heart. He wrapped his arms more snugly around her, trying to block the guilt building in him at the thought of what had almost happened. "If you hadn't helped me knock out that illusion—"

Her hand went to his mouth, her fingers pressing against his lips. "You wouldn't have killed me." Her voice was husky with sleep.

He pressed his face into her hair, relishing the scent he now associated with her. "Didn't you feel my hatred?"

She sighed and lifted her head, propping her chin up on her hands so she could look at him. Her face was lit by the rays of dawn coming through the tree branches, tinting her skin a soft golden hue. "Give me a break, Quinn. You weren't going to kill me. All I did was remind you of that little fact." She patted his cheek and yawned. "I'm your *sheva*. You can't possibly kill me, remember? Some things are even stronger than an illusion." She found his hand and entwined her fingers in his. "Until we bond and have to destroy each other, we're a team, in every dangerous and deadly sense of the word."

He was quiet for a minute, letting himself absorb the feeling of Grace's body draped across his, trusting him. "Does it bother you? My life? What I do? All the killing?"

She hesitated. "Yes."

He couldn't stop the stab of disappointment. Had he expected anything else? Here was a woman who'd been haunted her entire life by one accidental death. What made him dare hope that she wouldn't have a problem with who he was?

"But it's okay."

He frowned. "What does that mean?"

"It means..." Grace wrinkled her nose while she tried to think of how to explain it, and he found himself tensing. Hoping. "It means that it's part of what makes you who you are. Without it, you're not you. And that would be wrong. It's your whole package that I like." She rolled her eyes. "But, seriously, Quinn, what woman *wouldn't* be a little wigged out by your life? Zach nearly got decapitated tonight! By a friend! And Gabe?" She shuddered. "He's going to be the last face I see before I die. Or maybe it'll be Ryland. It's clear you guys are expecting him to go rogue at any second. Or even Gideon. He's ready to do his job." She dropped her head and pressed it to his chest. "God, I'd blocked all that out. I take it back. It's not okay. Your friends scare the daylights out of me."

He smiled. "If it's any consolation, you scare them more."

She studied him for a minute. "And how do *you* feel about all of it?"

He met her gaze. "Sometimes I find myself wanting to forget that I'm not supposed to let myself care about you."

The intensity in his voice went straight to Grace's heart, and the tension she'd been holding all night finally began to uncurl. Despite his harsh edges and the rules he lived by, Quinn was her rock in a world that was sliding out of control. Her kindness in a world where too many people wanted her dead. Her support when she felt like she couldn't take it anymore.

Grace was so used to expecting betrayal from others, especially after what had happened with her fiancé, that it was such a gift to be able to count on Quinn. Having his support was empowering her in so many ways. He'd given her a place, albeit it a temporary one, with the Order and with himself, which had given her the courage to stand up in front of all of them and admit what she was and what she could do.

Yes, Grace was aware that at least a large part of Quinn's loyalty was to the bond, but she was beginning to be okay with that, because it meant she could count on him. With her sister's life at stake, it was an unbelievable feeling to know that Quinn would stand by her, even when he was half-crazy.

Of course, were they to complete the bond, it was back to her old life of having people betray her, but for now, it was a gift, and she was taking advantage of everything about it. She was going into this with her eyes open and her heart protected, knowing that Quinn's dedication to her was because of the bond and not because of who she was. She wouldn't lie to herself about the future, but for today? She wanted to live and breathe what he gave her.

"Kiss me, Quinn," she whispered. "I need you to kiss me."

He didn't ask why. He simply tightened his grip on her, moved her higher up on his chest so he could reach her, then kissed her.

The moment the tender softness of his mouth embraced hers, her insides unclenched. She sighed with relief and pleasure. *This is what I needed.*

His hands tangled in her hair, and he deepened the kiss, his tongue sliding in and out, his lips coaxing her to respond. *I need it too,* sheva. *God, I need this right now.*

The earnestness underlying his words flowed through her, triggering a spiral of heat, warmth, and something else: a *belonging.* Grace moaned his name as his hands slipped beneath her jeans and his knuckles kneaded her bottom. Her body began to move against him, desire blossoming deep in her core as he hardened beneath her, responding to her, *needing her.*

She sat up and straddled him as she tugged her shirt over her head, his hands sliding up her ribs and over her breasts as she exposed them to the cool morning air. His gaze settled on her breasts, and she felt a shiver of excitement at his intense perusal, her nipples hardening at the first touch of a breeze.

Quinn cupped her breasts, then pulled her down so he could kiss each one. A tender kiss that made her tremble, then shudder when he scraped his teeth across her nipple. His hands supported her lower back, and she leaned back into his grasp, the muscles of his forearms hard against her sides. She drank in his strength, ran her hands over the tightness of his biceps, and relinquished herself to him.

Sheva.

Grace trembled at the endearment, at the tenderness of the word as it spilled through her mind. That's why she was safe with him right now, because she was his *sheva*. Not because she was Grace Matthews. The thought sobered her, and a little part of her wished that it was different. That he was there with her because of who she was, not because they were connected by some bond.

No. She was too wise to yearn for a fairy tale. She was lucky to have this moment, the unfailing commitment from Quinn, a warrior so honorable and brave. A man who truly wasn't fazed by who she was. A partner who had brought her into a world where no one was daunted by her powers, where her value actually increased because she was an Illusionist, instead of her talents being a black mark that qualified her for hatred, disgust and fear.

So what if this magical moment was because some archaic destiny had forced them together? So what if he didn't love her? Grace couldn't let it matter. That wasn't her life. It wasn't her future. She sighed, realizing that she was lying to herself. Before Quinn had showed her what it was like to be able to count on someone, she'd convinced herself she didn't need it.

But she did. She wanted the dream. She wanted the fairy tale.

"Grace?" Quinn paused, his dark eyes searching hers. "You okay?"

She shook off the melancholy, refusing to lose this moment because of some naive longing for something she'd never have. "It's perfect," she said.

He narrowed his eyes. "Why are you lying to me?"

"Just kiss me, you fool." Grace pressed her lips to his, and Quinn kissed her back, instantly taking over the kiss. His mouth was a sensual decadence, calling her out of her brooding and awakening a rush of desire that was like liquid heat crashing through her.

Quinn shrugged out of his jacket, never ceasing his seduction as he trailed his lips over her collarbone, nipping and scraping, sending chills through her body.

He tossed his coat behind her, then eased her down on it, his motions so gentle and tender, as if he were afraid to break her. "This time, it will be the way I've wanted to make love to you since the beginning," he whispered as he bent to lave her belly, his tongue teasing into the crevice of her navel as his fingers unfastened her jeans and he began to slide them over her hips with a sensual intimacy that shattered the shields around her heart.

"Yes," she whispered. This was what she wanted. To be made love to as if she was his entire world and always would be, as if the magic between them was simply them and how they felt about each other.

"Oh, yes," Quinn agreed as he kissed her again, harder now, demanding her body's response.

Excitement flared through her and she lifted her hips as he trailed kisses down her belly, following the path of her pants as he pulled them off her. His mouth tangled in her curls, and then his hot mouth between her legs made her jerk as he swept his tongue through her folds.

Let yourself go, sheva. His voice was a commanding whisper in her mind, but she felt his tremor as he fought to keep his own desire under control. He tightened their mental connection, and her body convulsed when she felt his need for her, his lust, his raging desire.

She grabbed for him, the bare skin of his shoulders flexing beneath her grip as he wrapped his hands around her legs and parted them further, stretching her as far as she could go, exposing her until she had no defenses, no protection, nothing. She was at his mercy, and she loved it, loved that she could trust him completely and know she was safe in his arms.

She shivered at the knowledge, at the awareness that he controlled her, that she was putting herself into his hands. She thrilled in the sensation of giving herself over to him.

You are mine, he growled as his fingers thrust into her.

The orgasm was instant, rising up from the depths of her soul so fast and so unexpectedly she screamed. Quinn kept his fingers deep inside her as he caught her mouth with his, driving the orgasm on and on, as her body shrieked with the pressure of the release, the cycle of power seizing her until she thought she couldn't survive it.

The moment it faded, while her body was still vibrating with the aftershocks, Quinn rolled off her long enough to ditch his jeans, and then he was back between her legs, his skin sliding against hers. No fabric between them, just the tantalizing, vulnerable feel of flesh to flesh. Arousal surged through her, and she grabbed his hair and pulled his face to hers as his lean hips settled between her thighs. His skin was hot and slick against hers, and his upper body loomed over her. His chest was wide and ripped with muscles, decadently hard beneath her hands. A man who could keep her safe from anything, if he chose to.

I'll always protect you, he growled. *Never, ever doubt that.*

Her throat tightened at his declaration, and she wished this moment would be forever.

Quinn reached between them and guided himself into her, and she welcomed his length and thickness into her body, shuddering at the connection as they became one, at the sense of absolute rightness as he breathed her name as he sank more deeply inside her.

She wrapped her legs around his waist and lifted her hips to meet him as he drove into her again and again. Tension coiled deep inside her as his rhythm intensified, as his control began to slip, as he fell into the desire building inside him, his need, his commitment to her. For her.

It was against everything Quinn had been for the last five hundred years, for the duration of his existence, yet his walls had fallen to her, to their bond, to his *sheva*. She felt his dedication to her in every trembling muscle in his body, in the glistening sweat as he struggled to keep control, in the tender way his fingers caressed her hair and in his reverent kisses as he staked his claim on her body, spirit, and soul.

Grace clung to his shoulders as his hips thrust even deeper, penetrating to her very core. She lifted her knees to draw him further into her, needing more. Emotions swelled in her chest, emotions that were so pure and powerful, she could almost imagine that there was nothing metaphysical pulling them together. Not this time. This time, it felt like it was simply them.

God, Grace. His groan was of complete capitulation, of total surrender as he thrust again, and her walls shattered.

I put my life in your hands, for now and for always. The words sprung unbidden from deep inside her, and his body instantly went rigid as the orgasm hit him, then ripped into her. She clung to him as the culmination of desire claimed her, and his arms held her tight against him as they rode the final crest together. As one.

The final tremors faded as he eased them to the ground, tucking her into the shield of his body. She snuggled into his heat and smiled as he pressed his lips to her hair. For now, for this moment, she would crawl into the shelter he gave her.

For it would all be over far too soon.

CHAPTER 14

Several hours later, Quinn paused as he approached the gathering at the campfire, appreciating the sight of Grace huddled up with his team. It looked....right. They'd spent the last several hours searching the Internet for any information on Nate, or how to bring down Ezekiel's walls, and they'd come up with nothing. *Nothing.*

Kane had teleported back from Ezekiel's prison, confirming what they had already assumed, that the walls were indeed weakening. He and Ian hadn't been able to find any reason for it, but he'd left Ian there to keep searching while he came back to report.

Zach had woken up, still under the illusion, and the Order had made themselves scarce until Gabe had hustled him off to get Drew. Gabe had checked in several times to let them know things were proceeding and that they'd found the kid and the uncle.

But since then, there'd been no contact, and Gabe hadn't responded to Quinn's attempts to contact him. It had only been an hour, but it was long enough that Quinn was starting to get edgy.

As soon as Ryland finished relaying what he'd learned from Dante's *mjui*, Quinn was going to pack up the team and head out after Drew if they hadn't made contact with Gabe by then.

Grace was sitting by herself on one of the logs, so Quinn slipped in behind her, positioning himself so his legs went on either side of hers. He wrapped his arms around her waist and rested his chin on her shoulder, needing to feel her body against his. Needing her to rebuild his foundation before they went to war.

This morning, in the woods, Grace had given him sanity and humanity when he'd needed it most. She'd embraced him, given him all that she had and was, and her gift had branded him deep inside. She'd given him life, on her own, not because of any metaphysical bond driving them into each other's arms and bodies.

He pressed a kiss to the side of her neck, and smiled when she set her hand on his thigh. Thano raised his eyebrows at them, but Quinn didn't move away. Grace was his, and he wasn't in the mood to hide it. His team would just have to accept that she made all of them stronger.

Ryland stood up, pacing restlessly, more on edge than Quinn had ever seen him. The warrior was already close to rogue. How close were they to losing him now? "I finished reading Dante's *mjui*," Ryland said. "Three Calydons and a woman approached the fishing shack. The short one walked up to Dante, and Dante greeted him by name, calling him Nate."

Well, that was interesting. Quinn rested his chin on Grace's shoulder while he considered that bit of information. "Dante knew Nate?" If so, there had to be information about Nate available somewhere. They just had to find it.

He laughed softly, thinking of the one person who they needed right now: the pain-in-the-ass self-proclaimed Calydon expert, Professor Lily Davenport. She'd gone underground a couple years ago, and they'd all been relieved to have the internationally known speaker off the radar. But shit, they could use her now. She could probably answer a lot of questions that they used to rely on Dante for.

Hell. Maybe they should try to track her down.

Ryland nodded. "Seemed as if Dante had invited Nate to come. Dante wanted to know what Nate knew about Ezekiel's prison."

Kane narrowed his eyes. "Why would he suspect Nate was involved? Who the hell is this guy?" He looked at Quinn for an answer, but Quinn had none.

"Nate said he'd found the tablet," Ryland said.

"What tablet?" Thano asked.

Ryland shrugged. "Dante knew what he was talking about, though, and he demanded Nate give it to him. He was furious Nate would even mess with it. I've never seen him lose his cool like that."

Quinn rubbed his jaw in Grace's hair. "Did he get the tablet from Nate?"

"Nope. Nate didn't even flinch," Ryland said. "He invited Dante to join him, to give his weapons voluntarily so that Ezekiel could harvest his power and bring down the walls. After making the offer, he simply waited, as if he knew Dante would say yes."

"An illusion," Grace said. "He was trying to put an illusion on Dante to make him agree."

Kane stood up, switching his flail restlessly from side to side, his scars vivid in the afternoon sun. "Dante's too powerful to be affected by an illusion. He'd never betray us. Ever."

"He didn't," Ryland said. "He told Nate to walk away while he still had the chance, said he was a fool to be messing with the tablet and Ezekiel." Ryland looked around at the team, his body rigid as his voice leveled, going carefully, devoid of emotion. "Then there was this hellacious screaming, like millions of innocents were being tortured. Dante stumbled. Nate went for the kill, so Dante struck first and threw his weapons at Nate. The other two Calydons took the hits for Nate. Before Dante could recall his weapons, Nate got the killing blow in while Dante was still reeling from the screams."

Kane spun to face him, his eyes haunted, his scars standing out on his body. "Dante really died? You saw his death?"

Ryland nodded. "Hell, yeah. I saw it. I lived it with him." His jaw hardened. "He's gone."

Kane threw back his head and let out a visceral howl of anguish. Grace dug her fingers into Quinn's thighs, and she started to rise, to go to Kane.

But before she could get to her feet, Ryland set his hands on Kane's scarred shoulders and gripped him. Kane cut off his howl and jerked his head down to look at Ryland. For a moment, there was silence, then Kane dropped his head so his forehead was pressed against Ryland's.

Both men closed their eyes, and simply stood there in silence, as the truth they'd been trying to deny finally became unassailable. There was no way to hold out hope any longer. Their leader was gone.

No one else moved or even breathed while the two warriors, the ones who owed their lives and their sanity to Dante most deeply, faced the brutal truth of their mentor's death. Quinn met Gideon's gaze, and he knew they were both remembering Elijah. Grace entwined her fingers with his and squeezed. He didn't let her go.

Finally, Kane lifted his head, and Ryland did the same. Their gazes met for a long moment, then Kane gave a slight nod. Ryland thudded his shoulder once, then dropped his hands and turned back to the group and continued his story as if he hadn't been interrupted. "As Dante died, he looked right at Nate and laughed. He said Nate would fail because he couldn't get Dante's weapons. He said the Order would hunt him down before he ever got another chance."

"Damn right, we will." Kane's fist was bunched around the handle of his flail. "He's mine."

Quinn thought about what Ryland had said. "Nate couldn't get Dante's weapons because Dante used them to kill the Calydons and hadn't called them back before Nate killed him, so there were no weapons in his arms for Nate to harvest. Dante did that on purpose."

"Hell, Quinn. We're up to our eyeballs in shit, we've got no idea what the hell's going on, and the only one who would know is dead." Gideon stood up, kicking aside the ashes from their fire.

Quinn surveyed the group. "Calydon weapons are being stolen, and it has something to do with why Ezekiel's walls are falling. I bet Nate wants Drew because his weapons would have the same powers as Dante's, since Dante is his father."

"But why Dante? Why you? Why not the rest of us?" Ryland asked. "What's the difference?"

Quinn frowned, and then he looked at Gideon. "The trainee that was killed at my house. You read his tag, right?"

Gideon nodded. "Yeah. Alex Drachman. Weapon was a spiked club. Lineage was—" His eyes widened. "Oh, *hell*."

Quinn punched his fist into his hand. "That's *it*." Triumph coursed through him as he swung back to the team. "It's the original twenty-one."

Thano whistled softly. "You mean, the twenty-one men who teamed up with Caleb to take down Ezekiel two thousand years ago? The ones that made up the original Order?"

"Yeah. I'm a direct descendent from them. So were Dante and his son. And so was the trainee whose weapon he stole." Quinn was psyched. He knew he was right. His instincts were vibrating, telling him he'd nailed it. "The stories talk of the ritual that bound Ezekiel in the prison. The legend is that it required a weapon donated from each of the twenty-one men who took him down. I'll bet Nate wants to reverse that ritual, and he needs the same weapons as before. All of the originals are dead, so the next best thing is the direct descendants."

There was a rustle among the men, a rumble of satisfaction that they were moving forward. "And the tablet?" Ryland asked. "Instructions on how to do it?"

"Makes sense, doesn't it?"

"Hang on." Gideon paused. "You're the only one whose weapon he took that is still alive. Does that matter?"

Quinn frowned. "Nate wanted Dante to donate his weapons voluntarily so Dante would be alive when Nate used them to free Ezekiel. It was Dante's being alive that was key." Their gazes met. "Nate will use my power instead, since I'm still alive."

Ryland rose to his feet. "The Order was created originally to protect the innocents from Ezekiel. That's our number one priority." His machete snapped out of his arm and into his palm. "We can't let him use Quinn's power to free Ezekiel."

"I agree." Quinn swung his leg off the log and stood up. "Our goal is still to find Nate and kill him, and to get my sword back. But now we also need to find the tablet, whatever it is. But if that fails and Nate gets away with my weapon and the tablet...." He looked around. "You have to take me out. We can't afford to have him use my weapon to free Ezekiel."

Grace's shock hit Quinn like a sword in his gut. *No.* Her words were sharp with fury. *Don't you dare sacrifice yourself.*

He was startled by the depth of pain in her beautiful eyes. *It has to be this way. It's part of my oath.*

But that's ridiculous! Killing each other isn't some moral sacrifice. It's just insanity. What is wrong with you?

Surprise coursed through Quinn at her intense reaction, at her anguish. He wasn't sure how to respond.

It was automatic, the willingness of Order members to sacrifice themselves if necessary. No one would ever care about him more than their goal, not enough to try to stop him. *Grace*—

"Quinn." Gideon interrupted their conversation as he set his hand on Quinn's shoulder. "I'll wield the blade."

Quinn met Gideon's gaze. "I'll look into your eyes at death." It was a promise they'd made a thousand times, and he hadn't really given a shit at the time. What the hell was the point? That was his life. He was a walking testament to the brutality of the Order, with his uncle's blood on his hands.

But now, as his gaze slithered across the fire toward Grace, and he saw her tormented expression, his first thought wasn't about doing his job. It was a raw fear about what would happen to Grace if he were killed. Who would protect her? Who would help her find Ana? Who would keep her from having to face all her burdens alone?

Shit. He shouldn't be thinking like that. He should be focused on his mission.

But he damn well couldn't.

Ryland lingered at the edge of the fire. "I'll back up Gideon if he can't pull it off." His eyes flickered with bottomless torment. "I can do it, no problem."

"Stop it!" Grace jumped to her feet. "Are you guys serious? You'll just knock off one of your own without another thought? How can you do that?"

Gideon's expression was stoic from years of practice in shutting down his emotions. "It's not without thought, and it's not without a great deal of pain. We'll do everything we can to prevent that outcome, but we do what we must. We protect innocents from rogue Calydons at all costs, and Ezekiel is the greatest threat there is to innocents. To all of us."

"You do 'what you must?' What kind of crap is *that*? Try standing up for those you care about, for God's sake! How can you sleep at night, knowing that you killed one of your own?" She shoved at Gideon's chest as Quinn slipped his arms around her and pulled her back against him, bracing himself against her blows.

"It's who we are, *sheva*," Quinn said, but the words felt foreign to him. They pissed him off in fact. Why the hell did this have to be the Order's mode of operation? Killing everyone first instead of looking for answers? Grace's questions made sense to him, but they shouldn't.

He couldn't afford to be thinking like this. He needed to be focused. He knew that containing Ezekiel was of utmost importance. He *knew* that.

"It's *crap!*" Grace wrenched herself out of his grasp and he let her go. Her eyes were haunted with pain that jabbed Quinn deep inside. "I felt your grief when Elijah died and I know you care about each other and about living. And yet you'll roll over and die? Admit you failed, give up, and take the deathblow instead of fighting?"

Quinn ground his jaw. "It's not failure if we defeat Ezekiel. It's success."

Her mouth dropped open for a split second before she recovered. "You're telling me that by allowing Gideon to kill you, you come out the grand winner?"

There was a time when that statement would have made sense to Quinn. When all his boundaries were clear and simple. But now, looking into her silver eyes, glistening with the pain of his betrayal, he didn't know anymore. "We do what we have to do. You'll do it for your sister, and I'll do it to save the damn earth if I have to." He caught her arm as she tried to whirl away. "But hear me out. I'll do everything in my power to make this shit go down right and to walk away standing, but if it comes down to it, I'll make the choice I have to make."

Grace shook her head. "I don't understand you. I don't understand how you guys can murder people you love, no matter what the reason."

Quinn swore. "Grace—"

"That lovemaking session we just had was a lie, wasn't it?" Her face was filled with hurt and the grim reality of who he was. "It wasn't about you and me. All that intimacy was because of the bond. It wasn't real, because you don't have the ability to really care about me or anyone else, do you?"

She was wrong. He knew she was. He'd felt a connection that had nothing to do with the bond. "It was real, Grace. It couldn't have been magically constructed, not something that intense."

"Of course it was, because you wouldn't let yourself connect like that on your own." She flung her hand toward the rest of the group. "That's why no one can break that *sheva* bond! Because you guys spend so much energy on doing your duty that you forget that the source of all your power comes from inside your heart! Damn all of you and your arrogance! Of course we're going to fail. You're all so damn tough that you won't succeed." She shoved past Ryland and Gideon, punching their shoulders to get them out of her way.

They both stepped aside and let her go.

Then the warriors looked at Quinn, waiting to see if he was going to go after her.

"This is good," Ryland said. "Distance between the two of you is safer."

Quinn gritted his jaw as Grace stopped at the edge of the trees, her hands over her face and her shoulders shaking. He knew she was giving him one last chance to make it right. To step up and say screw duty, he was going with his gut, which would mean claiming his right to live, hanging onto her, and charging into battle like an adrenaline-charged lunatic.

Hell, yeah, that sounded good right now—

Quinn. Gabe interrupted his thoughts with his swift interjection.

Where the hell have you been? Quinn turned away from Grace, focusing his attention on Gabe. *I was ready to come down there after you.*

We ran into problems with the uncle. Sorry, mate, but I think he's down for the count. I did what I could, but I couldn't stop Zach from eliminating him without arousing his suspicions.

Grace's shoulders stiffened, and Quinn realized she was hearing the conversation. He knew what she was thinking: another asinine and callous sacrifice for the greater good.

Quinn understood her point. He was well aware of the magnitude of the loss of Vaughn. He was a hell of a man, honorable and tough... Hell. Quinn couldn't afford to think like that. He had to be ready to do what he needed to do. Grace was wrong. Their ability to shut down their emotions was what made them powerful warriors. *We'll check on Vaughn as soon as we can. Did Nate contact Zach?*

Grace's disgust was evident in the look she gave him, and Quinn forced himself not to respond to her. He had to stay focused.

I didn't notice any contact between them, but Zach appears to know where he wants us to take the kid. We're on our way now.

Quinn's adrenaline kicked on. This was it. It was time. *Where to?*

The Gun Rack, where Nate killed Elijah. Must bring back good memories for the bastard. The delivery is set for eleven tonight. Can you get there first?

We're leaving now. We'll pick up Ian from Ezekiel's prison and beat you there. They cut off their connection, and Quinn repeated the conversation to his men "Kane, can you teleport all of us at once?"

"Of course." Kane's energy crackled through the air like hot wind on a desert night, and the team immediately moved together until their shoulders were touching. They had to be physically connected to Kane in order for his power to work on them.

Quinn held out his hand to Grace. "Kane's going to transport us. Are you coming?"

Her face hardened with resolve, but she ran over and slipped in between the warriors. "I'm coming." There was no warmth in her voice anymore. Just fury and reserve, and Quinn knew he'd failed to be the man she'd wanted him to be.

Shit. He was trying here. What the hell did she want from him?

The air began to hum as Kane prepared to teleport them to Ezekiel's prison. Quinn caught Grace's arm and forced her to look at him. "We need to be on the same team right now," he said, keeping his voice low. "Don't shut me out."

There was such soul-deep pain in her eyes, anguish that tore at his soul. "I have to, Quinn. There's no other way."

"There's always another way," he gritted out.

"Then you be the one to choose a different path," she snapped. "Caleb and Ezekiel fought for love so powerful that it transcended everything. That's why they were so unstoppable, because they fought with their hearts. You guys fight from duty. It won't be enough." She slammed her palm into his chest. "Don't be a fool, Quinn."

Anger rippled through him. "I'm not a fool, Grace. I'm your best damn chance."

"They aren't mutually exclusive, Quinn." She glared at him with exasperation. "You have it in you to be more," she said. "I know you do. Break the rules, Quinn. It's the only way."

He shook his head. "You're asking me to be weak."

She raised her brows. "Am I? Are you so sure about that?"

Before Quinn could answer, the woods vanished in a blur of energy, and Kane relocated them to Ezekiel's prison.

⬦⬦⬦⬦⬦

Grace stumbled as her feet reformed on the hard earth, and only Quinn's grip kept her upright, her chest still falling through the vortex that had caught her when the world had disappeared.

They were in the Columbia Gorge, a huge area of cliffs, mountains and a massive river, like a miniature grand canyon. Huge walls of old red clay rose before her, no windows, no doors. The prison? A faint glow emanated from it, leaving no doubt that it wasn't simply clay that was holding Ezekiel hostage. Little pieces of clay were crumbling, falling to the ground.

Surrounding them were acres and acres of dying vegetation. Leaves were brown and spotted, plants were curled with disease, and the pungent odor of death and rot permeated her nostrils. Even the ground was crusty and rancid under her feet and she felt her skin crawl. She suddenly wanted nothing more than to get away as fast as she could. There was something terrifying and evil here, and she could feel it working its way beneath her skin.

Quinn's hand settled on the back of her neck, and she didn't shrug him off. Somehow, even an overly heroic warrior destined to break her heart and gallantly sacrifice his own life didn't seem like such a bad choice when compared with what was permeating the air around her.

Grace moved closer to Quinn, relieved when he looped his arm around her neck and positioned her in the shield of his body. They exchanged no words, but the message was clear enough between them. They might not agree, but that wouldn't change whether she could count on him to stand by her.

Ian strode into sight as he rounded the north corner

of the prison. His gaunt face and disheveled clothes were covered in red clay, as if he'd been scaling the walls. "The structure is weakening." He gestured at the dead vegetation. "This destruction is from Ezekiel. His evil's leaching out. But I can't find a single explanation for what's going on."

Grace hugged herself and shivered as the men's tension jacked up. All this was from Ezekiel, with the walls only weakened? What would happen if he actually got out?

Quinn cursed. "There's no clue as to what's causing it?"

"I can't see a damn thing." Ian's flange mace was clenched in his fist, the three-pronged blade glinting in the sun. "But there's something else going on. Something's been stalking me since I got here."

The warriors immediately fanned out, weapons out and ready, and she sensed a vibration in the air as their adrenaline kicked on and they searched with their senses.

"Is there an illusion?" Quinn asked.

Grace did a quick check of the men, using Quinn's mental connection to each of them. "Just Gideon's, but it's fading already. Nothing in the air."

"Then let's check it out," Quinn commanded his team. "Start with what's on the other side of the ridge. The air feels heavier in that direction, but I can't identify exactly what's causing it." *Grace, I need you to stay here until I can make sure it's safe.*

She could feel the threat as well, a thickness in the air, and she knew he couldn't afford to be distracted by her. *Okay. Be safe.*

He winked at her, and then, without a word of further instruction, the warriors split into two groups and moved out, with Thano staying behind with Grace, his halberd out. The long staff with the intricate double blade on the end was intimidating, but his grip was relaxed, a man at ease with his weapon. "Take cover." Thano pushed her against a small cliff, then spread his legs and gave her his back, clearly standing guard over her.

Grace's heart started to pound. "You should go help them."

"Let me do my job, *sheva*."

The tension in his voice was unmistakable, and there was no endearment in his use of the word *sheva*, unlike when Quinn used it. She pressed her body into the cliff and then she heard a crack so loud it sounded as if lightning had exploded just over the ridge. "What was that?" she asked. "It was too loud to be a weapon."

"Not too loud to be a hundred weapons being called out at once," Thano said.

"A hundred?" From over the bluff came the swell of a battle cry, followed by the reverberating clash of weapons. Sparks flew in the sky, like fireworks of hell. "Quinn!" She started to run toward them. "It's a trap—"

"Stay here!" Thano shoved her back. "Don't call out Quinn's sword, or you'll leave him defenseless. If you distract him, he can't fight." Thano sprinted off in a blur and disappeared over the crest, brandishing his halberd and sounding his own battle cry.

Grace frantically looked around for something she could use as a weapon to defend herself if the battle came near her. She grabbed a rock, hefting it to her hip, because that would so help save her life if some Calydon came streaking toward her with a battle axe in his hand.

Sheva. Are you safe? Quinn's distracted voice floated in her mind, and she caught a flash of pain from him.

I'm fine! Don't worry about me, please!

He checked out immediately, and Grace sank down against the cliff, gripping her pathetic little rock tightly. She listened to the battle raging just over the hill, wincing at each scream of death, and praying it wasn't one of the men she knew.

Then excruciating pain exploded in her gut, and

she gasped and doubled over, knowing it was Quinn's pain, so intense that it had blown through the shields he'd put up to keep her out of his mind while he was fighting. He'd just been hit. *Quinn.*

There was no response.

"Quinn!" She scrambled to her feet and ran.

⁜

Quinn jolted back to consciousness just in time. His instincts burning a warning, he instinctively jerked to the left before he even got his eyes open. A weapon thudded into the earth where his head had just been. He thrust his sword, and it embedded itself into his assailant. He called it back before the Calydon had even fallen, armed and ready again.

The world spun from the blow he'd taken, but Quinn still staggered to his feet as his men battled. All of them were bloodied and damaged, fighting against the onslaught of warriors who kept coming.

Hundreds of Calydon warriors, lying in wait for the small group of Order members.

They were losing. For the first time in history, the Order was losing, and he knew they had only one chance to survive. *Grace. We need an illusion.*

Grace's relief flooded him. *Quinn! You're okay? You're alive? I felt you get hit!*

Yeah, cool, that she was worried about him, but not the time for mushy shit. *Grace! An illusion. I'll warn the men so they can prepare to resist it.* He sank his sword into the gut of another assailant, then spun back barely in time to fend off a blow that would have decapitated him. *Now, Grace!*

Quinn knew what he was asking of her. He knew how hard it would be. He wasn't blind to the panic that hit her as she registered his orders, but it didn't matter. *You believe in fighting with passion? Then fight with yours, sweetheart, or we're going down.* Another Calydon rushed Quinn, and he blocked the blow with his sword. He ducked as a dagger hurtled through the air at his head, and it whizzed past him and plunged into the throat of his assailant. *Now, Grace!*

><><><

Grace couldn't do it. She couldn't summon an illusion on purpose. Not to kill. Not to hurt. *Don't ask that of me, Quinn.*

She tripped, her hands scraping on the rock as she crested the ridge and saw the carnage before her. The fight was raging, like the ancient battles of centuries long past spread across the high desert. Warrior against warrior. Hand to hand combat. Sheer, raw muscle and force of will their strongest weapons. The din of metal clashing was deafening, and the air filled with the grunts of men fighting for survival.

She located Quinn just as a spiked flail slammed into his back, knocking him to the earth. He rolled to the side, blood pouring from the wound as he kicked the feet out from under his assailant. His sword flashed before sweeping through the warrior's midsection.

Her stomach recoiled in horror, and she felt the pressure of an illusion, rising to protect Quinn the way it usually came to life to protect her. Instinctively, she fought it, and then she saw three weapons streaking through the air toward Quinn, more than he could fend off.

He was going to die.

"No!" She screamed her denial and dropped her shields. For the first time in her life, she stopped fighting the illusion. *Save my sister for me, Quinn. I trust you.* She'd never survive the illusion, and Quinn would have to finish her mission.

The illusion ripped out of her and she threw out her arms, embracing everything about who she was, as the power exploded from her into the world. A cold chill settled on her as icy darkness bolted up her spine, and she fed it with everything she had to give.

Unafraid. Unbound. *Free.* The wind howled and her hair whipped around her face, lashing at her skin. Black clouds rolled in and thunder crashed, shaking the very ground she was standing on.

The earth shook again, and she realized it wasn't a storm. It was the very earth coming to her aid. She gasped as she saw smoke pouring from Mt. St. Helens in the distance. Dear God, she was triggering a volcano. *Quinn! Turn off your senses!*

The mountain exploded, throwing her backwards into a cliff fifty yards away, crushing her against the rock with brutal force. She crumpled to the ground as fiery heat swept across the barren earth. Trees leapt into flames, and the earth burned from the intense heat that was racing toward them.

She gaped at the destruction from the mountain as the earth was incinerated by its fury, as the volcano's rage swept down toward them. Her face began to burn from the heat and the wind became even fiercer. A glow rose in the distance...the melted rock, sweeping toward her, to wipe them out...

She heard the screams of men as the boiling rock hit them, incinerating them, sucking them into its cauldron. The odor of burning flesh stung her nostrils, making her stomach turn. Grace tried to scramble up the rock face, away from the rolling tide of melted rock. She jammed her fingers into the crevices, desperately trying to gain traction as the heat burned through her clothes. She lost her grip, falling to the base of the cliff as the crush of melted rock swept toward her. She threw her arms up in a useless defense...and then the world went black.

Utter silence.

The pungent odor of death vanished, replaced by

nothing.

Pain was gone too.

She was in a world of nothing. A void.

Was this death?

No. It's me, Quinn said. *You risked your life to save me, and it strengthened our bond enough for me to tighten our connection. I can manipulate your senses the same way I can manipulate mine. I've blocked them for you, so the illusion can't hurt you.*

God, Quinn was alive. Touching her. *You're okay? But I saw those weapons—*

You acted in time.

Grace's relief that he was safe shook her to her core. She felt the tears deep inside her and knew they were falling on her cheeks, even though she couldn't feel them.

Sheva. The tenderness in his voice struck her, and she felt something inside her break at the endearment that felt so heartless.

No. Don't call me that. I'm tired of all this crap about duty. My name is Grace Matthews, not some nameless woman to mate with. See me for who I am, Quinn. Feel who I really am. I'm not a magical bond. I'm me, dammit! I deserve more. Grace knew why she'd called that illusion, why it had been so powerful. It had come from the very depths of her soul, triggered by all the emotions she felt for him. The fact that after all that, she was still simply a *sheva* to him? No more. She wouldn't accept it anymore.

She felt Quinn's regret. *You do deserve more, Grace, but I can't give it to you. I'm not wired like that. Right now, we need to focus on the mission. The Order needs you. Your sister needs you.*

Her sister. God, he was right. She couldn't leave Ana just because she hated the rules Quinn lived by.

I heard you accept your death and put your sister's fate in my hands. You trusted me with her.

She bowed her head, knowing she would do it again. Despite everything, she would trust Quinn with the one thing in life she held most dear. *I had no choice.* She'd had to save him. She couldn't have let him die.

As you said earlier, there is always a choice, Grace. There is always a choice.

I hate you for making me care.

You should hate me, but you don't.

She sensed his smile in her mind and wanted to hit him, to pound at his chest for seeing through her lies. *Damn you, Quinn.*

Curse me all you want, Grace, but you changed the rules today when you offered your life for a greater cause. It's exactly what I'm willing to do. We're the same, Grace.

No! It's different! I did it for you! For love! Not to fight off some stupid enemy— Grace stopped as soon as she realized what she'd said. Did she really love him? Was it true?

She felt Quinn's wonder and shock, sensed him probe her mind for the truth of her words.

Screw that. Grace slammed up her shields to keep him out of her thoughts, and to keep herself out of them as well. Loving him was a path she refused to travel. She was too smart for that. She was a survivor, not a lovesick female willing to put her heart out there for dreams that would be crushed.

Grace had saved Quinn because if one of them had to go solo, he had a better shot at saving her sister than she did. That was why. Not because of the aching loss that had torn through her at the thought of him dying. Definitely not because of that.

Quinn's frustration rumbled through her. *Don't shut me out.*

I have to. She closed her mind to his, and she felt the emptiness of his absence. Yearning swelled in her to reconnect with him. The need to touch him, to hold him, to reach out for him burned through her mind. Having him so completely cut off...it was as if he'd died.

Grief caught Grace unprepared and crashed into her, and her heart ached with loss and loneliness and a bitter, horrible feeling of utter desolation. She let the tears come, let the devastation consume her, certain that to let him back in would make everything worse.

⋈⋈⋈

Quinn was shaking with Grace's grief by the time he tested to see if the illusion was past. When he heard nothing but the sounds of vultures calling, he dropped his shields and opened his eyes. Grace was the first thing he saw, his eyes not resting until they found her.

She was huddled on the ground at the base of a cliff, her skin raw and red from the burns, her body trembling as sobs wracked her body. But she was alive, and the relief that shuddered through Quinn at that realization was tremendous.

He sent a message to his team that the danger was past, and they came to life around him with groans and the clank of weapons. The remains of their assailants littered the ground, piles of charred ash drifting in the wind. They'd been destroyed by their own belief in the deadly illusion, an illusion that would have killed Quinn and his men if they hadn't known to prepare before it hit.

Quinn hauled himself to his feet, then nearly went down again as pain rushed back into his body. Too many blows from Calydon weapons, too many he hadn't been able to avoid. Warmth trickled down his back, and he knew he was still bleeding.

Willing strength into a body in desperate need of a healing sleep, Quinn forced his way across the rock toward Grace as he released his hold on her senses.

Grace lifted her head and looked around, her gaze

coming to rest on him as he staggered toward her. Her face tightened. "Leave me alone." She dug her bleeding hands into the dirt and tried to pull herself to her knees. "Can't you just leave me alone?"

"No." His legs gave out and he went down on his hands. Grace let out a small cry of distress. Blood was running down his arm and over his hand. Too much blood. He needed to get it stopped.

"Oh for God's sake. Would you stop already? You're killing me." Tears made her voice rough as she crawled over to him and sank down beside him, slipping her hands around his shoulders. "I'm here, okay?"

He groaned as he fell into her touch. "You're...all right?"

"Yes, I am." She wrapped her arms around him as he willed himself to crawl the final few inches until his head was in her lap.

He threw his arm around her waist and closed his eyes, burying his face in the warmth of her body. Grace was safe. Finally, he could focus on the process of healing. "Don't let me go," he mumbled. "I need a minute to stop the bleeding."

She pressed her lips to his hair. "I should throw you over a cliff." But her arms tightened around him, and he knew she'd keep him safe against her for as long as he needed. He knew, because he'd felt the words she hadn't been willing to say. She hated him, yeah, maybe, but she loved him too.

The thought scared the crap out of him, but at the same time, he wanted to lock her down and never give her a chance to retract it. "Merge with me," he said. "I can heal you, too."

She shook her head. "I'm healing on my own. The illusion was so powerful that it's healing me."

He grimaced. "Damn. I wanted you to need me."

She released a soft laugh. "I do need you. I need

you to save my sister."

"That's all you need me for?"

Grace looked past him, and he knew she was watching his team recover from the ravages of battle, tying off their most severe wounds and trying to staunch the flow of blood. They were gearing up for the final battle, and they knew they were out of time. Quinn felt her realization that this might be their last moment together, that the end was coming now. Her fingers tightened in his hair. "No, Quinn, that's not all."

He managed a grin, despite the grit stinging his eyes and the damage to his body. "You need me to give you purpose in life, don't you?"

She wiped some blood off his forehead. "You drive me crazy."

"And?" He wanted her to say the words. To hear her speak it. To know what it felt like to feel that love directed at him. He wanted it. Now.

"Quinn!" Gideon's voice was gruff, laced with pain.

He swore as his team descended upon them. His personal moment with Grace was over. It was time to go after Nate and Ana.

CHAPTER 15

Grace watched warily as Gideon walked up, followed by the rest of the team. What would they think? They'd just witnessed her at her worst, her most deadly. She'd just murdered hundreds of men. Grace glanced at the field of bodies and felt ill. Had she really done that?

It had seemed so right at the time, and even afterwards, when she'd seen Quinn alive. But now that she thought of what it would look like to strangers, the judgment they would reap, suddenly she saw it the way they would see it, what the world always saw her as. A murderer. Death. Someone not to be trusted.

You did good, sweetheart. Quinn was still lying heavily across Grace, his arm tight around her waist, his body lax with exhaustion.

Thanks. But she got more and more nervous as the rest of the Order approached. The warriors were covered in blood, their clothing ripped. They loomed over her like five black angels of death. Their gazes were dark, their eyes heavy with battle.

"Grace." Gideon crouched beside her.

She lifted her chin, preparing for the condemnation.

Gideon grinned and slugged her lightly on the shoulder. "You did good."

She blinked. "Really?"

"Hell, yeah. That was impressive as hell," Gideon said. "I'm damn glad you're on our team."

There were grunts of assent from the other four, the stoic team looking at her with respect and admiration, not condemnation or horror.

"Well, okay." Grace felt stupidly pleased by the compliments. Yes, it shouldn't matter what anyone else thought, and she knew she would have done it all again, but still. This was a first, having her curse generate compliments and admiration. Warmth spread through her, beautiful, amazing warmth. They'd witnessed her at her worst, and they'd accepted her for who she was. She grinned even wider, almost wanting to leap up and start dancing. What a glorious, amazing feeling! "Thanks."

Gideon inclined his head, but there was a twinkle in his eye. Yeah, this was a good moment.

Quinn shifted on her, and he lifted his head. His gaze swept over his men, taking inventory as he rolled to his side with a wince. "How's everyone?"

"Good enough. No one's about to bleed out, so that's a plus." Gideon eyed Quinn's shoulder. "Not so sure about you, though."

"I'm fine. I'm healing." He tried to sit up, but Gideon had to help him. "You think Dante had all these men here to protect the prison? In case Ezekiel got out?"

"Could be. More likely they were already working for Ezekiel, ready to be his servants when he gets out," Gideon's voice was grim.

"Well, if they were, point for us. They're all dead now." Quinn glanced around at the bodies littering the earth. Hundreds of them. "Decent work, considering the only reason we came here was to pick up Ian on our way to The Gun Rack." He rubbed his forehead wearily. "We weren't prepared for this attack. Without Grace, we would have died. It would have ended today." He shook his head. "I don't like it. There's too much shit going on that we don't understand, and if we don't figure it out fast, we might not get lucky next time."

"The Order is the only group of Calydons who've learned to work together, and even then we still have pissing contests," Thano said. "There's no way we could have predicted hundreds of Calydons teaming up."

"Dante would have. We have to think like he would. We have to think back to what Ezekiel did two thousand years ago, and expect him to do the same." Quinn tried to rise to his feet, but he hesitated with a grunt of pain.

Grace caught his hand and helped him up.

"What's the time?" he asked, releasing Grace's wrist, his fingers brushing over the wound on her wrist that was finally beginning to heal.

"We've got less than an hour until Zach and Gabe arrive at The Gun Rack," Gideon said. "Barely enough time to figure out what we're going to face and try to deal with it."

"Illusions," Quinn said. "He'll have those going again, I'm sure of it."

Grace rubbed the healing skin on her wrist from the copper band. Now that it was healing, it was itchy. She noticed her forearms were burning, and she tugged up her sleeve to look at her mark. The outline of the sword was almost complete, with only the final design in the middle of the handle remaining. Only half a stage to go, because she'd killed for him.

She'd *killed* someone. Hundreds of men. For him.

But she didn't feel regret. Or grief. She knew, in her heart, that she'd had no other choice. She'd do it again, and again, and again. To save him. Because she loved him.

And that made it all right. Somehow, making that choice to save someone she loved took away the horror of what she'd done, of the choice she'd made. It had freed her.

The choice she'd made had bound them even tighter, and that felt good, too. So right she didn't want to question it. Not now. Just for this moment, she wanted to bask in the feeling of being connected to him.

Because it would all be over soon.

As he directed battle strategies with the other warriors, Quinn traced his fingers over her mark. He raised his eyebrows at her, and she knew he'd realized that they'd done another stage. They were close. Too close now. And the worst part was that it felt good to be bonded with him, increasing the allure of closing that final stage.

For what purpose? Sealing the bond would bring the death and destruction of all they cared about. For her, that meant Ana. For Quinn, it was saving the world. If they bonded first, before they accomplished their goals, what then? Not only would they die, but so would everyone they were trying to protect.

It was a race now, a sprint between destiny and themselves.

Quinn's face was grim as he studied the mark, even while he continued to discuss the plan for intercepting Zach and Gabe when they were handing Drew over to Nate. *All that's left is for me to kill to save your life.*

The chances of Quinn having to kill for her when they took on Nate were high, and they both knew it. *I'll take your sword and do the killing myself.*

He touched her cheek as the discussion ended and the men separated to finish preparing for battle. "I don't want you to have to kill for me."

She lifted her chin. "If that's what I have to do to make sure my sister's safe, then I'll do it."

Quinn cupped her face with his hands, deep sadness in his eyes. "I've brought violence into your life, and I'm so sorry. Because of me, you've been forced to kill, to repeat your worst nightmares. I've destroyed you already."

She wrapped her fingers around his wrists. "No. It's because of Nate. He's the reason." But she saw the self-recrimination in his eyes, and knew he didn't believe her. She tightened her grip. "You helped me survive my illusion, you helped me control it. You're giving me the courage to accept myself, to stop fearing who I am. That's giving me the gift of life, right there. When we save my sister, everything will be worthwhile." She stood on her toes and pressed her lips to his. "Loving you will always be worthwhile."

He stopped breathing for a full minute. "You love me?"

"I wouldn't have killed for you if I didn't."

He closed his eyes and whispered something she couldn't decipher, then opened his eyes again to look at her. "You're a gift," he whispered. "You don't belong in my world."

She managed a rueful smile. "A little late for that, don't you think?"

"Hey." Gideon stuck his face between them. "We don't have time for this touchy-feely shit. You ready?"

"Yeah." Quinn turned to survey his team. "Any concerns?"

"The illusions," Kane said. "Not the one by Grace's sister because we can shut down our senses with those, but the ones that made Zach try to kill you. We don't seem to have protection against that. What if he makes us turn on each other?"

"Grace will watch for it," Quinn said.

"But then what? You saw what happened when she told Zach. It didn't matter," Kane said. "Dante was able to resist, but he is..." He grimaced. "...*was*...a hell of a lot stronger than us. I don't want to go in there and find myself fighting off Ryland."

Grace frowned as the men debated how to deal with Nate's illusions, then realized she was rubbing her injured wrist. She stared down at it, then suddenly thrust it in front of the men. "This. It might work."

Ryland scowled. "Your wrist?"

"No, no, the band that made the mark. It keeps me from doing an illusion, but maybe it would work to protect against one being done on you."

Quinn frowned. "Have you ever heard of it being used that way?"

She shook her head. "It wouldn't work for a typical illusion, because those are external. The bands are intended to stop the build of illusions from within, so I'm thinking it might work with the ones that are being created inside you guys."

Quinn took her wrist and studied it. "So, where do we get them?"

"My house. I tried them when I was younger. They made me sick, so I didn't use them. But I kept them as a security blanket, in case I ever felt one coming on I couldn't control." Her gaze darted to Quinn. "Better to be sick than to accidentally kill someone."

He squeezed her hand.

"You're sure they'll work?" Gideon asked.

"No. I'm not sure at all. I'm not even sure how many I still have. And I think mine are different than this one. Not as powerful..." She frowned. "I don't know. Maybe it's not such a great idea."

Ryland spoke up. "We'll try the bands. Maybe they won't work, but it's worth trying. We don't have any other options."

The rest of the men nodded their agreement, but no one said much. What was there to say? They'd have to go in and see what happened.

"Everyone ready? We'll go by Grace's place first and see what we can scavenge in the way of copper bands, and then we head to The Gun Rack to get into position." Quinn put his arm around Grace's shoulder as the men moved together to get within Kane's range.

Grace's heart tightened at the intense look on Quinn's face. He was fully prepared to die, either at the hands of his men if they failed, or in pursuit of his goals.

Why did it have to be like that?

"We're ready," Kane said. "Let's do it."

Quinn met her gaze. *I know it's not enough for you given the extenuating factors, but I offer you my heart. For always.*

Tears filled her eyes and her throat thickened. For all that they had faced together, it was ending now. There were too many risks that could lead to one of them dying at The Gun Rack. If Quinn's weapon wasn't recovered...if the bond was consummated...if the battle went to hell. She knew she'd do whatever was necessary to save her sister, and Quinn would sacrifice himself to stop Ezekiel from getting out.

She and Quinn as a couple would end at The Gun Rack. One way, or another. There was no out.

Grace. Quinn's voice murmured in her mind, and she knew he'd heard her thoughts. And she knew he also believed this was the end for them. Destiny would come for them, and it had never been defeated. They were too close now, and the call to complete the bond was too strong.

In the fight, Quinn would kill for her, the bond would be sealed, and then destruction would come.

"Hang on." Holding off Kane for a moment, Quinn took her by the elbow and pulled her to the side. His dark eyes were intense. "I think you should stay behind."

Grace blinked. "What?"

His hands tightened on her shoulders. "Do you know how badly I want to finish that last stage? To make you mine so completely that the world bows at our feet? To seal you as my woman forever?"

Grace's heart began to pound at the raw honesty in his voice.

"If we go, if you're with me, I *will* kill for you, and I will complete that bond. There's no other option." Quinn dropped his hands and stepped back from her, sweat beading on his brow. "I spent my entire damn life believing that I was stronger than that damn bond, but now that I'm in it? Hell, Grace, I've got nothing to fight it. I get it now. I understand why Ezekiel brought down the world because of Evangeline, and I understand why Caleb went insane after he lost his wife. I might be the toughest damn member of the Order of the Blade, but I'm lost to you."

Tears filled Grace's eyes. Finally, for the first time in her life, she'd found her place. She'd found the man who loved her unconditionally, who would give up the world for her, and it was the wrong time, the wrong man, the wrong situation. "Quinn—"

"Stay behind. Don't come with me. Walk away. Save us both, because as hell is my witness, I'm not strong enough to do it."

Grace was aware of the Order watching them, utterly silent, waiting to see what she would do. "You're right," she said. "I should walk away."

"Should?" His voice was strangled.

She nodded, trying to ignore that devastating ache in her chest at the idea of leaving him, because it was trumped by the even more horrific idea that by staying with him, she was sealing his death. "If I do," she said, "can you guys handle the illusions yourselves? Can you promise you can save Ana?"

There was silence, and she saw the agonizing conflict in his eyes. If he set her free, he would lose her forever. If he didn't, she would die.

It was Ryland who broke the stalemate. "Screw that," he snapped. "We need both of you or this whole mission is going to fail."

Grace started at the interruption, but Quinn didn't even react, he was staring at her so intently.

"This is not about some freaking love fest," Ryland continued. "It's about Dante and Elijah, and saving the world and your own damn sister. The only thing that matters is finishing what we've started, and you both know it. We have a job to do, and it happens now."

Grace shivered at Ryland's interjection, at the truth of his words. He was right. Completely right.

Had she actually considered walking away from Ana to save Quinn? How would Grace have lived with herself if she spent the rest of her life alone, knowing that she'd given up fighting for her sister and Quinn because she'd been too afraid of some stupid destiny that wanted to control her. Since when had she gotten so sucked into the Calydon lore that she'd forgotten how to fight for what mattered to her? That wasn't her, and she was taking control back. "I'm not giving up. I'm coming."

Fierce respect fired in Quinn's eyes. He said nothing, but he took her hand, his action a silent statement that he also agreed with Ryland. They had to go forward and risk everything.

There was a low murmur of assent from the Order as the team closed around them, preparing for Kane to relocate them.

Quinn took her hand and pulled her against him, pressing a kiss to her mouth, not relinquishing the pressure until her lips parted, taking a private moment in the middle of the crowd. The moment she welcomed him, he groaned and thrust his tongue deep inside. His hands dug into her hair as he assaulted her mouth with a desperation that shattered all her shields. She threw her arms around Quinn and kissed him back, throwing all she was into the kiss, telling him with her kisses and her body all that she didn't have the courage to say to his face.

Grace pressed her body against Quinn. She basked in the hardness of his muscles, the sharp edges of his leather jacket as it cut through her shirt. She tasted his mouth, the warmth of it, the musky flavor that was him. She breathed in his scent, memorized the way it curled through her nose and softened her belly. She ran her hands over his shoulders and his chest, sank her fingers into his hair.

Then the world began to hum, and she knew Kane was transporting them. She scrunched her eyes shut and shut out everything but the feel of Quinn's mouth on hers, the heat of his body as he loomed over her, enfolding her in his bulk. For this one moment, for this last moment, it was only them.

Quinn tucked Grace into the curve of his body and called out his sword as they arrived in the dark woods behind The Gun Rack after a quick stop at Grace's place to adorn the men with copper bracelets. They'd ended up finding sixteen stashed around the house.

He couldn't stop thinking about the fact she'd had so many of those bands: torture implements that nullified who she was and made her violently ill. It had made him think about how much burden she'd been dealing with, spending her life worrying about her powers and heritage killing herself and others. He hated that she'd suffered, despised that she'd had to fear herself. And now he was going to be the one to deal her the final blow?

Screw that. There had to be another way. *There had to be*.

He thought again of that brief moment during his uncle's death. That whispered plea. The red glow leaving his eyes. Had Felix come back from being rogue or had it been the imagination of a young, traumatized rookie? Was there really a way, or was Quinn lying to himself? Lying to Grace? Would he be her doom after all she'd survived?

Son of a bitch. He didn't want to be that man.

A cold rain was pounding through the trees, beating down on their skin like daggers. Mud was ankle deep, and the wildlife was silent. The Order members were still as they arrived in the woods, reaching out into the night with their senses to search for threats as they held their weapons ready, copper bands tight around their wrists.

"Everyone set?" Quinn asked. The bracelets had been too small for the men's wrists, so they'd had to slice them open and jerry-rig them back together. Gideon had shoved the extras in his back pocket to slap on Zach if they could get close enough. Gabe would be warned ahead of time and they'd stash one for him to pick up once they got there.

"We're good," Gideon said. "Let's do it."

Quinn checked with Grace. "Do you feel your sister?"

"No. I'd feel her only if she were doing an illusion." Rain was already plastering Grace's dark hair to her head and glistening on her cheeks, so like how she'd been the first time he'd seen her. Still that same small frame, those tremendous silver eyes, that fierce determination. But now, Quinn felt none of the angst and despair he'd felt before. Just calm, confident focus.

He grinned. "You know you make me hot when you get tough."

She wiped water off her forehead and flashed him a look of aggravation. "You never change, do you?"

His smile faded. "Just trying to lighten the moment. It's what I do."

"Well, instead of lightening the moment, why don't you try something different?" She met his gaze. "Like fighting with passion instead of restraint. Weapons didn't win this battle before, Quinn. Love did. Opening your soul and letting it all burn so fiercely that it strips you of everything you have left. If you were fighting with your soul, you never would have asked me to walk away before we came here. I won't be like you, Quinn. I'm in this with my heart and my soul, and if I crash and burn, so be it. At least I'll know I gave it everything I had."

Her words reverberated in the air, a challenge not only to him, but also to his team. It was the same one she'd issued at the campfire. The same one they'd ignored.

Only this time, it felt different. This time, the brands on his arms burned in response. Quinn recalled that passion that she'd unleashed when she'd generated the illusion that had saved him. He'd never felt that kind of intensity of emotion before, and it had galvanized him, giving him the strength to reach out to her and use his own abilities to protect her from the illusion. She'd made them stronger by not fighting what she felt, by making a choice based on passion, not intellect.

Quinn. Gabe touched his mind. *We'll be there in ten. You guys set?*

Not quite.

Well, get on it.

Quinn relayed Gabe's ETA to the team, then added, "Gabe thinks they're meeting with Nate, but he's not positive. Keep an eye out for Nate, and for anyone else as well." He pictured Nate in his mind as he'd seen him in Elijah's *mjui*, then touched the minds of all his men, showing them the image. Since they were standing so nearby, it was easy to connect with them, especially since they were all tuned into him. "Grace, check for illusions on everyone."

He held the bridge to the other warrior's minds for her as she checked.

"Everyone's clean. Even Gideon's is gone."

Quinn's brands began to burn, his instincts shouting a warning about a threat that none of them could sense yet. "We're going to be surrounded soon. Vanish."

The Calydons slipped off into the darkness, melting into the underbrush, their footsteps silent even in the mud.

Quinn wrapped his arms around Grace and took her up into the trees. "You'll be safe up here. Let me know if you see Ana." He was gripped with sudden fear for her safety, and he was filled with the ridiculous urge to haul her against him, keeping her in the shield of his protection, where he could keep her safe. His brands were burning fiercely at the thought of leaving her behind, screaming the warnings he couldn't afford to abide by.

He had to focus. He had to do his job. He could not afford to be ruled by passion. He saw that now, despite his moment of weakness a minute ago. Passion would mean making choices that would doom his team, and even her sister. The strategic choice was to stash Grace in the tree and go do his thing, not whisk her off to some safe zone where he could keep her protected.

But he couldn't shake the sense of foreboding at choosing to leave her behind in the tree. "Promise me you won't come down from here."

"Absolutely not." Grace's eyes blazed with determination. "What if you need my help? What if Ana does?"

His fingers tightened on her hips. "If you stay up here, I won't have to kill to save you and complete the bonding."

There was no softening of her stance. "I'm fighting for what I want, Quinn, and you don't do that by hiding. If I need to come down, then I will."

"Dammit, Grace!" He shook her slightly, his body vibrating with the effort of trying to contain his emotions. "I'm not giving up on us either. If we don't complete the bond, we still have a chance." He met her gaze. "I want that chance, Grace. I want us."

※※※

For a brief moment, Grace was undone by the intensity in Quinn's words, by the urgency of his tone, by the fierceness of his hold on her. She felt herself tumbling into his vortex, her heart beating with emotion she'd never let herself feel before—

"No!" She pulled back, wrenching herself away from his plea. "What chance do you want, Quinn? The opportunity to separate after all this is over so we can spend our lives in agony, craving each other, living a half-life because we're incomplete without each other, and yet can't afford to be together?" She shook her head, her eyes stinging with tears. She felt herself break apart inside at the thought of leaving him. "I know that was the original plan, but that doesn't work for me anymore. I can't separate from you, Quinn. I *can't*."

He stared at her, then cursed. "Dammit, Grace. We have to." His hands slid over her shoulders and cupped the sides of her neck, his touch a caress that made her skin burn. His voice was raw with emotion. "If I never kill for you, then I'd have you *forever.*"

"It wouldn't be a life, Quinn. I've lived my life terrified and broken since I was a child. Afraid of who I was. Afraid of feeling any kind of intense emotion that might trigger my illusions. But since I met you?" She pressed her hand to his chest. "I can't fight what I feel for you, and it feels amazing. I'm alive for the first time ever, and I'm not going back. I want it all, Quinn, and I'm going to fight for it."

"So, you're willing to die? To lose it all?"

"You're the one who's been saying all along that we can beat the bond. Why are you giving up now? What has changed to make it so powerful that you want to run away instead of taking it on?"

Quinn's eyes flashed. "Because I love you, Grace Matthews, and I know that I would give my life to save yours. I won't try to stop that bond because there's nothing that matters to me more than you. *That's* why I've changed. Because I know I'm not stronger than the bond. I want it. I want everything it will bring me."

"Death? Destruction?"

"No." He took her hand and pressed his lips to it. "I want you, completely and forever. Nothing can stop me from falling into your soul, no matter what the cost, no matter what the future holds. I'd rather die in your arms than live without you. That's exactly what destiny will offer, and instead of fighting it, I'll take it if that means I can have one more minute with you. That's why I've changed my mind."

"Oh." Her defenses crumbled. They just disintegrated right there, completely and entirely. "I love you, Quinn."

"I know. I can feel it." He took her hand and laid it on his chest. His heart was thumping like crazy, burning with passion. "Stay in the damn tree, Grace, because I've got no willpower when it comes to you."

"No," she said, digging her fingers into his muscle. "It's that love that makes us powerful. That's why we can win."

She heard Gabe in Quinn's head. *We're here. Drew's between us, and we're heading down the embankment into the woods behind The Gun Rack. You guys in place?*

Quinn swore. *We're ready.* He looked at Grace. "I have to go. Stay in the tree."

She didn't give him an answer. She just grabbed the front of his jacket, and pulled him close. "Just so you know," she said fiercely. "I'll be extremely mad if you get yourself killed."

He wound his fingers through her hair and pulled her against him, sinking his mouth onto hers in a deep, hot kiss. Then he pulled back, slipped out of her arms, and was gone.

<hr/>

Quinn was stretched out on his stomach in the mud as Zach and Gabe slogged down the hill from the parking lot toward the woods. Drew was between them, rain matting his hair to his head. His face was drawn and his were eyes sunken with hopelessness. Vaughn wasn't there, and Quinn scowled at the thought of what they must have done to Vaughn to get Drew away from him.

Zach cursed, and Quinn jerked his concentration back to the present. Zach had a fresh wound on his face and was limping, and Gabe was holding his arm as if it were broken. Vaughn hadn't gone down easy.

Drew tripped and Zach yanked him upright, his face so stoic and expressionless that Quinn knew he was still under an illusion. Drew tried to yank his arm free and grimaced when Zach tightened his grip. Quinn brushed against the kid's mind with a quiet reassurance.

Drew stiffened, and he looked around sharply. Then he straightened up and clenched his fists.

Quinn smiled, then faded into the bushes as the trio passed him. Drew would be ready. Quinn didn't move to follow them, knowing his men were in place.

He touched Grace's mind. *You still in the tree?*

Yes.

He didn't say anything else, and neither did she. What was there to say? Too much, and nothing at all.

My wrists are burning and I feel like shit. Gideon's voice was tense. *Same with Kane. I don't know about the others.*

Grace answered. *It means an illusion is trying to penetrate the protection the copper's giving you. I think the burning should be an indication that the bands are blocking it. If you tell me where you are, I'll come find you and check it out for sure.*

No. Did Grace really think he'd let her get down and run around in the woods? No chance. *Gideon, go to her.*

I'm on it.

There was silence in the night again and Quinn checked in with his team. All of their wrists were burning. He waited impatiently until he heard confirmation from Grace. *Gideon's clean.* Grace sounded pleased. *The bands are working.*

Yeah, frying my damn wrists right off, Gideon muttered.

Quinn passed the word onto the others, and felt a shift in the night as they gained confidence that they were safe from the illusions.

With any luck, Nate would think they were all under the influence and get careless. The illusion attack showed that Nate had been expecting them, ready to manipulate the whole team. Quinn's instincts began to tingle, and he knew danger was imminent. *Almost here.*

About damned time, Ryland said. *I'm bored as hell.*

The forest grew quiet, except for the pounding of the rain on the leaves, on the pine needles. Animals stopped moving, and even the wind seemed to stop.

Shadows emerged from the trees just in front of Quinn. Two Calydons. Neither of them were Nate. *Incoming. Not Nate. Stand down 'til we locate him.*

The pair moved almost silently through the woods toward the clearing where Gabe, Zach and Drew waited for them. Where was Nate? He had to be there, somewhere. Quinn had a feeling they'd be in serious shit if they didn't find Nate before he pulled the trigger. *Anyone have a lead on Nate?*

All answers were negative.

⊠⊠⊠⊠

Ana braced herself as Nate faced her, a smile on his face that made her stomach lurch.

She was drenched from hours of standing in the woods, waiting for the Order to show up. Her legs were shaking, her body was icy cold, and she was so hungry her stomach was killing her. Her ankle was shattered, courtesy of Nate's rage after she'd tried to get away on their way here, and now she had no hope of escaping. She couldn't even walk, let alone run. The pain had settled into a numb throbbing, except when she accidentally moved it.

Tears burned in her eyes, and she knew she was beaten. There was no escape.

Then she thought of Lily back at Nate's place. Waiting for Ana to come back for her. She recalled the broken look in Lily's eyes even as she'd gripped Ana's shoulders and given her the strength to fight.

Ana clenched her fists and set her jaw. The marks on her forearms burned, and she knew she wasn't alone in the woods. Elijah's spirit was still with her. *I won't let you down, Lily.*

"Everyone's waiting, my darling," Nate said. "Are you ready?"

She shifted her weight, trying to keep her foot off the ground, and gave no answer. Yes, she was ready, but not in the way he meant it.

Nate grabbed her arm and yanked her over to him, forcing her weight onto her broken ankle. She yelped and fell to her knees, then gasped as he pulled her to her feet again, forcing her to step on her right foot again. The forest blinked out of focus, as her ears began to buzz. *No, Ana. You can't pass out. You have to stay conscious.*

"No fainting. I need you conscious to do your thing." Nate tossed her to the ground and his knife appeared with a sharp crack. The night hummed as the Order members honed in on the sound, trying to track it.

"They heard that," she said. "They'll find you."

"Not in these woods. They'll never be able to pinpoint it. I'm playing with them." Nate grinned. "And go ahead and yell, my dear. I want them to hear your pain. Those Order boys are so protective of innocents. It'll be a nice distraction."

Ana bit her lip. Was he telling the truth, or would her screaming help them find Nate before he could kill them? Or would it lure them to him, one by one so he could pick them off? "I thought Frank said I didn't need to do an illusion."

Nate shrugged. "I know what needs to be done. Not him." Then he got that look on his face, that one that made her body start to shake in fear.

Ana scrambled backwards across the ground and her ankle twisted, sending shards of pain through her body. She shouted for help as she fell over the underbrush, trying to run, knowing Nate would grab her whenever he got tired of watching. He knew now that her anticipation of what he would do was as powerful as the actual beating, because her emotions were what caused the illusions, and he was intentionally goading her into terror.

Ana yelled for help again when he didn't stop her. The Order was all around. She'd never get a better chance than this one. This was her moment. It was now, or die. *Please let someone hear me.*

The marks on her arms flared, and she gasped at the feeling of them searing her skin. Then Nate stomped on her ankle, and she forgot about everything but the pain.

※※※

Grace's heart stopped as Ana's screams rent the night. "Ana!"

She immediately dropped to her belly and wriggled along the branch until her feet hit the one below her, her hands trembling so much she could barely hold onto the branches. *Did you hear her? Quinn, did you hear Ana?*

I'm on my way.

I'm coming. She winced when a branch dug into her belly, and she eased down to a lower branch.

Stay in the tree! Two Calydons are right near you! Dammit to hell, Grace! Stay in the damn tree!

Quinn's fury hit her so hard she jerked and lost her grip. She grabbed for the branch, but her fingers slid off the mossy bark. Branches ripped at her face as she crashed through them, landing hard in the mud, her face sinking into the thick sludge. The cold mud oozed into her mouth. She slithered up to her knees, slapping at her face to get the mud out of her nose and mouth so she could breathe.

Grace!

I'm okay—

The underbrush rustled and a beefy Calydon stepped out of the bushes, a long, curved knife clenched in his fist. "Who are you?" he demanded.

She scrambled backwards, the mud sucking at her feet as she tried to stand up. "Grace Matthews. Ana's sister. Take me to her."

He lifted his head and sniffed. "You're a *sheva.*" His eyes narrowed, and dark hostility made his face contort. "An Order of the Blade *sheva.*"

"Um..." So, yeah, kind of thinking that wasn't a mark in her favor right now. "We're just friends—"

"The Order killed my brother after he met his mate." She saw the rage in his eyes, the anguish for the loss of his brother, and the unrelenting, soul-deep hatred of the Order.

She was startled by the sudden realization of how the Order was treated in their world. Hated by their own kind, hunted, and having to live with the knowledge they killed brothers and friends day after day. Funny how that was almost exactly the life she lived as an Illusionist. No wonder Quinn hardened himself so much. That was the same lesson she'd learned. "I'm so sorry about your brother," she said. "I really am."

"You probably are. It's not your fault you belong to one of them." He touched her jaw. "Just like it wasn't my brother's fault he found his mate."

But there was no comfort in his words or his touch. Rage burned deep in his eyes, and his body nearly vibrated with the hatred of the Order. He grabbed her wrist and yanked her toward him.

She caught her breath as he jerked her sleeve up so he could see her arm. "You're almost fully bonded." He scanned the woods, and she knew he was searching for Quinn. "The bond's strong enough that it'll destroy him if he loses you now."

Um, Quinn? I think I've got a problem.

Almost there. Stay alive.

Trying.

The warrior met her gaze. "He'll feel loss unlike anything he has ever experienced before. He'll suffer, as no man should ever suffer. Except for a man such as him."

Grace knew there was no point in running, or trying to escape. She'd have no chance against him. Her heart was pounding, but she faced him, knowing that words were her only defense. "Actually, he's still planning to kill me, or to have his Order members kill me to keep the bond from finalizing, so really, you'll just be helping him out."

The warrior lifted his brows. "Then he is a fool."

"Yeah, well, that's true. Quite frankly, they're a little cold-blooded for my taste, but well, it's not like I can be choosy right?"

His eyebrows went up. "What?"

"So, yeah, I was thinking, maybe you could piss him off by simply kidnapping me instead? That would still be loss but you wouldn't have to kill an innocent like your brother. Because if you did kill me, then are you so different from them? Really?"

"It's not the same." Apparently unconvinced by her logic, he gripped his knife and thrust it toward her heart—

Oh, crap—

Quinn's sword appeared in her hand with a crack. She didn't even have time to register it before she plunged it deep into the warrior's abdomen. "Oh, God." She dropped the sword and staggered back as he grunted and went down on his knees.

His tragic eyes focused on her. "I'm not the enemy,"

he whispered. "Your mate is."

"I'm sorry." That damn sword was so bloodthirsty! Why did it have to kill everyone? What was wrong with this stupid world? Why was there so much violence? Why did everyone try to solve their problems by killing people?

A roar of outrage bellowed through the air, and she whirled around as a second Calydon rose up out of the bushes, his arm cocked to hurl his spear at her—

"No!" Quinn burst through the trees, his palm extended as his sword shot off the ground by Grace's feet and slammed into his hand. He shoved his sword into the warrior's chest just as he threw the spear at Grace. Her assailant crumpled lifelessly to the earth as Quinn called his weapon back, his eyes fastened darkly on her face.

Grace's body swelled with an intense heat, a longing so unbearable she gasped. She was consumed with a sense of completeness so overwhelming that tears burst free and streamed down her face.

Then Quinn was on his knees before her, pulling her into his arms, kissing her so fiercely and so deeply that she forgot everything else. She sank into his mouth, desperate for the feel of his tongue, crazed by the powerful grip of his hands on her hips. Deeper, harder, he kissed her, consuming her until there was nothing left of her. His hands on her breasts, all over her body, desperate to touch her. She buried herself in the hardness of his body, desperate to be closer to him, to consummate the emotions burning inside her—

He broke the kiss and held her face, his dark eyes searching hers, brimming with a passion and a possession so deep that it reached out and consumed her. "It's done," he whispered.

"The bond. You killed for me." She pressed her face to his neck, inhaling the scent that was him...the scent that belonged to her, for always. "You're mine."

His fingers tangled in her wet hair and he tugged

her head up. "I'm yours," he agreed, his voice rough and ragged. "For now, and for always." Then he kissed her again, and it was a kiss of deep love, of an eternity of connection, of a commitment that never, ever again would she be alone, even in her dreams, even in death.

He pulled back, streaks of rain glistening on his cheeks, rivulets matting his hair. His face was grim, but his eyes were raging with such commitment and such love that she knew she would be safe forever.

Which was the greatest illusion of all.

Quinn's face darkened at whatever expression he read on her face, and she saw the warrior come to life. No longer the man afraid of his feelings. A passionate warrior who understood that the situation had gone critical, and there was no longer any room for fantasies of separate lives or unfulfilled longing. They were in it, and the end was coming for them now. "Screw destiny. We're not giving up." Quinn stood up, then grabbed her hand and pulled her to her feet. "Come on."

Another scream rent the night, the agony of her sister's torment. "Ana!"

Quinn shoved Grace forward as he looked behind them, his sword clenched in his fist. "There are more Calydons coming. Go find Ana, but *don't* confront Nate." He pointed her in the right direction. "I'll catch up."

She hesitated. "Be careful."

He swept his arm around her waist and kissed her hard. "Always for you, *sheva*. Always for you. Now go!"

Grace turned and ran without another word.

CHAPTER 16

Grace had left Quinn far behind when she heard the distant clash of weapons, and she knew he'd found the Calydons that had been chasing them. Fear knifed through her and she stumbled, terrified for his safety. She hesitated, fighting the compulsion to go back and help him as the bond tried to force her to eschew all but Quinn from her heart.

No. She would not give herself over to the manipulations of some force that deemed itself the goddess of the universe. Grace scrunched her eyes shut and forced herself to picture Ana as she'd been in Elijah's *mjui*. Battered, bleeding, lost.

Grace welcomed the rush of anguish for her sister. She breathed in her fear for Ana, her guilt that she hadn't been able to protect her, her agony at the idea of losing the only member of her family she had left. She didn't try to be brave. She didn't try to hold off the pain. She let it fill every inch of her spirit, igniting every drop of grief that she'd been hiding since her parents had died, filling herself with her love and commitment to her sister.

Resolution filled Grace, deep, powerful determination to save Ana, and she knew she was over the hump. One for the good guys.

Don't die on me, she ordered Quinn as she started

running toward her sister again, squinting against the driving rain on her face.

He didn't answer, but she felt his concentration, and she knew he was still alive and fighting.

She kept a hold of that connection, touching his mind, but not distracting him, needing the comfort of his presence as she headed toward Ana.

✕✕✕✕

Ana shouted again, her voice raw, her stomach retching from the pain as Nate came toward her with his knife. Blackness flickered at the edge of her vision, but she fought it off, focusing all her energy on the knife in Nate's hand. Willing herself to stay conscious long enough to get his weapon.

Nate grinned at her. "Just a little more, darling, and then you should be ready to make the illusion powerful enough and deadly enough to take down the Order." He laughed softly. "Those arrogant bastards don't understand what it means to save the world. They don't get it, but Ezekiel does. It's time to get things properly aligned again. Ezekiel saved me from hell two thousand years ago, and now it's my turn to repay the debt I owe such a magnificent man."

Ana looked at him through slitted eyes and thought of the only threat she could that he might react to. "Frank's coming for you. For beating me. You know he is."

Nate hesitated for a fraction of a second, and anger rose in his eyes. "Screw him. He works for me, not the other way around." Then he brought the knife down and plunged it into her thigh.

She screamed and grabbed for her leg, her fingers closing around the handle of the knife as it protruded from her thigh. Dear God. She had it. This was her chance. She had to distract him before he took it back.

She looked at Nate's smug face, and all her anger

and fury at what he'd done to her and Lily welled up inside her. Not just fear. Hate. Anger. Pain. "You want a dark, powerful illusion? Well, you can have one."

Ana harnessed her anguish at having been forced to kill Elijah, drank in the agony of the knife in her leg and thrust it out into the night. She gave up on the dream of reclaiming the person she used to be, the woman who brought goodness and kindness into the world. She relinquished her resolution to hang onto the gentleness that made her happy. She let herself become the monster he'd tried to turn her into.

Instead of fighting the dark illusion, she threw all her energy into it, built it and fed it, praying she would be able to make it so strong that it would finally break through the shields Nate had learned to erect and finally affect him.

She didn't need to fool him for long. She only needed long enough to make him forget to take his knife back.

As the illusion began to build, Nate cocked his head to listen. The air was vibrating and the wind began to whip, the rain driving hard into her skin as the pressure built in the atmosphere.

Nate scowled and rubbed his arms, and she realized he was feeling the illusion. *It was working.*

He gave her a suspicious look. "What are you doing?"

"Fighting back." And then she let it go.

Power swamped the night and electricity crackled through the sky. Nate looked up and his eyes widened in shock, and she knew she'd done it. Victory triumphed through her. He'd finally fallen victim to her! She'd done it!

Then she saw what he was looking at and she forgot about everything, horrified by what she'd conjured up. Her worst nightmare had come to life. "Oh, God."

Nate whirled around and sprinted for safety, jerking her free of the shock of the illusion and back to her situation. She could agonize later. Right now, she had to act.

Ana gripped the stone handle of the knife and pulled, grimacing with pain as it came free. It slipped out of her trembling fingers and she lunged for it, scooping it out of the muck before it disappeared. Her hands numb with exhaustion and cold, she managed to hide it under her shirt just before she collapsed back into the mud.

He still had his other one, but one was all she needed. With a groan, she rolled onto her stomach and forced herself to her knees. "Come on, Ana! Go!" Summoning strength she knew wouldn't last, she began to crawl through the mud toward the clash of weapons, to where the Order was fighting Nate's men.

She'd done all she could. It was time to let someone else save her.

◆◆◆◆◆

Grace hadn't made it very far when the air pressure suddenly skyrocketed. *The illusion is active, Quinn. Be ready.*

Ducking against the wet branches slapping at her, Grace ran even faster, desperate to reach Ana before the illusion could distract her. She'd never tried to break through Ana's illusions before, since butterflies and puppies were what she'd wanted to see, and she had no idea if she'd be able to do it. She ducked under a branch and then smacked her forehead on the next one, pitching to the forest floor.

Reeling from the impact, Grace lay in the mud for a few seconds while she waited for the pain to subside enough to stand up. Ow. Yes. Princess Grace, she wasn't. Excellent timing. Clearly, warrior girl all the way.

The wind began to pick up, and the rain started to pour even more heavily. The weather was too extreme, and she knew it was the beginnings of the illusion, on its way across the woods toward them.

She realized Ana's screams had silenced, and Grace's stomach twisted with fear of what that could mean. "Ana! Where are you?"

No sound except the howl of the rising wind and the pounding of the rain. She stood up, staggering at a wave of dizziness. "Ana!"

Quinn brushed her mind. *We've taken care of the Calydons for now,* sheva. *Kane and I are following behind you. Keep going. We'll catch up.*

Okay. She started to run again, but her feet slipped in the deepening muck, and she fell again as the rain pooled at her feet. Her hands disappeared into the puddle, and the black water closed over them, hiding them from view.

The water was too warm. Grace's knees sank into the mud as she lifted her hand up, and thick, black water dripped off her hand in the dark night. Her stomach turned as she caught the faint metallic scent of blood. Oh…that wasn't good. *It's raining blood. Like Ana did to Elijah.*

Quinn snorted with disgust. *It's not raining blood. It's raining water. You know that.*

Not blood. It wasn't blood. Right. She did know that.

Grace lurched to her feet, grateful that it was too dark to see the color of the rain. It looked black. Mud. It looked like mud. She wiped her hands on her pants and slogged forward, her boots sinking in the thick sludge. "Ana!"

A shadow leapt out of the woods in front of her and took the shape of a Calydon warrior. She recognized him instantly from what she'd seen in Quinn's mind, but she couldn't believe it. "Elijah?"

✖✦✖

Quinn vaulted over a log, following Kane as they sprinted through the woods. They'd gotten a fix on Ana's screams, and they were closing fast, knowing Nate was probably the one making her scream. The rain was pooling at their feet, ankle deep as they splashed through it. Quinn wiped his hand over his eyes to clear them, then nearly crashed into Kane, who'd stopped suddenly.

"Elijah?" Kane sounded shocked.

Holy crap. Elijah was standing in front of them, a knife sticking out of his throat, the same knife Quinn had seen Nate thrust into his neck. Blood was running down his chest, the wound gaping open.

Kane held his flail ready, the spiked metal balls swinging at the end of the chains. "Talk to me, Elijah. You on our side now?"

Quinn reached out with his mind, trying to connect with Elijah, but he wasn't able to touch Elijah's mind. It was as if his teammate didn't exist. There was no link, no response. Simply nothing.

Elijah suddenly moved, so fast that Quinn and Kane had time only to hit the dirt before Elijah's throwing stars whizzed past their heads. Quinn cursed and hurled his sword. The handle smacked into Elijah's head and he dropped.

Quinn and Kane leapt up, then another Calydon stepped out of the woods in front of them.

Kane's mouth dropped open. "Elijah?"

Quinn caught a whiff of danger behind them and he tackled Kane to the ground as throwing stars whistled past where their heads had been. Elijah was behind them now, his arms raised as he called his stars back.

"What the hell?" Quinn jerked his gaze to his left, just in time to see three more Elijahs bolt out of the woods, throwing stars in hand. Son of a bitch. "The illusion is Elijah," he told Kane. "At the moment of his death."

"Do we kill him or not?" Kane rose to his feet and swung his flail, blocking a throwing star aimed at his throat. "How do we know if one of them's really him?"

The woods erupted suddenly and dozens of Elijahs charged, the throwing stars whizzing through the air. "Elijah's dead. Kill them," Quinn shouted. He sliced the midsection of the nearest Elijah, and his heart clenched as he dropped to the ground with a howl of death. *God help me if I just killed my friend.*

Then another throwing star pierced the front of his shoulder. He roared with pain, ripped it out and charged.

<hr/>

Grace's heart pounded as Elijah stood in front of her. She eased back a step as she tried to tap into his blood bond with Quinn to see if he was under an illusion. She softened her vision to access her Illusionist powers, just as she'd done with Quinn to see inside him. A faint glow started at his torso, and she grimaced. "You're under an illusion—" She stopped as his whole body lit up, a bright orange glow. Not just his gut. His entire being.

Holy cow. He wasn't carrying an illusion. He *was* the illusion. *Quinn! Elijah's the illusion.*

Got it. Thanks.

Grace flinched at the flash of pain she got from Quinn, then Elijah raised his throwing star and hurled it at her.

She had no time to duck, no right to call Quinn's weapon when he was using it. She had only one way to defend herself, and that was with her own powers. She channeled all her focus on the orange glow rising off him, on the irrefutable proof that he was an illusion. "You aren't real. I don't believe in you."

Her mind went still, and utter calmness took over her, and he seemed to glow even brighter as the throwing star hurtled toward her heart.

She looked in the eyes of the man who seemed so real, and she took back her power. "You can't hurt me."

The throwing star whizzed straight through her

chest and disappeared into the woods behind her.

She gasped with relief and her hands went to her ribs where the blade had hit. She'd done it. She'd broken through the illusion. By reaching out with her own powers, she'd been able to recognize the truth. It had been there all along, her ability to see through illusions, but she'd been fighting who she was so fiercely that she'd never embraced the talent she already had.

Quinn had given her the courage to face her true self, to not fear her abilities. And it had given her mastery over who she was. Never again would she have to fear herself.

She kept her gaze fixed on the illusion as three more Elijahs emerged from the woods. All of them were brandishing throwing stars, and all of them glowing. Hot damn! She was doing it!

She marched resolutely toward them, keeping her mind calm and focused, embracing her ability to know truth from illusion, *believing* in her instincts. The throwing stars whizzed past her, through her, causing no harm. Exhilaration rushed through her, and she broke into a run as more and more Elijahs emerged from the woods, attacking her and failing.

She heard the roar of blades crashing in the woods and realized Quinn and the others were being attacked by more Elijahs. With Nate nearby, she knew Quinn and the others couldn't afford to shut down their senses to avoid the illusion. Nate would leap at the opportunity and take them out. Could she help them? Could she hold the truth for them the way Quinn had done before?

Hurrying toward where she thought Ana was, Grace scrambled up an incline, her feet slipping in the mud. *Quinn. Let me into your mind.*

Little busy here, Grace. But he pulled her right in, and she could see he was surrounded by Elijahs, far too many to fight. She stumbled and went down in the woods, as she felt the fatigue in his body, the crippling pain as he fought through his injuries. "Oh, God."

She pressed her hands to her forehead and reached out over their link, focusing on the Elijahs he was seeing and sharing her power with him. The Elijahs surrounding him began to glow orange. *Do you see that?*

Shit. Yeah. They're all illusions. I can see it. A throwing star whizzed at Quinn, and she caught her breath when he didn't try to block it with his sword. He let it fly right at his shoulder, and it whipped through him without injury. She sensed his exhilaration, and then he focused again. *Can you do that with the other men?*

She let out a shuddering breath. *I don't know. If you can get me into their mind, I might.*

Quinn started running toward her, and she kept focusing on his illusions, even as she was surrounded by her own. He reached out with his mind and contacted the rest of his men. She saw what they were seeing, and she used her powers to reach into each illusion and expose the truth. The moment she did, all the Elijahs they were fighting turned orange.

Quinn explained what the orange meant, and the men's faith in their leader was so absolute that they didn't question it. They simply stopped fighting and started running for Ana and Nate. The throwing stars hit them, and went right through their bodies.

She was shocked by their faith in Quinn, by their ability to rapidly assess the facts and make instant decisions, like accepting that Elijah was an illusion. Maybe there was something to their stoic focus. If they'd been writhing in fear of death or fury at Elijah for turning on them, they couldn't have made such a quick shift.

Maybe she was the one who'd been wrong—

Oh, come on! She didn't have time for this now. "Ana!" She lurched to her feet and started forward, her muscles screaming with exhaustion. She tripped several times, having trouble holding the focus for all the men as well as herself, and still see where she was going—

A set of hands grabbed her and hurled her to the forest floor. She looked up to see Nate looming over her.

And he wasn't glowing.

◆◆◆◆◆

Quinn felt a rush of danger so intense he lost focus. Grace's presence vanished from his mind, leaving him unprotected from the illusions. *Grace!*

Nate found me. Her voice vibrated with fear, and his body went numb.

Jesus. His knees buckled and he went down hard in the mud. *Stay alive, Grace! I'm coming!* He lurched to his feet and was up and running before he'd even realized he'd fallen, his heart racing, his head pounding.

The trees blurred as he bolted through the woods, calling upon his preternatural speed as he never had before. Elijahs kept leaping out to stop him. They weren't glowing anymore, and he didn't care. He ran right through them, consumed by his fear for Grace, unable to focus on anything other than the gut-wrenching image of Grace at Nate's mercy. "Grace!" His mouth was dry, his lungs were tight as he ran, blind to the branches whipping across his face. *Where are you?*

He's got a knife.

Quinn's bellow of fury shook the night. He called to the blood bond between them, and instantly knew her precise location. He sent her position to his men and hauled ass toward her, vaulting over rocks and dodging trees, taking out branches with his sword instead of wasting time ducking beneath them. "Grace!"

He crested the last hill and saw Grace and Nate at the base of it. Grace was slumped at his feet, and the blade of a knife glistened in Nate's hand. Son of a bitch. Was he too late?

I'm okay. Her faint voice touched his mind. *I'm here.*

Nate looked directly at Quinn, a defiant gleam in his eyes as he grabbed Grace by the hair, jerking her head back and exposing her throat.

"No!" Quinn hurled his sword, and his blade cut through the air as Nate brought his blade down toward her neck. Nate ducked with the lightning quickness of an ancient Calydon. Quinn's sword flew harmlessly past Nate's head, but Nate's quick movement made him miss his target. His knife hit Grace's stomach instead of her throat.

Grace's agony hit Quinn so hard he crashed to his knees, his body convulsing from her pain. "Grace!" He leapt to his feet as dozens of Calydons swarmed from the woods, cutting him off from her. Real ones. Not illusions. Warriors keeping him from his woman.

"No!" White-hot rage exploded in Quinn's mind. He recalled his sword and charged into the fray, ripping through the enemy, his sword flying as he fended off attack after attack, not even feeling the pain when their weapons sank into his flesh. "Grace!" His shout was wild, ripping out of his throat.

"Quinn!" Gideon was right behind him. "Don't kill Nate! We have to get information from him first!"

Quinn whirled around and slammed his fist into Gideon's face, then spun back and took out another Calydon. He had to kill Nate. *Had to kill Nate.*

"Quinn!" Kane's voice was distant as Quinn continued his annihilation, able to think of nothing but getting to Grace and killing Nate. "You're going rogue! Focus, man!"

The words pulsed at Quinn's subconscious, and he threw them aside. He didn't want to hear them. Didn't care. Nate's death was all he could think about. It was consuming him, black rage savaging his mind and his heart.

The last Calydon fell and Quinn charged for Nate,

ignoring all the Elijahs in his way. Nate's eyes widened as Quinn charged through the illusions. At the last second, Nate dove to the right, and Quinn's blade sank into Nate's hip instead of his heart. Quinn ripped his sword free and raised it to plunge the fatal blow, then Gideon tackled him, taking them both down. "Come on, man! Give us two minutes to get answers out of him!"

Quinn brought his blade down onto Gideon's throat with so much force that he shattered Gideon's throwing axe when Gideon flung it up to block the blow. "Get out of my way, Gideon!"

Something careened into the side of Quinn's head and he fell as Kane's flail dropped to the earth next to him. Quinn grabbed the flail and hurled it back. Kane ducked as it whizzed past his head and embedded itself in a tree.

Quinn spun back to Nate with his sword, then froze mid-swing when he saw Grace had crawled in front of Nate, clutching her hands to her stomach.

"Don't do it," she whispered, her voice ragged. "We need to find Ana. Your weapon. The tablet. Only Nate has answers. Don't kill him."

But Quinn couldn't stop. He couldn't stop replaying the moment when Nate's knife had sunk into her body. Nate had to die. There was no other way. Quinn raised his sword to plunge it for the final blow, and she held out her hand and called his sword out of his hand.

It plunged into the flat of her palm with a smack and she held it up, tears streaming down her face. "I can't let you do it. Don't you see? It's the bond. Destroying everything we care about. Killing Nate makes us lose it all. You have to stop," she shouted. "God, Quinn, stop."

Quinn heard Gideon and Kane trying to stagger to their feet behind him, their weapons out and suddenly he knew. This was their moment. This was their destiny.

"I love you," she whispered. "Please don't make me kill you."

His heart beat for her, and he felt a flicker of humanity inside him, of hope.

Then Nate moved and his knife flashed as it headed toward Grace's neck. With a howl, Quinn called his sword back from her to take the final step toward their destiny.

※※※※

Grace saw a flash of metal behind Quinn as Nate's knife descended toward her. Quinn's sword flew out of her hand and into Quinn's palm. Then Gideon's axe clobbered Nate's hand. Bone shattered and his knife flew off into the mud.

Nate screamed and writhed in the mud beside her, holding his hand, no longer a threat.

But Quinn was still going after him. "Quinn! Stop!" His eyes were pulsing red. *Rogue.* He'd crossed the line into insanity, as destiny had commanded, and she knew he was going to kill Nate. With one swipe of the blade, he was going to start the chain of events they'd been fighting this whole time.

Gideon and Kane charged up behind him, and she grabbed Nate's knife out of the mud. His team got within reach, and Quinn whirled and smashed his sword into their heads with the quickness of a man possessed. He spun back to Nate as his friends fell to the earth beside him and whipped his blade back to bring it down for the final blow.

"No!" Grace screamed the words at his blazing red eyes, knowing he'd never hear her. Her hand shook as she raised Nate's knife, knowing she had to stop him. She was the only one left. It was up to her.

Time froze for an instant as she realized that Quinn would still kill Nate before he died from her blade even if she struck now. Nate would die without revealing Ana's location, without telling them where Quinn's weapon was, or how to stop Ezekiel from getting out. They would lose it all, and Quinn would die by her hand.

As it was destined.

His eyes met hers as he brought the sword down, and she held up the knife. His gaze went to the blade, and there was a flash of awareness on his face. Understanding that she would kill him now, and the end would be upon them.

"I love you," she whispered. "I believe in you." Then she opened her hand and let the knife fall to the ground, relinquishing her only way to stop him. Giving up her only chance to kill him. Trusting Ana's life to his heart, which had to be strong enough to thwart destiny

She stared in aching disbelief when he didn't stop. His sword whizzed past her head and thudded into its target, her heart breaking for all they'd just lost.

They'd failed.

Quinn fell to his knees in front of her and caught her face in his hands.

She stared at him through her tears. "I thought it would work. I thought if I didn't kill you—"

He turned her head and pointed to the ground. It took a minute for her to register, but then she saw that his sword was plunged deep in the earth beside Nate's shoulder.

He hadn't killed Nate.

New tears sprung and she threw her arms around Quinn's neck. He wrapped his arms around her, burying his face in her hair as his body shook. She held him as close as she could, unable to stop the sobs, his arms so tight around her she felt like he'd never let her go.

Grace heard Ryland shout as he approached with Ian and Thano, but she ignored them as they grabbed Nate and dragged him away.

She simply held onto Quinn as tightly as she could, until she couldn't hold on anymore. Until weakness started to take over her. Her hands started to slide down his chest and she leaned into him, too exhausted to hold onto him. Her adrenaline began to subside, and a sharp pain began to pulse at her. "Quinn." Her voice sounded weak, even to her. "My stomach..." Too much effort to talk...

※※※

Quinn cradled Grace to his side so he could look at her stomach. He took one look at the dark stains, at the blood dripping off the hem of her shirt, and he felt his heart stop. So much blood. "*Grace*." His voice broke as he pressed his palms over her stomach, trying to staunch the flow of blood. "Don't move. You'll make it worse." *Gideon! She's bleeding out!*

Take her into a healing sleep. You have to calm down. Focus.

Calm down? Are you shitting me?

Quinn. You're a warrior. Think like one, for hell's sake.

Quinn groaned and pressed harder against the wound, trying to find his equilibrium enough to focus. Grace flinched at the pain and leaned against him. Her body was cold. So still. "Ana," she mumbled. "Where is she?"

"No, no, baby. Stop talking." Quinn carefully eased onto his back, trying not to move her, keeping his palm pressed to her stomach as the warm blood oozed between his fingers. "I'm taking you into a healing sleep." *Gideon. I'm going to need help. I can't focus.*

I'm with you.

"No." She tried to push him away even as she sagged more heavily against him. "Not until I know Ana's okay."

Gideon. Do you have answers about Ana yet? Quinn glanced at the five Order members clustered around Nate. Gideon was standing above Nate's head, his face bloodied and beaten from Quinn's blows. His gaze was focused on Quinn, his brow furrowed in concentration.

We're working on Nate. He'll talk. Gideon sounded grimly confident. *We'll get it. You need to focus on Grace.*

"Quinn?" Her whisper was so faint.

"They'll have answers in a minute." He touched her mind, then he went cold with horror when he felt how weak her mind was, how distant. *Hell, Gideon. Can you feel that? We're losing her. I can't lose her.* His chest tightened and he couldn't breathe. *I can't—*

Shut up and calm down. Gideon's voice was steady. *You can heal her. Close your eyes, keep her warm, and let your mind quiet.*

Gideon's strength flowed into Quinn, and a sense of calm focus cocooned his mind. His heart rate began to slow down, and he settled back in the mud, wrapping his coat tightly around her. He felt her pain ease as she settled against him, letting him pull her into his healing sleep.

You got it. Gideon's voice was ruthless and unyielding. No emotion. Just determination. Exactly what Quinn needed. *Give her peace. Take away the pain first so her body can relax. It's the same thing you do to yourself. You know how to do it.*

Quinn wrapped his mind around hers, merging with her so his gifts became hers. But the minute he merged with her, he realized she wasn't asleep at all. She was passing on. *Gideon! She's dying! I'm losing her!*

I know. I'm here with you. Talk to her, Quinn. Call her back.

Quinn immediately turned his mind to hers. *Don't you dare give up, Grace. Ana needs you.* He gave her his healing strength, showing her body how to repair itself, but there was no response, and he sensed her sliding further away.

There was a ripple of impatience from Gideon. *Use her love for you, Quinn. Not her sister. You. You're burning so brightly for her it's making my head hurt.*

Grace. Tears burned in Quinn's eyes. *I love you, dammit. I can't live without you. I need you. Feel my heart. It's breaking for you.*

There was a tremor from her, and he caught his breath, but then the moment was gone. His chest felt like someone had sunk a dagger into it and his voice broke, his concentration began to shatter as panic started to consume him. *Dammit, Grace! I need you!*

We all need you, Grace. Gideon reached out for Grace, using Quinn's link to touch Grace directly. Gideon's intense healing strength flowed through Quinn, filling Grace with his power. *The Order needs you. You need to come back to us.*

Quinn opened his mind to give Gideon more access to Grace, and then was shocked when Kane chimed in. *He'll be a total ass to live with if you die, Grace. Spare us the burden of having to kill him because he's such a pain in the ass.* Then Kane's power flowed into their sleep.

Quinn's throat tightened at the support from his Order members. *Do you feel that, sweetheart? They all need you. You've won them over. You belong with us. Come back.* He stopped, blinking back the tears as her life force became even fainter. *Come on, Grace. I love you. Can't you hear me?* He turned his mind to Gideon, desperate and lost. He'd never felt helpless or impotent in his life, but he was losing it, losing his chance, losing her. *I don't know what to do, Gideon. Tell me what to do.*

Then Thano was there, sending his own healing strength. *If it's Quinn that's driving you to die, I'll be glad to step in and take his place. I'm here for you,* sheva.

Ian joined them, his powers heavy with his own grief, but reaching out for Grace. *Don't let it end like this, Grace. You have a chance I never had. Don't give up.*

And then there was Ryland. He said nothing, but Quinn felt his presence as he lent his own strength to the sleep.

Quinn was completely overwhelmed as the five warriors joined together, offering their healing strength to his *sheva*. His Order members, sworn by oath to destroy the very woman they were trying to save. Their power surged through Quinn, so strong, so adamant that Grace not die. Warriors, demanding her recovery, allowing her no room to refuse.

And still her life force weakened, and grief roared inside him. *It's not enough! There has to be more!*

Quinn. Gideon's voice was raw with regret. *I don't know what else we can do.*

Agony ripped through Quinn, and he roared with anguish, holding her cold body against his as he thrust every last bit of his soul into her. Everything he had. Everything.

CHAPTER 17

The stench burned Grace's nose and made her eyes water. She stumbled over the dirt road and tripped, landing next to a man with his neck twisted, his eyes staring blankly. He was wearing tattered trousers of an ancient style, no shoes or shirt. His ribs were sunken, as if he hadn't eaten in months. "Oh, God."

By the side of the road stood a small shack, held together with boards and branches. Another body in the dirt. Grace noticed a small child peering around the door, her eyes wide with terror. Then the child bolted out the front door and sprinted away from the cottage, dirty legs and bare feet flying as she raced down the street, crying and screaming in an ancient language Grace couldn't understand.

Grace staggered backwards. *Quinn? Where are you?* She couldn't hear his voice anymore, couldn't feel him calling for her. There were bodies all around her. Decay. Rot. Doom. Hopelessness. The ravages of war. It was destruction. It was death from thousands of years ago. *Quinn!*

Someone clasped her shoulder and Grace spun around, her hands going up to protect herself.

"No, Grace. You don't need to fear me." A huge Calydon warrior was standing before her. His hair was black with gray streaks, cut short against his head. He was wearing blue jeans and boots. A gray T-shirt was loose around his muscular shoulders. His dark green eyes were kind, but they were also cold, so much like Quinn's. His forearms were bare, and she could see brands burned into his skin. Spears. His grip was warm on her shoulder, real. His touch was a comfort, chasing away the horror surrounding her. "My name is Dante."

"Dante?" She frowned, confused. "You're dead, aren't you?"

"I am."

Oh…that couldn't be a good sign. "Am I?"

"Mostly."

"*Mostly*? What does that mean?" Tears filled her eyes as she thought of Quinn. She'd never see him again—

"Look around you." Dante gently turned her and gestured out at the carnage around them. "What do you see?"

She swallowed hard, trying to blink back her tears, trying to steel her heart against the grief, the terror, the desolation surrounding her. "Death."

Dante turned her toward the fields. "The crops. Do you see?" His hands caressed her shoulders, and she was able to catch her breath again, and some of her panic eased.

She knew he was numbing her pain, and she gratefully accepted it as she stared across the fields. They were acrid and dry, acres and acres of brown, withered stalks. The ground was dry and cracked.

"The people are starving to death. Turning on their families. Killing their children." Dante's voice was hard. "Do you see?"

"I see." Oh, yes, she saw it. She felt the desolation and loss in every cell of her body.

"This is what life was like when Ezekiel was free, before he was imprisoned. His taint spread across the lands, consuming all goodness and life wherever he touched. He's rising again, and now he's two thousand years stronger than he was when he was imprisoned."

Oh, wow. That wasn't good. "Why are you showing me this?"

"Because you are part of the new future. You and Quinn have changed the course of destiny, and the future is now open." His voice deepened and she felt a change in the air, a clarity, and suddenly she could feel Quinn's spirit again. Not just Quinn. All of the Order. *Quinn? Can you hear me?*

But there was no response from him.

"The world is growing dark again," Dante said.

There was a shift of surprise from Quinn, and she heard him whisper Dante's name in confused awe. The other men had the same response, and she realized Dante had brought them all together, and he was talking to all of them. "There is a new future, and you all are a part of shaping it. You must all join together to create a new destiny for the world. You could still fail, but there is a chance now. The fight is upon us, and it is yours to win or lose. Quinn and Grace created a crack, and now you all must pry it open before it closes forever. Before the world descends into a darkness from which it cannot be retrieved. Gideon, you must learn from Quinn and Grace, for your time has come to step forward."

Dante's energy rolled through her, filling her with light and strength. He fastened his gaze on Grace. "It's time for you to go back."

Her heart leapt. "To Quinn?"

He nodded. "You're part of our new destiny. If you die, it will break the fragile thread that is being woven. You must go back."

Relief rushed through her. "You're sending me back?"

He touched her face, his fingers gentle and warm. "No, you have to find your way yourself. I can't do that."

Oh, come on. Seriously? "I have no idea how to get back. I've never been almost dead before."

"You do." He laid his hand over her heart, and a warmth filled her. And then he was gone.

She looked around and saw the village was gone as well. There was nothing around her except sparkly blue light that bounced around her in all directions, disorienting her. "Dante?"

There was no reply, just the faint sound of bells in the distance, coming at her from all directions. The bells were calling to her, beckoning her, and her spirit began to drift toward them.

Oh...she had a bad feeling about those pretty little bells. She focused all her thoughts, all her energy, all her love on the man she loved. *Quinn. Are you there? I need you to guide me.*

There was no response, no sense of him, and she drifted further, the bells getting louder.

Yeah, please, no bells today, thanks so much.

Grace imagined her spirit coming together with Quinn's, becoming one. She embraced her love for him, for all that he was; a warrior, a killer, a man of honor and courage.

Dante had shown her a truth, and now she finally understood Quinn's commitment to the Order, to the greater good. *I'm there with you, Quinn. I believe in all that you are.* And she did, with every fiber of her soul, she knew she loved him and everything he was without reservation. To be willing to harden himself against his love for her to protect the world from the horrors of Ezekiel... she finally understood.

She admired him and the strength that enabled him to make such a sacrifice, and the power of his love that had enabled him to thwart destiny and let Nate live. *I love you, Quinn, truly and completely.*

Grace? Quinn sounded so hopeful, so desperate,

so disbelieving that she wanted to shake him. And then hug him and never let go.

Yes, it's me! I need your help. She clung to the thread holding them together. *I love you, Quinn.*

There was a whisper of hope from him. *I offer my life for you, Grace. Accept my gift. Take all my strength and use it to heal yourself.* His voice was blurred with tears, with love, with forever commitment, and her heart swelled in response.

The bells began to fade, and the blue lights started to blink out, one by one. *I'm coming back, Quinn. Don't let go of me.*

Never, sheva. Never.

The world began to tumble and spin. Sounds blurred and faded and grew, and suddenly the hard warmth of Quinn's body was beneath her, his arms tightly around her, his lips pressed to her temple.

She was back.

⋈⋈⋈⋈

Quinn knew the moment Grace's spirit had returned to her body. Disbelief and elation swept through him. He kissed her and tightened his arms around her as life flowed through her body again. *God, woman, never do that to me again.*

"She's safe now," Gideon said. "We'll finish with Nate."

They departed, giving Quinn and Grace their privacy. Quinn opened his mind and his soul and let her feel his love, showing her his raw need for her. It was so powerful the way it beat through him, unlike anything he'd ever experienced. It was electric, like life shooting through him with fierce abandon.

I love you, too, Quinn. Her voice was a quiet, exhausted whisper in his mind.

He rested his forehead against hers, skin to skin, too

drained to do more than simply hold her. He managed a smile, his body shaking with relief. *I think we beat destiny.*

Of course we did. It was only a fairy tale anyway. No truth to it at all.

He placed his hand over her arm, over his mark that would forever be on her skin. *No truth at all?*

Not a bit.

He felt her struggling to wake up, so he released her from the healing sleep and opened his eyes. She lifted her head from his chest and blinked at him, her cheeks glistening with raindrops.

Raindrops. He'd forgotten they were in the woods, and it was raining.

"You brought me back."

He wiped the moisture from her cheeks, his thumb drifting over her cold skin. He'd never seen a sight as beautiful as her face, those silver eyes, gazing at him with such love and such life in them. "Dante brought you back. I heard him. He came back for you."

"He came to speak to all of us." She kissed him softly. "But your love brought me back. Happily ever after now?"

He ran his fingers through her hair, untangling the strands, desperate to touch her wherever he could, afraid to hurt her when she was so barely healed. "Shit, I hope so. I can't go through that on a daily basis."

"Me neither." She pushed off his chest and rose unsteadily to her knees, then winced as she pressed her hand to her belly. "We have to find Ana."

"My team's on it." He was instantly on his feet, carefully helping her up. She leaned into him, and he wrapped her up in his arms and kissed her gently, reveling in the taste of her mouth, the warmth of her lips, the fullness of who she was. She pressed herself against him, returning the kiss with a passion that declared her never-ending need for him.

His hands slipped around her lower back, and he lifted his head. She met his gaze, and he saw the worry on her face as she clenched the waistband of his jeans. "Until we actually stop Ezekiel and save Ana, we haven't truly beaten our destiny, have we? We could still lose everything. That's what Dante meant, right? That we created a crack but could still fail?"

"No. We made it this far." His jaw tightened. "We're not going back."

She met his gaze, and he saw the determination he admired so much rise to the surface, chasing away her exhaustion, and he knew they could do it.

They had to. He couldn't accept anything less.

※※※

Gripping Grace's elbow firmly, Quinn helped her walk over to Nate. The Calydon was pale, his breathing shallow, but his jaw was set and his eyes were narrow. Mud and blood caked his clothes and skin, and he was surrounded by a bunch of pissed-off Order members.

Quinn's fury rose, his fists curling with rage at the sight of the man who'd sunk the blade into Grace. Then she set her hand on his shoulder, and he glanced down at her, feeling his insides unfurl again.

"He won't talk," Gideon said. "I don't think he cares if he dies."

Grace knelt beside Nate. "Where's my sister?" she demanded with the fierceness of a woman who had been through more than she could take. "Tell me where she is!"

His mouth curved into a slight smile, and his body jerked as if he were entering the throes of death.

"No!" Grace grabbed his shoulders with desperation. "You can't do this. Where's my sister?" She started pounding on his chest, screaming at him, and Quinn finally pulled her back and wrapped his arms around her.

He pressed his lips to her hair as he met Gideon's

gaze. His blood brother shrugged, saying that they'd exhausted all resources to get him to talk. "We'll find her, Grace. We will."

Holding her tight, Quinn studied Nate, looking into the eyes that were so black and so evil that he almost recoiled. Those weren't the same eyes he'd seen on Nate at the bar. Those were the eyes of ancient death and centuries old evil.

Those were the eyes he imagined Ezekiel would have.

Quinn opened his mind to Nate to see if he could pick up anything. He instantly caught a faint vibration he recognized. "The fool has my sword with him." He called to his sword. Nate immediately clutched at his back as Quinn's weapon wiggled free of a sheath hidden between his shoulder blades. The blade flew into Quinn's palm. "He kept it against his skin so it wouldn't disappear and return to me."

Gideon grinned. "One down."

Quinn flexed his hand in satisfaction as the weapon settled into his arm, carefully watching Nate's face. It was full of pain but unrepentant. And there was deep fear in his face. "He's afraid of someone, someone besides us."

"Ezekiel?" Gideon asked, coming to stand beside Quinn.

"Maybe." Quinn's instincts pulsed and he jerked his head up and reached out for Gabe. *Gabe? Everything okay there?*

No response, and Quinn felt his body kick into assault mode. "Go check on Zach and Gabe," he snapped.

Ryland and Kane took off, weapons out, while Gideon and Ian stayed behind. "We can't kill him until we find out where the tablet is," Gideon said.

"And Ana," Grace said, clutching his arm.

"He's dying. Maybe he won't be strong enough to keep me out." Quinn wove through the barriers in Nate's mind, using the connection that they shared as Calydons.

Nate was old enough that he should have had the defenses to keep Quinn out, but he was so close to death that he couldn't fight it. Quinn slid easily past Nate's defenses and into his mind. The moment Quinn was connected to Nate, darkness crashed into him. Evil so deep and so penetrating that Quinn recoiled and instinctively started to pull out.

Then Grace's hand slid into his, calming him, and he let the evil brush past him, using his shields to keep it out of his own mind. *Where is Ana, Nate? Show me Ana.*

He repeated the command and Nate's thoughts shifted involuntarily to Ana. Quinn saw her, lying in the mud, less than a mile from where they were. Hot damn. Two goals accomplished. Only one left.

The tablet, Nate. Show me the tablet. Show me how Ezekiel's walls are falling. He felt Nate's struggle, his sudden elevation of terror, then there was a flash of malevolence, of death, of true, pure evil. It gripped both of their minds and clawed at their spirits.

Ezekiel.

Quinn jerked himself out of Nate's mind and broke the connection. Nate's body convulsed and he screamed, and then he was dead. His body disappeared a split second later.

"I think Ezekiel just killed him." Quinn's body was numb from the force that had attacked Nate. He pulled Grace into his body, seeking her warmth and goodness to chase away the darkness in his body from that brief touch of Ezekiel.

"How old was Nate?" Gideon asked. "A thousand years?"

"More than that." He looked over at his friend. "Do you think he's been helping Ezekiel for the last two thousand years?"

"You think Ezekiel's been controlling someone on

the outside for that long?" Gideon raked his hand through his hair. "Hell. I thought he was isolated in there."

"He was supposed to be." Quinn tightened his arm around Grace. "If he could connect with Nate, then he could probably access others."

Ian cursed suddenly and held up his wrist. "It's burning again."

"Shit." Gideon looked down at his wrist. "I am, too."

Quinn shoved Grace behind him as all the warriors called out their weapons. "Who the hell's doing this? Nate's dead. Who's doing the illusions now? Ana?"

"No, it's not her," Grace said. "I can tell."

"So, it's never been Nate." Quinn said. "There's been someone else working with him all along...someone who has the tablet? Someone who would want to follow up where Nate left off with Ana and Drew." He swore and took off up the hill, toward the spot Nate had showed him Ana was, Ian and Gideon on his heels. *Kane. Ryland. Be careful. I think someone else is going after Drew. Get to him fast!*

We're on it, came the terse reply.

Quinn sprinted over the hill and down the other side.

Shit! Kane's voice ripped through his mind. *Zach and Gabe are down. Drew's gone.*

The tight grip of destiny closing down on them. *Find the trail. Find Drew. We can't let them get him.*

We're tracking him, and right now, he's heading straight toward you.

Which meant he was heading toward Ana, who was between Quinn and Kane. Damn! Had they gotten this far only to have destiny still win by destroying everything he and Grace cared most about? Ana, Ezekiel...had they lost after all?

No! Grace's voice was sharp in his mind. *You have*

to get there first! You have to save her! We can't fail! Hurry!

Quinn renewed his focus and lit out through the woods. He could hear the whisper of footsteps up ahead, and he knew he was in a race for Ana. He couldn't pinpoint the location of his opponent, but he could hear him bolting through the woods, going for Ana, trying to beat Quinn there. Quinn was the one in the rear, and he knew he was going to lose the race.

The mud was cool, soothing Ana's battered body. She was too tired to keep her eyes open, so she let them close, allowing the rain to wash over her face. It hurt to breathe, it hurt to turn her head, so she stayed immobile, waiting for the sound of Nate's footsteps returning.

She thought about her illusion.

Her darkest illusion had been called forth, and it had been the moment of Elijah's death. Elijah's death was her biggest haunting. He'd tried to help her, and then he'd died because of it. Because of her. She groaned softly, knowing that even the men who'd died tonight wouldn't torment her the way Elijah's death would.

And Lily. She'd failed Lily—

She heard the sounds of feet sloshing through the mud, and she tried to shrink into the muck so Nate wouldn't find her. So his Calydons wouldn't see her.

"Ana."

Her eyes cracked open and she saw Frank squatting next to her. He was breathing hard, and sweat was dripping down his temples. He had an unconscious man slung over his shoulder. A young man, really.

Frank wavered in and out of focus as she tried to make sense of what he was doing there, but her mind was too fried to think.

"Nate's other knife," he said quickly. "Do you have

it?"

Her head hurt. "His knife?" she echoed. Did she? She thought maybe she did, but she couldn't remember. She frowned and tried to think, but it was too hard. Couldn't concentrate.

"Ana! Focus! Where's the knife?"

"Don't know—"

He grabbed her wrist and pulled her hand up out of the mud. "Empty." He tugged her other one up. "Where's the damn knife, Ana?" He reached for her shirt, and she tensed, suddenly remembering that was where the knife was. At the same moment, she realized with sudden, instinctive certainty that she couldn't let him have it.

But she knew it was too late.

⌘⌘⌘

Quinn bolted up the small hill, Gideon and Ian hot on his heels as they burst out of the woods and sprinted into a small clearing. A man was bent over the mud-caked body of a young woman, and he had Drew slung over his shoulder.

The man leapt to his feet at Quinn's approach and took off instantly, disappearing into the trees in a split second. Quinn bolted across the clearing, saw the flash of movement in the woods up ahead and hurled one of his swords as his feet splashed through the mud.

His sword cut through the forest as Quinn reached the girl, and he heard the blade thunk into a tree. Ian sprinted past him in pursuit and Kane and Ryland came in from the other side after him. Quinn straddled Ana and held up his sword while he called the other one back.

Gideon set up behind him, and so did Ian until they were back to back to back, Ana between them, facing the woods, weapons out.

Ready for the bastard to claim his prize. Quinn could hear the heavy breathing, but it sounded like it was all around him. "Can you pinpoint his location?"

"No." Gideon said. "I can't get a read on him."

Quinn ground his jaw. "Hold your fire. I don't want us throwing our weapons at air and have him come at us while we're unarmed."

There was a crash and Kane burst out of the woods, weapons up. "Did you get him?"

"No."

Kane cursed. "The trail ended at the edge of the clearing. We lost him."

"He's around here. I can hear him. Find him."

Kane nodded and disappeared back into the woods, Gideon held his position while Quinn knelt to check on Ana. She had a pulse. *Grace. She's alive. We have her.* He smiled at Grace's sob of joy, then he gently lifted Ana onto his lap. Her hair was black like Grace's, matted with mud and sticks. Her thigh was drenched with blood, and her ankle was limp and twisted. What a bastard. Quinn gently brushed her muddy hair off her face. "Ana," he said softly. "It's okay. Nate's dead."

She stirred in his arms and her eyes opened. They were glazed and foggy. "Nate's dead?" Her words were so weak he could barely hear them, but he nodded.

"You're safe. Grace is here."

Tears filled her eyes, and his throat tightened. "Grace," she whispered. "She found me? Is she okay? She didn't get hurt, did she?

Quinn smiled at her concern for Grace's welfare, so much like Grace's worry about Ana. Sisters, so much alike. "She's fine."

There was a shout from the edge of the clearing and he looked up to see Grace running across the muddy ground. "Ana!" Grace fell to her knees beside her sister, and pulled her onto her lap. "I'm here."

Ana let out a small sob and raised her finger, touching Grace's face. "Grace?" Her voice was raw. "Is that really you?"

"Yes, it's me." Grace leaned over her, her cheeks glistening with tears. "You're safe now, honey."

"Safe?" Ana echoed.

"Safe." Grace's voice was so firm, but her body was shaking with exhaustion, belying the strength in her voice. Quinn wrapped his arms around her to hold her up, nodding at Gideon to take Ana.

"Safe," Ana mumbled. "That's good." She managed a faint smile and let her eyelids close. "Get Lily," she whispered.

"Lily?" Grace frowned as Gideon knelt beside them and slid his arms under Ana to pick her up. "Who's Lily?"

Ana's eyes opened as Gideon leaned over her. She looked right into Gideon's eyes and grabbed his shirt, her knuckles white with the fierceness of her grip. "Swear to me you'll get Lily." Her voice was fierce with sudden energy, with desperation.

Gideon nodded. "I'll get Lily, I promise."

Ana touched his cheek, and then slid into unconsciousness, her head landing against his shoulder as he stood up with her in his arms. He looked at Quinn. "Who'd I just promise to get?"

"No idea." Quinn helped Grace to her feet. "But I have a feeling neither sister's going to let you back down from your promise." He wrapped his arm around Grace as she pulled her sister's hand toward her.

Then she gasped. "She's marked!" She pushed Ana's sleeve the rest of the way up, and Quinn saw the marks on her arm.

Gideon cursed. "That's Elijah's mark. How the hell did that happen?"

Quinn met Gideon's gaze. "From when he tried to protect her instead of running. He died to keep her safe."

Grace set her hand protectively over her sister's belly, glaring at both of them. "Don't even tell me you're thinking about killing her because she's Elijah's *sheva*. I swear—"

"Elijah's dead, Grace. There'd be no reason," Quinn interrupted before she could get upset. "She's safe." He slid his hand over Grace's where it was resting on Ana's stomach, then frowned when his fingers brushed against something hard hidden under Ana's shirt. He lifted the shirt, then saw Nate's knife tucked in the waistband of her pants. He recognized it from the battle they'd had with Nate earlier.

He gently pulled it free. "She has Nate's knife? Why?" He flipped it over, then noticed it had a stone handle. "Calydon weapons are always full metal—" He noticed writing inscribed on the handle in an old language he couldn't decipher. He showed it to Gideon. "Can you read that?"

"Not a chance."

Quinn closed his fist over the knife as Kane, Ryland and Ian emerged from the woods. Their faces were tense with frustration, and their weapons were sheathed.

"We lost him," Ryland said. "We followed him to a set of tire tracks, but his truck was gone by the time we got there. He took off with Drew and whatever he knows about the tablet."

Quinn cursed softly as he tucked Grace protectively against his body. "Dante was right. This is just beginning."

※※※

Hours later, after Kane had taken all of them to Dante's house, a veritable fortress that masqueraded as a mansion, Grace leaned on the bed beside Ana. Her sister was resting under a light sedative prescribed by a doctor Quinn had brought in. The doctor had taken care of Ana's thigh wound, her shattered ankle, and her numerous cuts and bruises.

Even the Order members had been shaken by how badly injured Ana was, and it had taken all Grace's strength not to fall apart. Her sister needed her now, and she would be strong for her.

Kane and Ian had recovered Vaughn from the cabin, and he was in another room, but it was doubtful whether he'd live through the night. He was currently unconscious, too out of it to even ask about Drew.

Quinn had ordered the best care for him, his guilt over Vaughn's plight apparent.

Grace closed her eyes and held her sister's hand, trying to tell herself that it would be okay. That her sister would survive.

Physically at least. Mentally and emotionally? Did Ana have a chance of ever recovering who she used to be? Would she ever regain her beautiful illusions, that gift that she'd cherished so much? Grace buried her face in her arms, overwhelmed by what had been stolen from her sister.

A warm hand cupped the back of her neck and she lifted her head, smiling despite the tears. "Quinn."

He wrapped his arms around her and pulled her against him, kissing her hard. She sighed and buried herself against his chest, in the strength that he gave her. "I love you," she whispered.

"I love you, too." He tangled his fingers in her hair and tugged softly so she had to look up at him. "You're exhausted."

She smiled. "You are, too."

"There's a bed in the next room. You'll be able to hear her if she needs you, and the team will keep checking on her." He kissed her forehead. "Gideon's antsy for her to wake up so he can find out what he's supposed to be doing about Lily, whoever she is. I have a feeling he'll be checking on Ana every few minutes." He tugged her wrist. "Come on, *sheva*. You need to rest."

Grace glanced at her sister, but realized he was right. Her whole body ached, and her legs were trembling. "Okay."

He took her hand. "Before we rest, the men have something for you."

She frowned as she followed him across the room. "Do I want it?"

Quinn didn't answer. He simply opened the door and led her downstairs to the family room where the men had set up command. They were sprawled on the couches eating when she walked in with Quinn. Huge men in black leather who dwarfed the oversized couches. They were still covered in blood and mud. No one had taken the time to shower yet. Had they been waiting for her?

Gideon saw her first, and he stood up.

Thano glanced over his shoulder at her, then he set his plate down and stood, turning to face her. Kane, Ryland, Zach, Ian, and Gabe followed suit, until all the warriors were facing her.

Silent.

Her heart began to beat faster and she tightened her grip on Quinn's hand.

"You saved all of us at Ezekiel's prison at risk to your own life," Gideon said, his deep voice reverberating through the room. "In the history of our kind, no *sheva* has done anything like what you did."

She straightened at the formality of his tone.

"You resisted your destiny to kill Quinn. By doing so, you broke destiny's hold on Quinn." Thano's tone was rich with respect. "No *sheva* has ever done that."

Kane stepped in front of her and went down on one knee. "Dante came back to save you." His voice was reverent. "You have Dante's blessing."

Ryland nodded. "You're part of this destiny, part of all our destinies right now. Call out Quinn's sword."

She felt Quinn's approval of the command, so she did as he requested, the blade flashing to life in her hand. Quinn wrapped his hand around hers where she gripped the handle and steadied the blade.

Gideon walked over to her, then opened his hand and pressed his palm down on the blade.

She instinctively tried to pull the sword away, but Quinn's grip on her was too tight, and he didn't let her.

Gideon held the blade until blood trickled from his palm.

The other warriors followed, one by one, until they all knelt before her on the rich oriental carpet. Gideon nodded at her. "Your turn."

She tensed. "Mine?"

The corner of Gideon's mouth turned up briefly. "Yes."

Quinn grabbed her wrist and turned her palm over, his gaze flicking to hers for permission.

She leaned back into his chest and closed her eyes. "Okay."

There was a sharp prick in the palm of her hand, and she snapped her eyes open as blood trickled over her skin. Gideon was first, clasping her wrist with his hand. She wrapped her fingers around his wrist, the blood from her palm smearing onto his skin.

"You belong to all of us now, Grace Matthews."

Then he released her, and Kane reached out. She locked wrists with him, and he repeated the words. Then Ian and Ryland. Gabe. Zach. Thano.

Then they fell silent. Waiting for her response?

Quinn's hand tightened on hers. *Accept their declaration,* sheva, Quinn whispered in her mind.

She nodded. "I am honored, and I accept."

Each warrior bowed his head in a show of respect, and tears stung the back of her eyes. "You all are my family now, aren't you?"

Gideon smiled. "Yes, we are."

She watched the men as they rose to their feet one by one, their broad shoulders and muscular bodies towering over her.

Quinn took her hands and turned her to face him. "If you die, a part of all of us will die with you. We will be with you always, for eternity. You will never be alone again. Not anymore. Not in life, and not in death. Forever, an Order member will be your escort through the Afterlife and all eternity. You are one of us."

Her heart swelling, Grace looked back at the men. All of them were smiling. Deadly killers, covered in blood. Grinning like dorks. Even Ryland. Her men. Her guys. Her family. She finally had a home.

She smiled back as Quinn's hands went around her waist. "If you guys keep this up, I just might end up loving all of you."

Ryland gave a groan. "Well, shit. I take it back, then."

She laughed as the deep sound of male laughter echoed through the room.

Quinn leaned forward. "I don't think I've ever heard you laugh like that," he whispered. "It's beautiful."

She turned to smile at him, and was met by his mouth as he caught her lips in a kiss that made desire flare to life deep inside her.

Something soft hit her in the back of the head. She broke the kiss as another pillow sailed toward her head before Quinn knocked it away.

"Get a room," Thano said.

Quinn grinned. "I hate to say it, but the kid's finally right about something." He took her hand. "We'll be back in a few hours."

Thano winked at her. "We'll get you if we need you."

Gideon nodded. "And we'll keep an eye on Ana, don't worry."

Grace saw Nate's knife still sitting on the table, the one they'd found on Ana, and she realized that it wasn't over. Even Dante had said the worst was still coming.

Quinn's hand went to her lower back, and she smiled up at him at the kindness and love in his eyes as he returned the smile, realizing that no matter what came now, she could handle it.

Because she'd found her place. She wasn't alone. Quinn would always be there for her. In her heart, in her soul and in her life. She smiled up at him as he took her hand and led her out of the room. "I love you."

He gave her a wicked smile full of sensual promise. "If you love me now, just wait until I get done making love to you properly. You won't believe what I can do in an actual bed."

She laughed and linked her arms around his neck as he swept her up. "You're impossible."

He bit her neck playfully. "And you love it."

She smiled as he carried her over the threshold into a gloriously decorated guest bedroom. "I must admit, I do."

He grinned at her, those dark eyes dancing with laughter and lightness that she would never have predicted when she'd first met him on that rainy night. "I do, too, sweetheart. I do, too." He kicked the bedroom door shut and tossed her on the bed. "Naked mud wrestling is about to become your number *two* fantasy, my love."

Grace giggled as she scrambled back on the bed, watching him peel off his shirt and reveal his rock-hard body that was all hers.

This was going to be good.

Sneak Peek: Darkness Seduced

The Order of The Blade
Available Now

Lily ducked past her assailant and sprinted up the cement stairs, her bare feet slapping on the concrete, her heart thundering in her ears as she vaulted up the steps toward the open door. She jumped through it then whirled around and threw it shut, catching a glimpse of the Calydon warrior as he came after her. She slammed the bolt home then tore down the hallway. There was a shuddering explosion behind her as the Calydon burst through the wooden door. She skidded around a corner as her mind whirred. She'd never make it to the kitchen. She needed to stall him—

She screamed as a heavy, sweaty body tackled her and her chin smashed on the wood floor. Her head rattled with the impact as she was flung onto her back, and Lily saw the Calydon leer at her chest. Lust flared in his eyes, the raw, uncontrollable sexual greed of a Calydon. She jerked her gaze down and realized he'd torn her shirt when he'd tackled her.

Terror, raw visceral terror, tore through Lily, and for a split second, she was too numb to move, too terrified by the memories, by the moment, by what had happened before. Just like this. Again. God, not again.

He reached for her breast, and the sight of that hand coming toward her jerked Lily out of her stupor and galvanized her into frantic self-defense, a chance she hadn't had all those years ago. "No!" she screamed. She slammed her foot into his crotch as hard as she could.

Her attacker shouted and doubled over, and Lily scrambled out from under him, lurching to her knees—

He grabbed her ankle and dragged her back toward him, his grip crushing her leg. "I have to bring you back alive and able to perform," he ground out as he tried to catch his breath from her blow. "But those are all the limitations I have on what I do with you."

She fought, she kicked, she tried everything, and she was no match for his strength as he yanked her across the floor, back toward him, toward the lust gleaming in his eye—

Oh, crap. *His eyes.* They were glowing red, pulsating with evil, and her heart stuttered.

He'd gone rogue. He'd crossed the line from sanity into raging, crazed killer, a beast who would feel no pain, have no empathy, ravage mercilessly until there was nothing left. There was no compassion, no humanity left in this warrior. No matter what his orders, she was doomed now. He wouldn't be able to stop himself.

Again. It would all happen again. Just like before—

"Get off me," Lily screamed, scrabbling desperately for a handhold to try to get away from him. Her fingers hit a table leg and a cord. Tears streaking down her cheeks, she yanked on the cord and covered her face as a lamp crashed down on both of them, shattering glass everywhere. Oblivious to the glass, he grabbed her other calf and hauled her until her legs were around his waist, her back slicing across the broken glass as she fought him, desperate, frantic—

"Get the fuck off her!" An enraged bellow blasted through the hallway.

Her attacker didn't even flinch, lunging for her skirt with the furious insanity of a rogue Calydon. She pounded on his shoulders, then heard the whoosh of wind behind her. Lily looked up as a throwing axe spun past her head and slammed into her assailant's chest. The fatal blow flung him backward against the wall, a gaping wound opening over his heart.

Lily scrambled back, barely noticing the glass sinking into her hands and her feet as she struggled to get away from him. He hit the floor with a thud, and the axe yanked itself out of his body and sped back past her head. She heard the slap of it hitting someone's palm.

Another Calydon.

She whirled around, and her breath caught. At the end of the hall stood the largest Calydon she'd ever seen. He had to be close to seven feet, and he was wearing all black, even his heavy boots and his tee shirt that barely covered his broad shoulders.

Everything was dark about him, except his dusty blond hair hanging raggedly about his angular face and the shiny metal throwing axe in his right hand, stained with blood on one of its blades. His face was wrenched with fury, his blue eyes raging, his stance wide and ready, prepared to take on all threats. He was darkness, he was danger, and he was death.

His eyes weren't red, but Lily could sense he was far more dangerous than the Calydon that lay motionless behind her. This new warrior radiated danger and heat and something she couldn't identify. Something that eased the terror beating at her. Something that calmed her need to flee. Something that made her want to rush over to him and throw herself in his arms, just to feel his body against hers...

Oh, crap. What was wrong with her?

He held up a hand for her silence and cocked his head, and Lily realized he was listening for others. Oh, God. Others?

She lurched to her feet, staggering as a wave of dizziness caught her and she nearly went down. She braced her hands against the wall, holding herself up as she stumbled away from him, toward the kitchen. Glass cut through her feet, and a cry of pain slipped out.

"Lily!" he commanded. "Don't move!"

Lily? He knew who she was? Was he also working with Frank? Had he killed her rogue assailant to ensure she made it back to Frank?

The Calydon was striding toward her, his face dark with fury. Energy was swirling off him, and his well-defined muscles were taut with rage. He was terrifying, but at the same time... he was pure, elemental beauty. He was pure grace, reminding Lily of a wild cat loaded with sinewy muscle and a lightning-fast strike that would bring instant death to his enemies, but one that would curl around her and protect her, keeping her safe, claws safely sheathed just for her.

He was all male, a testosterone-laden specimen of strength and aggression, a threat to all she was as a woman. He was ruthless temptation calling to her deepest, darkest desires, the ones she'd hidden away even from herself. In his presence, everything that made her female flared to life, longing for this man, this warrior, this *enemy*.

Lily backed up as he neared, holding out her hand in a pathetically useless attempt to stop him.

"My name's Gideon. I'm here for you." His voice was forceful and unyielding, but to her surprise, he eased himself to a stop several yards away from her. He spread his hands as if he were trying to appear harmless. Hah. There was *no chance* he could ever be mistaken for anything harmless, and it wasn't simply the weapon in his right hand or the axe-shaped brands burned into his forearms. Danger bled from his pores, darkened his expression, weighted his broad shoulders. "Don't run," he said. "You'll slice your feet."

There was no remorse in his face for the body on the ground behind her, yet at the same time, heated desire brimmed in his eyes as he studied her intensely. He was a Calydon, a warrior of hot passions and cold death, both of them hopelessly intertwined. His overwhelming presence was stirring up heated feelings of longing deep within her, even as her heart froze in fear at all he was, for how her life could fall at his hands in a split second.

Lily tugged her torn shirt closed over her chest, knowing it would do nothing to protect her from the raw sensuality pulsing from him, from the painfully intense yearnings rising within her, responding to his call, desperate to fall into the fire he was already kindling between them.

She'd met dozens of Calydons in the past. She'd always felt their pulsing sexuality, their intense stares that made desire rush through her, preying on her heritage and how it called her to their kind, but this was *different*. With all those others, she hadn't felt anything for them. It had been easy to turn them away, to ignore the beastly desires of her kind.

But Gideon was different. He was stripping her raw, branding her with his gaze, making her body ache with need for him, for all that he was and could offer her.

His eyes darkened, and she knew he could sense her reaction, the need pulsing so strongly within her.

Her cheeks flared with embarrassment, and she began to slide along the wall away from him, using it as a support to keep herself vertical. She winced as her foot landed on something sharp, and she jerked her foot off the floor, brushing off the glass by running her foot over her calf.

Gideon's jaw tightened, and his hand went up, as if to grab her, but he stopped himself when she flinched. "Lily. There are more Calydons outside that my teammate is dealing with." There was an urgency to his voice. "We need to go." He snapped his fingers impatiently. "Come on. Now."

Lily gritted her teeth against the almost uncontrollable urge to drop her shields and bolt into his arms. To give herself over to him. Gideon was death, but he was also temptation. As she stared at the hand he was holding out to her, she felt an unshakeable conviction that he was her sanctuary. For the first time in years, she could be safe, if she would just reach out and take what he offered, his violence, his sensuality, his overwhelming desire, his *protection*.

But she'd trusted Nate when he'd invited her into his house so she could interview him for her latest research project, and she'd wound up his captive for two years. Despite all Lily knew about Calydons, she'd forgotten all her lessons and walked into Nate's house and paid dearly for it. She wasn't stupid enough to trust a Calydon again.

Never, ever again.

Not even the warrior who'd killed to save her. Next time, it could be she who fell victim to Gideon's weapon. Or it could be Gideon who turned that uncontrollable lust onto her.

And if he didn't turn on her next time, he would eventually. Of that, Lily had no doubt. The warrior standing before her was her salvation, her passion, and also her ultimate destruction.

SNEAK PEEK: NOT QUIT DEAD

NIGHTHUNTER
AVAILABLE NOW

With a sigh, Jordyn spun her chair toward the dining tables, propped her elbows on the counter of the bar, and leaned back against the battered wood. Slowly, she examined every person in the room, going through the same process she'd used at every other bar she'd visited in the last three hours to see if the man she was looking for was present.

Even as she did it, she was aware of the low odds of success. Did she really think she'd find Tristan this way? No, but he'd lived here for at least six months, and he had to have had an impact, right? Somewhere in this town, he'd left a clue before he'd disappeared. According to Eric, this was the last place he'd been seen.

Her gaze wandered over to the Gaston brothers, and then the door to the bar swung open, drawing her attention. The screen door slammed against the wall, and a dark shadow filled the doorway. The man who stepped inside was tall and broad-shouldered, with dark hair. His presence was so powerful that the energy in the room actually shifted, rippling as it tried to accommodate the sheer force of his being. She sucked in her breath and sat up, chills racing down her spine.

Eric.

He was there.

She stared at him, her fingers clenching the seat of her stool. He was so much bigger than she remembered. Taller, wider shoulders, a more dominating presence. He seemed to loom over the entire bar, an unstoppable force of power. He scanned the room slowly, starting with the

Gaston brothers.

A part of her wanted to leap up, race over to him, and throw herself into his arms. She was riveted by the raw strength of his body, and she knew exactly how much power radiated from him. He'd been wild and untamed in the jungle, but here, it was as if he were part predator, a feral beast constrained by no one and nothing, stalking through civilization in search of the prey that he would conquer. She recalled his claim that he wasn't a man, and she suddenly believed him. Yes, a man, but there was something else as well. Something more visceral and dangerous. Something so graceful and lethal, physicality far beyond that of an ordinary man.

His hair was longer now, disheveled and ragged as it hung over his forehead. His eyes were blazing and dark, his jaw taut, his muscles flexed. The man standing in the doorway was nothing like the flirtatious, irreverent man she'd met a month ago. This man was moody, dark, and pulsing with an energy so intense that it slid down her spine and settled right in her lower belly. This man was a warrior, and he was pure, unfettered *male*.

Her heart started to hammer, thundering against her ribs, as she watched his gaze slide over the patrons, moving inexorably toward her. She knew then why she was still wearing her business suit. It hadn't been to prove herself to the town that had once been her home. It had been for Eric.

The only time she'd met him, they'd been deep in the Brazilian jungle, and she'd been wearing boots, jeans, and a ponytail. He'd overpowered her with the sheer force of his person, and she'd wanted to reinforce her shields this time by putting on her work persona, the one that was about the power and strength of a woman.

It wasn't working.

She felt sucked into the vortex of his power, every cell in her body tightening with each passing second as she waited for him to notice her. In the jungle, she'd been so worried about finding her friend that she'd had no emotional space to really let Eric affect her, but now it was different.

Now, she was so deeply aware of him that she couldn't stop thinking about how it had felt during that brief moment when he'd kissed her in the jungle. Fast. Passionate. Intense.

His gaze penetrated the darkest corner of the bar, his brown eyes alert and vibrant. He'd looked rugged and athletic before, but now, he looked rougher, like he'd been spawned by the earth itself. His jeans sat low on his hips, dripping wet, as if he'd been submerged in the bayou for hours. His boots were thick with mud, and there was dirt streaked across his face. His dark hair was damp and tangled, shoved ruthlessly aside so it was spiked and messy. Droplets slid in a wet sheen across his forehead, the sweat of a man who'd been working hard at something, even though it was the middle of the night. Whiskers were heavy on his jaw, and she had a sudden ridiculous urge to run her fingers over them.

So much for thinking that four weeks in Boston was going to make her immune to the effect he had on her. It had gotten worse, exponentially more intense, since they'd parted ways.

She wasn't ready for this.

She wasn't ready for him.

She wasn't ready for any of it.

Jordyn swallowed, her heart almost leaping out of her chest as he turned his head toward her. His eyes met hers, and she knew instantly that, unlike the town that had known her for the first sixteen years of her life, *he* didn't have any trouble recognizing her. The flash of awareness was instant, and she felt like her skin was on fire. She swallowed, her mouth suddenly dry, and her fingers tightened around her stool, as if she could keep herself from tumbling off it and into his arms.

Instantly, he shoved away from the doorway and headed straight toward her. His jaw was tense, and his stride was long and purposeful, rippling with languid strength. His gaze was fixed on hers so intently that she wanted to look away...except she couldn't take her eyes off him.

She tensed as he neared, sitting up straighter and trying to get a cool expression on her face. "Where have you been—?"

He gave her no time to finish her sentence. He just swung his arm behind her lower back, hauled her up against him, and kissed her.

Sneak Peek: Darkness Possessed

The Order of the Blade
Available Now

The jungle smelled rich with the dampness of fertile soil. The trees were alive with the chatter of birds and the rustle of animals. Rhiannon closed her eyes and breathed deeply as she let the power of her birthplace roll over her and seep into her body. The freshness of the air seemed to cleanse her of all the grime and pollution that had accumulated during her years of living in civilization. She could almost feel her cells coming back to life and embracing the deep nourishment of the land she was meant to live in.

She went down on one knee and crumbled some dirt between her fingers, watching the rich, brown loam fall back to the ground from which it had come. To her surprise, she felt her throat tighten, and tears burned in her eyes. She hadn't realized how much she'd missed being home. It had been two days since she had left Boston. After much hard traveling, she'd almost reached the region that had once given her life...and then betrayed her.

A sudden sound broke through her focus and she went utterly still, listening intently. Another sound, quiet yet heavy, came from her right, and she recognized it instantly as the footstep of a creature that was too big to be a human, but could easily be a heavily armed Calydon. Without taking time to stand, she pivoted on her knee as she swept an arrow out of her quiver and pulled her crossbow off her shoulder. In less than a millisecond she nocked an arrow and had it pointing at the cluster of bushes from which the sound had come.

She knew she was in the open more than she wanted

to be, but relocating into the trees would attract more attention than staying completely still. Her mottled brown and green cargo pants and jacket would help her blend into her surroundings. Even her crossbow still retained the colors of the jungle that had once been her home.

There was silence. No movement followed the steps that she had heard, which made her tension rise even further. Whatever it was had become aware of her, and it was waiting for her to move in the same way she was anticipating its next step.

Penetrating silence prevailed, each trying to outwait the other. The muscles in her arms began to tremble, and she realized how out of shape she was. There had been a time when she had been able to hold her bow at the ready for hours, outwaiting even the most patient of enemies. Now, it had been less than a minute and already her arms were shaking. Her hamstring was cramping from the uncomfortable position she'd frozen in. A trickle of sweat was slithering down her brow, and she knew it wouldn't be long before it went into her eye. It wasn't even hot compared to what the jungle often was, but she could feel the steam rising off her body, curling her hair, and dampening her clothes.

With grim trepidation, she realized she had gone soft. She was in no condition to take on José and think she could walk away. She'd lost to him even when she'd been fit and in her prime. Now? She couldn't even hold an arrow ready for more than a minute. Her pulse began to hammer in her throat, and she willed it to quiet, knowing that José would be able to hear her heart pounding if he was the one in the bushes.

Please don't let it be José. She wasn't ready to face him yet. If she met him now, she would have no chance. A cold fear gripped her, and her fingers tightened involuntarily around the arrow, even as she fought to stay relaxed. Physical tension would throw off her aim. She had to stay loose.

Then she caught a scent, drifting to her over the complex smells of the jungle. It was the scent of a man. Not José. A stranger. He smelled of sweat, adrenaline, and something else. A deeper scent that seemed to reach inside her and unfurl in her belly. She instantly recognized her response as attraction. Desire. Lust. Dear God, *she wanted this man.* Fear gripped her with sudden cruelty, freezing her muscles and obliterating all thought from her mind except for a raw terror that screamed at her to run. *Run. Run!*

Her instincts knew she had to stay utterly still, but the fear of her attraction to a man was so deep that she could not make herself stay. Attraction was a trap. Desire could be twisted to hurt her. Lust was a cruel lie. Wanting a man was doom, torture, and a hell she'd never survive.

Instead of staying still and hidden as she should have, panic forced her to act. She leapt to her feet, spun around, and ran blindly through the forest, her boots thudding noisily on the ground. Branches tripped her and plants seemed to spring up out of the earth to grab her ankles. She couldn't even focus enough to ask them to help her instead of hurting her. Her mind was a swirling miasma of terror and memories, screaming at her to run and escape while she still had the chance.

"Hey!" The man shouted at her, his deep voice booming through the jungle.

The rich bass of his voice plunged through her flesh and ignited a fire inside her. A fire of want, longing, and the urge to turn and charge right toward him instead of away from him. "Oh, God, no. Not again." Tears streamed down her cheeks as she sprinted through the jungle, not even paying attention to where she was going. She couldn't remember the layout exactly. Her mind was fragmented with fear and terror, just as it had been so long ago when she had run for her life through these very woods. She stumbled over a root and tumbled to the earth, barely getting her hands out in time to cushion her fall. Her crossbow jammed into her jawbone and she gasped as the pain shot through her.

She hadn't even finished falling when she was already back up on her feet, stumbling as she tried to keep going. Trees loomed above her on all sides, but the branches were too high for her to reach, and she couldn't focus enough to ask the trees to help her. Everything she had as a weapon was gone, disintegrated by the fear ripping through her.

Then she realized there were heavy footsteps thundering after her, getting closer and closer. He was chasing her! She put on another burst of speed, her breath burning her lungs as she fought for air. Her legs were trembling, shaking with exhaustion as she asked her body to do things it hadn't done in so long.

She frantically tried to focus enough to take in her surroundings and understand where she was. She couldn't keep this up. She had to find a way out. She had to—

A hand closed on her shoulder, and fingers dug into her flesh, pulling her to a stop.

With his touch, all conscious thought fled from her mind. She grabbed the dagger from where it sat on her hip and spun around, striking as she turned. Her blade hit flesh, plunging deep inside thick muscle before she'd even finished her turn to see who was after her.

The dark brands on his forearms told her all she needed to know. It was a Calydon, and her dagger was in his heart. She spun the rest of the way around, facing him as he fell.

"Shit!" The warrior's dark eyes widened in surprise as he stumbled and went down to his knees.

Rhiannon ripped her dagger out of his chest and went still, bracing her legs in a ready position as she held the dagger ready. She knew she had to keep moving, but she couldn't run anymore. Not yet. She needed time to recover. She had nothing left. Her breath heaved in her chest as she desperately tried to get air.

She saw the blood pouring from his chest, and realized she'd struck a clean blow into the heart. Instinct had shown her where to find a heart on a Calydon, taking into account his height when she'd made her blind strike. Maybe she wasn't a total loss. Maybe she still had some of her old skills. Maybe she still had a chance to survive.

She took another deep breath, trying to recover from her run. She knew the respite from his injury wouldn't last long, but the heart had been a good place to hit.

He looked up at her as he pressed his palm to the wound on his chest. "Why the hell did you do that?" His voice had the same effect on her as before. It slithered through her body like a warm, seductive caress of pure temptation. And now that she could see what he looked like, it was even stronger.

His eyes were dark brown, flecked with bits of gold. His stare was intense, sinking deep into her very soul as he gazed at her. She felt herself flush under his stare, her body pulsing in response to the heat of his attention. For a moment, the world seemed to freeze, and she was caught in his spell, in his raw masculinity and strength. His cheekbones were sculpted, giving him a regal appearance, despite the heavy growth of whiskers and the disheveled dark hair, which gave him an aura of danger and lethalness that should have terrified her…but she found herself riveted by him instead.

His shoulders were broad, but not as broad as José's. Unlike José and his men, who wore camouflage pants, lean boots, and sported bare chests as if impersonating some ancient warrior, this Calydon was wearing the garb of civilization. His blue jeans were dirty and torn. His black T-shirt was loose and ragged. He was wearing hiking boots, but they appeared to be heavily insulated as if they were meant for trekking through snow and ice instead of the brutal heat of the jungle. He didn't look like he belonged to this jungle or to José, but the twin dark brands on his forearms told her all she needed to know.

He was a Calydon, and that meant he was a threat, no matter how intense her reaction to him was. In fact, he was even more dangerous *because* of the way she wanted to fall under his spell. Men knew how to take advantage of a woman's attraction to them. They preyed upon it, twisting it to their advantage. She knew better than to want a man, but her fingers actually twitched with the need to lay her hand over his wound and take away his pain, to feel his flesh beneath her palm, to move closer, and lose herself in the incredible strength and power of his being.

"Yeah…" he said softly, his gaze locked onto hers, as if he were having the same intense reaction to her that she was having to him. "Who are you?" he asked. "What's your name?"

"Who am I?" The question jerked her back to the present, to the very real danger he presented. If he'd been sent to find her, his quest would have to end now. Even as she thought it, resistance pulsed through her, and she realized she didn't want to kill him.

Grimly, she took a step back as she pulled another arrow out of her quiver. She set it in the bow and aimed it right between his eyes. "What do you want?"

She needed to know whether he had stumbled across her accidentally, or if José already knew she was here. Then, once she had her answers, she would do her best to kill the man kneeling before her.

She ignored the stab of regret at the notion of killing him. Sure, he smelled incredible and had eyes that had momentarily melted right through the fear of men that she kept wrapped so tightly around her. That didn't mean she was going to make the same mistake that had once almost killed her. Never would she trust the wrong man, or any man, again.

Never.

He would have to die. There was simply no other option.

SNEAK PEEK: DARKNESS UNLEASHED

THE ORDER OF THE BLADE
AVAILABLE NOW

Ryland spun around, engaging all his preternatural senses as he searched the graveyard for Catherine. He knew she had to be close. He'd touched her backpack just before she'd vanished right in front of him.

"Catherine!" he shouted again. He'd been so close. Where the hell was she? All he could sense were the deaths of all the people in the graveyard. Women, children, old men, young men, good people, scum who had taken their demented values to the grave with them. The spirits were thick and heavy in the graveyard, souls that had not moved on to their place of rest.

They circled him, trying to penetrate his barriers, seeking asylum in the creature that would be their doom. "No," he said to them. "I'm not your savior." Not by a long shot. He was about as far from their savior as it was possible to be.

Dismissing them, Ryland focused more directly on Catherine, opening his senses to the night, but as much as he tried to concentrate, he couldn't keep the vision of her out of his head. He'd finally seen her up close. She'd been mere inches away, the angel who had filled his thoughts for so long. Her hair was gold. *Gold.* It must have been tucked up under a hat when he'd seen her before, but now? It was unlike anything he'd ever seen before. He'd been riveted by the sight of it streaming behind her as she ran, the golden highlights glistening in the dark as if she'd been lit from within.

Her gait had been smooth and agile, but he'd sensed the sheer effort she'd had to expend during the run.

Another few feet, and he would have caught up to her easily, but she'd sensed him while he'd still been a quarter mile away, giving her a head start that had gotten her to the graveyard first.

Shit. He had to focus and find her. Summoning his rigid control to focus on his task, Ryland crouched down and placed his hand on the dirt path where he'd last seen her. The ground was humming with the energy of death, but again, he couldn't untangle her trail from all the others. He realized that she'd mingled her own scent of death with those of all the other spirits, making it impossible for him to track her. He grinned as he rested his forearm on his quad and surveyed the small cemetery. "I'm impressed," he said aloud. "You're good."

There was no response, but he had the distinct sensation that she was watching him.

Slowly, he rose to his feet. "My name is Ryland Samuels," he said. "I'm a member of the Order of the Blade, the group of warriors that you protect. I'm here to offer you my protection and bring you into our safekeeping."

Again, there was no answer, but suddenly threaded through the tendrils of death was the cold filament of fear. Not just a superficial apprehension, but the kind of deep, penetrating fear that would bring a person to their knees and render them powerless. Fear of him? Or of the fact he said he wanted to take her with him? Swearing, Ryland turned in a slow circle, searching for where she might be. "There's no need to be afraid of me. I would never hurt an angel."

The fear thickened, like the thorns of a dying rose pricking his skin.

Ryland moved slowly toward the far corner, and smiled when he felt the terror grow stronger. She might be able to hide death, but there was no cover for the terror that was hers alone. He was clearly getting closer to her. "Look into my eyes," he said softly. "I don't hurt angels."

There was a whisper of a sound behind him, and he felt the cold drift of fingers across his back. *She was touching him.* He froze, not daring to turn around, even though his heartbeat had suddenly accelerated a thousand-fold. Her touch was so faint, almost as if it were her spirit that was examining him, not her own flesh. Was she merely invisible right now, or had she abandoned her physical existence completely and traveled to some spiritual plane? He had no idea what she was capable of. All he knew was that he felt like he never wanted to move away from this spot, not as long as she was touching him. He wanted to stay right where he was and never break the connection.

He closed his eyes, breathing in the sensation of her touch as her fingers traced down his arm, over his jacket. What was she looking for? Was she reading his aura? Searching for the truth of his claim that he would not hurt her? She would get nowhere trying to get a read on him. He never allowed anyone to see who he truly was, not even an angel of death.

But even as he thought it, he made no move to resist, his pulse quickening in anticipation as her touch trailed toward his bare hand. Would she brush her fingers over his skin? Would he feel the touch of an angel for the first time in a thousand years? He felt his soul begin to strain, reaching for this gift only she could give him.

He tracked every inch of movement as her hand moved lower toward his bare skin. Past his elbow. To the cuff of his sleeve. Then he felt it. Her fingers on the back of his hand. His flesh seemed to ignite under her touch. A wave of angelic serenity and beauty cascaded through his soul, like a breath of great relief easing a thousand years of tension from his lungs.

At the same time, there was a dangerous undercurrent beneath the beauty, a darkness that he recognized as death. A thousand souls seemed to dance through his mind, spirits lodged in the depths of her existence. Her emotions flooded him. Fear. Regret. Determination. Love. A sense of being trapped.

Trapped? He understood that one well. Far too well. Instinctively, he flipped his hand over, wrapping his fingers around hers, not to trap her, but to offer her his protection from a hell that still drove every choice he made.

He heard her suck in her breath, and she went still, not pulling away from him. Her hand was cold. Her fingers were small and delicate, like fragile blossoms that would snap under a stiff breeze. A hand that needed support and help.

Ryland snapped his eyes open but there was no one standing in front of him. He looked down and could see only his own hand, folded around air. He couldn't see her, but she was there, her hand in his, not pulling away. "Show yourself to me," he said. "I won't hurt you."

Her hand jerked back, and a sense of loss assailed him as he lost his grip on her. "No!" He reached for her, but his hands just drifted through air. "Catherine," he urged, as he strained to get a sense of her. "I—"

Select List of Other Books by Stephanie Rowe

(For a complete book list, please visit www.stephanierowe.com)

STEPHANIE ROWE BIO

Four-time RITA® Award nominee and Golden Heart® Award winner Stephanie Rowe is a nationally bestselling author, and has more than twenty-five contracted titles with major New York publishers such as Grand Central, HarperCollins, Dorchester and Harlequin, and more than fifteen indie books. She believes in writing stories where characters survive against all odds, fighting their way through to personal triumph, while discovering true love and sensual, hot passion along the way.

Stephanie is an award-winning and bestselling author of adult paranormal romance, and has charmed reviewers, receiving coveted starred reviews from Booklist for several of her paranormal romances. Publishers Weekly has also praised her work, calling her work "[a] genre-twister that will make readers...rabid for more."

In addition to her vibrant paranormal romance career, Stephanie also writes a thrilling romantic suspense series set in Alaska. Publisher's Weekly praised the series debut, ICE, as a "thrilling entry into romantic suspense," and Fresh Fiction called ICE an "edgy, sexy and gripping thriller." Equally as intense and sexy are Stephanie's contemporary romance novels, set in the fictional town of Birch Crossing, Maine

Stephanie is a full-time author who has been an avid reader since she was a kid (she even won the blue ribbon at her town library for reading the most books over the summer). She wrote her first book when she was ten, but abandoned that fledgling career when people started asking to read it. Fortunately, she now delights in people reading her work, and loves to hear from readers. With more than fifty completed novels to her name, Stephanie is well on her way to fulfilling the dream that started so long ago. Some of her favorite authors are Lisa Kleypas, Dick Francis, and Julie Garwood, but the list goes on and on

In her spare time, Stephanie loves to play tennis, take her rescue dog for walks in the woods, and to make up stories about the people she sees on the street with her daughter. Yes, the author's imagination is always at work.

Want to learn more? Visit Stephanie online at one of the following hot spots

WWW.STEPHANIEROWE.COM
HTTP://TWITTER.COM/STEPHANIEROWE2
HTTP://WWW.PINTEREST.COM/STEPHANIEROWE2/
HTTPS://WWW.FACEBOOK.COM/STEPHANIEROWEAUTHOR

Made in the USA
Lexington, KY
01 June 2016